ANDREA JONES

REGINETTA PRESS

The Reginetta Press
www.reginettapress.com

Distributed by:

PublishingWorks, Inc.
151 Epping Rd.
Exeter, NH 03833
1-800-738-6603 or 603-772-7200

Interior design by Anna Pearlman
Book Jacket designed by Erik Hollander
www.HollanderDesignLab.com

LCCN: 2009923735
ISBN: 0-9823714-9-7
ISBN-13: 978-0-9823714-9-7

Printed in the USA

*For those who harbor pirates
in secret coves.*

For Lisa,

Welcome back
to Neverland,
via Port
Washington —

Andrea Jones

Contents

Once Upon Never-Time 1

The Enchanted Queen 4

A Pirate's Passion 21

Ship's Company 24

The Story of Red-Handed Jill 27

Pearls from the Lagoon 39

Taming the Beast 46

Harvest at the Fairy Glade 56

Beasts' Accord 61

The Inquisition 67

Growing Pains 77

Camp Meeting 86

The Open Door 94

Shades of Black 102

Passion Play 111

Back . . . and Forward 119

The Revel Master 129

Cravings and Sweet Nothings 140

Dark Hunting 152

War of Attrition 156

Revelations 168

Deliverance 178

Workings of a Damaged Man 194

All or Nothing 212

Rites and Rituals 224

Death of a Legend 235

Duel on Deck 251

Taming the Boy 265

Other Oceans 277

The Seas of London 285

Never, Again 293

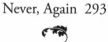

Once Upon Never-Time

When she woke, she was the woman in the bed on the ship in the sea, and she used to be Wendy Darling, who dreamt in the bed in the nursery of Number 14.

Now, the rhythm of the waves had overtaken the rhythm of her dreams. But when? When had she become accustomed to the swaying of the ship? At what point in time had she grown used to the bed that mocked the rocking surface of the sea?

She knew now that the presence behind her, cradling her, would bind her forever. How had she become one with that presence, possessing it and possessed by it? By the arm thrown to rest across her own. The heavy arm that protected and confined her. That powerful, handless arm ending, hideously, at the wrist.

Hook.

Her eyes flew wide and it happened again. The reality of the man seized her breath and tore it away. Waves of shock rushed up her body, panic gripped her heart. The girl she had been was swept away, her shell refilled with surging waters, assaulting her from within.

Even now, Hook, made real, ripped her to pieces and recreated her, all at once.

She tried to breathe.

Even now he afflicted her, when she was sure so much time had passed.

Think. When had she called him into being? First spun his tales? Ages ago. Lifetimes. *Breathe again.* But in the Neverland, time had no reckoning. Her custom of keeping it lost to its lack of regulation here. Yet she had clung to it, while other familiarities fell away to lie derelict at the bottom of Neverbay.

Remember to breathe. Where were the boys now? With her parents, becoming gentlemen. Wendy alone had chosen, been chosen, to stay. Wendy alone had arrived in the land of eternal childhood only to find she was already growing up. It was here she had escaped the bonds of uncaring youth. In her new freedom, she had begun fully to live here, as a woman. The woman she had chosen to be.

The woman in the bed on the ship in the sea.

Breathing evenly at last, she lifted her hand to his mutilated stump, caressing it, once. Her eyes fell closed and she slept again, swaying in his arms to the perpetual timelessness of the rocking sea.

Hook was awake. He was always awake when she was. He knew her thoughts; he never feared them. She was thinking about time again, as he used to do. One day his own thoughts would be as open to her as hers were to him. In time. Time, which ticked on forever here, and simultaneously held no meaning at all.

True to his own code of chivalry, Hook allowed her the illusion of solitude. But he would never allow her to be utterly alone. For all his buccaneering, it was being alone that had corrupted him. He had ensured that he wouldn't be alone again.

He was intensely aware of her reaction to him, the shock she endured in those moments when his reality struck roughly. Really, it was quite gratifying. Now she was relaxed, once more at rest under his arm—his gashed, ghastly arm. Interestingly, it was the hand that was no more, not the hook, that had caught and closed the door to her escape. And opened a new way.

It was said of Hook that he flinched only at the sight of his own blood. In sheer nerve she was fast becoming his match. How could she be otherwise, who had dreamt life into a man like him? It often amused him to think how thorough she had been. He was a perfect Pirate: flawlessly ruthless, cutthroat, arrogant, without shame. All these things, and crowning the lot, the jewel of his nature, that refinement which won success where more crudely-made men might fail.

In innocence she had created him, a tale to frighten children. Too late she discovered his truth, and once begun, his story had continued. Now, completed, he was returning the favor.

Her courage made the effort at once easier and more difficult, but he didn't care. He was a man who didn't care—about a great many things. Thus, his one-handed grasp closed more firmly upon the few things he did hold dear. Winning. Living. His ship. Jill.

Always, now that he had taken her, Jill.

Then he woke her, and moving in Time to the rhythm of the sea, they began their dance.

The Enchanted Queen

This moment was Wendy's once-upon-a-time, when she believed Peter Pan was her dream come alive.

She spiraled as high as she dared in the air, dancing above the Island. Her hair whirled with her, and she laughed when it caught up to her face, tangling in her eyelashes and hiding the kiss that hung waiting at the corner of her mouth. Peter would find it today. She was sure of it.

But neither Wendy nor her kiss would be captured. She turned toward the wind and it helped her fingers shoo the snare away. The wind shared her passion—to fly was joy. Danger, too, of course, but she had only to beware the cannon, Long Tom, wherever it played dark games with pirates, and to avoid arrows loosed by Indians among the trees. After that, the sky was her own, and she shouted to it of her happiness.

Once upon a time, when she believed.

Peter had taken her on impulse. Unmeasured months ago, he lured her from home at Number 14 in London with the double temptation of adventure and domesticity. He taught her to fly as he guided her here. Peter liked to portray his theft as a triumph, but his 'Wendy-bird' had followed wholeheartedly, eager to taste both pleasure and peril. That first night—under fire from Long Tom—Wendy tamed her fright with a spirit that made Peter's eyes gleam, and she trusted no matter where on the Island he led her, Peter would never let her come to harm. While he was just a boy he might not admit it, but with an inkling of woman's intuition, Wendy understood; from the very beginning, she was more to him than just a girl.

Whatever the risks, now it was second nature to her to soar above the Neverland's flamboyance, loving it. The sea circumnavigated the Island, hoarding secret coves of emerald and sapphire, stowing waterfalls and languid lagoons. Wendy's isle anchored mountains, forests, creeks and encampments. And her own little house, built by the Lost Boys at Peter's command. She could just see it below, its tiny roof flickering with sunlight as the breeze agitated its leaves. Appraising the Neverland like a jewel, Wendy could as yet only guess at the complexity of its facets. With her new perspective of inhabitant, she divined both haven and hazard. But what was benign, and what was sinister? In spite of Peter's reassurances, Wendy had begun to wonder.

She felt safe for the moment as a familiar blur rose up to meet her, formed into Peter, and rose higher to eclipse her. Peter often moved so swiftly one couldn't distinguish his features, which in themselves fascinated Wendy. In appearance Peter was both boyish and aristocratic. Whenever he held still, the first things to catch her attention were the bright green eyes almost covered by his golden hair and the bright silver dagger at his belt. Now he checked his ascent to look down from his eminence and beam on her.

"Peter, were you in the forest?" A quick inspection answered the unspoken half of her question. Wendy's shoulders relaxed and the sudden dread that had gripped her retreated. His blade was still shiny. He hadn't been hunting.

Peter descended, hanging almost near enough to touch. Hiding one hand behind his back, he smiled in his most intriguing manner. "Wendy. . . !"

She sparkled. "What is it? Oh, Peter, what now?"

Pushing himself backward, he launched into a somersault. As he righted himself, he stretched out an arm and offered her a garland woven of perfect roses, trailing ringlets of green tendrils. "Yellow roses for your yellow hair. I cut the thorns off. Do you like it?"

Wendy didn't, in fact, particularly care for flowers; they tended to wither and die too soon to suit her eternal tastes. Nor did she desire to touch rose barbs again, that pierced her skin and caused her fingertips to blossom, too, with blood. But Peter had gone to some lengths to please her, and she *was* pleased. "It's lovely. Did you make it yourself?"

"Of course! And while I was there at the Fairy Glade, I showed the fairies how to make one, too." Peter drifted nearer and taking the wreath in both hands, held it reverently over her hair, an earthy halo. Wendy breathed in the fragrance. The blooming circle smelled dewy, almost cloying. She stifled a cough.

Peter crowned her. "Queen of the Lost Boys! Your Majesty." And he bowed, as only Peter could bow. He was a superb make-believer, the most wonderful boy Wendy knew. But of course, she admitted in her truthful way, he'd had much more time to practice than other boys. She curtsied in return, as grandly as possible in a nightdress and without benefit of flooring, then floated toward him. Regal, she ignored the pricking of the thorns, which, as usual, he'd missed among the roses.

"You shall be rewarded, Sir." Disguising her longing, Wendy extended her arms in what she hoped was a commanding fashion. "I grant you the honor of a dance."

With the knight's deed accomplished, the boy Peter grinned again. "I don't dance." His voice was bold, unashamed to be heard. "I fly!" He promptly rushed away, escaping into a cloud.

Grateful now for the snagging thorns that secured her garland, Wendy sped after him, her viney ribbons fluttering and the cloud shredding in her wake. As she grabbed for Peter's heels, he veered into the next puff, surprising two boys. Wendy narrowly dodged them all and pulled herself upright, halting her flight to laugh as ordinary Michael and John tumbled out of the froth exclaiming, "Peter, Wendy! Oh . . . !"

Wendy's laughter ended when her brothers lost control and shot down toward the Island. Nightshirts riffling in the wind, the two boys struggled to regain flight, kicking, flailing, and yelling, but all the while falling. As she realized their predicament, Wendy's eye caught the flash of movement among the trees. Indians!

"Peter, an arrow!" She dove after her brothers.

"Leave it to me. Nibs, take charge of the boys!" With a grim smile, Peter darted toward the forest to draw fire away from the others. He flew low, then lower, and the strings of ivy and the leaves he wore became one with those of the trees. He and his dagger shimmered into the forest.

Nibs, Curly, Slightly, the Twins, and Tootles heard trouble coming. Having hung below playing tag, they now stopped short to goggle up at the onrushing brothers. It was possible Peter's boys possessed enough sense between them to avert disaster without his guidance. All three of the Darling children were counting on it.

"Boys, catch them!" Wendy was yet too far to help John and Michael, but as she streamed lower, her arms reached for them anyway.

Nibs was Peter's best strategist. He took command as ordered. "Ahoy, lads, all together!" He signaled them closer and the boys bunched themselves to form a motley flock. Wendy shut her eyes and winced, hoping. She counted the seconds until she heard the collective "Oof!" and knew at last the fall was broken.

"Thank goodness!" Wendy's ready smile reappeared and she righted herself to float down, touching her garland. She laughed to see the tangle of boys. "Do hold still while I sort you all out."

"Where's Peter gone?" asked the shaggy, brown-eyed Twins, the only ones who still had breath in their lungs.

"Plundering booty from the enemy, of course." Tootles recovered quickly and his sturdy arms handed Michael to Wendy by the collar of the nightshirt. "I hope he'll bring back weapons."

"Aye," Nibs agreed. Satisfied that his leadership had succeeded, he now considered that Peter, too, might need the boys' assistance. A plan of attack was already forming in his mind. "And if he's not back soon, we'll go after him."

John straightened his nightshirt in an effort to regain his composure. "Wendy, what do you think? Shall we follow Peter and see if he wants help?"

"No, John. He gave instructions to leave it to him. Peter will keep us safe from the Indians."

"Wendy lady?" Curly's freckled face looked thoughtful as he asked politely, "Are there Indians in the forests of London?"

"Papooses, too?" asked the Twins, always curious.

As the eldest, Slightly remembered more clearly than the other children. "No, London is where the nurses push prams in the park. You know." With wise looks, the Lost Boys nodded to one another. At some point in their infancies, every one of them had fallen from such a pram. Iron bars bordered the park's trees and pathways, and if, after the gates were locked, a lone little boy roamed the grounds in search of fun, the fairies would find him and deliver him into Peter's care. Except for Curly, the allure of the Neverland far surpassed the park, and on the rare occasions the Lost Boys thought about it, they laughed to think the place had ever seemed a wilderness.

Seeing their smiles grow, Wendy looked askance at the children, a spark of mischief in her eye. "The question *I* want to ask is, did you boys fall out of your prams, or did you jump out and run away from home, like Peter did the day he overheard—"

A distant whoop sounded below, followed by a fierce cry, the kind of cry that stops hearts. The boys froze. Wendy wheeled toward the horizon, scanning for Peter. . . . Nothing more could be seen there. She clenched her hands into fists and waited, searching, while the boys crowded closer together.

Far-off drums erupted in a savage beat. All the children's hearts started up again to match it. Slightly interpreted its meaning, and his voice was hushed. "War drums!" The boys looked with wide eyes from one to another, waiting breathlessly for Time to catch up.

Time obliged. Within seconds they heard a lusty crowing. The next moment, Peter burst through the forest roof. His band of boys released sighs of relief and Wendy's eyes lit up. He sped back to them, hair wild and green eyes glowing, victory personified, the Indian arrow between his teeth. Everyone waved and cheered for Peter, including himself.

Slightly eyed the arrow hopefully. "Can I have it, Peter?"

But with ceremony, Peter raised it in salute to Wendy and presented it to her. The scents of sweat and myrtle leaves lingered about him. "For my Indian princess." He was, indeed, a superb make-believer.

And Wendy equaled him. Entering his game, she changed roles without a hitch.

"Big Chief Peter! Many thanks." The queen-turned-princess received the tribute with dignity, but spotted a smear on her brave's forearm. Her eyebrows drew together. "Are you hurt?"

"Just warpaint, nothing to worry about. Look, boys, a badge from the Indians!" Peter thrust his marked arm in the air, showing it off.

Deprived of a good fight, Nibs led the charge notwithstanding. "Hurrah for Peter!"

"Hurrah! Hurrah!"

As her fears for Peter calmed, Wendy smiled indulgently. It seemed she was the only member of his band glad to have avoided a skirmish. Looking him over, she found that neither he nor the arrow was bloody—but his dagger was.

She recoiled.

A sudden wind whipped her, passed right through her, flapping her gown and binding her face with her hair once more, and with the tendrils of the garland, too. She shuddered with cold and shoved them away, one-handed now because of the arrow, and asked no more questions. Peter would tell of his adventure later . . . if he thought of it again.

His sharp eyes caught her reaction. "What are you shivering for, Wendy? I told you, I'm fine."

"It's just the breeze. It's getting cool now." She tried on a smile.

Peter knew he was a wonderful boy and he seldom hesitated to boast. "The wind can't catch me! I never feel it."

"I feel it always. I can't help but feel it." Wendy's gaze strayed, drawn toward the trees from which Peter had emerged, but they masked their mysteries. Another gust fluttered her nightdress.

Eager to tell the news, Michael waved his hands. "The Lost Boys saved me and John, Peter! They catched us from falling!" He was a schoolboy bred in captivity, released to the wilderness.

"We thought we were done for!" John was an older schoolboy, released a bit too late.

Peter crossed his arms, disapproving, his fine features severe. All the boys drew back and lowered their chins.

"You two were flying too high. You've been here long enough to know the rules." Peter's gaze darted. "The rest of you were too low! The Indians could have shot you, and then I'd have had to avenge you all."

The boys were solemn. They knew Peter to be most foreboding when his rules were broken, the primary one of which was the rule against growing up. It was rare that his boys knowingly disobeyed. Peter's laws hampered independent thinking somewhat, but Michael, as the littlest, was least grown-up and not as self-conscious as the others. He still asked questions. "Avenge! Our honor? Like in Wendy's stories?" Michael often fell asleep before the happy endings and missed important bits, but even he knew the importance of keeping up with Peter's decrees.

"No. *My* honor, for leading a pack of fools!"

The boys squirmed, not knowing whether to display amusement or shame, so in a practiced effort to appease their leader, some did one and some the other.

Wendy came to their rescue. She turned from Peter, his dagger, and his wrath, to the jumble of children. Hugging Michael, she assessed the damage. "It's all right, everyone is safe now. We've learned to take better care of ourselves next time. But Michael, John, how damp you are! Hanging about in clouds . . . "

And Peter permitted Wendy's motherly role to assume its authority. She gathered the family together. "Time to go home, children." She was relieved to see Peter's ill temper dissipate as swiftly as it had appeared, and they both hustled the Lost Boys toward their underground hideout. Wendy clutched the arrow, feeling even now that its tip pointed to danger. But no. That couldn't be. She was living happily ever after with Peter Pan, in once-upon-a-time, and the adventure of the arrow was over. Surely, she reasoned, Peter would make everything all right again.

As the band flew over the colorful Island toward home, the children took care to remain at the proper height, throwing occasional glances at their chief. Peter flew freely, shooting like the arrow after the tail of a parrot and wobbling comically alongside butterflies over their bushes.

Wendy, too, watched him. He plucked a large leaf and wiped his dagger clean.

Wendy looked away.

Amid her circlet of roses, the hidden thorns stung her again as over her shoulder she searched the darkening forest. No creature moved there. Only the Indian drums beat on, slowly and solemnly now. A dirge for their fallen warrior. The arrow grew heavy in her hand.

Wendy reminded herself that Peter had kept the children from danger. That always made it all right, afterwards.

Soon they would be safe with their suppers, chattering and quarreling about the day's adventures. They would gather before the fire to hear another of Wendy's tales.

Wendy shook herself and smiled uncertainly.

It would be all right, then. Everything would be fine.

It would be only a story.

That evening's adventure tale, punctuated by gasps and sighs from the children, proved worthy of Wendy's reputation. As it unfolded, even her brothers sat blinking. The Neverland was a mine of riches for Wendy's inspiration, and it lent her plenty of material on which to draw.

She had removed the uncomfortable crown with no loss of rank. Although none of her subjects appreciated the fact, Wendy remained a graceful, slender queen as she recounted her stories. She liked to imagine she had been enchanted by a gnome chief, to sit upon his throne in his underground cavern each night, inventing tales for the greedy ears of his gnome band. They were surrounded by walls of twining tree roots and leafy hangings, wooden flutes and animal bones, bows, quivers, and one sword. A pleasant loamy smell pervaded, perfect, her majesty thought, for a gnome chief's den.

This queen's clear blue eyes always spoke the truth. Now they were lit by the hearth fire, and her fair hair fell over her shoulders. The boys squatted in a half circle at her feet, cozy on the earthen floor as she gathered the straws of each day's experience, twisting the strands with nursery stories, to spin golden rings to hang upon their ears. Wendy's words cast a spell that, as yet, even she didn't fully understand. A blending of truth, myth and magic.

If this lady had a secret, it was in her smile. She didn't need enchantment to call it; it flew naturally, willingly to her lips at the slightest excuse. It was just the right shape for a queen's smile, and it cradled the hidden kiss, visible only to the few who could read her heart. Wendy's smile seemed impatient to bestow its kiss upon her prince. But as yet, her desire remained as arcane to Peter as her kiss.

Although the prince declined to come forward tonight, the smile presented itself as Wendy looked around at the faces of her listeners. "Don't be afraid, children, it's just a story." She had given free rein to her imagination, and the ride had gotten a bit rough. At her reassurance, the gnomes breathed more easily. The difference between them and their chief was that Peter did not distinguish between the real and the make-believe, and yet he was not afraid. He was exhilarated.

Only Tinker Bell, that moody bit of fairy, seemed unaffected. Here was another queen, and one not inclined to share power. Tinker Bell was proud, perhaps because she was different. Her wings, instead of the fussy, lacy affairs so common among her kind, were luxuriant like a butterfly's. Wings such as these didn't merely move through the air. They moved the air itself. And they were blue. The intense, iridescent blue of the peacock.

Tinker Bell disdained to honor 'the Wendy' with her presence at story time. Scorning to be found among the gnomes, the fairy hid herself away in her niche to sit unseen and unheard with chin in hand and ears pricked throughout the narrative, hanging on every syllable. Tinker Bell listened assiduously to the big girl's words. She stored them up and stacked them to use against her later, like cannonballs. The battleground was Peter. The Wendy was the enemy.

As Wendy's story concluded, Peter jumped up on his chair, exulting. "Nobody tells a story like Wendy!" Then, usurping success, "That's why I chose her to be our mother." Many nights, in what to Peter seemed the distant past, he had hovered outside the nursery window, listening with rapt attention to Wendy's tales, especially those about himself. Now she was here and she was his. Peter had made up his mind; she must never go back and grow up. To that end, he discharged an appreciative smile.

Enchantment not yet broken, Wendy was flattered by Peter's warmth of feeling. Manners, however, dictated a show of modesty. "I only came to look after you poor Lost Boys. Peter told me you had not one pocket among you, and no medicine. Someone had to mother you." The tale of her first meeting with Peter and his insistence that she come away with him was one of Wendy's favorites, recited on many an evening. But as she remembered that long-ago night, a questioning look crossed her face, and she dropped her playful air to stare into the fire. The matter had begun to trouble her of late. How long ago? Exactly when had this enchantment seized hold of her?

The boys were familiar with Wendy's story of pockets and medicine, and accustomed to performing their part in it. They picked up their cue, and only Peter noticed their mother's change in mood. "Thank you, Wendy lady! What would we do without a mother?" In a body, the boys poured themselves over Wendy, ending her distraction and earning Peter's approval.

Wendy recovered, laughing, and pushed her boys away, rising from the throne to light the nightlight. It was an opaque shell the size of her hand, spiraling into nothingness at the center, its inside sprinkled with fairy dust. Such grains of Tinker Bell's magic had enabled Wendy, John and Michael to fly from home. All it took to master the air was fairy dust and happiness. For Wendy, Peter supplied both.

It hadn't been easy to get Tink to part with more dust for the nightlight, but Peter had persuaded her, knowing it was important to Wendy. He had explained that it was important because Wendy wanted her brothers to remember their home. Michael and John might go back, someday, if the nightlight in the nursery still burned by the open window. Tinker Bell had demanded a good deal of Peter's attention until the subject was exhausted. Ultimately, she permitted herself to be swayed, surrendering the dust in hopes the Wendy, too, would remember home—and exit with her brothers.

Wendy lit a twig in the fire and touched its flame to the grains of gold in the shell. With the gentlest of breaths, she blew on it, and the powder ignited to glow with a warm, dancing light, exuding a fragrance of fermented apples. As she placed the nightlight on the table next to the bed, John studied it, remembering something from far away. "Wendy, are you and Father going out tonight?"

Wendy's eyes glowed like the fairy light. "Peter, shall we go out like real mothers and fathers? We could go to the Fairy Glade!" In her excitement, she forgot and placed a hand on his arm.

But he didn't shake it off. He bent his elbow like a high-born gentleman and escorted her. "We shall go to the theatre, Madam, and wear chimney hats." Everyone laughed while he strutted around the room with Wendy on his arm. Her fingers met the toned energy under his bare skin and she looked up at his well-formed profile. Although it was impossible to determine an age for Peter, Wendy knew herself to be petite for her own. As he allowed her to press against him, she observed again that Peter was just taller than she, and in her opinion, they were a perfect match.

Only one boy had grown taller than Peter. It was Slightly, light-haired and lean, who now interrupted their promenade. "I think I remember the theatre. Isn't that a story-place?"

Peter stopped. "We have the best stories right here. And mothers and fathers don't leave the children at night, do they? Afraid they'll fly away." He dropped Wendy's arm and turned to face her, breaking the connection. For a moment, she had been wearing her mother's white evening gown. But it was gone.

Curly, named for the nature of his rusty hair, was fascinated with the world the Darlings had left behind. He turned to Wendy, too. "They can leave the children as long as a dog is there, right, Wendy?"

"Not a dog, Curly. A nurse, or a nightlight, like ours. Now it's nighttime, boys. Into bed."

Peter propelled himself into his chair by the fire and watched while Wendy presided over the ritual.

"Give me your hats . . . clothes for mending . . . weapons. . . . Now here's your medicine." Make-believe medicine was gulped with genuine distaste. "I'd think you'd be used to it by now!" Wendy was amazed at how her boys resisted it, aware as they were that it was only water. But she excelled at dispensing it. It had become a challenge. "I spent all morning working out how to get you to take it." She released her grip on the nose of the last boy, who happened to be the tough, solidly-built Tootles. He rubbed his nose and appealed to Peter.

"If we take our medicine, will we get strong enough to wear boots? To stomp around in all day and stow by the bed at night, like pirates?" It was Tootles' greatest sorrow that there was not one pair in the hideout to polish after adventures.

Peter leaned back, his answer casual. "We'll have plenty of boots, once we've slain the lot." He directed a meaningful stare at Wendy.

Wendy ignored the hint and nudged Tootles toward the rest of the children on the bed. "Make room for Michael tonight, boys. He's just outgrown—" Wendy stopped short and shot a glance at Peter. He eyed her sharply, then looked up at the basket hanging over the bed, in which Michael had slept . . . until tonight. Squinting at Michael, he sized the little boy up, then laughed.

"He's got a ways to grow yet. I'll keep him a little longer!"

Wendy promised herself to be more careful. Her rapid heart-beat slowed.

"Peter!" Slightly tossed a tiny missile. "Here's another baby tooth. I think I've only two left now." Peter caught it and held it up to examine in the light of the fire. Wendy's heart sped again. A mystery was at work here, in spite of Peter's rules. It had something to do with growing up, and as Slightly's mother, Wendy would one day have to guide him through it. She had recently begun to wonder who would guide herself when the time came.

"I don't know why you boys can't keep your teeth. I still have my first set." Peter shoved his dagger aside and stowed the tooth in his pocket, the first Wendy had fashioned on the night she was initiated as mother of his hearth. It was too tricky to fasten a pocket to his skeleton leaves, which in any case were perpetually falling off and regrowing themselves—such leaves were rare, only to be found in the Neverland, and so far found only by Peter—nor was it feasible to fasten a pocket to the ivy vines he liked to wind about himself. But Wendy was resourceful. Now Peter's pocket had a flap to secure its contents when he flew upside-down, and she had made it of leather and strapped it to his sword belt, which he always wore whether or not he carried the sword, for he was never without his knife.

At last the boys lay piled on the one bed in the hideout. It was comfy, and big enough for all, including Michael, and there they wiggled under the furry skins provided by Peter's forest kills. Hunting was Peter's favorite sport and he kept the hideout well supplied. Tonight the animals seemed still alive until Peter sprang from his chair and advanced with face aslant and dagger drawn. "Do I have to slay those beasts again?" At which the boys immediately lay still.

With the children settled, Wendy moved about, listening to the breathy music of Peter's pipes and putting the hideout to rights, making it feel like home. From time to time she studied Peter. One of the few places he sat still was in his big chair next to her own, while playing father to the boys or prince of the palace. Peter had woven his throne from willow boughs, and their greenery clung to it yet. Wendy watered it every morning with the dregs of the medicine bottle. It, too, thrived under her care, lending to the cavern a foresty touch from the upper world.

Peter noticed her watching him and cocked his head in curiosity. Smiling, she kept her voice low. "I was thinking how you sit enthroned on your seat of honor, like a prince in his feasting hall. You rule your realm from that chair."

"I like being prince! It's even better than being father."

Wendy gathered up the discarded clothing and joined Peter at the hearth. She advanced with caution, as always, for instinct and experience informed her that, prince or not, he might startle when approached, like some woodland creature.

Maybe if she made it sound like a story he would understand her this time.

The fire spoke first in soft pops and crackles, then Wendy. "One night, I was sleeping in my bed in the nursery and a wonderful boy whispered in my ear."

He was listening.

"You wanted me to come away with you, so you taught me to fly. Do you remember?"

Peter remembered. He remembered how, with the promise of flight and something else he didn't yet understand, he had cunningly drawn her out the nursery window—just before her mother and father burst through it, breathless, reaching vainly into the night to pull her back. It had been a grand adventure!

"It's one of your best stories!"

"It's *our* story, Peter, and it really happened."

Peter shrugged. "They all really happened."

"No, no." She leaned closer. "In London, I longed for adventure. I couldn't wait for it so I made up stories to tell Michael and John. It's only here the stories are true," except, so far, the love stories. "Most of them."

She had long ago returned his acorn for the thimble kiss she had given him. Peter didn't understand what a kiss was, and when Wendy quite shamelessly offered one that first evening, he simply held out his hand to accept it. Not wishing to embarrass him, she had slipped her thimble into his fingers instead, and with an honorable sense of obligation, he'd given her an acorn in exchange.

The acorn saved her life once. It still bore the scar of the arrow Tootles had fired at her. Wendy didn't blame Tootles for being bloodthirsty. It was the way he'd been brought up, and of course he was urged to shoot by Tinker Bell before Wendy had the chance to be introduced to the Lost Boys. But that was all in the past. These days, Wendy got more practical use out of the thimble than the acorn, so the acorn lay on the mantel, displaying its wound.

Like most of the furnishings in the hideout, the mantel was crafted by the enterprising Twins with their building skills. Carved from a hunk of alder, it was constructed to exhibit Peter's array of trophies, from beadwork to buck racks, with a brass button winking here and there. The mantel dominated the room and dwarfed the acorn. But Wendy wasn't deceived by dimensions. Like her love stories, the tiny seed might yield a forest yet. Neglecting her mending, she stared at the mantel and fidgeted with the thimble.

Peter said, "As long as I'm in the stories, I don't care if they're true or not." His eyes grew bright. "I had a fine adventure in the woods today, Wendy. I killed that Indian!" He bounded up to seize the arrow from the mantel and struck a heroic pose. "He threatened you and the boys." With its shaft in his fist, Peter shook the arrow above his head in a victory rite. Leaping from the fire, his shadow played along, arching over the earthy ceiling.

"Peter! For no better reason than that?"

He stopped, indignant. "Should I have let him kill one of you first?" The arrow came down. "I have to protect my family."

"You're full of courage, and a good father to the boys. But sometimes you frighten me." Wendy peered up at his shadow, looming, but momentarily still. "Just like the forest beasts."

He tossed the arrow and perched close again, his shadow condensing. "You never act frightened. You're always very brave on adventures, even if you won't let the boys and me kill any more filthy pirates." But Peter's instincts about Wendy were alert, too, and now he offered rare credit for her cunning. Admiration oiled his voice. "You've managed to keep the pirates at bay so we haven't had to fight them. Even Nibs and Tootles have piped down about attacking them. And we'd have gobbled that cake if you hadn't warned us it was a pirates' trap."

Wendy nodded like a sage. "Only a mother knows how subtle pirates can be." She herself had invented the dangers, conjured them up, in many a story. Wendy knew danger, intimately.

"You're a wise one, Wendy."

Peter's praise warmed her as heartily as the fire, yet as she gazed into the flames, she found herself puzzling. "The danger is real now. But once upon a time it wasn't." Her forehead creased. "Even Time behaves differently here. It's the only thing that *isn't* real." She looked up at Michael's empty basket and thought of Slightly's tooth in the maw of Peter's pouch. "I sometimes think the crocodile swallowed Time right along with that clock. I never know where it will pop up next." As she spoke of the crocodile, the image of its teeth caused her to wince. Like a row of knives, each committed to slaughter, they triggered an uncomfortable memory of Peter's dagger, and his hands wiping a man's blood from it this afternoon. The warmth receded, and Wendy felt much older than the girl she had been the night she arrived here.

"You can tell the croc's story tomorrow night!"

Wendy's posture sagged. "But how many tomorrow nights will come? How many have passed? I used to be so sure about Time. I could rely on it. But I keep trying, and I can't think how long we've been here, away from home."

Innocent as he might be, Peter recognized dangerous ground. She'd worn that same look the night he flew back to the nursery to retrieve her china tea set. Peter would keep Wendy, no matter what he had to do, and he'd whispered that message to Wendy's mother where she dozed by the window. He'd even shed a few of his skeleton leaves to be discovered by Mr. and Mrs. Darling in the morning, underscoring his determination. Peter didn't know as much about parents as he pretended, but he suspected they could read an omen almost as well as he could.

"You're right, Wendy, Time isn't real here, so it doesn't matter how many nights." With his sly smile playing along his lips, he scooted closer. She scented the lingering leaves, just as she had when he'd first awakened her, and his next words thrummed the memory. "I knew that first night how much you wanted to fly."

Her face cleared. "Yes, Peter. I wanted it very badly. You were clever to see that." She gripped the thimble tighter.

"The cleverness of me!"

"You're clever enough to see there's something else I want badly, now." She watched Peter's face take on the alert expression he wore whenever she began a story. So many stories.

She had been patient such a long while, anticipating the natural response of boy to girl. Wendy couldn't gauge the time, but she'd grown at least an inch waiting for it. It had to come sooner or later. Setting the thimble aside, she held her breath. They were close now. No more delays.

Slowly, Wendy reached for Peter's hand. She cradled it like a fledgling and lifted it, placing it against her cheek, barely touching his thumb to the kiss at the corner of her mouth. "Can you see it?"

Alive to danger again, Peter didn't move. Wendy willed him to read her heart as she watched his wary eyes considering her. The time might be right at last. If she believed. For one long moment, she held hope in her hand.

Then, like sunlight, Peter slipped through her fingers. He leapt to his feet and spun away. Snatching his sword, he darted toward the tree trunk at the end of the room. At a safe distance now, Peter, the superb make-believer, assumed his best paternal manner. "I'll go up on guard, Wendy, now that the Little Ones are abed. Good night!" He nodded with authority, then snaked his way up through the hollow tree to the forest floor—to guard *himself* until such time as Wendy no longer threatened.

Wendy sighed, her hand lingering on the hidden kiss. "Will he ever see it?" She frowned, and immediately heard a familiar mocking tinkle from a niche in the wall. Her eyes shifted toward the sound, the frown formed a line of determination, and her hand moved stealthily down. The slipper slid off her foot and sailed in Tinker Bell's direction. A musical retort followed, after which both females put out the lights and retired, each harboring dark thoughts about Peter Pan.

A Pirate's Passion

A dark man harbored dark thoughts about Pan.

The night was black, the cabin blacker. The man was darker still. His hair spread in waves on the silken pillows, like the midnight surface of the sea. It parted at the ring hung upon his ear, a delicate filigree, yet solidly golden. The beard was trim, but further growth of whiskers darkened his face and neck with unsuppressed masculinity. Small beads of moisture lay stagnant on skin too taut to allow retreat.

The dark thoughts interrupted his existence, punctuated it, so that he lived in broken segments of desire, urgent but never concluding. . . .

Hook lay alone, hating it.

Barely controlled hostility filled his eyes. Forget-me-not blue eyes, beautiful to look upon, deceptively blue. They'd be blood-red as he watched Pan die.

The ship shifted as the sea tempted her. Small creaks and stretching groans sounded as she strained at the ropes of her anchors. Footsteps fell, and muted shouts, while men worked to confine her. A bird of prey, she was jessed but menacing.

His hook lay at rest upon the couch, the peelings of a ravished apple scattered round it. The apple's seeds languished where he'd spat them. Its sweet taste lingered, its last drop on his lip. He drew it in with his tongue. He was finished with it.

When would he finish Pan?

He ached to finish Pan. Pan's destruction was his passion. The kind of passion only pirates know, the bloodlust, to be slaked at the thrust of a blade.

And at the end of passion, victory. How deeply this man desired victory, prized it above most other things. The urge to win must be satisfied—at the expense of the boy. Only a man would live to see the conclusion of the blood feud. And already, much blood was spilled.

His throat constricted. He couldn't taste the apple any longer. That old, bitter loss of blood overwhelmed its flavor.

But the hour of triumph was coming, and soon. It beat ever closer. Hook's instinct felt it; his pulse throbbed with the feeling. His moment of vengeance for all the damage wrought by that arrogant boy.

And now, a girl. Pan had taken a mother for his boys.

The throbbing shifted lower.

'The Wendy,' they called her. She had the sense to keep them away from bloody pirates. With good reason. Hook considered the fate he and his claw would mete out to those tender throats when he had them. His good hand gripping the hair at the base of the skull, persuading a stretch of neck to lay itself bare. The blade lightly applied, coaxed, for maximum pleasure. And a ruby trail. Bloody boys.

They were far from innocent, Pan's accomplices. In unguarded moments he'd lost good men to those whelps. They'd made attempts on his ship, as well. Yet that girl protected them as if they were lambs. What to do with her? No doubt she, too, had a tender neck.

But she had shown herself to be no fool. He would have to be subtle. With an untried female at his mercy, so many possibilities arose.

Necessity decreed he begin by plucking her from Pan's circle. She'd interfered with Hook's plans. No boys abroad after dusk, watch posted at the Lagoon. She'd never even let them touch Smee's poisonous cake. He'd finally had it thrown to the croc.

Hook's face contorted. He couldn't abide the thought of the croc. He sat up quickly, apple peelings fluttering to the floor. He couldn't abide the thought of his own dark blood, to remember it oozing through the teeth of that beast—and over the bright blade of Pan.

The memory took him instantly. Blades clanging, metal flashing, blinding sun, swooping sword song, clattering, thick dark blood warm everywhere, sleeve, breast, eyes, hair, boy, boots, deck. Slipping on it, knees smashing. Unimagined pain, white hot, sparkling ring on white flesh flying into air, raining red, green monster snapping. Excruciating. Searing. Jeering face of insolent boy, crowing, crowing. Needing to strangle but unable—only one hand. . . .

By the time he stopped shaking, another taste lingered on his tongue. Dark crimson drops stained the rug. His own blood. The only thing in the world at which James Hook flinched.

He mastered his ragged breathing, controlled his face.

Soon.

Teeth clenched, he raised the hook to forget-me-not eyes. Staring beyond it into the Darkness, he hissed his vow to the unseen enemy.

"I'll tear you!"

Ship's Company

The tip of the knife severed the threads, tearing its way to the top of the seam. Mr. Smee replaced the knife in his teeth. He concentrated, positioning the cloth under the needle of his sewing machine.

The fabric was robust. Hearty, like its handler. The red Irishman sat on deck this morning mending the flag with its skull over crossed swords, the Jolly Roger. Proud work, and Smee's hands were skillful. The grinning standard would wave once again, inspiring fear in faint hearts and loyalty in black. Smee hummed along with the machine, his tall, muscular frame at odds with the homeliness of his chore, his boot beating time as it pumped the wrought-work treadle.

The pirate vessel lay at anchor in Neverbay, a favorite haunt of both captain and crew after weeks at work on the sea. The great ship returned there time and again between her experiences on wilder water. After her most recent flight, she'd come home to roost again. The bay's refuge allowed for repairs to the *Roger* and fresh paint for her gilded accoutrements; the Island offered leisure for the pirates and the sport of destroying its resident enemies. Of fish, fruit, and game the Neverland yielded plenty, and for those who knew where to find it, female companionship—although not abundant—was avid. In these men's opinions, no more welcoming port existed.

Nor sailed a more effective officer than Mr. Smee. Although the *Roger* was anchored in a port of pleasure, its immaculate deck spoke for Smee's efficiency, as did its polished fittings. Confident his fellow crewmen would execute their duties even in the cheer of a sunlit morning, he felt no need to prod them. Smee paid little heed as the sailors hustled about the deck, performing their tasks and swapping tales with mates. These men knew his reputation. As he labored over his sewing, not one of them would invite the consequences of baiting Mr. Smee about his domestic talents. He had demonstrated that his skill at cutting and stitching was not restricted to inanimate objects. He'd cut with the knife if the matter was personal, or the cat-o'-nine-tails on captain's orders, and then he'd stitch the sailor up again and see him fit for duty.

Not many shirked their duty. And none begrudged Smee his position of bo'sun to Captain Hook, in charge of the ship. It placed him within a proximity to that magnificent and volatile man that would have tested the mettle of the best of them. No, Mr. Smee, reputed to be as strong and as sweet as rum, was respected.

But now his mates subdued their banter. The sunlight hadn't dimmed, yet the men's aspects darkened as if thunderheads scudded in. Nudging one another, they found work elsewhere, deserting Mr. Smee on the deck while they melted away toward safer posts. The sloshing of the bay waters filled the void, and the gait of fine boots on the boards, all unnoticed by Mr. Smee humming at his machine until a shadow slid over the cloth, staining it blacker. A sharpness on Smee's shoulder cut song and motion short. His knife thumped onto the flag. Carefully, he heeded the low, silky voice.

"You neglected to attend me last night, Smee. I was alone."

Alone. Smee heard the echoes ring within that word. "Aye, Cap'n." The bo'sun's eyes peered sidewise over his spectacles, the only part of him daring movement. He was a brave man, but not foolhardy. "The ship was restless last night. The lads had a time keeping her to anchor, Sir." He hoped he'd find smooth sailing in these waters. Smee knew better than any of his mates that in the absence of fellowship, the vessel was of highest concern to her captain.

"I know. I felt it." The hook lifted. It snagged and snapped a thread of Smee's striped shirt. Hook's gaze on his bo'sun was keen, and it shifted to the banner where it lay stabbed by the needle. Silently, the white teeth grinned accord with the legendary captain. Hook's handsome face leered back at it. Living on the edge of crossed swords wasn't comfortable. It was invigorating.

The flag called the Jolly Roger was his ship's namesake and Hook's sole companion among this crew, for the elegant Captain James Hook had no mate. His men were good pirates all, fierce and lusty, and Hook valued them. But even Mr. Smee, with his many talents and well knowing his captain's ways, was a common man. These sailors had championed Hook and sworn oaths of loyalty to the death—but they were so far beneath him. They toiled below while Hook rode high like Roger, alone, regarding the horizon.

Hook regarded it now. Silver seabirds sailed above him, their thoughtless flight appearing so easy. Of all the creatures on and above the earth, Hook envied only the birds, which possessed the final freedom of flight. But he didn't need to be airborne to view the arms of the bay cradling the *Roger*, nor the open sea reclining beyond them, shamelessly tempting men of appetite to partake of her offerings. And the Island behind so full of promise, burgeoning with life and color. The captain breathed deeply, relishing the salt-scented breeze that dared to twine his hair. Its boldness brought a smile to his lips. "The horizon looks well today."

It was time to unfurl the scheme. His hook prodded black Roger, needling him like Smee's machine. "Rattle him back up, Smee. We've work to do."

Smee's shoulders loosened a bit. He liked the smile on his captain's face. So cold it warmed him. He ventured a quick inspection of his threadbare sleeve. He'd have to run up a patch for that—later.

Smee's red beard spread with the grin. "Unrip your plan, Captain!"

The Story of
Red-Handed Jill

By the standards of the Neverland, the day had been an uneventful one, and Wendy was obliged to tap her creativity for fresh material. This night's tale would be new—one of those that hadn't as yet come true.

"Tonight I'll tell you the story of Red-Handed Jill." She inspected the crew gathered at her feet.

"Oooo!" Every nook of the cavern filled with anticipation, and Peter and the boys leaned into the firelight.

"Red-Handed Jill was a Pirate Queen. She was known far and wide for her prowess in swordplay, and she was a crack shot. The first time she fired a pistol, she shot the eye of a parrot at fifty paces." Wendy aimed a make-believe pistol in both hands, and fired. "She wore sturdy boots and sailed on a fearsome pirate ship. And she left terror in her wake."

Big eyes all around the circle.

"Red-Handed Jill got her name from her very first adventure. She killed a beast when she was only a girl—"

"Not even grown-up?" piped Michael.

"Not even. But that did it. She was a lady from then on." Wendy put her back into her task. "You see, Jill had gone rambling through the forest one day, looking for fun—she was quite a bold girl—and a tiger scented her out and followed her, creeping until it could get a good jump at her. But Jill was too clever for that. She heard that tiger stalking her and she hid behind a tree, and when the beast passed by, she waited for its tail. Then she grabbed it. She yanked on it, and the animal was so surprised that Jill laughed—it had such a funny look on its face."

"Like this?" Slightly had been a boy longer than most of the others, and he always knew how Things looked. He'd had a lot of experience imagining them.

"Yes, Slightly, only not so human." She licked her lips. "Jill whipped the knife from her belt." Wendy whipped it. "And slashed that tiger's throat." Wendy slashed it. "But not before the animal dragged a sharp claw across her wrist, drawing blood." Gripping her arm, Wendy began to 'bleed' profusely. "And when she saw her own blood mix with the blood of her first kill, she dropped her knife and went all savage and got the blood-rage!"

The boys clutched at each other's shoulders. Wendy heard a ripping in the shirt she'd be mending that evening.

"Jill dropped down on her knees by the pool of blood and plunged her hand into it. She raised up her arms and whooped and danced until the rage left her. She knew no one would believe she'd killed a tiger all on her own at such a tender age, so she cut off the tiger's tail with her gory knife and tied it round her waist."

"Eeeww. . . ."

Peter rolled his eyes and scowled at Curly.

"And her right hand never came clean again. It was stained with her first blood—the blood of the beast that stalked her. When the people of her village saw her red hand and the tiger-tail belt, they knew she was fierce and they named her Red-Hand. They thought of her as a tiger herself, and they were so afraid that they wouldn't come near her. She was beautiful, too, and she took to carrying a whip and she used it to bring down any boy who tried to tame her. Well, as you can imagine, even her mother and father didn't want such a headstrong girl any longer. She left the village with a reputation and stowed away aboard a barge on the river. And eventually she got out to sea and joined up with pirates."

"The pirates let a lady join them?"

"Yes, Nibs, but she had to prove her valor first."

"I thought women are bad luck aboard ship?"

"Oh, no, Tootles. That's just girls. She was a lady by then, as I told you. Pirates love ladies." Tootles nodded with an understanding he didn't yet own.

"The Pirate King didn't even try to take her whip away and tame her. He knew she was too magnificent for that, like her tiger. They sailed together and had lots of adventures, and the Pirate King fell in love with her. He made her his Queen and took her to Paradise. In the end they kissed . . . just like the end of all great stories."

Sighs all around. When Wendy roused herself from her magic to speak to the boys again, she noted their wistful expressions; they were learning to appreciate the finer points of her stories. And the boys weren't alone. A musical breath issued even from behind the curtain of Tinker Bell's niche. As always when Wendy spoke, the fairy was aloof. But she was listening.

With renewed enthusiasm, Wendy surged ahead. "Red-Handed Jill and her Pirate King had more adventures—" She glanced at Peter. Framed by his willow chair, he was cleaning his nails with his dagger. Wendy bit her words. "But I'll tell the rest of the story tomorrow."

"Tell it tonight!" shrieked the Twins, their brown eyes eager as they clamored for more. Since there were two of them and only one of Wendy, they could never get enough of their mother's attention.

"You heard Wendy, boys. That's the end of Jill for tonight. And tomorrow Wendy can tell a better story. I don't like lady pirates."

Wendy frowned. "Peter! It's a lovely story." The boys shouted in agreement. Like Peter, they knew what they wanted and how to get it.

But Peter was firm. "It's a *love* story. Anyway, Paradise is right here in the Neverland." He tipped his head and grinned at Wendy. In the light of his smile, even an underground hideout took on idyllic attributes.

She nodded, brightening. "Yes, it could be here. I believe it is."

Considering the idea, Peter thought for a moment, then said, "But I've never seen this Jill with her tiger-tail belt here." Wendy imagined he might be intrigued with the lady after all, but just as her hopes began to rise, his eyes narrowed. "Nor do I want to."

"She's only a legend. But why don't you like her story?"

"Because she grew up, of course."

This time, Wendy couldn't suppress a smile. "Most people do, Peter."

"But what kind of adventure is that? I'll never grow up!"

The response from his crew was immediate.

"Nor us, Peter."

"We won't, either!"

Secure in his authority, Peter challenged all comers. "Who wants to grow up?"

His band of boys shook their heads emphatically. "Nobody!"

"Who wants to leave Paradise?"

"Not us!"

Peter seized his dagger and jabbed it upward. "I say death to lady pirates!" His henchmen roared approval, and when their cries began to fade, he whipped them up again. "Death to *all* pirates!"

Partial to the lady she'd brought to life, Wendy opened her mouth to protest, but Curly hopped up and laid a finger above his lip to indicate a mustache. Crooking his other arm, he hunched over and mimed a burly pirate, stamping his boots along the floor. The boys giggled, but not nearly so hard as when upon his 'death' by Peter's knife, Curly smoothed his hair and dusted off his sleeves, which, in spite of Wendy's care, were so patched as to render the gesture ludicrous. Even in make-believe, Curly was such a gentleman that the boys rolled around the floor, laughing and holding their bellies while the melody of Tinker Bell's mirth flowed from her hidden room. Shaking off the sting of Peter's remarks, Wendy, too, smiled again.

Peter placed a hand on Curly's head, pushing him down into the circle and reprimanding him in mock severity. "You've heard too many of Wendy's tales about ladies and gentlemen in London. From now on, no more love stories. Only children who are getting too old like romance, and nothing is worse than growing up."

Cozy as it was, the cavern seemed to Wendy to constrict, and she felt an urge to spread her arms to hold its walls at bay. Compelled to speak her mind but reluctant to dispel the others' humor, Wendy hesitated. Time in the Neverland was so slippery. She couldn't guess how long she'd been thinking this thought. Weeks maybe, or months. It was a simple idea, but not an easy one to suggest to Peter, for it ran counter to his law. Fingering the nightgown she was outgrowing, she looked around at the gap-toothed grins of the boys' missing baby teeth and decided that, however capricious Time might be here, there was no escaping it. Her proposal's moment had come. She placed her faith in Peter's zeal for adventure and captured Jill Red-Hand's boldness. The woven roots that formed the walls appeared to recede along with her reticence, and although her stomach flipped itself over, Wendy didn't flinch.

"Growing up might be an awfully big adventure, Peter."

Stunned, the boys solidified. They sat like stones. Peter stilled, staring as if Jill's whip had struck him. The hideout waited and even the hearth fire died down to listen. In the silence, Wendy dared further. "When you grow up, you can fall in love and do important work and see the world and be independent and free." Pausing, she looked intently at Peter. "I want to do all those things."

Peter's eyes reflected the fervor of her own. "I'm independent and free, but I have no use for the rest of it!"

Wendy loved the passion that stirred him. She wished she could believe the passion was for her. For the moment, she took what satisfaction she could from simply inspiring it. Inhaling a calming breath first, she accomplished a reasonable tone. "You're a wonderful boy, Peter. You've always been independent. The rest of us are different. We'll have to depend on you always, unless we choose to grow up."

The children blinked. They were used to hearing Wendy soothe Peter. She often teased him. She had never incited him before.

Peter jumped to his feet and bent over her while the boys shrank back. "That's how it should be! I'm the captain of our band. You do as I say and you'll always be safe."

Supporting herself on the arms of her chair, Wendy rose and stood to face him. "But there have been times when the boys and I had to depend on ourselves." Accustomed to attributing the noblest motives to Peter, she softened her voice. "I know you want to keep us safe. You care about us." Care might grow up to be love, in Time. Seeking evidence of this notion, she unearthed it, not from his words but from the intensity of his regard.

"And it should never change. We're a family, make-believe or not." He plunked down in his chair and flung a leg over its arm.

Wendy was touched, yet determined. "But I'm learning all the time how to get along. One day I'll want to do as *I* decide, like Red-Handed Jill." Each boy stared with open mouth. "That is the day I'll grow up."

Peter leaned forward. "If you're to stay with me, Wendy, you won't ever grow up. That's my law. I'll never be made to be a man! Not one of my boys *ever* has! What about the rest of you?"

Peter's troops mustered. Like him, they knew what they wanted, and how to get it.

"Aye, aye!"

"Never grow up!"

"Peter's our captain! Hooray!" The tension broke like a dam, and the boys bathed in the waters of their former security.

Wendy sat down. She wouldn't allow him to see that she was shaken. "All right, Peter. I understand. I hope you'll try to understand, too."

Peter did understand. He understood submission. Whether it was real or imaginary didn't worry him. Glad once again to rule unchallenged, he smiled broadly. He darted to the mantel, and applying the reverence he awarded all his trophies, elevated his acorn. Holding it out to Wendy, he waited, then lifted her hand and placed his offering on the pale altar of her palm. He brought his face close to hers so that she felt his hair brush her own. "You belong here. In Paradise." He drew back, and his green eyes cajoled her. "You must stay with me, Wendy. We'll always need a mother." That much, he understood perfectly.

"Yes. You all need mothers." Every one of her brood, after all, was just a boy. But what did Wendy need? She looked down at the acorn in her hand. Wrapping her fingers tightly around it, she felt the arrow's notch eating into her skin. With his kiss in her hand and his needs clearly satisfied, Peter winked at her and resumed his throne.

John, amazed at his sister's nerve in sparring with Peter, could see she required cheering up. He administered the best medicine he knew. "Tell us another story, Wendy."

"Yes, yes! Another!"

She had grown fond of these boys. Still rebellious, she wondered if *that* form of growing was against Peter's law, too. She struck the thought aside and sought a smile for them. She found it, one of those that was always so ready. She lost it, and found a fraction of another. "All right, dears, I see that you should have a story. A mother knows." She aimed the acorn at John and fired it with force. John caught it and hurried it back to the mantel like a hot potato while the other children awaited their mother's next yarn.

Wendy gritted her teeth, but she was magnanimous. She was a queen. Buying time, she pretended to search her mood for a story, but quite naturally, the darkest one of all came instantly to mind. "I'll tell another pirate story. And to make Peter happy, this one involves no ladies—yet."

A hush fell over the hideout. Peter was unaware he'd just been bitten by a certain Pirate Queen's tiger, and his faith in his Wendy was restored. Her breathing was shallow, but she began, fiercely.

"Now I'll tell you the tale of the blackest pirate of them all."

Collective gasp. The boys knew who was coming.

"This is the tale of the terrible Captain Hook!"

The fire spat, the Twins sniffled and Michael cried. The power of the man was that strong.

"Be brave, my hearties, for you never know when you'll meet him. You must be prepared—if anything can prepare you for that kind of shock. Captain James Hook, the lion of the sea, the scourge of sailors everywhere. The tyrant of the *Jolly Roger*, which lies at anchor, even now, in Neverbay."

This was too much for Michael, who ran screaming to Wendy's lap. She held him, but she was merciless.

"Hook is handsome and haughty. He has a mane of wavy hair, like a lion's, only black and more civilized. He cultivates a glossy goatee, and wears a heavy golden earring. Hook displays perfect manners, being very well-bred. His voice is silken, his costume beautiful, ever so elegant. But looks can be deceiving. As beautiful as he appears, his heart is cold. And as cold as his heart is, his smile is warm and gracious. He could melt you with it."

The boys thought this a bit much and became restless. Wendy, however, was a consummate storyteller. She knew her audience. "And his eyes are the blue of forget-me-nots—until he strikes to kill! Then, they burn red! That is when you know you are about to die. . . . "

Now all were crying, except Michael, who fell asleep. Peter glowed.

"The young James Hook was bo'sun to Blackbeard. Buccaneering was mother's milk to him. When he'd looted enough booty and learned all the pirates' tricks, he jumped ship to go his own way. But Blackbeard challenged him to a furious duel. By that time, Hook was a master swordsman, and he carved a mark on his captain's cheek. Then Hook struck out on his own and commandeered the *Jolly Roger*, that infamous ship, the savage of the sea, with its powerful big gun, Long Tom. He took on the crew, but chose no mate, for Hook is a solitary man, and beset by Darkness. He brought with him his own bo'sun, the brawny redheaded Irishman, Smee. Mr. Smee is like rum, they say—strong and sweet—but after a fight, he'll wipe his spectacles before his sword.

"Hook's crew is a treasure trove of miscreants who, in admiration of their ingenious captain, have sworn loyalty to the bitter end. Among them is the handsome Cecco, an Italian brigand, bedecked with jewelry and full of bloodlust. And there's Cookson, and Alf Mason and Gentleman Starkey—Starkey is one of the most horrible of Hook's pirates. His face is scarred from teaching fencing, and he still carries the ruler he brandished among the terrorized children he once taught at school. And there's Bill Jukes, tattooed from stem to stern. And the huge black man, whose name is so dreaded in his native Africa that no one but Hook dares to speak it, even here! And oddest of all is Noodler, whose hands are on backward. But . . . at least he *has* hands . . . for Hook has but one!" Wendy, always the professional, paused for effect. It arrived on cue.

"Where Hook's right hand ought to be is a deadly iron claw. As you can imagine, he uses it to great advantage in dueling. That hook is feared by his enemies and his own men alike. But, you're wondering how he lost his hand."

Breathless, the boys bent to hear.

"He lost it in battle, with Peter Pan!"

The children jumped up and cheered. "Hooray for Peter! Brave Peter!" Peter went further and crowed. Michael drooled.

"Hook is afraid of almost nothing." Wendy mixed metaphors in her excitement, "Only one sight curdles his black heart. The only thing in the world Captain James Hook can't abide is the shedding of his own blood. That is why he dreads the crocodile, who tasted it once before, when Peter fed him Hook's hand, rings and all. That croc would like nothing better than to finish him off. Which would draw a lot of blood and cause Hook to faint.

"So you see, the wily pirate captain had his bo'sun, Smee, wrap a ticking clock in a bundle of meat and bind the lot in one of his fine linen handkerchiefs, for scent. Smee threw it to the crocodile. The greedy beast swallowed it, and now Hook is warned by the ticking whenever the croc is on his trail. Thus it happens that the notorious captain lives on, searching the Island without respite, seeking to cut down a certain wonderful boy and his band."

Wendy allowed time for the drama to sink in, then couldn't bring herself to break the mood. "Swallow your medicine, boys, or I'll take out my whip and make you walk the plank! Now, into your bunks."

Peter bounded up, and in token of a hook, shook a crooked finger. "Avast, maties! Belay that order. It's to the brig with you swabs. Stay below or, shiver me timbers, I'll give you ten of the best!"

"Aye, Cap'n!"

"Aye, aye!" But Curly tripped over the Twins, and Peter towered over him, wrathful in his play.

"Mr. Tootles! Fetch me the cat-o'-nine-tails!"

Tootles looked to Wendy, inquiring. It was becoming a habit for the boys to seek her approval before carrying out Peter's more questionable schemes. She complied with Peter's directives whenever possible, and since the cat was only pretend, she fell in with this one, sanctioning the command.

"Captain's orders, Mr. Tootles. Bring out the cat!" But Wendy was glad Peter was too busy buccaneering to notice his authority being challenged. As it happened, the dreaded punishment proved unnecessary, as all the children vaulted into bed without its persuasion, pursued by Peter's imaginary hook. Unnaturally soon, they fell quiet, huddling together under the skins and shivering, for Hook and his pirates loomed. Neverbay was much too near.

Sighing after her exertions, Wendy collected her sewing and settled next to Peter, who had already lost all traces of piracy and sat smoking a make-believe pipe by the fire. She watched the light flickering on his face, first bright, then dark with shadows. It lit the room in the same way, she noticed, establishing safe havens, then causing foreboding figures to appear in farther corners. The interplay of cheer and gloom didn't seem to affect Peter, but for some reason it made Wendy uneasy. She must be tired.

"I wish we hadn't quarreled, Peter."

"Quarreled? We only said it wrong. We really agree, don't we?"

"People can't agree all the time, but it doesn't change how we feel about each other."

With all his accustomed confidence, Peter smiled at her. "I feel the same way I did that first night, when I made you mine."

Wendy felt the blood rush to her cheeks. The way he talked!

Squinting at her, Peter cocked his head. "You look a little different, though."

"Something about my mouth, maybe? Can you see it?" Lightly, she touched her kiss.

He laughed. "I see your mouth, it's still there!" Her words sparked his curiosity. "Is that the beginning of a new story?"

"I hope so." But Wendy shrugged. She didn't really expect a different answer any longer, but she still believed. She went on with her mending. Everything *was* the same as that first night. And yet there was something new, something both terrible and wonderful hanging over her. She couldn't identify it. Had it started with the quarrel, or just before? The changing firelight brought it near to her mind, then danced it away again. It was just a feeling.

Wendy's spirit sought to overcome it. "Pirates are dreadful creatures, but I would so like to go to sea like Red-Handed Jill. Imagine the grandeur of the sea beneath our feet, the white wings of sails above. Only think of climbing aloft to taste the wind, casting off toward adventure!" But when Wendy saw Peter's eager face, she regretted whetting his appetite with this flavor of the maritime. The sensation she sought to banish only stole closer.

"That's a good idea! I'll commandeer the *Jolly Roger* for you, Wendy! And this time we'll win her."

"But, Peter—"

"You weren't here yet when we last attacked. We only killed a couple of pirates that day, but once the boys and I have slain Hook and the rest of his men, we'll sail the Seven Seas and have nautical adventures. I despise all pirates, but it's great fun pretending to be a pirate captain!"

Pretending. Wendy smiled, pretending she meant it. "Valiant Peter, to dare such a thing for me."

But the feeling crept out of the shadows, and now it was fear. Peter did not distinguish between real and make-believe. He might in truth make another attempt on the *Jolly Roger*, and the story she told tonight was one of the true ones, much too dangerous to enter.

She couldn't warn Peter of the risk. He was a boy, he was so full of himself. Warnings would only make him more eager to prove his daring by rekindling trouble with the pirates. She didn't understand the intensity of his feeling about them, either, why he couldn't leave them—leave Hook—alone. Instead of the cautionary talk she usually employed, she tried a different tack.

"Peter, why do you hate the pirates so?"

"Huh! Because they *are* pirates. They don't play by the rules."

"Your rules? Because they're grown up?"

"Any rules!" He scowled, his countenance black as any buccaneer's.

"You mean because they're free to do whatever they choose?"

Peter rallied, more earnest than she'd ever seen him. She thrilled to witness the fire blazing in his eyes. "I mean they are the only creatures on the Island I can't find a way to tame."

Wendy's pulse froze. "Oh! Oh, yes. That's why I dread them, too! You can charm practically anything, Peter, but no one can control those men."

"Hook can. He does." Peter's expression was almost envious.

"And you want his power? But your attacks on him have only led to your hideous blood feud."

Peter laughed. "Yes, I drew blood. Hook's! I'm not like him, afraid of a little blood."

"But you took far more than blood. You took his hand! He'll never forgive you that. And while Hook hunts you down, all of us are in danger."

"All the more reason for me to kill him."

Wendy closed her eyes and heard the wind whistling down the chimney. It wasn't easy, but she had managed thus far to guard her boys against the feud. She learned the terror of it in the moment she first hung in the air over the Neverland, in that moment when the concussion of Long Tom pounded against her chest and nearly exploded her heart—when from afar she spied Hook's ship at anchor in the bay, and the violent gusts had taken her by the throat and rasped into her ear that the story she had created—Hook's story—was not a dream. She had felt the cold wind hissing, hissing that Hook was here, and he was real, terribly real, after all.

She whispered. "The terrible Captain Hook."

Wendy drew her mending closer to the fire. She had suddenly gone icy cold. Neverbay was much too near.

Pearls from the Lagoon

It was a cold place if you were a pirate's prisoner. It was a basking place if you were a mermaid. If you were a boy, it was perfect. Hook determined that all elements of this place would come into play this late afternoon.

Mermaids' Lagoon was a deep curve set into a cliff, with craggy shoreline and spraying waves. A rock shelf lined part of the coast, high enough to provide dry footing—until sunset. When daylight deserted the lagoon, no safe step remained. The mountains on either side of the cliff face were covered in moss, saturated and slippery. Here and there lay basking rocks, the biggest of which was a distance from the shore, in the deepest waters.

That was the notorious Marooners' Rock, dreaded islet employed by ruthless sea captains in need of an executioner. Rusted shackles bored into the rock, staining it in streaks, the only evidence of victims abandoned there as tide went in and boats went out.

Only those long familiar with the Lagoon knew its secrets. The mermaids knew them, of course. Pan did. So, also, did Captain James Hook.

Mermaids were curious creatures. One couldn't count on their cooperation, but one couldn't discount it, either. Rarely did their scaly-backed hands release the condemned from the rock. They remained unmoved by human passion, however much they inspired it. Pan was friendly with them, but the most involvement ordinary people could expect was a splash and a glimpse of scales disappearing into the depths.

Yet a glimpse of a mermaid, like her song, was tantalizing. Hook was not immune. Unknown to Pan, he had insinuated himself into the good graces of one or two of the maids. His persistence and his inestimable charm won success there. No female on whom he turned that charm had yet resisted it, tail or no. In addition, the mergirls coveted jewelry—they wore little else—and a pirate as successful as Hook had swag to spare. These ladies of the deep weren't what he'd call companionable, but they would do, in a pinch. He'd been known to carry home a pearly comb after an afternoon's bask. Today he would profit again from those stimulating hours, watching, and listening.

Hook now stood leaning into the wind, one foot planted on the prow of the *Roger's* dinghy. He cast a sharp look about the area as the craft thrust itself into the Lagoon. Bill Jukes lunged back and forth, shirt meeting tattooed skin in damp patches as he plied oars to part the waters. Surges of wind tugged at Hook's hat, inviting its feathers to fly free, but Hook imposed his will on it, removing the hat and taking it and its plumage captive under his coat on the bench. The wind retaliated by flinging pungent wafts of seaweed and kicking up the current. Hook stood firm.

At the ripened moment, Hook called over his shoulder to ship oars. He scanned the shoreline, rolled his boots to the thigh, then sprang over the gunwale into the shallows. Commanding Jukes to vanish until dusk, he headed toward shore. The wind died down but Hook's blood quickened as he discerned exotic eyes watching his progress. He splashed his way with assurance through the rock pools as Jukes hauled on the oars. Slowly, the boat withdrew.

His senses heightened, Hook paused at the end of the rock shelf where it overlooked an inlet. A series of small caves riddled the wall at his back. Here he removed an object from his breeches pocket. He lowered himself down near the water's edge, resting arms on thighs. Working his fingers with delicacy, he hung a golden chain upon his hook, and metal slid on metal with a barely audible, singing rasp, until it dangled from the steepest angle of the curve. The sound was exquisite.

They heard it.

He lay down on the sun-drenched rock, the hook suspended over the edge. Warmth spread throughout his long body. The round, rich gems in their settings swung, glinting with sunlight. He waited.

Assured of secrecy by a few very pleasurable exchanges, Hook had removed himself to one of the dark fissures behind him. He was near enough to observe Marooners' Rock and yet deep enough to conceal his deeper purpose. Satisfied he was hidden, he made himself comfortable and waited again, passing the time extricating seaweed from his hook and drying his mustache. To the dampness of his attire he paid no heed.

At last his mergirl's signal slapped the water's surface. Reminiscing about the past hour's delights, Hook regarded her intriguing tail until it slipped out of his sight. Only then did he raise his gaze to the human creatures forsaking the element of air to enter that of water. They touched down on the rock, bathed in sunshine. Hook envied the ease with which those children moved about the Island. The deeds he could perform if he could fly, if he could sail the sky as he sailed the sea, master of the air. Perhaps he'd spy out insight into that mystery, as well.

He observed.

Ah, a bonus. A streak of light resolved itself into Pan's fairy. Tinker Bell had accompanied him. Hook didn't have to watch long to see that this creature was a liability to Pan. A vulnerable spot. Hook's half-smile slid to his lips. May the Powers bless all females, marine, fairy, or human. So useful.

It started simply enough. 'The Wendy' tested the temperature of the water. She scooped back her tangled hair and poised herself on the edge of the rock, considering her toes. Then Pan dove in and mermaids bubbled up all around him, inviting him to play games. As expected.

Stripping to various stages of undress, the other boys waited, anxious but respectful, until the Wendy withdrew her toes and pronounced the water safe. With a lot of noise, they jumped in and frolicked about in a tiresome manner. Their antics bored Hook.

As a breeze rippled her skirt, the girl watched after the boys, warning off rogue mermaids with voice and shooing gestures that showed little success. Occasionally calling to the children, she assured herself of their safety. Especially the two new lads. Who were they? They looked as if they had at one time attended school, an observation one would never make about the other boys. There was something prim about the bigger one, and they wore nightshirts.

The Wendy, Hook noted, raising one eyebrow, was clad in night attire, as well. So Pan had snatched her from her bed! Time had clearly paid a visit; the gown was too short . . . among other insufficiencies. Add a jewel or two and she'd be well on the way to becoming a mermaid herself. Hook's lip twitched.

The captain's eye was distracted from the subject of his musing by the fairy, who continually bobbed above Pan's head, rushing any mergirl who came too close. Hook would have swatted the little nuisance in short order, but Pan bounced up and down unconcerned in the waves between heads, tails and Tinker Bell. The Wendy, more ladylike in her methods than the fairy, sat on the rock kicking up sprays of water at the maids—although she wasn't above letting fly a smallish stone.

Hook didn't miss the sentry posted on the far arm of the cove. At irregular intervals, Pan appointed a different boy to relieve the one on watch. The Wendy's work, of course. Be wary of pirates. Be wary, indeed. Hook wore a satisfied sneer, invisible to her sentinels.

As oblivious to female admiration as he was to his foe, Pan swam over to slither up the rock where he shook himself, like the dog he was, spraying the girl. She suffered him with humor, maintaining an even keel. The fairy, on the other hand, buzzed around the pair in a temper. She berated Pan and every so often seized the opportunity to pinch the Wendy or yank her hair—most especially when the girl and Pan were intimately associated, as when the girl drew fruits from her basket to dangle over his lips, or lingered over a stubborn strand of seaweed caught round his waist. The Wendy dodged her persecutor, and when, on occasion, the boy noticed the fairy's hostility, he might pick the creature out of the air and cast her away. Mostly he didn't notice.

Nor did Pan demonstrate awareness of a more interesting circumstance. Hook perceived that he was witness to a dance: the Wendy stepped close to Pan, the fairy countered, and Pan backed from both. The steps were repeated time and again, neither lady winning advantage because Pan, his hair bright in fairy nimbus and his chin stained with juice, never completed the dance. Foolish boy, Hook smirked. He doesn't know.

Of a sudden, Hook's attention deviated to an eagle above the Lagoon, wheeling toward the cliff top. He watched the eagle for a second or two, and as he returned his focus to the Wendy, she spied it, as well. Gazing skyward, she deserted her companions and, running the length of the rock, flung out her arms and leapt into the air, soaring up and up, speeding after the bird.

The eagle exhibited no hurry to complete its circle. Catching up to it, the girl hung at a respectful distance, just behind and below the regal tail. She flew as naturally as the bird, for all the world as if she owned the air. Growing ever more eager to execute his design, Hook gazed at the creatures. The two flew in tandem, wings spread wide, gliding free over the affairs below. Indulging in the timeless image, Hook renewed his determination, easing himself back into patience.

The Wendy-bird swooped down, snatching at the air, and rounded to form her own circle, drifting to perch at the cliff's top. Hook squinted up at her. Poised on the edge, with the relentless sea winds tugging at her nightdress, she thrust up a fist clutching what could only be a feather. Her clear voice rang among the rocks as she cried to the children to see, waving her treasure in triumph.

Slowly, Hook shook his head. He was learning.

During the course of his observation, Hook absorbed every nuance. His time was well invested. On the whole, the girl favorably impressed him. She assumed an air of tolerance for all parties, yet Hook would swear that in guarded moments he'd seen her strike at the tiny moving light. He tapped the sickle of his claw against his boot leather, considering. Judging from all he had witnessed, the Wendy was ripe for his harvest. All according to plan, he now knew his enemy.

He could almost taste her.

Pluck. And abandon. Exactly the traits he required of her. He nodded to himself. Exactly the things he would do to her.

As the last brilliance of afternoon sparkled on the Lagoon, Pan, in his self-important manner, straddled the big rock, hoisting his boys out of the brine one by one and slinging them onto it, where they stretched out to dry. A handsome eagle feather was twined into his dirty hair. Her treasure, plundered. Never had Hook been more disgusted by that boy.

Forming his final impressions, Hook observed as the Wendy stood still, apart from Pan, seeming to engage the fairy in banter. But as soon as Tinker Bell ventured within range, the girl blew at her, creating a gale that wafted the sprite several yards out to sea. Afterward the girl was wise enough to dive off the rock and disappear—until her streaming head and shoulders emerged from the sea, directly in front of Hook's lair.

She was near enough for him to hear the gasp as she sucked first air. Her hair floated on the water, rippling in its eddy. She swam, and her arms sent water churning to bounce against the ledge not far from his feet. The Wendy clutched and hauled herself onto the very shelf of rock on which he had lain with wet, gaudy trinkets, savoring the salt on their skins.

His arm jerked. He held his breath. He could have touched her.

Do nothing rash. Keep to the plan.

He lowered the hook.

Her breath came in bursts as she rested. Her hair and her gown clung to her body while, for a few moments, she lay luxuriating, like a mermaid. Upon sitting up, she tossed her head, bent, and gathered the hair into her hands, one fluid motion. She wrung the water from her hair and the droplets plunked on the rock surface, spattering it. A sudden rivulet snaked toward Hook's boot. As he drew himself deeper into shadow, his shirt whispered against the wall.

Just a whisper, but she heard it.

Immediately, she pivoted to discover the beast that stalked her. For one instant, as her eyes challenged the darkness, her features were revealed to him.

Taken aback, he stiffened, his brow creasing in incredulity.

He recognized her face. It belonged to him, and he to it. Her face had been carved from his dreams.

Everything connected. He knew who she was. . . . *Wendy*.

A laugh thrilled the air and Wendy spun around. A mermaid beckoned to her, just feet away. The lovely tail waved, lazily, tauntingly. Wendy leapt to her feet, her mouth opening in awe. The mermaid raised up, an array of round, rich jewels shining on her breast, and she let loose a song of piercing beauty. As she fell back to stroke the water, her melody pulled Wendy with her, enticing the girl to return to the sea, and even her wake was succulent. Enraptured, Wendy rose lightly on her toes and with one twist of her shoulders, floated up.

Hook didn't move. He stood staring at the glistening drops falling from her gown as she pursued his lady of the deep from the medium of the air. For the first time, he resisted the lure of the siren song.

He hadn't even heard it.

By twilight, the treacherous tide of Mermaids' Lagoon was rising, its waves ceaselessly concealing and revealing its secrets. As intended, all elements of this infamous place had come into play that late afternoon. Those who could escape the tide had done so.

One remained, changed forever.

At the shadowed entrance to a womb of rock, a seaman waited for a dinghy. The sea rose, whispering as it came, pulsing in and out of the cave, swirling over and then laying bare his boots. He watched, but didn't see.

All those dark thoughts, broken segments . . . She would join them together. With a tale. An intriguing tale.

He looked up, and far out to sea. The wind made free with his hair and toyed with the golden earring. He stood firm.

Now he had his bearings. Captain James Hook observed the new stars and fixed his course.

Wendy was his storyteller. And so much more.

Taming the Beast

The course of Time being so erratic, Wendy couldn't be sure, but by her uncertain reckoning, weeks had passed since the Lagoon adventure, and still Tinker Bell was prone to twinkling fits of hysterics. The memory was fresh for Tink, who was drenched before it was over, and although it was no one's fault but her own, she chose to blame the Wendy. Even Peter hadn't curbed her vitriol, and Peter could tame almost anything.

Wendy had been mesmerized, deep under the spell of the mermaid, but some instinct had guarded her. She took to the air first in her pursuit of the creature, instead of diving into the maid's own element. Her sudden flight alerted Peter to the situation, and he kicked off the rock to her rescue. Tinker Bell, still vigilant, streaked after, fearing for Peter's affection, hoping for the Wendy's demise.

Entranced by the song, Wendy flew nearer, lower, trying to capture the sound before it sank into the sea. She was so close as it submerged, she felt it must be near the surface still. Just as she pitched to dive, Peter blazed in front of her, breaking the flow of sound. Abruptly, she halted to watch in bewilderment as Peter plunged in to warn the mermaid away. Tinker Bell was so determined to ward off competition that she plunked right after him, spraying a tiny jet of spume as she immersed herself in the merworld. Thereafter, the haunting song ceased altogether, and laughter broke the surface in a cloud of effervescence.

Tink was too airy to swim. She bubbled back up and floated, a soggy bit of flotsam. As she spluttered, glowing particles of her fairy dust ebbed away, and the sight of it frightened her. She panicked, her wings waterlogged and beating against the sea, unable to attain flight nor make her way through the water.

Only moments passed this way, for as soon as Wendy came to her senses, she awoke to Tink's dilemma. She reached down and formed her hands into a raft. In spite of the fairy's ill will, Wendy found the grace to respect her proud nature. She allowed Tink to climb on deck by herself, dragging aboard a single shred of dignity—whereupon Tinker Bell aimed and spit.

Dignity remained tattered yet and frequent hair pulling was the order of the day, so Peter cocked an arrow and pretended to shoot Tinker Bell down, while Tink reversed herself and escaped up the tree shaft to the world above. A hollow tinkling echoed in the chute, and Wendy awarded her hero a smile, grateful to him for both recent rescues and her belief in him confirmed again. She was relieved, and now at liberty to discuss the idea of the day.

Any good idea that wandered into the hideout became Peter's in the end, by right of domination, and Peter decreed that today should be a hunting day. Living among the trees, one lived among the beasts. It followed naturally that one would hunt the beasts from the trees. The logic was Peter's own, and because it was his, it belonged also to the Lost Boys. But it didn't really matter whose logic it was to begin with, anyway. Everything became Peter's.

Therefore it was Peter's idea, not Wendy's, to hunt today. And that afternoon in the hideout he announced, "Take up your bows and knives, boys, the forest is too full of beasts. We must thin them out."

Knowing his enthusiasm for the hunt, Wendy had qualms about the suggestion. She remembered the fates of other creatures at Peter's hands. But there was need for the excursion on several levels and, condescending, Peter yielded to her request that he slay only beasts this outing, "But if trouble arises, or even Indians or pirates, I'll not stay my hand!" He was never more happy than when hunting.

"I'll come along, then, and keep a lookout for trouble." Wendy vaguely hoped to warn trouble to keep low before Peter could have at it.

But all the children, excepting Peter, harbored the terror of pirates that Wendy's stories inspired. Even those boys who'd killed a pirate or two in their time wondered now how they'd done it. The children had been rummaging for weapons, but at the mention of trouble, they hesitated. Beasts were the least of their worries.

"Shall we hunt waterfowl today?" asked John. All the boys knew Peter slew birds in the marsh only as a pretext for spying on the pirate ship. On more than one occasion, Peter had changed quarry in mid-hunt, aiming for felons over feathers. His band was loyal, but leery. John, having at one time lived among the civilized, had developed a different stripe of courage from the rest. He dared to bluff. "Near Neverbay?"

"No, we'll stalk big game in the underbrush. Wendy needs fresh skins."

Silence fluttered down like the last leaf.

"A large family does go through them," Wendy affirmed.

The boys looked up, down and sideways. Constructing a tepee had seemed such a good idea at the time. But because of avenging arrows, Wendy's precautions forbade the family to fly over the Indian village, and the children had no recent image of a tepee on which to draw. They had, however, discovered that animal skins made a cozy tent when you lashed them together and suspended them from the bedposts.

It was the campfire beneath the tent, on the bed, that went all wrong. The stench still hung about, which was in fact the real reason for vacating their home today. Vacating was also in fact Wendy's idea before it was Peter's. Peter liked the smell of burnt fur. It reminded him of burning and pillaging. It reminded Wendy never again to slack her responsibilities and leave the children alone. For very different reasons, both Peter and Wendy determined the children should examine the Indian village next time the natives moved up to their mountain camp.

Opting for discretion, those children offered no comment. With the energy of acquitted suspects, Peter's boys fell to smearing their faces with mud for camouflage—an unnecessary precaution for those who had been smoked with the skins—and up the tree shaft the family went, away through the forest and even farther up into the treetops, with Peter in the lead sending parrots shuddering off, appropriating an eyrie among the leaves from which to spy out their prey.

Wendy always seized an opportunity to fly, but the children climbed this time and became tangled between quivers, bows and branches, and for several minutes their quarry, which were no doubt anxious to begin the charge, refused to come close to the snapping, dragging and rustling. It wasn't the nature of the big game on the Island to tolerate such noise, even from easy targets. The beasts might do better, all things considered, to engage in the Indians' hunt, now in dependable progress on the other side of the Island. One could count on the natives to observe tradition.

Once they won freedom from the foliage, the children chattered like the monkey families scampering deep in the forest, whence these primates could be heard screeching and screaming in delight. Thinking themselves above danger, the monkeys audibly defied it, prompting Wendy to wonder if such innocence, whether in boys or in beasts, could long survive this wilderness. The boys, at least, seemed bit by bit to learn caution.

The family settled in, Wendy and Peter screening themselves in the shade of branches and the others perching above them or nestling in trees on either side. Tinker Bell appeared, flying down from a parrot nest she'd been trying on, and settled on Peter's shoulder. Wendy sent her a suspicious look. Peter picked off a few orange feathers and addressed his fairy sternly. "You can stay, Tink, but only if you're quiet."

"Quiet and at a safe distance from me." Wendy narrowed her eyes, leaving it to her rival to work out the ambiguity.

"And see that you don't go near the beasts, Tink. I don't want any loose fairy dust on them."

Wendy turned to him in surprise. "Why, Peter? What harm can it do?"

The Lost Boys caught Peter's meaning and regarded Tinker Bell with anxious eyes. They had never thought of this scenario, and their expressions transformed as it revealed itself to them in horrifying detail. They were too well acquainted with the fairy to believe she wasn't capable of it, or—to put it charitably—unthinking enough in her blue rages.

"You know what fairy dust can do. It made you fly."

"But how can it hurt the animals?"

"Not the animals, Wendy. Us. The animals could chase up here after us, if they could fly."

She didn't want to believe it. "But they'd have to think pleasant thoughts, too!"

"I can't think of anything more pleasant to a beast than to fly up here and tear into us, can you?"

Eyes widening, Wendy looked again at Tinker Bell. "Oh." A monkey shrieked in the thick of the wood somewhere behind her. Tink crossed her arms, sat back on Peter's shoulder and smirked. Her movement shot off a few of the sparks that a moment ago seemed so innocuous, and something uncomfortable prickled inside Wendy. She kept her voice slow and even. "I think, Peter, it would be safer for the children if Tinker Bell would please go home."

Careless once more, Peter shrugged Tinker Bell off. "Go on, Tink, leave us to hunt."

Tinker Bell beat her wings and recovered herself. She hovered for a time, glaring her malevolence, first at Peter, but especially at the Wendy. The fronds enclosing the girl stirred in the breeze as she returned the fairy's stare. Tink darted off to the forest, chiming madly, but Wendy's prickly feeling did not go with her.

The boys, at least, were happier at her departure. They began once again to look forward to the adventure ahead. Nibs and Curly, just above Peter, were debating the anatomy of the beasts about to be slain. Curly asked Wendy if they might wish on the wishbone. "You said your mother let you pull one in the old life. I'd wish to see London."

Nibs' wiry frame sat the branches easily, like a sailor in the rigging. "I'd wish for a sword, to fight pirates." His swarthy face lit with a grin as he threw Tootles a salute. "And boots, of course." Wendy assured them that the hunt wasn't likely to produce any wishbones.

Remembering an island chieftain in one of Wendy's stories, John and Michael hankered after boar's tusk bracelets. Peter assured them that wild boars inhabited the far side of the Island, near the Indian camp. "We're more likely to shoot tigers here than boars." Wendy was certain the plural of boar was boar, but didn't bother to correct him.

Slightly's branch bounced as he mimed impaling a boar on an Indian spear. "Let's go there tomorrow. We could make a pact with the Indians to declare peace while we hunt together. Then we could celebrate at their village, feasting and dancing around the fire for three days and nights!"

Excited by any new idea, the Twins swayed on limp and limper limbs. Their precarious roost didn't bother them. They had already discussed the limitations of this tree and designed a structure to support a hunting blind. "We'll have to look bold to impress the Indians. Can we grab a tiger's tail like Red-Handed Jill?"

"Who?" asked Peter with airy nonchalance, and Wendy scowled at him before replying.

"Of course you may, Twins. I've brought plenty of bandages and medicine for the wounded."

"I'll cut you a tiger-tail belt, Wendy, since you like the story so much," Peter said, proving his perfidy. He knew perfectly well who Jill was. But he looked so brave and casual, Wendy felt her heart swell, and she had to smile.

All this time the beasts put off their entrance. By now they were probably tapping their claws and chafing as the boys whooped their approval of Peter's or Wendy's tiger-tail idea. Wendy's eyes shone as she thought of it, for once forgetting the creatures' proximity.

She would feel so fierce and wild sporting a tiger belt. How gallant Peter was to understand what she wanted and promise it to her, in spite of his own distaste for the story. Whatever his feelings for romance, his pledge was a token of his care for her. And one day soon, he might show it again and ask to hear the adventures Wendy itched to invent for Jill. As if picking up the thread of her thoughts, Tootles carried her hopes further. He ribbed his captain, exclaiming, "Peter, you do respect lady pirates after all!"

"No, I never will. Pirates of any kind are villains. But I respect Wendy. She's our mother."

With the sensation that her insides were empty, Wendy looked out at the forest, staring blankly. The belt would be nice, anyway.

As ever, Curly was a gentleman. Considering his old belt and the ragged shirt Wendy had mended many times, he asked, "How do boys in London dress to fight pirates? I want to look proper if I go there some day."

Peter tossed his head, dismissive. "London is no place for boys. Since I ran away from home, I only go there when I need something I can't find here." He flashed his smile at Wendy and immediately she felt the presence of her heart again. It always gave her trouble when he looked at her that way.

"Peter?" John asked, "You needed a mother when you came to our window. Have you ever gone back to your house to see your other mother?"

Peter's expression waxed grave, as it always did when he considered grown-ups. "Yes. Once. I'll never go back there any more." The boys pricked up their ears. They sensed a story coming.

Touched again, Wendy asked gently, "Why, Peter? Did she try to make you stay and become a man?"

"No." Peter's eyes spilled bitterness.

"What then?"

The boys were fascinated now. They hung on Peter's words as steadfastly as they hung in the trees. He rarely hesitated to boast of his adventures. This one must have been dramatic.

"It was a long time ago. I'd been away just long enough to want to go back. Not to stay, really, but for an adventure. And when I found the house, I remembered my mother used to sing to me. I wanted to hear her sing."

Michael interrupted, "Did she tell you stories, too, Peter?"

"She told me lots of things I didn't think were true. Were the untrue things stories, Wendy?"

Wendy didn't know how she knew. "Not exactly, Peter. Mothers sometimes tell us what they want us to believe. To keep us happy."

"She must not have wanted to keep me at all, once I'd gone."

"What happened?"

"When I went back to my window, it was locked."

Michael and John inhaled. The Lost Boys rolled their eyes at each other, and Wendy's heart bled.

"And it was fitted with iron bars."

"No!"

Peter resisted going on, but seeing the scandalized looks on their faces, he made a show of tapping his courage. Persevering, he tossed them another morsel. "But that's not the worst."

Curly sniffed, pulling a bedraggled kerchief from his neck. "What could be worse?"

"My mother had forgotten me!"

A mother herself, Wendy gasped in disbelief. "How could you think that?"

Peter lifted his chin, fixing her with his green gaze. "Because I saw her. I saw her in my room."

Wendy's spine stiffened. "Then she hadn't forgotten. She was waiting for you."

In a gesture worthy of the best London theatre, Peter shook his head. "No. She was sitting by my bed. Singing."

"But that proves—"

"To a new baby boy!"

The silence of the family's shock rebounded through the wood. The children dangled, speechless. It was the ultimate insult to run away from home and be replaced. One imagined, at the very least, that one was missed, and every boy in those trees hoped his absence had ruined the lives he left behind. If they hadn't wanted to be noticed, they would have stayed at home. The band of boys subsided into stillness while they indulged in the horror of Peter's tale, but having soaked up the effect of his story, Peter forgot it.

All quiet.

At last the forest fauna came to life. Roaring reached the children's ears, halfhearted at first, petulant . . . then, as the dinner hour advanced, swelling to the full fury of hunger. The leaves surrounding the children quaked as bows nocked arrows. Danger imminent, all ears were alert, all eyes expectant, hardly blinking. Tiny mudslides dribbled from the camouflage on their cheeks to plop on the ground below. Then, the soft sound of panting, almost a purring.

What was coming? Something more than a story. Something wild.

Peter's face was set, intense. He hung over his branch, muscles as taut as his bowstring, his arrow poised.

Wendy hoped the something was nothing. At the same time she hoped it was something fierce and feral. Something not even Peter could tame. She hoped it was Red-Handed Jill, brandishing her whip. She hoped it wasn't Red-Handed Jill because Peter might kill her. She shivered and then she stopped hoping because something had arrived.

Peter's arrow hissed and sang. Darts from the boys' bows whistled after it but bounced to a stop, unnecessary. Peter threw back his head and let out a mighty crow, his victory shaped into sound. It seemed to Wendy that his voice was his arrow, and it pierced her heart. Her hand flew to her breast and she cried out. "Oh! Oh, no!" The something died instantly. With only one shot, the hunter prevailed, in the space of a heartbeat.

Jubilant, the children loosed themselves from the trees and dropped in bursts to the forest floor. Wendy sought to descend also, but found she couldn't fly. Without focusing, she climbed down, fingers seeking purchase branch by branch until her feet touched the ground and led her to the death scene. Rubbing together, her palms tried to rid themselves of grit.

"It's a lion! A lion!" The boys danced around it. Wendy pushed through them and looked down. Her heart bled again at the sight—the powerful king of the forest, with a golden mane flowing freely to the earth. Its mouth gaped open, exposing its tongue and its deep teeth. In its silence, it spoke to Wendy.

She choked on her words. "It looks so proud, even though it's dead." She looked to Peter.

His countenance glowed with triumph while the boys shouted and cavorted around him. The image of pride, Peter flung his arm toward his kill. "Look, Wendy, I've made the forest safer for you."

She stared at the animal again. She didn't feel safer. Somehow the death of this splendid thing seemed only to bring danger closer. "It never really threatened us. . . . " But some other kind of beast crouched in Wendy's memory, a shadow looming over her from the light of Peter's hearth fire. It danced in a macabre rite, clutching an arrow for a trophy and celebrating the death of a man. She put out her arms to hush the children and knelt down next to that ghastly shadow's most recent prey.

Peter tugged on its fur. "He'll make a nice blanket now I've tamed him."

Wendy's face tensed in consternation. She had to stroke its mane, to caress its coat. It was warm and silky, contradicting the claws that fringed its footpads. Unable to comprehend its fate, she shook her head. "But it's huge, fully grown."

"The grown-up ones are the most dangerous, Wendy. The only law they understand is the law of the jungle."

"The forest animals can't obey rules, Peter!"

"Of course not. They're wild." He shrugged. "They have to be slain."

She dragged her gaze from Peter to the carcass and its equal horror. When she could speak again, she wondered, "How did you bring down such a magnificent creature so easily?"

Peter stooped over his victim, placed a foot on its shoulder and yanked the arrow free. Wendy shuddered at the drag of it. Dark liquid began flowing from the wound.

"I know where to aim! The heart is the weakest part, even in the meanest of creatures."

Wendy buried her fingers in the fur of the animal, gloriously unlawful—and dead at Peter's feet. Its blood marked his hands, and, although it couldn't be seen, its blood stained her hands, as well. She didn't look at them, and she didn't know how she knew . . . she wasn't innocent.

Watching the wind ripple through the mane, Wendy realized Peter's words were true. The heart was the weakest part. Because she still felt his arrow, driven into her own. She recognized the truth. She admitted it. And in her afflicted heart, she still believed.

Harvest at the Fairy Glade

Tinker Bell was no innocent. She was well versed in forest lore. She knew the warning signs. She should have heeded them.

But her small heart was breaking, and she fled from it. Tink streaked through the forest, away from her beloved Peter and oblivious to where she was going. The Wendy creature was taking Tink's place in Peter's world, and the world was gall to her. This Island was her universe, and there was no place on it that didn't remind her of him. She could settle nowhere.

Her thoughts ran rampant, as confused as her flight, and her aura burned angrily. Peter had brought the Wendy here on a whim, just a whim. He hadn't cared about the girl, he wanted to hear stories. He'd heard lots of stories now. Why was she still here? And the Wendy thought she was a queen, she ruled at the hideout, Peter commanded all the band to obey her. Adventures weren't risky and fun anymore, their mother ordered them to be careful! And every time the Wendy was careful about something, she got bigger. About this notion, Tink wasn't confused at all.

The Wendy wanted to grow up. She *was* growing up. Peter was one of the things the Wendy was careful about. With the clarity of air, Tink could see that the big girl wanted Peter to grow up, too!

Tink belonged to Peter. He must never grow up and away from the fairy world. Better that he never understand his Tink than that he should grow away from her. She didn't care that he didn't guess her secrets; he had secrets, too. As long as she remained his fairy, her hope persisted that one day, with the cleverness of which he boasted, he might unpuzzle her mysteries. But even if he never learned how to touch her, she belonged!

Swerving over the Island, Tinker Bell bounced from point to point, first high, then low, and always moving. She circled the house in the clearing, pulling faces and shaking her fist. She itched with an urge to pick it apart, leaf by leaf, but finding no satisfaction in threatening the girl's shell of a dwelling, zipped on again toward rarer scenes. She didn't slow, and some while later found herself zooming up the steep contour of the Indian mountain.

The air grew chillier toward the top, and Tinker Bell paused to pant and fan her cheeks. Perching at the pinnacle, she gazed on the mountainside, spying stone circles around cooking fires, waiting tepees and a long, low lodge built of pine logs. All uninhabited now, until the fields fell to harvest and the People moved with the seasons.

The Indians were Peter's enemies. Maybe she should run away and join them. Tink might be the first fairy to befriend the People, and how priceless a prize she would be to them! Conceiving in her bitterness what a trophy Peter's golden scalp might make, the fairy soared down the far side of the mountain to follow the river, watching for the telltale smoke that would lead an exile to the village on the plateau. For once, Tink would venture where Peter forbade her to go.

She heard it before she saw it. Chanting song, and flutes. Dressed in deerskin shifts, women knelt before their tepees, shaping dough for their dinners. Others were winding in procession about the camp, playing some game with the black-haired children in their wakes, and old ones with white hair sat on broad-striped blankets, cross-legged, and laughing at their antics. All the villagers took up the chant, even the men in buckskin leggings, congregating on the edge of the encampment to drop the fruits of their hunting and unsling their weapons. The note of harmony in their music struck so jarringly on Tinker Bell's mood that she grimaced, reversed tack and buzzed away. Cautious only to avoid the pirate ship in Neverbay, she tore in the opposite direction, careless of where it would lead, as long as it took her away from the noises of contentment.

Instinct eventually headed her homeward, toward the Fairy Glade. Dusk was falling as she neared it, and she glimpsed the webs of light her cousins wove as they flew about their homes and halls. Patches of buds and tall grasses lit up and dimmed as the lights passed over them, making the glade gay and rippling. The fairy community was enclosed by a ring of toadstools, more symbolic of a magic place than of fencing, as it kept nothing in or out. Fairies were not particular with whom they kept company, providing that the company was merry. Their musical language played on the air and echoed in their hollow tree stumps. Greeted by the sights and sounds of home, the wanderer approached.

Yet Tinker Bell wanted none of it. She closed her eyes and ears to shut it out. Had she not, she would have heard the squelch. A toadstool lay crushed.

The glade was full of life. Tink didn't want life. She yearned for stillness tonight. She veered away to rest on a knot in the apple tree. Often she sat here, watching Peter's fingers at work when he came to pick the fruit. The red apples were luscious and wholesome, but Peter sometimes picked one or two of the green ones as well. Protective of his safety, Tinker Bell had warned him of their potency, but he picked them anyway. The fairies tasted the unripe apples when they wanted to sleep before long nights of feasting. Just a bite or two would do it. To swallow any more assured that a fairy would never partake of future feasts, for although the glade possessed many healing properties, none could counter a lethal effect.

Desolate, Tink cast about for a fat green apple, one sure to be full of the fairy sleeping draught. She selected one, then hovered next to it, bracing her hands on it and rubbing her cheek against its skin. Its rotundity promised respite, of whatever duration she chose. But at length she sighed, shook herself, and headed instead for the garden, where her people grew herbs and flowers to flavor their dispositions.

She skimmed over the wild holly border and on above the blooms, finally sinking into a rose. It was cool, soothing. Pulling its petals around her as high as they would reach, she hid herself from the world. Her light faded to its faintest glow. The flower's fragrance overpowered her, but she wanted to be overpowered. She didn't desire merely to sleep. She wished to be taken over, completely, by some force of nature. She wanted her body to be so full of sensation that she wouldn't have to sense anything at all. Like her heart. So many emotions, and so little space for them. Subsiding, she laid her untidy head on her arms.

A shushing sounded in the grasses. Tinker Bell had no room in her heart to hear it.

She remembered living here, among her people. They were a joyful race of creatures, even flippant. They had never understood the moody Tinker Bell. She felt everything more deeply than others of her kind. They didn't experience life solidly; they breezed through their emotions, one of which was revulsion at Tinker Bell's intensity. They marked it and then they were gone, like bees from a bitter flower. In time she divined that she would never belong here.

So Tinker Bell had ventured into the woods alone, and there among the trees and tendrils was Peter, his green eyes enticing her, never letting her go. Her heart pounded, remembering. She hadn't even attempted to resist him. In him she saw a light burning with the same intensity as her own. She understood. It was because he was a boy.

She understood something else, too, that the Wendy was just discovering. As long as Peter was a boy, he would never fully experience the grown-up emotions he felt the beginnings of now, intense as those feelings were. But he didn't want to grow old, ever, and Tink was content. He and Tink were alike, were together—until the Wendy came.

The weaving lights within the fairy village stopped moving. They held still for one instant, then streaked in all directions and disappeared into trees, stumps and holes. The glade fell silent.

At last Tinker Bell pushed the rose's petals open. She swung over its lip and climbed down the stem to the earth below, stepping from thorn to thorn as if descending a ladder. She felt too heavy for her wings.

Her gaze fell upon a patch of herbs and her feet began to roam among the stalks. She would gather some chamomile to brew herself a drop of tea. Medicinal tea to heal her heart. She selected a petal and plucked it, folding it to fit her pocket.

Sighing again, she let her eyes wander. A soothing tea might remedy her pain. . . .

In the next instant, her gaze sharpened and focused. On something else. On another kind of remedy.

The Wendy liked medicine, she took it every day.

Tink could brew a medicine for the Wendy. A tonic that would make her want to go away. Something to kill her love for Peter, maybe.

Or, maybe, something to kill the Wendy herself.

A poison!

Tinker Bell's wings sprang apart, fluttering so wildly she rose several feet off the ground. She hovered for a moment, grinning. Her small heart held joy again, and she shot up high over the garden, her energy illuminating it. Eyes darting, she searched for the leaf, just the right shaped leaf, the deadly foxglove, that she would pluck and carry so carefully home to Peter's hideout. She was no innocent.

She saw nothing but the leaves. She laughed her shiny-bell laugh. She heard nothing but the laugh.

To think of herself being careful, like the Wendy! It served the girl right, Tink would use her own medicine against her! She thrust her hand in her pocket and yanked out the chamomile petal. She crushed it in her fist and flung it at the ground.

The right medicine, to cure both of Peter's girls. Like a snake, the lethal leaf slid into her pocket. She tossed her head to laugh again, her every sense restored.

The laugh died in her throat. She took it all in at once—toadstools lying crushed, a path of violated grass, the dwelling place dark and silence screaming, the pungent smells of salt and tar, gold teeth gleaming in her own blazing light.

Next came puzzlement, for the huge hands that seized her were all wrong.

Beasts' Accord

Peter's hands wiped his dagger clean, but did not sheath it. He stood, legs apart, surveying the skins stretched and pegged to dry in the clearing near Wendy's house.

"This game's too tame, Wendy. Not enough adventure in killing beasts with arrows." He grinned and jerked his head toward John. "Even John brought one down."

"And skinned it!" John stood tall with the breeze mussing his hair, wishing he had a dagger to clean. He had borrowed Nibs'.

Celebrating his brother's victory, Michael twirled a zebra tail over his head. "John, the Mighty Hunter!"

Wendy appraised John with a keen look. She hadn't imagined it; he did remind her of their father this afternoon.

She sat on the willow bench Peter had made for her, her back against the leafy wall of the house. A gentle wind rippled the leaves so that the little dwelling looked as if it were shivering. The top hat chimney emitted blue fog now, to match the sky, as it always did when Wendy was at home. Its lid flopped soundlessly up and down, mouthing alarm as the smoke pushed past it.

A creek concealed itself in the woods behind the house, forgetting the silence necessary to safeguard its hiding place. It gave itself away in constant babble. Wendy listened to it for a moment, counting the Lost Boys as they returned from washing there. "It was only fair to come down from the trees." Peter had his new-idea look on his face, meaning she must ask. "What's your plan now?"

He tossed his knife up, sending it revolving, and plucked it out of the air by the handle. "Hand-to-paw, boy to beast. That's adventure!"

"I don't doubt it, Peter, but the little ones have had enough adventure for one afternoon. Let them stay here." The mighty hunters, now all accounted for, were very glad to have a mother at times like this. They had hunted beasts with Peter hand-to-paw before, but sometimes now they wondered why they had done it.

"You'll come with me?" Peter's smile was beguiling, and Wendy's heart leapt. The idea of wandering the forest alone with him tempted her. But a parrot screeched its warning high in a tree across the clearing, its flaming feathers a reminder of the morning's disastrous campfire. Regretful, she shook her head.

"Best if I keep an eye on the boys. And my house! Will you mind going alone?"

"Favor me with your token, Lady, and I'll ride to hounds after my fox."

Wendy laughed. He knew so many stories nowadays that several often got jumbled together, but he posed exactly like a knight errant embarking on a quest. "With my compliments, Sir Knight." She proffered her handkerchief, sewn and scented for just such an occasion. "Make haste, Sir, darkness approaches."

Sir Peter bowed, the lady inclined her head, and the valiant strode into the early evening shadows, toward the creek. Wendy watched until he disappeared, then she stepped to the edge of the clearing and searched the trees all about it for signs of lurking danger. Seeing none, she turned back to the boys. "Shall we play hide-and-seek?"

There was no hesitation. "You're It!" The boys shouted, pelting toward the woods to shin up trees and burrow down holes, making enough noise to frighten off any unseen threat.

"Not too far from the clearing, boys!" Wendy leaned against a tree and buried her face in her arms. As she counted, she breathed in the dusky bark scent.

Tiptoeing, the Twins doubled back through the forest to slip into the house. They needn't have sneaked; Wendy knew they could always be found there, planning improvements. They recently built two chairs for her use, and a table to compliment her china tea service. A slight chinking sound escaped the house, from which Wendy surmised nimble fingers were invading the sugar bowl.

After the flurry of activity, the forest hushed. Wendy smiled to hear stealthy, rapid breathing. "Twenty! Here I come, ready or not!" She dropped her arms and immediately spied from the corner of her eye Slightly hanging by his knees several trees over, trying to blend in with hanging creepers. A clump of leaves attempted to disguise Tootles under the same tree. She pretended not to see and stole into the clearing where Nibs was making himself skinny under the stretched remains of the zebra. The thought struck Wendy—these boys weren't as adept at hiding as they'd once been. Their secret places were growing smaller. Or the boys were growing bigger. The realization stole Wendy's lightheartedness away.

She sought to regain it. As if preparing to fly, she dreamed of Peter. Her prince. Closing her eyes, Wendy lifted her face to soak in the last warmth of the sunshine. Here she was, living in the woods just like Snow White. But after a moment, Wendy sighed. That princess looked after a pack of dwarves, too, "But Snow White's prince wasn't sleeping." Would Peter ever awaken? Surely then their story would be complete, and they would live happily ever after.

An outburst of giggles located the Twins for certain. "You mixed it up, Wendy!"

"The prince never sleeps!" Two sets of identical brown eyes peered at her from behind the viney shutters of her window. "He kisses the princess and wakes *her* up."

"I'll tell it differently tonight." Wendy's smile broke through. "Snow White will give the prince a kiss before he goes looking for it. Maybe he's too busy adventuring to know he wants it!" She laughed. "There's still hope." She hunched down like a predatory animal and rushed at the two boys. "And I've found you, Twins!" They screeched and ducked out of sight.

The spirit of the game returned to her and she dashed about dispatching her quarry. "Nibs! Tootles! Slightly! I've found you, too!" They emerged and began beating the bushes for the others. The shadows lengthened and the recesses in which they searched grew darker. One by one, those who hunted returned to the comfort of the clearing.

Then Wendy stopped seeking boys and listened.

Tootles jerked his head up and gaped at Nibs. Nibs returned his look and they both froze. Slightly and the Twins gawked at Wendy, who stood tensed, all senses alert, staring into the woods behind the house.

"Curly, Michael, John! Come out at once!" She cast about frantically, searching for them, but they all heard it now. The three still in hiding hurried out, Michael rolling from a cluster of tree roots, John and Curly sliding down from high treetops on vines that burned their hands.

"Everyone! Into the house!" Wendy ran to it, yanked the door open and waved them in. Throwing herself after the boys, she slammed the door behind them, becoming aware for the first time how insubstantial the bark over the entrance really was. She had always felt safe here in the house Peter ordered built for her, and her first instinct was to run for his protection within it. Now, as Wendy's blood turned chill, the wind whipped through the leaves of its flimsy exterior. Too late, she recognized its frailty.

The eyes peeping at the window this time were several different colors, and all the eyes looked terrified. The children listened. Through the rustling of the foliage came a rhythmic beat. A beat not found in nature. The sound emanated from the woods behind them, and even the babbling of the careless stream seemed hushed to listen. The beat tapped constantly, mechanically, accompanied by the softest swish as a powerful tail dragged along the bank of the creek. Tick, tick. Tick, tick. Tick, tick. Tick, tick. . . .

The children deserted the windows to huddle together in the little house. Wendy held Michael, her hand over his mouth. It was a needless precaution. No one uttered a sound. There was no need; the ominous ticking of the crocodile was sound enough.

They waited.

And as the beat faded at last into distance, still none of the children had to speak, for Wendy's words spoke for them all, soft and terrible.

"Peter's in danger!"

With the stealth of a predator, Peter moved in the underbrush along the creek. An odor of decaying leaves hung in the air as his feet picked a path among roots and muddy patches. Hanging willow branches made his skin itch as he pushed through them. Leafy whispers blended with the stream's chatter. Detecting another sound above these, he halted to be sure.

A steady metallic cadence. A ticking clock. He turned around, a satisfied smile on his face.

Peter withdrew to a respectful distance, but did not hide himself. Instead, he squatted next to a tree trunk, knife at the ready. He had taken to the woods hunting his next adventure. Here it came.

The ticking drew closer. Close enough. Peter whistled once, low, in warning of his presence. He watched the edge of the creek as the rain of willow boughs trembled and gave way to a snout, then slid apart, exposing two florid eyes. The crocodile was already looking Peter's direction. It hauled its bulk along the mud bank into view. Such a creature had no need to hide from such a boy. It opened its mouth wide, a gesture at once yawning and acknowledging, and its teeth stuck up in contrast to their bedding of rosy gum. The ticking struck much louder now.

Peter's nod was curt, but he kept his voice low. "Hello, old brute. Shall we slay each other today?"

The ticking diminished as its jaws closed. The reptilian eyes remained watchful, but unafraid. A moment passed, then the croc shot forward—suddenly, effortlessly. It paused, one body length from the boy.

Peter hadn't moved. Here at last was a game that suited him. Not too tame. "Only one beast is safe from the blade of Peter Pan." He crept the least bit nearer. "One beast who is my ally." The crocodile blinked.

With slow footwork, the boy advanced, close to the ground. "We are bound, you and me, by a common enemy."

The stream tripped over itself, running, but couldn't escape the tick. Peter gazed steadily into the croc's ruby eyes. "Wendy wants me to keep away from pirates, but you're free to hunt them. And Hook has one hand left!"

The animal grew restless. Its head lifted and weaved. It slid forward a few inches, stopped. Within both creatures, a hunger gnawed.

"I know. It'll be time for another one soon. But for now . . . "

Peter inched within arm's length of the monster, then leaned forward to rest his open hands on the earth. It yielded, cool and damp, to his knees. He raised his hands and spreading his arms, held them out at his sides. A cocky smile formed on his lips. The knife lay on the ground. Peter's green eyes looked down at it, then up at the croc.

"Are we agreed?"

The croc hissed. The creek screamed its babbling alarm.

Two sets of teeth grinned. And the clock ticked on.

The Inquisition

The sailor's gold teeth were rimmed with a smile when Tinker Bell entered the candlelit room. Her heart quailed. She was in the one place she'd wanted never to see.

The odd hands grasped her yet. She was exhausted from struggling against them, her little legs ached from being pinned. By this time, her iridescent wings drooped in an attitude very unlike their peacock counterpart.

The burly man with glass over his eyes snapped the door shut behind them. "He's back, Captain!" He pushed her abductor farther into the room and gestured toward the side of the cabin, where a pair of boots could be seen on a silken couch. Perfectly polished boots. A velvet curtain concealed the rest.

Tinker Bell felt the tension of the hands increase. "Captain, Sir, the deed's done." Tink's light no longer reflected in the golden teeth. Now it was the light of abundant candles.

A silver sickle drew the curtain back and raked it aside, revealing a rich harvest for the eyes. His long body, dressed in cloth of splendid colors, reclined on a day bed. In a cascade of darkness, his hair lay in contrast against the brilliance of his robe, his jewels, his earring.

"Well, well. Our little treasure hunt in the Fairy Glade has proven productive." He laid down a leather-bound book with glittering gilt lettering. He took his time, placing his feet one after the other on the floor, and rising to stand with the grace of an aristocrat. He spoke as leisurely as he moved. "Tinker Bell."

Captain Hook strolled toward her. He lifted his hand, resplendent with rings, and held it palm up, offering his first finger in greeting. "Such an honor."

Tinker Bell declined with a violent shake of her head.

"Ah, I understand. Your feathers are ruffled. You've been shocked by our sudden invitation to the *Jolly Roger*."

She hadn't expected this smooth voice, this pleasant smile.

"But where are my manners? Allow me to present myself and my crewmen. We haven't formally met, although I have enjoyed the pleasure of beholding you from afar. I am James Hook, captain of this ship. Mr. Smee, my invaluable right hand. . . . As you can see, I am in some need of that service. And Mr. Noodler, at present acting as your captor, but I assure you, you are in good, albeit unconventional, hands." Both sailors beamed in admiration, not upon Tinker Bell, but upon their captain.

Tink did her best to glower. Hook continued his smile, framed to perfection within his glossy goatee. "Now that the formalities are out of the way, let us make you more comfortable." He aimed a brisk nod at Noodler. "Excellent work. Mr. Smee, batten the hatches!"

Smee sprang to the door and shot the bolt. He pulled down the glass covers of the bookcase next to it, then he skirted the opposite side of the cabin, inspecting the mullioned windows ranged along three sides, securing each one. Behind the couch the wardrobe door stood ajar, and he hastened to shut it, listening for the click of its brass latch. Lastly, he rolled up the oriental runner at the side of the couch and placed it against the crack beneath the cabin door.

Hook's eyes also scanned the room, inspecting. He drew a handkerchief from the sleeve just below his hook and fed it into the keyhole, tamping it with the tip of his claw.

"All secure, Captain." Smee withdrew to stand, tall and respectful, by the entrance.

"Very good." Hook turned to Tinker Bell. "I know what you're thinking, but it is no trouble at all. We would go to any lengths to make conditions perfect for entertaining such a lovely creature." The two crewmen eyed him; they knew him to be most dangerous when most polite.

"Mr. Noodler, please release our charming guest."

"Aye, Sir." Cautiously, Noodler uncurled his backward hands. Tinker Bell staggered a step or two, finding it necessary to cling to his thumb. Her legs were weak and her lower wings crumpled. In a sudden panic, she feared she might never fly again. She beat her wings to open them, then stamped each of her feet. A powdery cloud rose up, and it was then she noticed the coating of gold on the hands. Her magic dust. She looked warily up into the dark blue heaven of Captain Hook's eyes.

"Yes, my dear. I see it. How very interesting. It was really not necessary for you to bring me a gift, other than your own delightful presence. However . . ." Hook strode to a cabinet hanging on the wall at the foot of his bunk. The glass door flashed as he opened it, and he removed a crystal vial and a shaving brush. Returning, he indicated that Smee should handle the brush. He pierced the vial's stopper with the tip of his hook and pulled it free. The cork remained on the point while he held the vial to Mr. Noodler's hands to capture the golden glitter.

"Please excuse me. I hope I am not behaving in an ungentlemanly fashion if I sweep up your . . . essence, thus? You must forgive me, I'm afraid I am not schooled in fairy etiquette. Yet."

Etiquette be damned! she indicated in a reverberating ring as she flung herself away from the thumb and hurtled across the room. She was not yet mistress of her damaged wings, but she was determined to make them take her where she wanted to go. Tinker Bell thudded against every window, rushed under every drape, over every beam of the ceiling. Finding no exit, she bounced off gleaming paneling, ornate carving, satin coverlet, padlocked chest, mahogany desk. She threw herself pell-mell about the room, chiming a row of swords together and knocking over a decanter on the dining table, splashing herself in wine. She ended by skittering to a slippery halt on the keys of a harpsichord, pounding purple music from her feet. There she stayed, vibrating with its string as she stamped, screaming in C sharp.

The men looked to their captain, then guffawed. Hook laughed as heartily as they. Tinker Bell stopped the scream and covered her ears. She was bewildered. What to do next? She plunked herself down on B and folded her legs.

Hook knew what to do. "A woman of spirit, I see! I do so admire spirit." He turned to his men. "Well done, Mr. Noodler. Now away with you." He looked at Smee and jerked his head toward the door. Then, fondly, Hook replaced the stopper and tucked the vial into an inner pocket of his robe. He approached the harpsichord and lowered himself to its stool, positioning it between the fairy and the window, so that only he faced the exit.

At the door, Smee placed a hand on Noodler's arm, then leaned over him, speaking in an undertone. "Better fetch us that cricket cage, matey." Noodler touched a backward hand to his forehead and prepared to slip away. While Hook commanded the fairy's attention with solicitous attentions of his own, Smee quietly opened the door. He ushered Noodler out, taking care to replace the bolt and the rug.

Hook bowed. "Miss Bell. My apologies. You must find my crew very rude. We are not accustomed to such fine company." Detaching his gaze from his guest, he directed it toward the cabin entrance. "Mr. Smee, fetch me a fresh handkerchief. And wipe up that wine. We'll be wanting more."

He turned back to Tinker Bell. "Of course you are distressed. And not only because of me and my men. Am I right?"

She looked up sharply.

Hook kept his gaze on Tinker Bell but put out his claw to receive the handkerchief. He offered it to her with a flourish. She snatched it and began scrubbing the wine from her person. Then she wiped her feet on it, like a doormat, and kicked it into Hook's lap. He gathered it up.

"If I might take the liberty. You have overlooked a spot or two." Tinker Bell refused to flinch. With the reverence of a worshipper, he dabbed at the fairy. "Ah, that I had two hands to more fittingly attend you. Alas, I, like you, have been wounded, and suffer mightily. At the hands of Pan."

Avoiding her eyes, he folded the handkerchief and wiped the keys of the instrument. Tink watched him, her head tilted. He tossed the soiled linen over his shoulder and assumed a brave face. "But we must go on, mustn't we, making the best of tragic circumstances? Let me offer you some refreshment.

"Mr. Smee, have you a drop of nectar for the lady? My dear, we shall be more comfortable at the dining table."

Tinker Bell didn't trust her wings.

"May I escort you?"

She made him wait just long enough, then struck discordant notes on the keys as she climbed up the proffered cuff. Once aboard, she stretched out a tentative finger. She had never felt of velvet before. It was warm and yielding. She nestled in, evoking a memory of her grandmother's wings.

Hook stepped evenly to the table in the corner and placed his forearm upon it. Disembarking with some regret, Tink was surprised to find more velvet on the wooden surface. Smee's colossal form stood over an emerald-green cushion, grinning.

"Made it for you myself, Miss."

She limped a bit, then fluttered over it, undecided. The cushion invited her. Its dimensions were perfect for a fairy, the color glorious, and the velvet—so soft. Dispensing with caution, she sank into its luxury. The silver candelabra shed light and warmth. As its comforts seeped into her skin, she swept her gaze across the cabin. Perhaps it wasn't such a dreadful place, after all.

Smee bent to hold out a tiny ivory cup to her. "Nectar, Miss? In my own thimble? It would be an honor."

She accepted it.

The decanter sparkled in the candlelight as Hook poured himself a cup of wine. "A toast, to Tinker Bell. *Belle.* . . . Her name itself means Beauty!"

She liked the way he separated the two words of her name. Tinker, Belle. She drank.

It was sweet, it was tangy. It was gone, and Smee was there, refilling the thimble from a miniature jug. Hook lowered his eyebrows, reproving. "Now, Mr. Smee, pray be considerate of the lady. She is unaccustomed to spirits. We will set temptation aside for now." Hook removed the jug to a discreet distance on the table. Smee retired.

Hook leaned upon the board. "Preliminary pleasantries over, my dear, we progress to the business at. . .'hand.'" He waved his hook, his wry smile engaging as he enjoyed his own jest. "You wonder, no doubt, why I have sent for you in such an urgent and unconventional manner."

She nodded.

"I hate to disrupt our happy evening with any manner of unpleasantness, but I find it unavoidable. It has come to my attention that your consort—"

Here Tinker Bell chimed in surprise.

"Oh, yes, consort, a royal person's mate, for are you not royalty? A fairy as rare as yourself, princess or no, is one whom we common mortals envy with every unmagical fiber of our beings!"

Tinker Bell released a shiver of jingles.

"As I was saying, I have discovered that your consort, Pan, has taken a mother for his boys." The hook toyed with the jug of nectar and the china clinked in a dull, full way. "I perceive you are ignored, and worse, cast out of his good graces. How very distressing this must be to you, who are not accustomed, as I am, to being alone."

His sigh was heartrending. "Yes. I am a solitary voyager in this world. I understand what you're feeling."

Tink's loneliness rang out. If the sound of it resonated within Hook's own breast, he didn't bother with it now.

"To be sure. He has dealt you a grave injury, my Belle. And I, who have experienced the degree of damage Pan can inflict, offer you my deepest and most heartfelt sympathy."

Tinker Bell sniffed and watched the jug as the hook inched it closer to the cushion.

"But do not believe for an instant that I have brought you here in such a dramatic fashion only to commiserate with you." His gaze fell full upon her. "No, dear one. I have much more to offer your wounded heart than mere words, soothing as I hope they may be to your elegant ears."

Tink's wings lifted. She didn't know whether to look at the blue eyes, the sparkling rings, or the jug.

The eyes chose for her. "I, too, would remove the Wendy—yes, I know what she is called—from Pan's band. It suits me to cut them off from their mother," he cast a forlorn look upon his hook, "the way I was cut off, so to speak." The jug was in his fingers. "I have a plan—" Abruptly, he set the jug down. "But who am I to speak of plans to you? You have, no doubt, already devised a method of ridding yourself of this intruder?"

Tink looked sly.

"Oh, wonderful! Do tell me. How do you propose to do it?"

Tinker Bell directed a meaningful leer toward the jug and pulled the foxglove from her pocket. Fanning herself with it, she peeked from under her eyelashes.

"Poison? Really? Do have another dram." He filled her thimble. He was in no hurry, and he was enjoying himself. Disarming women was his forte. One had only to identify the weapon and use it first. Lifting his own cup, he tapped it to hers, and they drank together.

"Of course you know the situation best, my Belle. But I have reasons for wanting to keep the Wendy creature alive. Might you be satisfied if I simply . . . spirited her away from Pan?" With an air of nonchalance, he reached out and relieved her of the leaf, which had drifted onto the pillow. He held it up and looked at her sideways. "Saving your lovely little hands from any dirty work, as it were."

Tink's curious eyes peered at him from over the thimble.

"I might keep her myself, you see. As it happens, I have need of a storyteller. Dear Mr. Smee," he sent a look to Smee, who brought forth another jug, "has a weakness for love stories."

Furiously, Tinker Bell sputtered into her nectar.

Hook frowned. "Oh, no, don't tell me. Knights and ladies? Boys and pirates? No fairy tales?" He topped off her drink. "We'll remedy that. Very soon, we will each write our own happy ending, eh?"

Unnoticed, the foxglove fluttered to the floor. As Hook had foreseen, the fairy, wise to danger in the wood, was ignorant of this darker, more sophisticated forest. It flowered with kindness, flattery, luxury; it burgeoned with gratification. She was reveling in it. So was Hook. His smile was genuine now as he guided her down his path.

"Belle."

Unsteady, she perched atop her pillow.

"Tell me, my love, where might I find this Wendy, of a summer's afternoon. Alone?"

Giving a little hiccough, she floated up a few inches, then descended.

"She has a special place of her own, no doubt. All girls do. Perhaps . . . in the forest?"

Tink slowly indicated the affirmative. She didn't want to move her head too fast.

"Near any particular landmark? Say, water?"

Another nod.

"A stream?"

A lopsided smile. Her hand wiped a horizontal circle.

"In a clearing. Is there a cave or a structure of some kind, for shelter?"

Another levitating gasp.

An edge in his voice. "A way to mark it?"

Dizzily, Tinker Bell thought a moment, then puffed on an imaginary pipe. Her finger drew a curlicue above the bowl.

"Ah." His voice softened. "Smoke. Excellent."

She pointed to his eyes.

"I don't follow. . . . "

Pointing out the window, she indicated the sky. He diverted his gaze toward the glass, then returned it to her face.

"Blue smoke, like the sky. But how will I know when to find her there, by herself?"

Tinker Bell looked down.

"Belle?"

In an attempt at determination, she shook her head—then regretted it as the room reeled.

"Some mystery, love?"

Fighting the remains of her will, her eyes looked up.

"Ah, let me take over your care for you. A matter of such proportions, for one so petite!"

Absently, she stroked her velvet. Teardrops began to dampen it.

"You mustn't waste another tear on him. I won't allow it!"

She wiped her eyes on the back of her hand.

"Favor me, and I will be your champion. I will rid your kingdom of this heartbreak." He leaned closer and gazed upon her, tenderly. "When can I find her, in her secret place, alone?"

Tinker Bell hung her head.

"No. . . . No, I don't believe it! You surely cannot mean she has persuaded Pan to share this secret place with her—already?"

Tinker Bell's head swung up and she swayed, blinking for a moment, two moments. Her brow wrinkled and she studied Hook's face. Little by little her features relaxed, and she lowered her head once more.

Shaking her shoulders, she released a spray of golden dust. It settled on the velvet, glittering. She gathered a handful and blew on it so gently not a particle stirred. A thrilling, tingling sensation spread throughout her body and she responded to it, accepting a gradual smile. Her rare blue wings grew luminous, like the light of the full moon through stained glass.

Hook raised his eyebrows and slid his gaze toward Smee. They exchanged a deep look. "Do you mean, my darling Belle, that if I breathe upon your dust, I may summon you?"

Tink reclined on her cushion, nodding.

Hook continued to stare at her as he drew the vial from his pocket. When he looked down, it too, glowed, transmuted from gold to a vibrant iridescent blue.

Hook hardly drew breath. "And you, in turn, can summon me?"

A tiny tinkle sounded the answer.

"And if I should call upon you, you might be so generous as to grant me the honor of . . . doing as I ask?"

Helplessly, her shoulders rose.

" . . . Whatever I ask?"

She didn't move. She looked.

He pressed the vial to his breast. "Tinker Belle. You are a jewel. My own Jewel, far richer than any treasure I have yet discovered."

Her smiling eyes drooped sleepily. She heard the newly-familiar chink of crystal on wood.

And then Mr. Smee looked in awe upon his captain. In all his years of service, he had never admired James Hook more than at this moment. Truly, the man was a master. For with his eyes half closed and a smile that could melt gold, he bent lovingly over the fairy, and with one finger of one good hand, Captain James Hook did what no man, save himself, would ever do again.

He stroked her peacock wings.

"Just one more, insignificant question, before you rest, dear Jewel. Exactly what other properties does your . . . marvelous fairy dust possess?"

Growing Pains

On a night of a near-full moon, the village lay at rest. Nudged by silent paddles, the river waters stroked their pebbly banks and then subsided. When the tree frogs ceased their chirring, the old woman stirred uneasily. As she started to rise, her granddaughter hastened to her side, but the woman shook her head. Colorless as the moon, her braids barely moved.

"No, child. Strike the drum and run to gather the children. Boots are upon us."

The black eyes that watched her widened, and then the girl whirled to obey. Even as she threw open the flap and ran light-footed from her grandmother's tepee, the silence of imminent danger afflicted the camp. The old woman listened for the tom-tom, and when the shouts and screams erupted, she straightened her spine. With bony fingers, she drew her blanket closer to her shoulders. By the time the torch plunged through her doorway, her cloudy eyes were clear enough to see her enemies, and her back stiff enough to greet them with a proud indifference.

A swarthy seaman with large golden earrings followed the torch, poking his head under the flap and smiling at her with his even white teeth. He strode into her home, cast a greedy glance around, and finding no gold or silver, tossed his head back and laughed. His brown boots stepped near to the Old One, right on the skins of her pallet, and with the tip of his cutlass, he pointed to the open doorway.

"It is time to go, old woman." The red light of embers smoldered on his bracelets, turning them a bloody orange. He spoke with a strange accent, unlike the other white men's, and shrugged a set of muscular shoulders swathed in an embroidered shirt. "Do as you are told. I should not like to harm such a one, who reminds me of my own tribe's wisewomen."

It was the wailing and the gunfire that moved her to rise, but still she delayed, resolved to speak her words. "You will not find what you seek here. Tell your chief. His men may plunder their riches, but his own treasure lies elsewhere."

"Old One. He already knows this." In an incongruous gesture of chivalry, the pirate tucked his sword at his side and offered his hand. Through the open tepee flap, firelight illuminated the scene outside. The woman glimpsed her warrior son resisting the grip of an ebony-skinned giant bearing an ax in his belt. Refusing the pirate's assistance, the woman rose, gathering her robes and leaning on her staff. As the young girls shrieked and the babies cried, her son, like all the others, struggled with his captor.

The old woman's nostrils smelled the bite of gunpowder. Hastening into the flaring light, she felt the slap of cool air on her cheeks. Indifference grew more difficult to feign as flames tasted the sacred wood of the totem pole. Standing in the midst of strangeness, she wrapped her fingers around the familiar roughness of her staff. All about her, the dogs barked and the men fought. Trees bled from gunshot wounds, oozing sap.

Glancing toward the river, the woman spied the camp scouts lying bound next to the canoes, inert and senseless. A row of boats lined the water's edge, bobbing in the river's gentle eddy. Closer to hand, black-haired women knelt to shelter their children in their arms, their mouths open in supplication. When the braves who encircled their families finally threw down their tomahawks, the Old One saw him.

The Black Chief. The tall one, with his glittering earring and the sleek lion's mane flowing from his scalp. He emerged from shadow, materializing like a malignant spirit. Standing in the ring of crackling firelight, he drew a white cloth from his sleeve, raised a foot to dust his boot, then flicked the cloth and retired it to a pocket. When he was satisfied that all eyes rested upon him, he flourished what should have been his right hand toward a man near the totem pole. The sailor balanced a bucket, and at his captain's signal, he dashed its contents over the sacred carvings. Fire greeted water with a hissing scream that doused the most virulent of the flames. Only then did the Black Chief's shiny boots saunter forward. He wore a sneer on his lips and his eagle's claw dangled at his side. He hadn't raised it against the People, but its message was clear. That claw would slash any who disobeyed its master.

At the mercy of his men, the People obeyed. Under European eyes and the light of a near-full moon, the Indians began their exodus.

And as she hobbled toward the children to lay her calm, cool hands upon them, the Old One looked to the moon, and wondered.

Did it cast its light upon Rowan, or was he confined in the shadows?

"They're gone! They're gone!" Nibs came sliding down the hollow tree to land on his feet in the hideout. Before Wendy could ask the question, Peter did.

"Who's gone?"

"The pirates! I saw them weigh anchor and drop sails. The *Jolly Roger* is headed out to sea!" With his eyes still full of the sight, he sighed. "She's a beautiful bird." Nibs had been performing his morning lookout duty, another of Wendy's, now Peter's, ideas.

Peter crowed, then he shouted, "The pirates have set sail!"

More relieved than anyone, Wendy exulted, her ready smile sparkling. The boys bounced and yelled around them. When at last the tumult subsided, Wendy stopped to think. "I wonder what made them go?"

Peter got a shrewd look. "Nibs, was there any sign of the croc?"

"No, Peter, but I did see Tink at last."

"Tink? Where?" Peter was aware that Tinker Bell had been absent for a bit. Wendy was aware that Tinker Bell had been absent for exactly six days and seven nights, unless Time was misbehaving again, which no doubt it was, but at least since the afternoon of the hunt. Tink had not slept in the bed within her niche, nor was any trace of dust to be found in or near the hideout, nor indeed, on Peter, who had remained unaware even of that fact until the nightlight ran short of fuel and dimmed.

Nibs said, "I forget exactly where she was, but she didn't look herself."

By now Wendy was concerned about the fairy. Tink was part of the family, after all. "Nibs, please. Think where you saw her and tell us what you mean."

Nibs traced a finger in the air as he recalled his reconnaissance route. "I flew over the Island, keeping high, then I skirted the Lagoon and came round the far side, over the mountains and on to the Indian camp—the whole tribe was canoeing up the river—then I finally got over to Neverbay. That's when I saw the ship. I watched the pirates for a while and then came straight home to tell you about it, and—That's where I saw her! She was flying kind of cockeyed around Wendy's house."

Peter relaxed. "I'll go look for her after breakfast. You say the Indians have broken camp?"

"Looks like they're moving to the lodge up the mountain."

Peter's crow resounded again, and he punched the air. "Then today's the day! We'll raid their camp!" The children whooped and pranced until Wendy spied earth trickling from the ceiling. They were all excited to have a carefree day ahead. Everyone hurried through breakfast and rounded up supplies for their foray, slinging on quivers and sharpening blades.

John was no longer restricted to his bow and arrow. Peter had at last allowed him to fashion a knife from bone, and now John thrust it proudly into the sheath Wendy had stitched and which he wore around his naked middle. Wendy worried about John, not because he wielded such a weapon, but because Peter had sanctioned it. Peter, too, must have seen that John was growing. If John was old enough for a knife now, how much time was left before he was too old? As much as Wendy hated to think about it, the knife was a signal that his time was approaching.

Michael's, too. These days, Michael looked just like the older boys, in skins and leather. He certainly wasn't the baby of the family any longer. The other boys didn't advance at the same rate as the Darlings, perhaps because they'd lived their whole lives here and they were more accustomed to Peter's ways. No radical adjustments in thinking were necessary for them. Still, now that Wendy was their mother, they were growing faster than ever before. Slightly had yielded another tooth to Peter's pouch, and Tootles was becoming almost burly, redefining the meaning of his britches. Even the Twins were advancing, developing more sophisticated building skills, always seeking more complicated projects and crowding the hideout with wood and tools. They littered so much sawdust about the entrance above ground that they had designed a new round broom with which Wendy kept the tree shaft clear. Apparently Peter had been correct in his assessment but wrong in his assumption; the children *had* needed a mother, yet her effect was not to keep them young, but to encourage their growth.

In spite of this shortcoming, Wendy, like any mother, took pride in her boys. All was well and progressing naturally with them—yet that very circumstance was the source of her fear. She watched Peter, anxious to gauge his disposition toward them. When should she speak? And what, really, could she say? Peter's law against growing up was firm.

None of the children required a nightlight any longer, but Wendy kept right on lighting it so as not to call Peter's attention to their maturity. It was more difficult to conceal the status of their baby teeth. She didn't want to ask what became of them when they disappeared from Peter's pouch. Some shuddering impulse made her hide several of Michael's and John's teeth and wonder again if the nursery window was still open. In these moments, concern for her brothers' futures would fill her heart. Perhaps they were too unfamiliar now to be admitted through the window. Perhaps the old nightlight, weary of watching, had burnt itself out.

Still confident that she belonged in the Neverland, Wendy herself was changing, and she now wore a garment of her own design. She had found her nightdress becoming short and skimpy, and ragged from her many adventures. In her new gown she felt beautiful, and much more at ease with her person.

Peter had proposed a sneak incursion aboard the pirate vessel, where he supposed must be hoarded trunks of fine dresses and linens, stolen once and ripe for looting again. Nibs and Tootles seconded the idea, eager to seize any opportunity to board the ship. But Wendy of course would not allow Peter to endanger himself or her boys for the sake of mere clothing, and had applied her mind to finding other less risky solutions.

It was Tinker Bell who gave her the answer. Wendy admired the appointments within the fairy's niche. Tink enjoyed the finest furniture in the hideout, handcrafted to order by the Twins. Her best piece was the mirror they had carved. Wendy used to wonder how the mermaids fashioned their many mirrors. She now knew that like Tink's, the glass was water drawn from the Lagoon, left to harden under a full moon. But Tinker Bell's curtain, bed hangings, gowns and tapestries were made of some lovely fairy stuff, and Wendy had asked Peter to discover the source.

Wendy's new dress was loose and flowing, made of layers of various shades of gauze, ranging from the fresh green of new leaves to the emerald of the twilight forest. Peter had commissioned the fabric from the Fairy Glade. The patches of material woven by fairy looms bore a faint fragrance of ginger, and were so small Wendy had to piece the swatches together. Then she hemmed it and draped it, and cinched it at her waist with a girdle of softest doe skin.

The fabric was airy as gossamer, and the least bit sticky, so that it clung more lightly than cobwebs. And like a cobweb, it was hardy, resistant to the snags and snares of the woodlands. Although her needle pierced it readily, Wendy found the material unyielding even to Peter's knife, which she borrowed in an unsuccessful effort to trim the stuff. The fabric was deceptive. Light as it was, it simply could not be cut.

She looked more and more like the enchanted queen of her story-time, with her hair plaited into numerous braids and her cheeks grown slender. If not for the kiss waiting in the corner of the royal smile, Wendy's mother might scarcely have recognized her now, although her father would have known her at any time. Mr. Darling had often told Wendy she was enchanted.

Peter did not object to the changes in Wendy as he did to the changes in his boys. He felt she looked more like a mother was supposed to look. And he liked her new dress so well he went out to gather vines of ivy, like his own, to twine about her, complementing its shades of green. The wind sometimes tugged at the vines until they bound her too tightly, and when Peter wasn't looking, she would loosen them. If Peter noticed later on, he would bring fresh tendrils and twine them again to his satisfaction. Wendy thrilled to his attention and his touch but, for the sake of comfort, she became skilled at the art of discreet rearrangement, for although Peter could be distracted from the boys' changes, his sharp eyes detected every detail of Wendy's.

Now, as the children prepared for their outing, a soft glow lit up the tree trunk. It descended to glide into the hideout and become. . . Jewel. She remained suspended in the air, calm amid the chaos, waiting to be noticed. Tootles saw her first. "Tinker Bell! She's back!" Everyone greeted her, but she didn't answer. She just hovered with a secretive smile.

But this serenity wasn't the only change. Surveying the fairy, John said, "Look, she's different. Her hair's down."

Curly tried not to gawk. "I never knew her hair was curly, like mine!"

"Tinker Bell, you're looking lovely." Wendy studied her with the discretion she had learned to apply wherever her rival was concerned. "But the boys are right. You aren't quite the same somehow."

Peter reached out to tug the flaxen hair. "Tink, where've you been? We missed you last night." The fairy favored Peter with her regard, then swept by him, touching his cheek with her passing fingertips and continuing toward her niche.

Wendy was suddenly reminded of her father again. Wasn't that a trace of tobacco hanging in the air? As Jewel alighted, she turned to face Wendy, giving her an almost pleasant stare. Wendy had never seen that expression on the creature before. It was sort of assessing, sort of envious, but altogether unconcerned. The curtain slid closed.

Wendy turned back to the gaping boys. "Well, I'm glad she's home safe, anyhow. I wonder where she's been?" She mused for a moment, then said, "Remind me to tell you the story of the changeling this evening."

She watched Peter and the boys slither up the tunnel toward adventure. John was last, and he turned to her with one hand on his dagger and one foot in the tree. "Come on, Wendy, we— What's wrong?"

Wendy blinked. "I've just had an idea." Even the fairy might be growing up! "I think my story tonight will have to be a new one, after all. About the strange things that are happening today." Then she laughed, snatched up her basket, and flew up the tree trunk to greet whatever adventure lay ahead.

The young brave rolled up his blanket and prepared to end his journeying. The night had been another full one. He was glad. It was why he had come here.

He breathed deeply of the abundant air, turned his face to the morning light and recalled his dream. He fixed it in his mind, along with its brothers, born of other nights, so that he could relate it to the Old Ones. They would interpret his night visions, and determine his name and his future. He wouldn't question their wisdom. They were the ancestors.

His mother had called him Rowan. She was a wisewoman who had had dreams of her own, and in them she had seen her little son circle the rowan tree. He circled the tree until there were two of him, and then his twin flew up into the high branches. She had teased him as he grew, checking under his blanket every sun-up, and scanning the treetops, seeking the other Rowan. Rowan, the Life-Giver.

Rowan turned his back to the sacred rock, but it, too, was fixed in his mind. He would remember the breeze wailing in the forest on his left and the wind's fingers stirring the kettle of the sea on his right. He would remember the stars sleeping above him and the earth waking below him, and his tomahawk for company, its oaken handle in his fist. He would remember his dream of the good air being sucked from his lungs and an evil presence lurking in the darkness. The sacred place had granted a foretelling, and he honored it.

Rowan took the first step. He was going home to discover his place among men. He knew only that he had no place among women. His mother and his baby sister were gone.

Rowan took many steps, and when his feet began to ascend the slope to the plateau and he was in sight of the smoke from his village campfires, his dreamquest should have been at an end. But here he read the signs, learning that it was destined to go on.

Something was wrong.

Camp Meeting

Peter led his band over the trees, across the Island and into the territory of the Indians. Arrived at their destination, he signaled for all to fly low and dropped crouching into the wood that fringed the near side of the encampment. He listened, he watched, then he sprang into the air, launching himself end over end and touching down at the top of the totem pole. After a sweeping look around, he crowed the all-clear. The boys crept from the forest to gather in the center of the camp. Enemy territory.

"My totem is a crocodile!" Posing, Peter pressed his palms together to snap his fingers like jaws, hissing horribly. "Who'll give us a hand?" Then he laughed and jumped backward to slide down the pole. "Take a look around, but any booty belongs to the captain, to divide up later."

Wendy had performed her own ceremony, making an additional survey of the village, flying all around it to assure herself it was safe. She now called from the top of the pole, where the wind lashed her skirts. "Take only loose things left on the ground, boys, and no peeking in the tepees!" She tossed the basket down, leapt to the side and caught the pole, her fingers bouncing on its bumps as she spiraled all the way. "Put everything you find in the basket—unless it's breathing, of course." Feeling a film coating her fingers, Wendy looked down, surprised to find them darkened with char. Observing the pole more closely, she saw that it was black in places, as if singed in some ritual of fire.

The band prowled about the camp, listening to its echoes, exploring mostly, but picking up feathers, beads and bones where they lay abandoned here and there. Nibs found the tom-tom and was ready to awaken it with a fist when Wendy spread her hand on its smooth, stretched top. "No, Nibs. We'd best not call attention to ourselves. Let's just pretend." But she danced as wildly as the rest with their painted faces around the totem pole, Peter playing his pipes and the children drumming with their voices, leaping over the dead ashes in the pit and almost catching fire in spite of them.

Michael was the first to sit down and reach for the basket. "I'm going to decorate my bow to look like the Indians'."

"I'll show you how to bind the feathers around the handle." Pulling a skein of leather from his Wendy-pocket, Slightly sat down cross-legged next to him. If one overlooked his light hair, Slightly in his vest and leggings appeared more like a native than any of his brothers, and telling him so was sure to bring contentment to his face.

Peter took the basket from Michael and examined the spoils. "Don't worry too much about your bow, Michael. You'll be getting a knife soon. I'll see to it." Returning the basket, he smiled like a king doling out largess. As Michael whooped with joy, Peter felt Wendy watching him. "What?" he asked.

Wendy thought fast through the gust of anxiety. Her youngest brother was growing, and Peter had marked it. She brushed her hair from her face. "Oh, it's just that I'd like a knife of my own." But she was anxious on this point as well, sure she would be denied; Red-Handed Jill carried a knife.

Cocking his head, Peter grinned, teasing. "You don't have a proper belt for it, just a doe skin girdle. And I like you that way!"

Michael tugged Wendy's arm, pulling her down to sit next to him. "I'll let you use my knife whenever you want, now that I'm big enough to have one."

Wendy kept her eyes on Peter. "I'd hoped that wouldn't be for a long time, Michael. But I appreciate the offer." Peter settled to sit on her other side and blew on her cheek. She shivered and smiled, but soon after, she secretly loosened her vines.

The band set to work and before long, all their bows were enhanced with beads, bone and feathers, Peter's being the handsomest, with the best feathers as well as bits of rabbit fur above and below its grip, which was wrapped in leather. He crowed in high spirits, and shot several arrows swooshing off into the wood. Tootles watched them go, and at a signal from his chief, jumped up and plunged into the forest to retrieve them. As the stoutest boy, Tootles had become nearly fearless, and Peter might need those arrows back, for not even he knew what menace lurked among the trees.

The Twins finished their examinations of the totem pole and the frames of stretched rope the Indians used for drying skins. At present, they were wondering about papooses, having never observed these native children. Island lore maintained that papooses were bound to their mothers' shoulders, but the mechanics of the theory baffled the Twins. "Wendy, if we were Indians, how would you carry both of us on your back?"

"One fore and one aft!" Nibs employed nautical terms whenever possible.

Wendy laughed, imagining it. "It's lucky you can fly instead!"

Always respectful, Curly frowned. "But Wendy's a lady. She would have a pram to push you, Twins, just like the one you fell out of when you came to the Neverland."

"Only I'd have kept an eye on you in the first place, unlike your silly nurse."

The Twins started in alarm. "But then we'd never have come here! Indian ladies must be much more fun than nurses. We'd rather be papooses."

Peter got his new-idea look. "I'll tote you! John, help out with a Twin." The two boys slung the Twins onto their backs, John following Peter's lead. They teetered in a precarious dance all over the camp, thrilling the youngsters as they stumbled in a magnificent pantomime, dodging trees and nearly tipping the Twins into the cold fire, coming to an abrupt halt at the river on the far side of the settlement. Peter's new-idea look still shone as the ensuing splash resounded.

When the Twins emerged, dripping, they sputtered in excitement. "We've found treasure!" Squelching with their toes, they pried it up, and between them dragged forth a muddy lump which, sloshing to shore, they presented to Peter.

He looked at it sideways. "It's a blob of muck."

"No . . . " Taking it in her hands, Wendy examined it. "There's something else here." She knelt down on the bank to wash it, rubbing until the murk swirled away. The Twins bent over her.

"What is it, Wendy?"

"It's pottery, a jar." She kept scrubbing. "It's beautiful. Look at the painted figures, crocodiles and hawks, dancing all round it." It was wide at the bottom, narrow at the neck, red figures on glossy black. She held it out to the Twins. John, Nibs, Curly and Michael swam up for a look. They'd jumped in after the Twins, thinking a splash in the river looked like fun.

"Let me see." Peter intercepted it. He rinsed the mud out of the inside and poured it over Curly.

Diving at the muddy young gentleman, John ducked Curly. "Just getting the mud off!" John said as they both surfaced, spitting, then he broke into an imitation of his father. "I do apologize, young man, but your appearance was simply too shocking to allow in decent society!"

The 'young man' had the grace to smile, and to the society's delight, placed one arm along his waist and topped the incident off with a bow. "Think nothing of it, old man."

Peter laughed at Curly, then declared he liked the jar. "This will look fine with my arrow and my eagle feather. We'll put it on the mantel when we get home. Another trophy!"

Wendy turned to watch the Twins, but they didn't seem to mind. They set about scavenging along the bank for sturdy sticks, planning to dredge up more treasure. Perhaps, she thought, their mother and father were bringing them up well. These boys were accustomed to sharing.

Slightly wandered the encampment, drinking it in. Pausing in front of the totem pole, he studied its many hewn faces. He identified each symbol. Remembering Peter's snapping hands, he decided he wasn't comfortable with the idea of a crocodile as the family's totem. It suited Peter, but repulsed Slightly. He listened as the others slipped and slithered in the river below. He'd rather be a bird than a beast. Birds were right for this place.

Presently, he walked among the tepees. He stepped lightly, keeping a respectful distance, yet he was intrigued by the painting on the dwellings' tawny skins and the neat way their poles intertwined at the tops. He missed their welcoming smoke signals. The tepees were much bigger than he supposed when he'd snatched glimpses of them from the sky. They could hold whole families. Maybe there was room for another young brave in one of them? A 'slight' one.

Smiling at the thought, Slightly turned toward the woods. His smile faded and his face became alert. Two slate-gray eyes were staring at him, chips of smoked glass, so still and solid they seemed to belong to a sapling. They didn't blink. Neither did Slightly's.

More than eyes were here. It was an Indian boy, plainly a warrior in the making. Everything about him was rigid. Cheeks and chin were carved like a totem pole, his coarse black hair bound tight on either side of his face. At his naked thigh, he gripped a tomahawk. Slightly felt himself grow more substantial just looking at this boy. He didn't hesitate. He stepped into the wood.

"I'm sorry."

"Do you belong to the Golden Boy?"

"Yes. No! What do you mean?"

"I am of the People. Don't be sorry, I know your band didn't drive them away. I have read the signs. It is the work of boots."

"Boots?"

"The marks are everywhere. But I know where the tribe has gone."

"Our scout saw them canoeing up the river early this morning. I'm Slightly. What's your name?" But the splashing at the river stilled, and the native boy looked around for spying eyes. He crooked his hand at Slightly, and they both bent low, the dark head and the fair disappearing into the underbrush.

They settled on the far side of an oak, sheltered by its filtering leaves, and spoke again, softly. "I will be given a name soon. I am called Rowan. Why are you called Slightly? You are not slight."

Slightly smiled. "I was when Peter found me and named me."

"I see how you walk among my people's places. I will call you Lightly. It is more fitting."

Emerging from its vest, Slightly's chest swelled with pride. "I like that. I like your people's places."

"The Golden Boy, Peter you call him? He is not welcome here. He has brought sorrow to the People, with his knife and his pack of wild boys."

"I'm one of the wild boys."

"No. The woman came and guided your pack away from mischief. Except for your Peter, you have all grown." Rowan gestured toward the camp. "But I have seen her today. She is more like a fairy, and it is known how he leads his fairy."

As Slightly listened to these surprising observations, he turned thoughtful. "I guess you're right, we have grown. The lady, Wendy, is my mother." Then he laughed, but quietly. "But she isn't much like Tink!"

Rowan's face clouded. "My mother is gone, but I hope to bring her back to the People one day."

"Why is she gone? Did she come from an open window, like Wendy, and have to go back through it?"

Rowan sat very straight, his glass eyes glinting. "She is independent. Like me. I don't question the Old Ones. One day they will want her back."

"Peter will never allow Wendy to go away, like the older boys did."

"My people say there have been many boys. Where did they go?"

"Some were killed by pirates . . . " Slightly's face became tinged with red. "And your warriors."

Rowan didn't flinch. "It is my turn to apologize. But what of the others?"

Slightly shrugged. "I don't know. They must have broken Peter's law."

"My mother, too, broke with tradition."

"But Peter treats Wendy differently from the boys. I don't think he'll part with her, ever. Peter will keep Wendy no matter how she grows."

"That is what I believed, too, for *my* mother."

"Do you have brothers, Rowan?"

"No, I have no one now to share my tepee. This is not natural for me."

"You would find our hideout very natural!" Turning his head, Slightly listened for the sounds of his family. The breeze crackled in the limbs and leaves of the old oak tree, but the laughter of the others remained distant as they played their games. He had a little more time.

"Rowan, will we be friends now?"

Rowan smiled, his brown lips firm even so. "It was foreseen that I would have a twin."

"Like my brothers, the Twins?" Slightly's heart was floating, lightly.

Rowan's gray eyes searched within Slightly's blue ones, reading the signs. "Not twins of the body, but of the heart." Rowan held out his arm. Slightly joined it with his own. As their two hands clasped elbows, their arms embraced, and abided. "We will be friends."

The embrace lingered, and grew.

When the sun rode high in the sky, Rowan watched the Golden Boy's flock fly away, noting their direction. He felt light, as if he could soar into the air himself. But the signs had spoken to him, telling the story of what had happened here before the visit of the pack. Still watching the sky, he directed his steps toward the river, to begin his trek along its banks to the mountain camp, for it was there his people had fled.

He entered the cover of the trees, keeping the river at his left. Its sparkling played tricks on his eyes, appearing and disappearing as it peeped between the tree trunks. The tomahawk hung at his side, no longer his only friend. Rowan felt its weight tapping against his thigh as he stole along the shadowy path.

Then one of the shadows deepened, the river light vanished, and Rowan felt another weight, a tremendous weight, pound him from behind. Rowan sprawled flat out on the path, the earth pressing on his chin, the breath blown from his chest and the tomahawk biting into his leg. A huge, dark mass grunted and lay upon Rowan's back, reaching for his hands, to bind them.

When the brave was tied securely, the gigantic black man picked him up. Rowan felt light again, as light as a corn doll, his former rigidity now the brittleness of husks.

The work of boots.

The Open Door

The door was open, and it didn't matter today. Sitting next to it with her pleasant work, Wendy basked in sunbeams, stringing a bracelet from the cache of Indian beads in her basket. She had already made one for Peter and she had woven a few of the beads into her hair. She intended to gather pine cones on her way home, to place around the pottery jar on Peter's mantel. For now, she reveled in her freedom, hoping no boys or other disruptive creatures would interrupt it.

Wendy was spending the afternoon at her own little house. The Indians had decamped, the pirates sailed away, and she was ready to fly if she heard the tick of the croc. Peter deemed it safe for her to stay alone there while he and the boys flew over to the Lagoon to swim. Wendy liked spending time by herself here in the peace of her clearing. She liked to listen to the chatter of the brook for a while, instead of the chatter of boys. Leaning back on her bench, she watched the blue smoke curling up to become the sky. She gave no thought to the distress of the chimney hat lid, flapping away above her. She felt the quivering of the leaf wall, but her own exterior was calm.

A cup of tea was what she wanted. She laid the bracelet aside and slipped into the house. Out of habit, she reached behind her to pull the door shut. She could still hear the stream telling the world where it lived.

No other sound disturbed her solitude until, half dozing at her tea table, she thought she heard singing. It was only the creek's hysterical babbling. Her eyes opened. No. . . . It *was* singing. She listened more attentively. It was singing, but these were voices such as she had not heard since leaving her home in London long ago. Men's voices. But the Indians were on the other side of the Island, up on the mountain. Wendy sat up straighter. Who could it be? And why were they singing?

She began to hear branches swishing, and footsteps in the forest. A great many footsteps, and much nearer than she at first imagined. As her grip tightened on the arms of her chair, the voices grew louder. She caught a snatch of the song. She shot out of her seat and seized the window vines. Searching wildly, she saw nothing, only trees.

The song became clearer. Assuming shape, it struck into her heart. She made out moving splashes of color, bright within the greenery, flashes of silver and gold, swords swinging at long-legged sides and bracelets on muscled arms. They were so close now she could see pistols within easy reach of tattooed hands. Her mouth opened in terror.

No. No! It couldn't be! The pirates had sailed. . . . The *Roger* was gone! But here they were, ship's company invading the forest, bold boots stamping right into her clearing. Wendy's heart pounded. Loosing the vines as if they were on fire, she sprang away from the window, screaming inwardly but not daring utterance. She stood just inside the door, invisible behind it, immobile except for the shaking she could not control. She listened. It was all she could do.

There came a tap of metal on wood, then a vigorous voice rang out, "Hold up, mates!" The singing and tramping ceased amid a jingle of weapons. An exchange of low voices, then the same speaker, with a lilting cadence. "Get on with you, lads. Search ahead, you know where to go! Anything you find, bring it back to the harbor . . . *alive!*" It had to be Smee, the Irish bo'sun.

Wendy heard two steps on a wooden surface, then a noise like a door closing. Another low consultation. Then the awful words, "And men, if you find the lady, do what you have to do, but hands off. The cap'n wants her willing to parley, if you catch my meaning." A chorus of smirking joviality, and the marching began again as Smee urged the men off. "Get going, quietly this time! And mind those boys. They've the sharp arrows, you'll be remembering!"

Her worst fears confirmed. The pirates were after the boys. After *her!* The ship had sailed, and it was only a ploy. The enemy, Hook, was still here, waiting at the harbor. Where were the men off to? Surely they were headed away from the Lagoon?

But what of Smee? Why was he left behind in Wendy's clearing? He had to be only feet from the house. Was he to search it? She would be taken! She had nowhere to hide, no way to run, or even fly. She'd been shot down by an arrow once; she had no desire to tempt the ball of a pistol unless as a last resort. Truly needing that knife now, she cast about for a weapon. There was none. Smee could easily—

Wendy froze. Through the leafy walls and the whimpering of the breeze slipped a new sound. Had she believed her worst fears confirmed? How foolish she was a moment ago! Wendy quickly realized her mistake and a new wisdom dawned on her. She knew his voice.

She sickened as she recognized it. The voice she herself had spoken so often, in play. It mocked her now, the storyteller, hearing the real thing at last. The stuff of legends. She slid to her knees, helpless, on the cold, mossy carpet. The velvet voice of Captain James Hook continued to speak.

" . . . Mr. Smee. What a quaint place this is." He inhaled deeply. "A tidy little retreat for any person of sensitivity. I'll avail myself of it now."

"Aye, Captain. 'Tis a pleasant enough place. I don't wonder the girl comes here to get away from the menfolk, if you can call them that."

Wendy's eyes widened. How did they know?

"I hardly call them that, Smee. Boys are boys, and men are men. There is no confusing the two entities."

"Shall I check the hut, Sir?" The grass stirred nearby. Wendy stopped breathing. She heard another set of boots in the grass. They halted to loiter just outside the door. A soft swish and the click of beads against metal. *Her* beads—on his metal hook. Only a curtain of bark and living green separated her from the man.

"No need to bother, Mr. Smee, she'll not be here. She's with Pan somewhere, enjoying a happy day since the *Roger* sailed from harbor. I saw her scout flying overhead this morning. To think I've been after the wrong fox all this time! She's a crafty vixen, that Wendy."

He knew her name! And more.

"True enough, Sir, haven't we found? She's flummoxed our plans right smartly since she arrived on the Island. Can't get near those boys. But today'll be different, aye, Sir?"

"The outcome of today's incursion has yet to be decided. Never underestimate your enemy, Mr. Smee. The men are searching the Indian encampment because it is the perfect time for Pan to raid it, as the tribe has decamped and made for the hills. It would seem our little assault last night made the natives somewhat uncomfortable."

Wendy sighed silently. Here, at least, she could find relief. The pirates were searching the wrong side of the Island for Peter and the boys! On foot, they'd never get to the Lagoon before the boys left it, before the tide. She heard her bracelet drop into the basket.

Now she was free to fear for her own safety. What did Hook want with her? He was so near! She raised her hands to her face, and a new thought struck her as she touched the corner of her mouth. No, she was just a girl. And he wouldn't see it. He was a pirate, he couldn't read her heart. Never.

But she made herself smaller, there on the forest floor of her house.

Smee was speaking. "It beats me how she puts up with them, Captain. One girl amid a bunch of boys. Little savages, too."

"That is the circumstance on which I am counting, Mr. Smee. Surely by now the lady has wearied of mothering the little ruffians? After all, there are other, more mature ruffians in these parts who are in need of a . . . mother. It is time our crew felt the civilizing influence of the fairer sex."

Wendy heard the grass stir as he paced. "I am a man of sensibility, Smee. I am weary of the lack of manners displayed by my sailors. It is high time for a change. Perhaps the lady will feel the same way, and welcome the opportunity to branch out? She might even enjoy the freedoms our way of life would afford her."

"Aye, the call of the sea! And the men would appreciate a lady aboard, no doubt of that. With your authority behind her, she'd be respected right enough. I'll wager she'd get better treatment from us than she gets from those rough boys, so full of themselves."

Suddenly the grass was still. "Bravado, Smee, is the correct term. How like a boy to show off. Pan is the worst, of course. As much as I envy Pan his youth, I would never give my manhood in exchange. As a boy, Pan is a prisoner to his weaknesses; he must never show them. I, on the other hand, show my weakness to the world, and am, ironically, the stronger for it."

"Weakness, Captain?"

Wendy turned her head to hear better. She had detected a note of caution in Smee's question.

"Aye. You see it before you. The wound, caused by Pan himself. I am not afraid to own it. It is no shame to me. Rather, the shame lies upon he who inflicted it."

Smee declined to reply. It seemed he deemed it safer to hold silence.

"And therein lies the difference. A boy will hide behind his pride. A man will face the world."

"But a girl, Captain. Won't she fear to face the world with pirates? Do you think her bold enough to join?"

"When I make the girl's acquaintance, I will know. The men will not harm her, you made my orders clear. I need to speak with her, to learn her mind. If she joins us, I will find it in my heart to end the feud with Pan. I would consider her presence a peace offering. I have lived long enough to understand the value of compromise. I am proud, but not too proud to reach an accord, even with an adversary as hated as Pan."

"And if not, Captain? If she won't come, or Pan won't give her up?"

Waiting for the answer, Wendy moved not a muscle. Something sharp scraped the lower half of the door. Hook lingered just outside it.

"Of course it must be strictly her decision. Surely Pan cannot speak for her? She is her own mistress, I presume! If she is not inclined to join us, she must remain my enemy. Yet will I release her. It would be a pity, but honor demands."

Smee's lilt held a touch of pride. "Aye, Cap'n, you are a man of honor! I've never seen you force a female of any description."

"No. It's never come to that, has it?" They both laughed, Smee in a rollicking manner, and Hook's more throaty. Wendy jumped as a sudden crunching struck just above her head. Looking to the top of the door, she saw it, a sharp metal point piercing the bark. Razor sharp. Her heart raced. The point was yanked free and the door tottered, opening. It swung out a few inches—and rested. Wendy stared out the opening, appalled.

The laughing men moved toward the forest and she caught her breath and gathered her wits. She got to her feet. How she wished she dared peep through the crack of the door! But no.

"Off you go, now, Mr. Smee. I'll stop here a while and walk back. I shall enjoy a stroll in the wood. Report to me when you've any news."

"Aye, aye, Captain! The lads are bound to have snared something by now."

Wendy listened to Smee's purposeful steps directed the way the other men had gone, but she heard nothing more. Nothing to indicate the direction of a captain's boots. The silence prickled. She knew he had to be about. She could still feel his power. There'd been no indication of his departure. But where was he? How near?

The crack of the door beckoned. Surely she could push it open just a bit more, ever so gently? He must be in the forest by now, or at least at the edge of the clearing? The breeze tugged at the door, inviting her out. The stream's burbling sounded strangely complacent; it made no objection. Wendy felt the hard, uneven surface of the bark under her fingers. She touched the gored place, where the hook had violated it. A small wound remained there. Pressing her face close to it, she peered out with one eye.

The hole was so small and rough she could see only dimly through it. But a shadow loomed there. A large shadow, directly in front of her, separated from the door by only a few feet of air. Wendy lost her courage and pulled away. There she stayed, hands flat against the bark.

She reflected on all she had heard. It was very different from what she expected. Nothing at all about harming the boys. On the contrary, a way had opened to save them, and Peter too. If Hook meant what he said in confidence to Smee, he would accept Wendy in exchange for all the others. The feud would be at an end!

If he was a man of his word. Wendy searched her memory. Was he? Could Hook be trusted in any way, on any level? Yes. He could be trusted to preserve his own interests. And he considered himself to be above other pirates; although he would be ruthless if crossed, he often refrained from a fight if he could achieve his desires in a more civilized fashion. Yes, this certainly had been true of Hook.

Or was she just wishfully thinking? Would she really consider a life aboard the *Jolly Roger?* Even temporarily? She'd always wanted to sail . . . but not with a crew of buccaneers! . . .Hook would protect her? Yes. At least, he had that power. Absolute sway over his men. It was possible she could voyage in safety.

The freedom of the open sea drew her. Wendy's spirit sailed even now, just dreaming of it.

But Peter would never allow it. He didn't understand compromise—and he would kill or die before he'd see his Wendy among the pirates. She would have to make him see the sense of it, or make it his own idea. Another opportunity for adventure. He would still need her, surely she could come back to him when the terms of agreement were satisfied? Perhaps it wouldn't be so very long. And afterward, what stories she would be able to tell, to Peter and *all* the boys!

And then she thought of her brothers. They were growing, they needed her to guide them, protect them. But if she could return quickly, they would be all right. And she might keep in touch with them, somehow. John might join her if necessary, maybe as a cabin boy. He wouldn't have to become a real pirate. Neither of them would.

Wendy recognized that Hook had spoken truth about at least one thing. Boys were full of bravado. It was bravado that got them killed. If she could find a way to keep everyone alive, shouldn't she do it?

All these thoughts rushed through Wendy's mind as she stood, compelled by the open door. If the door had remained shut tight, such reflections may not have entered into her little house. She might have hidden away, enclosed and closed-minded. But the door was open, now, for good or for ill. And so was Wendy.

With a small, hesitant creak, the bark swung away from her fingers. She stood for a moment, hands remaining poised, then she lowered her arms and took one firm step over the threshold. She looked straight ahead at the man before her. He was dressed in black, his back to her. She took another step, then, oddly, reached behind her to push the door shut again. It made a soft bump as it closed.

His head raised up and turned slightly. The air stirred his hair.

The same air stirred her own as she faced the dark figure that had haunted her, that hunted her.

"I am Wendy. We have found each other."

Shades of Black

He concealed his emotions. He turned slowly to stare directly, unsmilingly into her eyes. He chose his first words to mirror her own.

"We have found each other. I am Hook."

Apart from his dreams, he had seen her only once before. Then she had been a girl. She was still young now, but now, she was his Beauty. Her hair, her gown, the ivy, all clung to a form that belonged in this woodland surrounding. Her eyes were deep and clear. They reflected truth. Hook showed nothing of his satisfaction.

Wendy felt rather than saw him. He was velvety black, his sword hilt sharply silver, dark hair sleek and flowing, his neat beard glossy. The heavy earring was rich, his eyes a piercing blue, more startling under the black brim than the gems studding it. She sensed that every part of him was exactly as she had described, so many times.

And there, the hook. Cold and barbed, incongruous with his finery. Barbaric. A stark hint of the cruelty he cloaked.

She could barely speak. She whispered.

"I know you."

But he was so far from what she expected. So much more. So much more real.

His voice held a touch of irony. "Yes, I am known."

An inner ache stabbed her. She reached to the house for support. Hook strode forward and caught her shoulders in his good arm. He guided her to the bench, swept the basket of beads to the ground, and seated her. Seating himself beside her, he tossed his hat on the gay colors that now lay scattered in the grass.

His touch, his proximity made everything worse. The ache within Wendy intensified. It was a force that gripped and pulled. Part of her that had been just a dream awakened and escaped, and the void it created burned raw. She tried to fill it with air, breathing fast. Hook perceived the violence within her, that she was immobilized by turmoil. Some moments passed before she was able to make herself breathe quietly. He watched, unperturbed.

He had already identified her weapon. He used it first. When she could hear him, he spoke to her, his manner grave. "Let me tell you a story, Wendy, while you recover yourself."

Wendy became aware that his hand rested on his knee, jeweled. The hook lay casually across his thigh. She was unnerved to discover that its inner curve was sharpened like the edge of a razor, and much as she would have preferred the diversion of the jewels, it was the hook that snagged her gaze and kept it.

His fairy had informed him. "I have heard of a little girl who flew away from home. She longed for adventure and knew precisely where it could be found." As his silken voice began the narrative, Wendy's gaze left the razor, drawn irresistibly to his face. She looked on him in wonder. Hook was telling her a story?

"And when she grew up, she became a complete and beautiful woman, having partaken in full along the way of both joy and pain." His eyes held her own, restraining them from the hook.

"She was marked by her experience, of course, but those markings gave the woman her strength. They blended with her beauty to form her soul, a work of art that lives on forever."

Her hands tried to stifle her response. "Ah!" Tears stung at her eyes. "You know."

Hook's tone was flat. "What is it I know, Wendy?"

"The end of my story. As I wish it." She looked away at last. "And I know what you'll do."

"Not even I know what I will do. Let us find out together." He rose and walked a few paces.

Feeling she had endured a great deal in a few moments, Wendy was grateful for the opportunity to collect herself. His bland demeanor, so unexpected, was calming. He spoke to her over his shoulder.

"Obviously, you were witness to my conversation with my boatswain. You know that I sought you, and why. I have no secrets. It is well." He turned to face her once more, his silver sword belt flashing from shoulder to hip, spearing her eyes with sunlight. "What say you to my proposition?"

She clutched the bench, and her courage. "Why should I trust you? Will you honor your word if I agree?"

"You know me."

Wendy released a scornful breath. "That is hardly reassurance."

"I am not here to reassure you . . . Wendy Darling."

Wendy blinked. He knew her full name. She would have to think about that later. "How much time will you allow for my decision?"

"Oh. No time." Hook shook his head, once. "Time doesn't exist here."

Her eyes widened. Time was what she needed. To her cost, it had never been on her side. She rose from the willow seat. "I—I must accept. But I will need time, to explain to Peter. I'm not certain what his reaction will be."

"I am certain. He will challenge me and I will kill him."

The implication of his words and the coldness with which he spoke them struck her like frozen rain. Her mouth fell open. As it all sank in, she became aware that it was much too familiar.

"You sound just like him!"

His gaze was cool. "So you begin to understand. Your boy is no better, and no worse, than the pirate he professes to despise."

Shock struck her yet again, but she tasted the truth of his bitter words. She wanted to spit them out. "So you will use me to provoke your duel!"

"What better provocation can I find?" In two strides he was in front of her. He gripped her upper arm and forced her face close to his. "When Pan loses to me, you understand, there will be no more choice for you. There will be no more boys to mother. I will not ask your 'consent' again."

Aware of his strength, Wendy saw, horribly late, that she was caught. The decision to be made was make-believe, had never existed. He was as wily as she had portrayed him. She should have seen it! But he had baited this trap too well.

"But why not kill me with the boys? Once you've snared Peter, I will be of no more use to you."

His icy eyes swept over her. "On the contrary. It will be most gratifying to watch you and Pan betray each other." She drew a sharp breath. Hook released her arm, observing as horror spread over her face. She backed away, but he stepped close again and looked down at her, sneering. "Yes, you play him false even now. I see the desire in your eyes. You are impatient to grow up."

Her heart beat with wild alarm. What else did he know?

"Pan must see it too. What will his reaction be to *that?*"

She cast her eyes down, silent.

"I thought so. You claim you are loyal to him, yet you break his law. And he will betray you, as well, when you most need him."

Her jaw jutted and she shot him a defiant look. "I don't believe you!"

He raised an eyebrow. "Yet you respect truth above all things. I will prove it to you. Easily."

She was dazed, but realized she must learn more of his scheme. "You talk of truth? Then tell me. You spoke to Smee of Peter's weakness. What did you mean?"

"The clever vixen, always trying to divine my plans." His eyes narrowed. "Or are you simply casting until you may inquire about my own weakness? To gain power over me?" The hook waved, negligent of its effect. "It matters little. I am an open book, to you." He inhaled deeply. He began to pace. "I meant that youth paints the world with a boring palette. Only two possibilities exist for Pan. Black, or white." He swiveled to face her. "Such children see only two shades."

Wendy looked past him, seeking some kind of help from the surroundings that at one time seemed so friendly, but had deceived her. She became aware of the dusky twilight of the woods, and the glare of the sun on his earring. "Dark . . . and light," she murmured. Against her will, as if a wedge of intellect was prying her from the boy she loved, she acknowledged this man's thinking.

"Exactly." His tone had grown shrewd.

She said softly, to herself, "There is nothing in between, for Peter."

"And you will betray him as soon as you are able to see the shades of black."

She stood transfixed by his piercing stare. He hadn't moved closer, but by some insidious means, he encroached. She felt his presence filling her, inky dark velvet and heavenly blue eyes. She had difficulty breathing.

"I behold you at this moment," Hook observed, "attempting to reconcile the twain. But according to Pan, all his deeds are light. Acting for what he believes to be good, he has never thought of consequences. He doesn't even know the pain he causes." Hook cast a gaze upon his claw, his lip curling. "The damage."

Wendy had already learned not to be distracted by his speech. But she must play for more time. "Damage . . . to you."

"You are young, but I will tutor you." He considered his hook. "There was terrible pain, for a very long time. And I had to relearn everything." His head jerked up and he glared at her. She stepped back.

"I was a master swordsman. Do you think it was easy to regain my skill? I couldn't wield a spoon, let alone a cutlass. I couldn't even sign my name!" Hook stopped and thrust his hand toward his side. Wendy braced her body, thinking he was about to draw his sword, but he pulled a small book from within his coat. "By the time I was able to scrawl my signature, even my name had changed." He tossed the book to her. "Look at it."

Wendy caught it and searched his face. Her fingers felt the giving relief of leather. She opened the book, dragged her gaze from his, and looked down. Then she understood.

Inside the front cover he had inscribed his name. The name his enemy had inflicted on him, along with his wound: *Jas. Hook.* The signature was flourished and bold, but barely legible. Her forehead creased; her heart bruised. Looking at him again, she closed the book and held it out.

"Keep it. You may find it to your taste . . . Storyteller."

She nearly dropped the book.

"Yes, I know that, too."

Of course he knew it. Wendy stared at the book's glittering letters for a moment before she could make sense of them. It was a collection of antique fairy tales.

She kept her gaze on the volume. He was so far ahead of her. As if he had read the book, and she was only beginning it. She would have to match his cunning. She opened her mouth to speak, but the words that had always been her allies wouldn't rally. She swallowed and tried again.

"What duties will be expected of me?"

He relaxed, but his expression gave no sign of his feelings. "That is as yet undetermined. The important thing is that you join me."

"But I heard you tell Smee——"

"Enough! Let us just say that I am weary of living alone, a man among animals."

The pounding of her heart made it difficult to keep her features calm, but Wendy mastered them. Surely Hook didn't mean he wanted—companionship—but only that his men needed manners. Uncertain, she set the book down as if it were made of glass. She waited for more information.

"My dogs are faithful, but mongrels, all of them. Your talents will bring a welcome change for us. I've seen what you've done for your pack of boys."

She sought to absorb this evidence of his observation. How had he seen, and when?

"You will be, perhaps, more welcome to my crew than you were to Pan's. After all, 'pirates love ladies.' How did you put it? Those who have 'proved their valor.' "

Wendy's knees went weak. Hook had spoken her own words, from the story of Red-Handed Jill! The realization rushed through her like the wind, to leave her reeling, her soul in shreds. Hook's perception delved far deeper than she'd supposed. Not only could he tell her story—he'd somehow lived it.

And he could touch it. He moved a step closer. With excruciating leisure, he raised his good hand and, as she shivered, lifted a lock of hair from her shoulder. Drawing it toward him, he released it, strand by strand, to her breast. "Seeing how lovely you are, I expect you'll be obliged to demonstrate *your* valor. Many times over."

He had played the card that broke her concentration. Her mind began to panic, her breathing grew rapid. She struggled to make one point very clear to him. "I know nothing of men. I'm just a girl."

"And innocent enough to believe in fairy tales. As if your tender age could protect you."

"If not my age, what?" She grasped at her last hope. "Will you protect me?"

"Wendy. You must have learned by now to rely upon no one. You must protect yourself. I daresay you always have."

She lowered herself to the bench, her head bowed, her thinking fast and desperate. Hook took advantage of her distraction to direct a glance and a nod toward the roof of her house. A burst of fairy light rose from it, and Jewel sped off on his errand in the direction of the Lagoon.

Wendy's thoughts raced. How to outwit him? He knew too much! He played his game as if the outcome was fated to his advantage, as if he had already won. She felt herself losing to a subtle mixture of force, inevitability and something else she didn't want to admit, even to herself. It was attraction, yes—physically, he was everything she had imagined, and he stirred her. But it couldn't be admiration. He was a pirate! A pirate, who envisioned her as a lady. A man who had called her lovely. It was almost as if he could read her heart. . . . Countered by her own reaction to this man, Wendy could not find a way to win freedom, for herself, for Peter, for the boys. And he must know that, too.

If only she could shut herself away in her little house one more time, and stay forever. But it was so fragile. And if she stopped there, her story would take no form. As he had foretold with maddening assurance, her experience was already shaping itself into her soul.

And then he was beside her. "Wendy Darling, what shall we call you? You must have a pirate name, hearty."

She turned to face him straight on. She summoned the fiercest name she knew and threw it at him. "Red-Handed Jill!"

"Red-Handed Jill. That's the one. You must tell me her story. . . one night . . . " His mouth twisted with insinuation. "When the children are abed."

He loomed over her, all black velvet. "What is *your* weakness, my Jill?" But he held two fingers to her lips. "No, I will answer for you." His fingers moved lower to caress her chin. "I have already used it against you, haven't I?"

He forced her chin up so that his incredibly blue eyes caught and kept her own. "And I will use it again."

The ache jabbed within Wendy. She thought surely he must have thrust his hook in her. She must be dying. But the hook crouched on her shoulder, cold and sharp. She made an attempt to turn her head toward it, but he held her chin. Her body began to shake, and she couldn't stop.

"I will use you again, and again, until I have satisfied my Darkness."

His hand lay on her cheek. "You know of my Darkness. You have told of it. Did it make a cozy bedtime story for your brats?" His thumb lingered on her kiss before his hand slid to her neck. He dropped his eyes as if appreciating how easily it fit around her throat. Something else he'd had to relearn. His thumb stroked her neck.

"As I say, I am an open book. Take care, lest one day my eyes burn red, and I close upon you."

But this day, his hand remained open, and his eyes remained blue. Wendy felt his grip release her.

"Jill."

Her throat closed of its own accord, her shoulder pricked, but when she dared to look, hand and hook were resting, harmless, on his thighs. She began to breathe once more. To think once more.

If she was destined to be Jill, she had better recapture her courage. She grasped it by the tail. "What is it you really want from me?"

Hook had drawn back and, head tilted, was studying her face. "At the moment, I want you to tell me a different story. Open your lips, and speak to me of this kiss." And without touching her again, he leaned toward her so that his lips lingered an inch from her own. She was certain, then, that he saw it, that he sensed its impatience, and that its waiting time was at an end.

And it was, after all, not a prince, no prince at all who had come to claim it. Hook was no prince.

He was a king. A pirate king. The king to break the queen's enchantment. He placed his open lips over her own, at the corner of her mouth, directly upon it. But he didn't take it.

She gave it to him.

And she felt the wind rush through her this one last time. But it wasn't the wind now who twined her hair in his fingers and gathered her kiss in his own until finally and at last, Time no longer existed for her.

Above them, the blue smoke ceased to billow. It puffed itself out and blew away in the parting breeze. And without warning, the chimney hat gave voice to its scream, for a clear, high shriek exploded on the roof. It sounded like crowing.

It was Peter.

Hook's blue eyes ignited. Wendy had never seen him smile before. "Right on time!"

Passion Play

Hook was up, he spun around, his sword shrieked from its scabbard and steeled his hand.

"Don't touch Wendy, Hook!" Peter stood straight, straddling the roof of the house. He held his bright dagger ready.

"Too late. . . . I *have* touched her, and long before today."

Peter leapt from the rooftop to stand a sword's length from Hook. "You filthy pirate! She's mine."

"She has just become mine. Is that not so, ah—what shall I call you?" He tossed a quick look to Wendy.

She sprang to her feet, shaking off her trance. "It depends who wins, doesn't it?"

"Precisely. Your 'Wendy' and I were discussing the future, Pan. Not yours," his brow creased in mock concern. "You have no future."

Peter advanced with his green eyes flashing. "I've future enough to rid the world of you forever."

"Peter, keep back! He doesn't want me, he only means to kill you."

Hook began sweetly, "A mother's weakness. A story to protect her young. But I do want her. Who can resist her?" He circled left, so that Peter's steps countered. "Can you, Pan?"

"I'll resist you, with my knife!" Peter hunched forward, holding his knife steady and beckoning Hook with his hand.

But Hook only scoffed. "Your knife isn't enough for her, now. She has agreed to join me, if I give her what she wants."

"You don't know what she wants!"

"Indeed? I have just delivered it." He regarded Wendy warmly, "And accepted her terms."

Peter turned his head to follow Hook's stare. Wendy's cheeks burned. The boy fired back, "Pirates don't honor terms with girls."

Watching Wendy, Hook's regard intensified. "But just as you suspected, she doesn't want to be a girl any longer." Wendy tore her gaze from Hook to look into Peter's eyes. She saw Peter falling for it. And she couldn't deny it; Hook had trapped her in the truth.

But Hook was cold once more. "Decide now, Pan . . . " He kept circling. His movement forced Peter to present his back to Wendy where she stood in front of the house. "How far will you go to keep her from me, your Wendy?"

"I'll fight you to the death, Hook."

Hook smiled genially, his tone conversational. "Yes, I know that. But whose death?" He lunged, and the two weapons collided with a rasping scrape. Peter's dagger was no match for the rapier. He could only deflect the charge—until a sword appeared from nowhere and fell into his outstretched hand.

Wendy was startled to see Nibs overhead and the Lost Boys flying toward her through the forest. Nibs had tossed the sword, and Peter's courage flowed into action. In one movement, he transferred the dagger to his other hand and seized the sword, parrying Hook's next thrust and launching his own attack.

Wendy fought her fear. She had to think. "No! Nibs! All of you, get away!"

But the band of boys paid no heed, settling on the grass to stand tensed around the duelists, with the little house forming part of their circle. Jewel, too, had streaked from the forest. She hovered above them, her light blazing. John and Michael looked pale and perplexed, as if awakened from nightmares, but the other boys were flushed and their expressions fierce. Each of their knives spoke its own lethal language. Hook marked their positions.

Peter's voice rang bold as ever, "Leave Hook to me, boys!"

Distraught, Jewel flitted from boy to boy, resonating with dismay.

Again Wendy cried, "Michael, John, go home!" She stepped into the circle to wave the band away, but all eyes fastened on magnificent Peter. And black Hook.

Peter glowed. "And miss all the fun? The boys and I have been itching for this fight, haven't we?"

"As have I, arrogant boy," Hook called. The enemies surged, clashed and withdrew, and surged again. Compelled by old animosity, they struck their swords together, making brutal music. Falling back only to renew his grip, Peter whirled and lashed out, slashing. Hook's rapier flew high and low, blocking Peter's blows. Boots and bare feet stepped wide, balancing the aggression of the blades, maneuvering within the ring of children. As Hook circled, he faced the house and never turned his back to Wendy. Reversing tack when necessary, he made certain Peter fought in front of her. The boys' weapons, held at the ready, surrounded the opponents but didn't interfere. Peter had spoken. Only he would fight Hook.

A grim fascination gripped Wendy. Driven by instinct, she evaluated the situation and found she understood it perfectly. Both parties were skilled swordsmen, but Hook's superior size and strength gave him the advantage. Clearly, he had mastered with his left hand the skills lost with his right, and far from exerting himself, he was taking pleasure in this fray. Peter was smiling. He was cunning and quick. But he was a boy, his reach insufficient to drive his blade home. His repeated attempts to close in and score were foiled by the slicing claw. Wendy watched, reluctant but intrigued, as it fended off any steel nearer to Hook than the point of his sword.

"Come, Pan, don't be shy. Shake hands with my hook!" It shot out and shredded a leaf at Peter's hip. Peter realized his disadvantage and took to the air in one exultant bound.

"You can't catch me, Hook, on the ground or in the air!"

The pirate snarled his disgust as Peter attacked from on high. Hook fought him off, jeering, "But I can bring you down!"

Peter darted forward and back. Hook beat him away. Finally snaring the boy's blade in the crook of his claw, Hook slid it down to the hilt of his own and flung it off with both arms. "Fly away while you can, boy!"

Peter sailed backward, then charged again. "Never!" Hook waited for the attack, dodged it, and spun to take up a position behind Wendy.

He raised his sword to her back. The boys gasped and John and Michael cried out, "Wendy!" She stiffened as she felt the tip pricking her spine.

Peter froze in mid-air. "No!"

"Afraid I'll pierce her with my blade? Do you even know what you're fighting for, Pan?" Wendy stood very straight, very still.

Peter eased lower, deadly earnest. "Give her to me."

Hook redirected the point, stepping close to Wendy and pressing the flat of his blade to her back. Resting his hook on her shoulder, he purred in her ear, "I do apologize, but needs must." He raised his voice to Peter. "I present her to you with my compliments. Try to take her." He shoved her with force, so that she tripped into the center of the ring. Hook smiled derisively at Peter. "Let us see if you are man enough to keep her from me."

Peter touched down to stand next to Wendy. Watching warily from under his hair, he tucked his sword in his belt, keeping his dagger alert as he returned it to his right hand. He grasped Wendy's wrist and pulled.

Wendy's heart sank. *Bravado. . . .*She knew what he would do, what both of them would do. "No, Peter, it's just a trap. He has it all planned!"

Peter kept his eyes on Hook. "I have to protect you, Wendy."

Nearly frantic, she exclaimed, "But he knows that, he knows everything! He's only using me to get to you. You have to listen!" She struggled in his grip. "I'll go to him and you can take the boys away."

Hook bided where he stood, poised but unmoving. His eyes glinted as he watched the drama unfold. Peter assured himself of Hook's stillness, then took his eyes off the man to glare at Wendy.

"It's true? You want to go to him, Wendy?"

The silken voice interrupted. "You can call her Jill Red-Hand now, Pan. I do."

Peter remembered the story of the lady pirate. He hated her. "Wendy?"

"I don't want to go to him, Peter. I *have* to. Remember that Jill could defend herself. Just get the boys to safety, now!"

Jewel jingled at the edge of the action. It seemed for once she agreed with Wendy. But Peter only gripped Wendy tighter. "You told me Jill was just a story."

"Time is running out!" Her urging grew desperate, "Hook's men may be surrounding us this very moment. You have to go!"

"Listen to her, Pan. She knows me."

Peter was listening. He was seeing, as well. He used all his senses. His eyes squeezed to slits. "You look different . . . and you stink of pirate!" He flung her away.

Wendy caught herself, and her shock showed on her face. "Peter!"

Hook was all modesty. "That would be the kiss."

"*That's* what you were doing? Together?"

Doubly betrayed, Wendy couldn't answer. But her eyes, as always, told him the truth. And it had nothing to do with thimbles and acorns.

Peter shook his golden head. "No. I don't care. I won't let him have you." He grabbed Wendy's arm and pinned it behind her. "She's still mine, Hook. Whatever you've done to her, I'll take her back."

Jewel's iridescence beat in front of Peter. She pleaded in musical hysteria.

"Away, Tink!" Irresistible as always, Peter knocked her aside with the back of his hand. She tumbled, flickering.

Hook looked askance at him. "Pan, you really must cultivate your way with women. Ask this lady her preference, to begin. She appears unwilling." He took a step forward.

Peter tugged Wendy back. His dagger shot out. "Don't try it, Hook."

The boys were confused. They banded together for comfort, breaking the circle. Dizzily, Jewel flew at them and bored into their backs, her tiny hands pricking them toward Peter.

Hook stepped again. "I don't have to try." He pointed his sword to its scabbard and thrust it home. "It's done." Advancing to the point of Peter's knife, he looked down at it, unimpressed, then swept his gaze to Wendy.

His voice was intimate, insinuating. "Jill? Open your lips . . . "
They opened in a gasp. He held out his hook to her. "Speak your
intention. Will you come to me now?" In a subtle movement, the
hook shifted, inclining toward Peter's wrist. "Or later?" The razor-
edged claw paused, hungry, only an inch away.

She lowered her eyes to focus on the danger. "Don't hurt Peter. I'll
come." Raising her eyes again, she locked his blue gaze in her own.
"Now." As she uttered the promise, the panic rushed inside her.

Peter acted swiftly. He drew back his arm and slashed the dagger
down, clanging against the hook. His blow met no resistance. He
dragged Wendy three steps backward while his dagger rebounded to
her throat. "I'll kill her before I let you take her."

Michael screamed and John seized him. "No, Peter!" Lowering
their weapons, all the boys stared. Jewel hung over them, her light
fading to its merest glimmer. John pulled Michael's face to his own
chest and wrapped his arms around him, holding firm as Michael
fought to free himself. Wendy couldn't see them, she could only see
Hook lifting his chin, triumphant. His gold ring swung upon his ear.
"So!"

Wendy grasped Peter's wrist with her free hand. He was hurting
her arm. Her head tipped up, her eyes turned toward him. She still
believed. "Peter, you don't understand what you're doing!"

"I do." His face hung close to hers, his hair scented with myrtle.
Keeping his eyes on Hook, Peter pressed his cheek against her own.
"I do understand." He brushed her hair out of the way with his lips,
never losing sight of his foe. He whispered in her ear, "I'd rather see
you dead than turned pirate." She inhaled sharply. Hook observed, his
muscles tensed.

"Not my throat, Peter. That's a pirate's way." Wendy sought to
regain his confidence. "You taught me, remember? The weakest part
of any creature is the heart." And the fairy gauze of her gown was
impossible to cut.

Peter turned his head. With his beautiful eyes, he looked into
hers. "I'll remember everything. But I'll pretend I never knew you."
Breaking Wendy's grip, he rotated his dagger to point it at her heart.
"I'm very good at make-believe."

He shot a look at Hook, then began to cut away the ivy he once, so gladly, twined about her body. His knife worked deftly. At each snap of the blade a tendril fell, until the garland lay in limp green pieces at her feet—the ever-after end of once-upon-a-time.

Wendy closed her eyes. She felt Hook watching, permitting the scene he had staged to play itself out. He had threatened her. He had embraced her. What did he really feel? It didn't matter any more. In one lesson, he had taught her to rely only upon herself.

She could hear the boys' restlessness in the grass behind her. She knew they wouldn't save her, either, nor would Peter's spiteful fairy. The creature was strangely quiet. No jealousy interfered now that Wendy's wish was granted. . . . At last Peter clasped her in his arms, and she had stirred him to passion.

He set his knife to her throat. "I promised you adventure, Wendy. To die will be the biggest one of all!"

His words cut into her like his dagger. Wendy grasped Peter's arm and fought against him. She had to act, to rescue herself. Jill would defend her life with any weapon at hand. Wendy would tell a story.

"Peter, let me tell you about the adventure." She stopped struggling, continuing the fight with words. John released his hold on Michael. All the boys stilled. Hook observed Peter, his gaze keen.

"Today the Pirate King used your Wendy to bait a trap for you. But you were too clever to fall into it. You saw that I was only trying to save you. I know now that I can't."

"I'm trying to save you, Wendy." He returned Hook's stare. "From yourself." The cold knife began to burn against her neck. She pulled hard on his arm, trying to tear it away.

It didn't stop.

Hook sprang at Peter, slashing with a vengeance, raking a red furrow from wrist to elbow. Peter let go of Wendy to double over, exhaling as he grasped his arm. Smears of blood marked both blades, and more tinted Peter's fingers. Wendy reeled away, clutching her throat. Behind her, she heard chiming alarm and high-pitched screaming.

Peter groaned and stumbled toward the forest as Jewel burned a trail to his side. Shouting, the Lost Boys scrambled to reach him. They gathered him up, each grabbing an arm, a leg, a vine or belt. Amid the skins, knives and feathers, his chest rose and fell with his gasps. His green eyes sparked, shooting hostility toward the pirate. He vowed through his teeth, "It's not over yet!" He didn't look at Wendy at all. The boys leapt into the air, to fly him to safety at last.

But before they were away, Hook strode after them. "You're right, Pan!" He reached up and snagged Curly's belt with his claw, plucking him easily out of the air. Curly screamed, still clinging to Peter, and the boys dragged him. They pulled together toward escape while Hook raised his head to hiss at Peter, "I've only begun! Now I see how well you care for her. She'll be better off with me—no matter what I do to her." He savaged the belt. It fell away to slither into the grass, and the flock of boys sped upward and homeward, led by the brightness that was Jewel.

Standing in the hollow of Wendy's clearing, Michael rubbed his wrist across his eyes. John yanked him along, and together they braved the black man and rushed to Wendy's side as he pivoted toward her. Placing an arm around each of her brothers, she let them lift her into the sky to float away from the little house, where the blue smoke would never rise again—because Wendy was no longer at home.

Warm drops slid down her cheeks. Other, thicker drops congealed at her throat.

She looked down into the clearing. She saw the man in black velvet watching her go. She saw him saluting her. There were the violated vines, the severed belt. There, the basket and its beads lying in the grass, the little brown book abandoned on her bench. She saw the colorful clothing of pirates emerging from the cover of the trees that had concealed them, and Mr. Smee bending over his captain's hat, brushing it off.

She felt her brothers' arms supporting her and then she supported herself and shook them off to raise her arms and embrace the sky. She dried her tears upon it and soared upward as high as she dared. There were no more limits.

This was freedom. Why did it hurt so badly?

She had so much to think about. So much to decide. Much to do.

It wasn't just a story any more. It was her life. And she believed in it.

Back . . . and Forward

Wendy lay on the chilly grass under a blanket of moonlight. She was listening to the music of the spheres, watching the fairies float above the flowers, like constellations evolving.

Harmony reigned within the limits of the fairies' circle. It was soothing to give herself up to the garden and the fragrance of its midnight roses, stargazing. How they fanned their way along, these creatures of air. They appeared to be a universe in miniature, but they didn't feel anything bigger than themselves. Life to these fairies was an airy, merry step such as Wendy used to dance, high in the sky above the Island, and believed she would dance again. She had almost found her smile, while watching them. Almost.

Wendy, in turn, was watched by John. Michael had fallen into a dozing dream. Passion was hard to hold for long in the Fairy Glade. It became one with the ether, and dissipated from the hands and heart. Wendy reflected that Tinker Bell, ruled by her passion, had forsaken this tranquil place. She, too, must be acquainted with its nature. . . . There it was; the smile lived. Like Wendy, it hadn't been murdered after all. Just changed.

John was relieved to see the smile. "Wendy? What shall we do now?"

Wendy breathed in slowly to steady herself. "We'll have to go back, John. There isn't anywhere else." The herb garden had provided a poultice for her wounded throat. She removed it and picked up another. "And I have to take care of the boys. They're all in much more danger than even I imagined." But she must have imagined it; she had begun the story. She no longer wondered how long ago.

"But what about Peter? Everything that happened!"

"What happened was a pirate's trick." She had tried to be rational about this, after the tears had dried. It was so important to understand. Peter was limited by his unlimited youth. It was—it was a weakness. . . . He lived adventure after adventure but didn't learn their lessons. Each one found him in the same place he started the last. And somehow, Hook perceived it.

"Peter is only a boy," she said, "and Hook laid his trap very cunningly. We all walked right into it, starting with the sailing of the *Roger*, and the Indians breaking camp. I should have seen it." She wished she could consider Hook in the rational way she had considered Peter, but doing so was impossible. The closeness of their encounter made her thinking unruly. Her pulse still beat unnaturally fast.

"But Wendy, he was so angry!"

"Oh, no, I never saw a man so horrifyingly calm."

"I meant Peter. He nearly slit your throat!"

"Oh. . . . Yes! But John, I won't be afraid any more. I'll explain to him, and you know how he is. By tomorrow he'll probably think it was all a grand adventure. I only hope he doesn't rush into revenge tonight." The next moment, she tensed. "What if he's already stormed the ship searching for us?"

"He and the boys might be at it again!"

John and Wendy looked at each other, faces white as the moonlight.

"Wake Michael quickly, we have to go." She stood and collected herself for her youngest brother's sake, and for her own, but her heartbeats refused to slow.

With a gentle nudge, John roused Michael. "It's time to go home, Michael. Can you fly?"

"To the nursery? I was dreaming of a nightlight." He blinked at the little moving stars. "It must have been the fairies."

Wendy took his hand to pull him up. "Not the nursery tonight. But maybe, if the window's open, you'll go back there soon."

"Are there fairies there?"

"If a fairy loves you, Michael, it will follow you anywhere."

"Wendy, you love Peter like Tinker Bell does, don't you? That's why you were so brave."

Her smile came through again. "You were brave, too, you and John. You saved my life."

John stood very tall and faced his sister. He had to look down to her by now; adventure after adventure had taught him lessons he'd have never learned in London. He shook his head. "No, Wendy. Captain Hook saved your life."

She hadn't thought of it that way. She thought of it now.

"Right after he nearly lost it for me!"

The fairy stars continued to orbit their budding planets as the two Darlings and their sister skimmed away over the dark, drowsing treetops toward the only shelter the Island afforded, the home that had formed and nurtured them. Peter Pan's secret hideout under the ground.

All alone and injured, Peter presided over the evening ritual. One by one, the Lost Boys had swallowed their medicine and now, with the nightlight burning, they slept in the one big bed. Their solitary chief reigned from his willow chair, surrounded by its leafy blades and trying not to coddle his wound. A grubby bandage wrapped around the slash. Jewel perched on his hand, which was far too still to be a part of Peter. But it hadn't been cut off. Its stillness was just a measure of his pain.

Jewel, too, was still and in pain, yet she was sure her part in the play would work out for the best. Her heart was too small to master the grand plan, but that didn't mean the plan wasn't at work. She had faith. The discomfort wouldn't last, and Time would arrange everything. Time and—

She and Peter swiveled toward the sounds only one of them hoped to hear. Three swishes in the tree trunk, and Michael, John and Wendy were back. Wendy?

Wendy! Peter leapt up grinning, ignoring the fire of his arm. Jewel fluttered, confused, to alight on the back of his chair.

"You came back!"

Wendy beheld the bright green eyes almost covered by his golden hair and the dagger, silver once more and, she was relieved to see, at his belt. Just like the first time she'd ever seen him. "We're back. Are the children all right?"

"Of course," he said, and gripped his elbow. "How did you get away?"

"We flew away right after you did." Wendy noted the bandaging. His wound was haphazardly wrapped in a cloth none too clean.

"Why didn't you come home? The boys and I tried to rescue you but we couldn't find the ship. Hook must be hiding from me."

"It will be back in the bay by morning, I'm sure of it. He—" But with chilling clarity, Hook had indicated his goal was to kill Peter. Why had he missed two opportunities in one day? Wendy shivered at the question; today's experience hinted how unfathomably deep Hook's motivations might plunge.

Then, with an effort, she stirred herself toward her duties. Touching each of her brothers on the shoulder she said, "John, Michael. Please go to bed." She remembered how, to a child, bed seemed the safest place to be. As of tonight she envied that feeling, and those who could believe in the shelter of the covers.

But John, no longer quite a child, threw Peter a distrustful look. "Wake me if you want, Wendy." He didn't hang up his knife tonight, but kept it with him.

Peter eyed him, then glanced at his own injured arm. "I got a scratch today. It was glorious, wasn't it?"

Wendy bit her lip, but found herself approaching Peter with less caution than had been her habit. Her instinct informed her now that he wouldn't startle any more. Tangling at the point of Peter's knife this afternoon, they had been too intimate to be shy. Still, she was glad to have business to tend, and she pushed Peter toward his chair. "I've brought you an herbal poultice from the Fairy Glade. Let me put it on." Jewel jumped to his shoulder, and with delicate motions, Wendy lifted his wrist to lay his arm on that of the chair. As she removed the red wrappings, he merely winced, and although she touched him, his demeanor continued bold.

He shrugged, boasting, "This is nothing. It won't slow me down."

Diplomacy had gotten her nowhere with Peter, and Wendy had had enough of it. "I'm tired of mopping blood off you boys. I'd like to draw some myself for once!" Like Jill, she thought. On any other day, the comparison might have startled her.

Peter brooded as he watched her hands. "I would have drawn blood. I would have killed him." Wendy straightened, her fingers hovering near the ruby line at her throat. Had he forgotten the blood he'd drawn, already? Loath to remind him, she didn't answer.

"I gave him the hook he used against me." He said it proudly.

Wendy saw the irony. She'd seen it all day. It had been intended that she should see it. "You do seem to have gotten back a bit of your own. But you still don't understand. Everything that happened is because of what you did to him. Everything that is still happening."

Peter looked mischievous. "He'd have done the same to me."

Wendy paused to get used to him again. With reluctance, she smiled. She shook her head and bent over his arm to dress the wound. It was not as deep as she had feared, but it would leave a scar, no doubt of that. How much uglier was the scar Peter had left on Captain Hook? That was a more difficult thought to get used to, and she shuddered and shoved it from her mind.

"Maybe, Peter. But today he had the perfect chance to do the same to you. He could have taken your hand, and he refused it. Why?" One thing she knew now. Hook had reasons for everything he did, or didn't do.

"Why did you give your kiss to him?"

Wendy looked up, surprised. "He wanted it." And she was even more surprised by her answer. Her eyes were drawn to the fairy, who glowed with a warm light that spilled onto Peter's wound. "I didn't think you could see my kiss."

"I can't. Tink told me." His face grew stern. "But I saw you giving it to him."

Wendy was wary. She kept her eyes on him. Jewel watched Wendy with her wings shut tight.

"What did he give you for it?"

"Give me?" Her insides lurched. "For a kiss?"

For her kiss, he had given her . . . his own.

Wendy caught up to her beating heart. "It really doesn't concern you, Peter. I'm sorry you happened to see it. You should never have known." But his knowing had been intended, as well.

"We should know everything about each other, Wendy. We're a family."

With a pitying look, Wendy studied Peter. He really was innocent. His wonderful belief in himself made her feel oddly sorry for him. Today's incidents had shaken Wendy, but granted her in exchange a valuable lesson. Peter, on the other hand, seemed unscathed even by his injury, and at the Fairy Glade Wendy came to understand that as long as his experience never changed his outlook, he could sustain his confidence. A naïve kind of Paradise, to be sure, but one in which, at least up to now, Peter made his home.

A peculiar silence attracted Wendy's attention, and the girl looked to his fairy, so close to him, whose downcast head gave evidence that this member of the family might have her own secrets to conceal. Wendy wondered if she'd gained an ally on this front. But the sprite remained quiet, and Wendy renewed her effort with Peter. Clinging to patience, she adopted a guiding tone. "People do keep some things secret as they grow up, even from those they love."

Peter winced again. At her words, or at the pain? "Another reason not to grow up. I don't want you to keep secrets from me."

Exasperated, she sighed. "Well, I seem to have none now!" Jewel released a grace note. Wendy sat on the hearth and threw the bandage in the fire. It burned with an acrid cloud that quickly dissipated, like a genie emerging from its bottle.

A genie of truth. Wendy did have secrets, as innocent as baby teeth. She had withheld the truth instinctively, loosening Peter's vines to be comfortable in her clothing, hiding evidence of the boys' growth to protect them. Yet those secret parts of her that she had tried to reveal to Peter—her love, her kiss—he hadn't accepted.

But Wendy's eyes were clear. If he had looked to see the truth in them, he'd have found it. He was too young, he hadn't the perception. It was no wonder he had been blind to the subtle shadings of this afternoon's design. Startled by that thought, Wendy stopped to consider her own perception. *Subtle shadings. . . .Shades. . .of black?*

Sitting rigidly still, she guarded the fire as if another cloud of candor might issue from it. Like Peter, Wendy desired truth but found it unsettling. Peter hadn't seen her variations, but someone else certainly had. Someone with an eye for color and a talent for arranging it. A man. A man had kissed her, awakening something primal within her, and now there were more hidden truths. What else would burst from the genie's magic bottle? Other richly-colored things, other stuffs and textures she hoarded and fingered but that she herself could not yet see.

The face she had watched so often in the firelight, Peter's face, was free of shadows now, and questioning.

"Why does Hook want a mother, Wendy?"

The ache began, pulling from inside. She drew breath. "You may never be old enough to understand that, Peter."

Jewel's light pulsed again. She sat up straight, tilting her head to one side and arching her back, like a being spellbound and drawn by an irresistible power. Her wings quivered, then blossomed, illuminated in a way Wendy had never before observed. The light of the fire shone right through them. Jewel smiled to herself, half closed her eyes and drifted above Peter's shoulder. Then, as if summoned by some mysterious force and compelled to obey, she formed an arc to the hollow tree. Wendy could still see the blue glimmer as the creature swooped up the shaft. It intensified to astonishing brightness.

Jewel let out one ringing note in farewell. It calmed Wendy to hear it, as had the voices in the fairy universe. It encouraged her to say what needed to be said.

"But understand this, Peter. I was afraid of you today."

Peter sprang from his chair and stood with perfect posture. "It's all right, Wendy. I forgive you."

Wendy's father couldn't have delivered the declaration better. The boy had to be pretending! "Forgive me?" she exclaimed. "I've done nothing wrong!"

"You said you would leave me."

"Because Hook threatened you!"

Peter grinned, wickedly. "For no better reason than that?"

Her mouth opened in amazement, then she laughed. "My own words! Clever you." Becoming serious again, she got to her feet. "But you know I was trying to keep our family safe. You nearly destroyed it."

Peter's enticing smile stole across his face, the smile that had drawn her from the nursery to the Neverland. "Wendy." And under the force of that smile, she remembered why she came away with him that night. He took a step forward to stand close to her. "You worry too much about what's safe." He leaned toward her, his eyes beguiling her, again. "Let's just do what's fun."

The walls of twisty tree veins seemed to Wendy to bear down, to be burying their roots deeper into the ground. She scented the earthy smell of their growth, and she heard the sleeping breath of the boys curled in the bed. The little cavern was warm, full of repose, full of promise. Did it promise what she wanted?

Peter was so perfect in his imperfection. Wendy admired his handsome face, wondering. She had to be sure, now that the spell was broken. She took his arms in her hands and, gingerly, so as not to hurt his wound, drew them around her waist. Peter's eyes gleamed with confidence, as if he could give her that something else he promised her when she first trusted him, whatever it was. She felt the vitality of his young body against her own. She felt his wish to keep her near. She wove her arms around his neck, touched her lips to his, and kissed him.

There was passion there. There was, and it moved her. But it moved her backward. It beat in a subtle tempo, like Time. It reminded Wendy of birth, of mortality, and of death. The smell of the cavern turned dank in her nostrils. She drew away. She knew now. She would move forward, or she would die.

Peter looked at her, curious. "Do I have to give you something?"

Released, she moved on to the next adventure. "Yes! I want a weapon. A dagger, or even a sword." She wouldn't look back.

"You won't need it. I'll protect you."

"I needed it today! I have to be ready to protect myself. And I'm sure I have the skills, it seems natural to me somehow. I never felt that before today." Like a lot of other things.

"Don't worry, Wendy. I'll kill him! Nibs and Tootles and I have formed a plan of attack. I'll take Slightly tomorrow and we'll call a pow-wow with the Indians. We'll make truce so we can defeat the pirates together. I'll get you the *Roger*, yet!"

"No, please. All I want is a knife."

"No. And don't ask me for a tiger-tail belt to tuck it in, either."

"All right. I won't ask. I'll get it myself!"

So much to do. She backed away and reached over the bed to gather up the lion skin. She wrapped herself in it and, this night, moved away from the bed, settling instead at the far side of the fire. The hide would keep her strong and warm during the darkness, help her to formulate her plans. And she didn't want to be alone.

Peter knelt down beside her. "Wendy, come back to the bed."

"No."

His myrtle scent encircled her. "I won't let Hook take you from me."

"I intend to have a say in the matter, too." A curious blend of dread and anticipation surged through her heart as she thought of the future. She was old enough now to realize that anything could happen, and without warning. Only one thing was certain. "Neither of us was prepared for today. For the boys' safety, we'll have to be ready for Hook's next move."

"I've always been ready to fight him. You held me back."

"And now I know how right I was!"

"And now I know Hook wants to steal you from me. But I chose you to be our mother, to tell us stories. The pirates can't have you."

The events of this day weighed heavily on Wendy, and it was only getting longer. "I believe I'll always tell stories. It's just that the ending of this one isn't as clear to me as it once was."

"I don't want it to end at all."

"But the boys—"

Peter tossed his head. "There will always be boys. I mean you." His voice resonated, unashamed. "I don't want you to go away again."

"Go to sleep, Peter."

"I felt so strange while you were gone. I've never felt that way before."

"I felt new things, too." But the fading fire revealed his features in a new light. Wendy had never seen Peter look so troubled.

"I don't like feeling that way."

"How did you feel, Peter?"

"I felt . . . alone."

The Revel Master

The fairy ran her hands through the velvet and relished the luxury of it. Reclining on her cushion, she worshipped at the altar of her new god, celebrating his mysteries. She was a true believer.

Hook looked down at the living jewel on his lap, sensing tremors in the feathers beneath his fingertips. This indulgence was so little to give the creature, for so much return. And a delight to give.

The black velvet was set aside now. He was stripped to an open shirt and breeches, his sword and boots waiting by his camp bed, his feet digging into the pile of the carpet. The silken tent was lit by a lantern sitting on the table next his chair, casting its light on a tomahawk. The wedge of rock on its shaft crouched grim and rugged under its feathering. Rude, by Hook's standards. But effective.

The captain had given the word. The sound of his men carousing echoed off the harbor waters and rang in the woods behind, accompanied by a fiddle and a reedy concertina. The bonfire on the beach had been torched. As it feasted on its fuel, the glare of it threw color sprawling on the tent floor. Outside it reflected in the sailors' eyes, flickering out only as their mouths tilted up to admit the contents of flashing bottles. The revels had begun.

Hook took a drink from a bottle of his own. He would join his men momentarily, after business. "So we advance to the next level." When he spoke to the fairy, she caught the sweet, potent scent and sat up to hold her thimble for another draught.

"Yes, my dear, all you want tonight." He tipped her a drop. "Our success!" They drank. When she had drained her cup, she looked up to him, quizzical.

"You wonder why the Wendy wasn't taken today. You must trust me, Jewel. The berry ripens on the vine."

Reverting to habit, she chimed the least bit rudely, whereupon his eyes narrowed and his voice smoothed. "You want to watch yourself." Tink subsided; Jewel returned. "Better." He relaxed. "Your beloved Pan is spared for the greater effect. I nudged him just sharply enough to move the game along."

The fairy flipped her hair out of her eyes. Hook raised the cushion and set it down on the table, bending closer. "He deserved at least that much, even you must admit." His frown exuded solicitude. "How ungallantly he handled my Jewel!" Vividly, his words resurrected the memory for Jewel. Still a martyr to the boy's blow, she rubbed her hand on her maltreated cheek, sighing.

"Pan can never give her what she wants now. She will learn." His half-smile stole to his face. "I have found her to be a quick study. Rest now, Jewel. I will send you home before the sun rises. But remember. . . he is also as yet unfit to deliver your own heart's desire. Sleep tonight, and believe in Time."

Jewel reached her arms toward him. Her high priest bestowed his little finger, and she squeezed it. Hook shook his head. Such simple faith.

Drawing the netting aside, he set her pillow on his cot, then closed it to shield her from view. "Smee." The tent flap rustled and the boatswain stooped under its opening, in his hand his own measure of the strong, sweet rum he was reputed to resemble.

"Cap'n?"

His captain's lip curled. "Put down the firewater Smee, and bring me the boy."

"Aye, Sir, begging your pardon." Moments later, the flap opened again to admit the native boy, steered by Smee's hand on one naked shoulder. Rowan stood erect, eyes fixed in front of him, hands bound at his groin by rope.

Hook faced him, equally uncompromising, but for his loose waves of hair. In the warmth of the evening, his voice struck chill. "In spite of Mr. Yulunga's eagerness to dispatch you, my hook in his flesh ordained otherwise. As you might guess from the ease with which he captured you, Yulunga is one of my best men. Yet for your sake, he now bears the mark of my mercy. You live, and my man is disfigured. Still . . . " His eyes probed Rowan's one last time. "It would be bad manners on my part not to thank you for your usefulness. You will not journey to your 'Dark Hunting' ground tonight." Hook lifted the tomahawk and swung it casually, experimentally. The boy watched, his slate-colored eyes impassive.

"According to your own custom, you are in my debt. I have no such honorable entanglements, so I will keep this. No doubt we'll meet again; I'll not say goodbye." He turned to Smee. "Take him to the forest and watch him go. Bring Yulunga with you. Leave the boy bound."

"Aye, Captain." As Smee prodded the young man from the tent, Hook tucked the tomahawk into his own belt. It suited him tonight. He aimed a last look at the cot, then he caught up his bottle and stepped into the night. Into the revelry.

The sea breeze was bracing. Torches blazed along the beach, the bonfire burned hot and high. Hook strode toward it, his men falling away to cut a path before his hook could do it for him. The pirates' eyes glinted in the firelight, appreciating the rare sight of their captain at their celebrations. Tonight he was among them, and he brought his own heat to the fire. Bare feet sank in cool sand, drinks rose in hands. The captain's claw called for attention. It pointed to the fire.

Silence stumbled among the crew, releasing the soggy slap of breakers on the sand. The dry wood sparked, sending fire moths to the moon. "Here's a beacon to fetch us our Beauty. She sails toward us now. It's back to work for us soon, on the high seas! To the *Jolly Roger!*" He drank deeply. The water bounced the pirates' shouts back to them, doubling the cheer and setting off the drumming.

The hook directed the raising of a driftwood target, and guns added their barking to the merriment, blazing into the night. The captain flung a bottle high and laughed as it burst into ringing stars. In habit born of experience, Hook cast his glance around the periphery of the festivities, on guard for peril. Two or three native women in fringe and beads loitered at the edge of the wood. Hook signaled to Mason, the forest-side sentry, to let them come. None of his company should be alone tonight. He circled the fire, master of the revels, leading not a pack of dogs this night, but men. Yet as they clapped their hands to one another's, all avoided their captain's. His hand was a legend, with a sharp reminder.

The women knew it, too. As they stole to the beach, they slipped amid the crewmen where they were welcomed with warmer hands. They smiled and returned the petting, enjoying the attention, but their dark eyes followed the captain as they moved among his men. Dancing and sipping, they flirted with danger as the night wore on, drawn curiously closer to the man of the claw, of whom they had heard in many tales. Subtly, Hook returned their smiles, biding his time.

Smee and Yulunga drifted back to the beach, and their captain watched as Smee selected his woman, wrapping his arms around her to snatch her off the sand. Smee beamed on her. "Lily! You've accepted our invitation, then! You're here."

She was pretty, with her dark hair in a braid, her figure pleasingly full. Her arms encircled Smee's neck and she laughed and looked up into his eyes, smiling. "Where else would I be?" Smee carried her from the crowd, away to the shadows at the edge of the sand. Gentleman Starkey's features went dark as the two passed between him and the fire, then his scar-marked face lit up again before he turned to lay a kiss on a second lady, the perfection of her cheek contrasting with his own. They hastened toward the trees, his arms surrounding her.

Hook made his move. He strode toward Cecco. With earrings swinging and bracelets jingling, the Italian sailor pulled the third woman in a dance around the blaze and headed for the wood. Hook snared him by the fine-embroidered collar. At the tug of the claw, Cecco halted. The others caught the motion in the corners of their eyes. Their song trailed away as they stared. In slow, guarded movements, Cecco looked around. "Captain? You wish?"

"I wish. But I'll return her, Mr. Cecco. Intact." A murmur rippled through the gathering as he unhooked his claw from Cecco's collar. Cecco threw his hands up and inclined his head to the lady. Moving off, he kept his dusky eyes on the captain, shoving away the elbows of his jovial comrades.

Hook guided the lady away from the fire and directed the company over his shoulder, "Broach a new cask, and give us another of your songs." Excepting Cecco, the men scattered. The fiddle struck up a rollicking tune. The concertina caught it up to wheeze along. Where the sand became moist under their feet, Hook turned to her wide black eyes. He waved his claw in a congenial flourish and smiled halfway. "Don't look so frightened. It hasn't had to tear a woman yet. I see no reason to begin tonight."

Releasing her breath, she smiled. Dimples played around her mouth. Her eyes darted as she wondered where to place her hands. He helped her, hiding his hook behind her waist and pulling her arm toward his belt. He pressed his hips against hers and began to sway to the rhythm of the drums. She followed, becoming more at ease in this familiar coupling. Feeling the tomahawk rub against her waist, she rested her hand on it. "This is a kind of weapon I have seen many times, but never before in a pirate's belt."

"It pleases me tonight. The outward indication of my mood."

"You are a warrior tonight? Not a lover?" Her dimples deepened.

"I will give you anything but my secrets."

"Maybe you are both! But you command many sailors." Her hand slipped from the tomahawk to his leg, stroking it. "You know. It is unimportant, what lies on the outside of a man." Her touch slid to the inside of his thigh. "It is what is hidden within that matters."

"This man has something hidden. For you." He stopped moving and appreciated the animal warmth of her palm on his thigh. "Within my pocket, that is. You may retrieve it if you so desire."

Her gaze lingered on his eyes; her hand felt for the pocket. Hook smiled while she searched for it, coy, and taking her time. Her fingers bestowed a delightful pressure as they readily surveyed. The lady's complexion took on a becoming flush that Hook found altogether agreeable, and he pressed closer, the better to admire it. The dimples lent her lips a kissable charm, and that charm increased with the attention she devoted to every nuance of his inclination. Standing near the water, neither he nor the lady took notice when the logs of the fire crashed, eaten away by flame, resettling their bones in the shooting blaze. The hidden prize awaited.

Her eyelashes fluttered; the pocket was found, and it was empty. Hook's lip twitched. "The other one. No hurry." She took him at his word, her own face sharing the look of pleasure on his as she fondled him, warming to the task once again, and tarrying over it. In time, the lady found something significant in a region no pocket could logically inhabit. Their two bodies as they touched thrummed with the drumming. She did not forget her quest, though in the course of it no avenue of opportunity went untried, no possible path neglected. The elusive prize seemed lost to limbo, but neither party repented. And when her fingers finally slipped into the pocket, his hand pressed upon them and trapped them there.

"Understand. I have no wish to offend you. It is meant as a gift, for you and your companions."

Released from his grip but reluctant to end the game, her fingers slowly sought the gift, found it and drew it out. She looked down. It was sharply pointed, glowing a lustrous white in the torchlight. The woman gasped with delight. "Where did you find this? It is the rarest of offerings!" She ran its smoothness through her hair, mussed by the men, and felt its luxuriousness. A solid pearl comb.

"It is from the Mermaids' Lagoon. I am gratified by your pleasure. Merely a token."

She tucked it into the pouch slung at her waist and clung to him. Her countenance shone. "It is much more than that, to me." Twining her lively, lissome fingers in his, she invited him with her eyes. "Will you walk with me? Please. I would like to give you a gift, also."

"I will walk with you back to Mr. Cecco. I perceive that he is most anxious for your gifts." He circled his arm around her tempting dimensions and started to turn, but stopped at her tug. Bracing her hand on his arm, she stood on tiptoe to brush feather-light kisses against his throat. When he didn't push her away, she slid her hands up his chest. He looked down at her, his lips set in a wry smile, waiting.

Her fingers spread apart, stealing higher. She caressed his upper body as deftly as she'd stroked his loins, and here, too, she found something significant. Yet this discovery was wholly unanticipated. As Hook had expected, her hands halted at his breast. She opened her mouth and quickly pulled away, disconcerted at what she'd found there. "Oh! I am sorry!"

"As you were saying, it is what is hidden within that matters. Never mind, my dear. There are many here who require your attention. See to them, if it pleases you, and give my warmest regards to your sisters." He took her arm and escorted her, flustered, to the dashing Cecco, who, concealing nothing within, had never ceased his vigil. "As promised, Mr. Cecco."

"*Grazie*, Captain." Cecco lost no time in waltzing his lady to the wood—while she looked back over the breadth of his shoulders and blinked.

Hook watched after them, feeling the heat of the fire on his throat and remembering her fingers in quest of his pocket. He kept moving, the insubstantial sand shifting under his feet, the moon over his shoulder, and as he mingled with the men, he observed the other revelers. The gunplay by the target continued, cracking the sky open in bursts of orange. Mr. Smee returned the woman called Lily to the fire and found her a drink while Yulunga, the fresh claw wound visible on his shoulder, engulfed her hand in his massive fist. In a gesture strangely tender for a man so formidable, Yulunga lifted Lily's fingers to his lips, and before long both hands had disappeared into the shadows, leaving only a pair of footprints behind. Other footprints tracked away and back, in sets of twos and threes. The singing and the banter grew steadily louder. Eventually the music stopped trying and the drums dominated the air. In his melodic accent, Cecco recounted stories to Lily, his hands waving in gestures that set his jewelry chiming. His first lady, the dimpled angel, flitted among the bunch of drummers, her eyes engaging the captain's again, her arms engaging the pounding hands of her current sailor. She entangled his hands so that the sound of drumming decreased until some time later, when it rebounded with renewed and vigorous force. The other woman, clad now in little other than her hair, hurried from the dark edge of the beach, laughing as she ran and turning backward to toss a colorful kerchief at Jukes, who pursued her, himself half dressed and revealing a good deal of his stem-to-stern tattoos. Hook heard her shrieks over the beating in his ears as Jukes caught her with little trouble. The pair rolled on the beach and into the waves, weaving their bodies together in the sloshing brine. Hook closed his eyes and still saw them, all of them. Revelers on a beach, knowing no shame.

Like himself. And he lifted his face to the breeze and recalled a pair of clear blue eyes regarding him with courage and just a hint of admiration. He envisioned a royal smile harboring a kiss, shameless and begging to be taken—but needing to be given. His pulse surged with the force of victory again, as it had done when he accepted that kiss. He breathed deeply while he flexed his shoulders and stretched his arms, then he hunted down another bottle and joined the men at the cask to fill it with rum.

He had hoped this night would pass quickly. It was only getting longer.

Cookson, the beachfront scout, turned his back to the fire again and felt of his weapon. He pulled his jacket tighter. It was getting cooler out here, as the party by the fire got hotter. His luck, to draw watch the night the captain led the fun. But better here than with the lads on duty aboard ship!

He tracked along down the beach. His feet were clammy in the wet sand, the swirling water renewing the feeling regularly. Every few seconds. Like clockwork. Sounded like clockwork, too. Or was it the drums? Squinting, he leaned to get a better view of the boats, keels up on the shore, hulked and prostrate, like penitent monks. Cookson smiled irreverently; they were missing the party, too. Then he jerked himself upright. Something slithered among the boats, and unlike his imaginary monks, this something was *un*repentant and smelling about for more sin.

Cookson flung his hand toward the fire. "Avast! Pipe down, lads!" Tugging at the lanyard round his neck, he pulled the whistle from his shirt. He blew shrill warning and dashed back up the shore. "It's the croc! The crocodile, Captain!"

The message spread and reverberated. "The croc!" Dead calm fell on the beach. All eyes searched the darkness, then looked to the master's face. Hook thrust his bottle away and froze, listening. Only his eyes moved, narrowed to pierce the night. Cookson came at a run, his jacket flying behind him, his finger pointing down the shore to a pair of red points on the beach.

Hook snarled and launched himself toward it, the men on his heels grabbing up the torches planted in the sand. The lights bobbed and streamed as the torchbearers ran, but it was hatred that lit Hook's path. Hatred for the senseless thing that sought to tear his life from his grasp. The relentless monster with no reasoning, and no mercy.

There, the flare of the beast's eyes . . . and the sound of ticking. Hook judged the distance, then halted, spraying sand. His men pulled up short and reached for their weapons. Flanking their captain, they formed a half circle on the water's edge, the croc at its center.

Hook breathed fast, staring at the brute. The blue of his eyes shifted, forget-me-not turning to violet. Seizing the head of the tomahawk, he yanked it from his belt. It was rough and primal, the ideal handler for this beast. The ticking assaulted him, then the croc advanced, scenting the excitement and gliding on its belly toward its prize. Hook steadied the axhead with his claw while his hand slid down its shaft. He raised it, feinted twice for aim, and hurled it at the monster with force so heavy the breath rushed from his lungs. His eyes mirrored the croc's, flaming red as he watched the hatchet revolve in a flying arc between his hand and his enemy.

It struck, true and deep. The beat of time submerged as the monster groaned and belched, and backed away. Red rivulets crowned its head and veined its face, the tomahawk its headdress as the animal writhed in a dance of pain and retreated down the beach, hoarding its tick and leaving behind it a slimy trail. It skulked into the darkness, hissing.

Hook stood among his jubilant crew, his shoulders heaving. Mullins cried out, "Did you see, mates? Captain made it jig! The croc's joined the revels!"

Hook turned his face to them and they stopped abruptly. The red of his eye was terrible to see. "Chase it down, Mullins, Cookson, find where it's gone!" Mullins sobered and pulled the nearest torch from a mate's fist, then both men pelted after the beast.

Violet returned to Hook's eyes, to ease into blue once more as his heart calmed and his breathing steadied. Then the smile spread, slow and satisfied. It was the signal they had waited for, the outward indication of his mood. The men broke into cheers again. Hook looked at every one of them, then released the pent-up power, throwing his head back and laughing. The revelers crowded near, but not too close, lauding him back to the bonfire and the waiting women, more raucous than before. The drums pounded again, and again.

And again.

The fire was replete, the crew's mood mellowed by women, drink and fellowship. Hook lay back on his elbows and considered the sea, a bottle tilted, half buried in the sand next to him. Smee materialized at his captain's side.

"Sir, 'tis a shame we lost its trail to the sea."

Hook inhaled the salt air. "As ever, we taste the bitter with the sweet."

"True enough. A fine idea it was, Sir, to feed the beast with a clock. Time's on your side, you might say!"

Hook raised an eyebrow. "Would that be the *in*side, Mr. Smee?"

Smee chortled. He was rarely treated to the captain's humor. "I meant that Time's in your favor, Captain."

"A mere superstition. Those who worship Time, Smee, must propitiate it, or fear the end of grace."

"Aye, Sir, and your fearlessness is well known. You showed that croc right well. But the Indian lad's time could've been up today. He should be half home by now, with the moon we've had. Lucky he left you a keepsake to ward off the crocodile. The debt's paid, now, isn't it, by his tomahawk?"

"Fortunately, he doesn't know that."

"Did you never get him to speak, Captain?"

"He spoke most eloquently, without language. Yulunga's report was correct. It seems the boy has befriended a comrade of Pan's."

Smee's eyebrows lifted. "Do you say, now? Then why did you not stretch him on the rock?"

Hook gazed at the shrinking moon. "Now, now, Mr. Smee. Nature must take her course. He is quite a handsome lad. Compelling. Given enough of your precious Time, he will render me service."

"Sir? But I thought . . . Oh." A smile whipped across his rugged face. "Captain, that's deep!"

" 'Each one to his own taste,' as the French are wont to say."

Smee modified his grin. "Nothing gets by you, Sir."

"What of the women? Did they accept my dispensation?"

"Aye, and a wee bit of my own!"

"Nothing gets by me, Smee. And?"

Smee nodded. "The ladies will be ready, with babes in tow."

"A most rewarding day." He could still taste it, that sweet, shameless kiss. Hook handed Smee the bottle. "Drink tonight, Smee, and tomorrow have my pistols oiled. The matched set."

Smee's jaw dropped open. The captain hadn't carried two pistols since—

"One of them is going courting."

Cravings and Sweet Nothings

Wendy sat up with a sharp intake of breath, clutching the lion hide. She had dreamed a deep dream, a vision of purple eyes, eyes the color of kings' robes. At first she had believed the eyes to be fixed to stare upon herself, but then they were her own eyes and before them hung a green spider, spinning a web beaded with dewy drops of blood.

She heard Indian drums beating again. She had heard them all night, but waking now, she recognized the sensation to be the unrest of her heart. Its rhythm was uncivilized, unfamiliar . . . something she was relearning.

Looking about her, she found Peter slipping his quiver over his shoulder, seeming to have forgotten the gash along his arm. He had seen her startle awake.

"Good morning, Wendy! We're off to the Indian camp."

Slightly waited for him with one foot in the hollow tree. Since the children's excursion to Indian territory, he wore a band of leather about his forehead, and looking more like a native than ever, he was eager to go and smiling to prove it. "Before the day is done we'll smoke a peace pipe and become blood brothers."

Still clinging to the hide, Wendy rose. "I won't try to stop you, Peter, but must Slightly go?"

Slightly's face clouded. "I have to go, Wendy."

"I know you can manage, but I feel uneasy about it." Maybe it was just her imagination. Alongside recent events, the dream had left her unsettled.

"Slightly's coming. I've taught more about the Indians to him than to any of the other boys. I'll be back by afternoon, with a good story to tell!" Impatiently, Peter brushed a willow leaf from his hair.

John was awake now, and seeing the two boys ready to go, he rolled off the bed. "I'd like to go to the mountain camp, too."

"Slightly is the oldest. Today is his turn. *You're* coming next time." Peter slipped a knife from his belt and tossed it to John, who caught it, surprised. Feeling for the sheath at his waist, John found it empty. He drew his eyebrows together to give Peter a doubtful look. He had meant to keep his knife with him during the night, to defend Wendy if necessary.

Peter returned John's look, grinning at him, then turned to poke a hand into the fairy's niche and shake her awake. She tinkled in a groggy way, and rolled over to go back to sleep. "Stay in bed, then, Tink." Peter opened his Wendy-pocket and captured Jewel's glittering residue as he dusted off his fingers.

After yesterday's conflict and strategy sessions, Nibs was alert and ready for anything. He handed Peter his bow. "I'll go part way with you. I have to go on lookout duty." The other children were climbing sleepily from the bed.

"No, Nibs, wait a bit. There's no hurry. I want you all to stay close to home today. Wendy, keep the boys near. There's no guessing what Hook has in mind. Boys, do what Wendy tells you. Those are my orders." He signaled to Slightly, who started to climb into the chute, thought better of it, and stepped aside for him. Peter breezed up.

Slightly followed, but more slowly, as he had to pull in his knees and elbows and wedge himself inch by inch. Wendy watched him, hoping the sinking feeling in the pit of her stomach was just the after-effect of her dream. As its image revived, the feeling became too much, and she ran to Slightly and set her hand on his knee to stop him. "Slightly!" She bent and peered up at him. "If you can't fit down again, I'll understand. I'll come out to you."

"I wasn't worried, but thanks!" He touched his fingers to his lips and tossed her a crowded kiss, then proceeded to muscle his way up to the surface and was gone.

Wendy looked toward John to compare his growing size to Slightly's, but the Twins seized her elbows and pointed to the mantel which, unless Peter was present, always took precedence over any other thing in the room. "Look, Wendy, Peter's jar!" Their eyes filled with anticipation. "If he brings more trophies from the Indians, we'll build a bigger shelf to hold them."

The jar was there. She had forgotten to find pine cones for it yesterday or a hundred years ago. It was Peter's now. The acorn, the arrow, the eagle feather, everything was Peter's—including Slightly's idea to make a pact with the Indians. For a moment, she imagined a chair sitting on the mantel, too, to display the Wendy.

But there was one thing, one sweet thing Wendy kept hidden. She had to get it back. It had to be kept safe. "Nibs, I want you to scout thoroughly this morning. As soon as you've reported back, I'm going out."

Nibs gave her a curious look and saluted. "Aye, aye." He vaulted onto the bed to help the other boys make sense of the skins and pillows. Wendy held the lion hide to her cheek, to feel its warmth and comfort one more time before the day began. Then she shook it, and falling to work as the boys had done, began to fold it.

She stopped. As her face contorted, she drew one of its legs toward her. She stared in disbelief, and then her gaze darted again to the mantle. What she sought wasn't there among Peter's trophies. She turned toward the hollow tree and shivered, all warmth and comfort draining away.

The lion's right front paw, with all its claws, had been hacked off the hide.

Rowan listened to the water rushing by, just out of reach. The sound had disturbed his sleep, but he had slept, in spite of the tantalizing trickling and in spite of the ropes cutting into his wrists. He would be a warrior soon. He could endure worse than this. The Black Chief with the eagle's claw could have decreed that he should endure worse than this. And now Rowan owed the Black Chief a life-service. It was fitting. Rowan was the Life-Giver.

But Rowan hadn't meant to give him his secrets. His slate-gray eyes had simply not been able to mask his emotions when questions were plied about his new companion. Rowan's shame was tempered by the force against which he had been set. Enemy though the man might be, Rowan had never questioned the judgment of the tribal elders; but only now did he understand why they had forbidden the hunting of the Black Chief's scalp. It possessed too much power. Such a prize might tear the tribe apart. It was taboo. And Rowan was no stranger to taboo.

The moon had lighted his path last night and determined it should end here. When the moon left him by this abandoned dwelling-place, the forest was too dark to search the stream for a rock to cut his bonds. By now, he craved a drink. He got awkwardly to his feet and shouldered the door, anxious to reach the water the moon had provided.

But he halted, listening: two pairs of feet brushing the grasses, then running, slowing to a walk, like geese touching down to earth. Now they stepped toward him. Rowan slid to the window. Another moment and the two boys were within view.

It was Slightly—Rowan's 'Lightly'—led by the yellow-haired boy with bow and dagger. The Golden Boy, who flew like the hawk, and who with those very weapons caused so much anxiety among Rowan's people—every bit as much terror as the crocodile. Rowan spotted the fresh red wound on his arm right away. It must be painful, but the boy's face didn't show it as he pulled an apple from his pouch and offered it to Lightly. Rowan tried to swallow, his thirst redoubling at the sight of the fruit and the snap of Lightly's first bite.

But even in his craving, Rowan wondered. Should Lightly be touching that fruit? The healers of the tribe revered green apples. They were strong medicine. The sleep these apples induced was profound. Ever since he was a child, Rowan's mother had cautioned him not to taste one. The Golden Boy must be careless indeed, to give them to his followers.

Rowan attended the boy's voice as it spoke in a low and earnest tone, " . . .always to be a boy and to have fun. And I want Wendy to never leave me alone. Don't forget . . . " As Rowan watched, unblinking, the pair disappeared into the wood behind the house.

Giving them time to move away, Rowan looked about the shelter. He wondered at the sight of white sand spread over the table. He smelled it. It carried a faint odor of strawberries. He pressed his finger in it, then touched it to his tongue. It felt like grains of crystal. It tasted sweet.

The taste clung to his mouth. He saw the bits of shattered glass, but he avoided them and scooped the stuff up with the swollen fingers of one bound hand, bending over it, mouthing it, then sucking at it, licking his fingers, the strokes of his tongue spilling it over his ropes, his wrists. It was so sweet, sweet as honey, but it crunched between his teeth. He dug for more and lapped it up. He didn't think he could get enough, and his mouth was too dry to try. He straightened, the white sand sticky, coating his lips, his chin, and tumbling like a sweet snow to drift rising and falling on his bare chest.

Then, Rowan Life-Giver followed another instinct, and his friend. He stole from the house, marking the beads on the ground in front of it, and entered the wood. Searching for footprints in the earth next the stream, he determined the direction he would pursue once he had tasted water and broken his ropes.

He savored his tongue. He didn't doubt his path, and he didn't question why the moon had brought him here.

Nibs slid down the tree chute. "All clear, Wendy. I flew high like we planned, and the *Jolly Roger* is back in the bay with the pirates aboard her."

"What did you see?"

Nibs paused to look Wendy up and down, blinked, then answered, "There was a pile of smoldering ashes on the harbor beach. Lots of broken bottles, and footprints all around. Looks as if they had a party last night. I found this, too." He flashed her a bold smile and pointed to the kerchief he'd tied about his head—orange, and knotted at the back.

Tootles looked up from the grindstone on which he was sharpening knives. "You look just like a pirate, except that you have no boots.

And a party sounds like fun. Wendy, can we have a party on the beach one night, with a big fire?"

"Only once it's safe. So that's where the pirates were! There are plenty of trees to hide them there, just off the beach. And they were celebrating?"

"There weren't any boats left, I checked under cover of the brush all around. But what did they have to celebrate? You got away, we all did, and Peter only got a scratch. If I was a pirate, I wouldn't carouse until all my enemies were stowed in the brig. Or until my sword had run them through."

"I would!" Tootles declared. "I'd celebrate any time I survived a raid! And then I'd polish our boots and sharpen our weapons for the next." He wiggled his thick, bootless toes and held up Curly's shining dagger as an example. "Pass me yours, Nibs, I'm ready for it."

Wendy reached for Curly's knife. "Let me borrow this again, please, Curly."

Forgetting to be a gentleman for once, Curly had been eyeing her. But habit was strong and he recovered his manners. "I was going to cut my hair this morning, but I can wait."

"Thank you. You can make yourself another belt to hold it. Take down Michael's old baby basket and use its strips to braid one. Michael can help you. Now I'm off to do some scouting of my own."

Closeted within the niche, Jewel rose from her couch, yawning. She fumbled for a thistle and brushed her hair.

John had thoroughly studied his sister. He now stood up. "I'll come with you."

Michael wanted to come, too; so did they all, but Wendy waved them down. She had her secrets. "No, thank you. I have to go alone this time."

Jewel poked her hand in a drawer, rifled it, and pulled out a tuft of dandelion. She buffed her nails—and listened.

Speaking slowly, John thought aloud, "Peter went to make peace with the Indians . . . " He scrutinized Wendy once more. "You're going to be Red-Handed Jill again and try to make peace with the pirates. . . aren't you?"

All the boys watched for Wendy's reaction, using John's question as an excuse to stare at her. Curly piped up and spoke for the rest. "We've all been wondering that. It's just the sort of thing mothers do, isn't it? You did it yesterday."

Behind the curtain of the fairy's room, two little dresses were hanging side by side. Jewel held her head slantwise and examined them. Even so, her miniature ears listened for the Wendy's answer.

"It's not come to that yet today! Don't worry about me, I'll be back soon. And remember what Peter said. Stay close to home. And no bonfires."

Still they stared at her, until Nibs took charge and forced them to pull their gaping gazes away. "Twins, go up with Wendy and stand watch. And you can make more arrows. We can't be too careful. I know how those pirates think."

Wendy raised one eyebrow and wondered if he did know. She tucked the knife into the belt she had made for herself while waiting for Nibs to come back. It wasn't a tiger tail, but it would do for now.

It was the tail of the lion with which she had slept the night before, dreaming of drums.

In spite of Nibs' all-clear, and maybe because of it, Wendy was cautious on her flight through the trees. She remembered too well the pirate colors blossoming within the wood as Michael and John spirited her from the house. Curly's knife in her belt didn't make the memory any less potent.

She alighted at the edge of the clearing. All was still. Walking toward the house, she pieced together in reverse the events of that day as she came across its remnants. She stopped to pick up Curly's belt, with its jagged scar. She ran her fingers over it, over the edge of leather both sharp and tender, and wondered if a scar of flesh would feel this way. Absently, she folded the belt and held it close. It was supple in her two hands, and the sun's kiss awakened its leathery scent. Would a patch of new skin feel tough like this? Would it grow to cover bone?

Another few steps. Here were the remains of the vine Peter had cut away. She didn't have to touch them. She already knew how they felt. Ivy was beautiful in the forest. It spiraled upward if left to thrive. She conceived an image of ivy twining up the mast of a ship, green, thick, and clinging, surging toward the sun. She began to sway as if on board, then remembered herself and looked down at her feet planted in the grass. Uprooting them, she moved to the next reminder.

The beads. . . . His hat had lain here. Its jewels couldn't rival his eyes. Wendy's own eyes narrowed. She angled her head. Where was the basket? He had swept it over here . . . the first time he'd touched her. Right here, with these beads spilling out.

Looking around for the basket, she saw something that shouldn't have been there, something that played no part in the scene enacted here. It lay on the bench, next to the book and two leather pouches. Her lips parted, and the rhythm of her heart was disturbed yet again.

It was polished and shining, made of both wood and metal, and very welcome. She dropped the belt and ran to kneel before it. Her hands hesitated above it for only one instant, then seized it and embraced it. Immediately, she felt a wave of power wash over her. Before she could think, she whispered fervently, "Thank you."

But who was she thanking, and for what? Her enemy, for lending her the means to destroy him? What arrogance, to place in her hands a weapon to use against him! Or was it confidence? Or was it . . . care?

Was he not her enemy? Wendy felt angry now. What was he to her, bringing her heart's desire, in whatever form? For Hook had read her heart; it was she who was the open book. Her tension relaxed as she searched within herself for the answer. She had longed not for golden apples, not silly flowers even. He had given her that which she truly craved, regardless of how she might use it. From any other man, that would be an act of love.

Wendy breathed carefully. What, really, was the link between them? How could he use it to suit his purposes? She didn't have to know right away, she was free of Time and its demands. She would discover truth as it was revealed. And now she had a tool with which to handle it, the one thing she had asked of Peter, and been denied. The return for one kiss.

She lowered the gleaming pistol to her lap and fondled it. It was smooth, its fine wood mellow like honey and warm from the sun. As she turned it over she stared, and it began to tremble in her hands. Inlaid on the stock were three initials in flowing script. Two were crafted of the shifting colors of mother-of-pearl . . . *J.H.*

The third initial was black, branded with iron between and over the first two, burned right into the exquisite handle. She smelled the acrid odor of charred wood, inhaled it to smolder next to her heart as she read his message, written to her in fire—his love letter. . . . *R.*

J.R.H. Very slowly, Jill Red-Hand raised the stock of the pistol to her lips and closed her eyes. And she answered his letter, with a kiss.

It was a hard lesson for Jewel, but she was learning it. Patience. Believe in Time, that's what he told her. And he was always right. He always knew what to do. Even when he hurt Peter, it was the right thing to do. Pain brings him closer to you, he said. She believed him. It was part of the lesson.

He never caused Jewel pain. His voice alone could bring her to bliss. But it was never his voice alone. . . . His fingers were gentle, velvet. She would have flown to his hand even if she had never gifted him with the secret of her slavery. But now she was inescapably his creature, and content to be so. She closed her eyes. Peter said he was a black man. But when he touched his fairy to make her wings radiate their rarest light, when she beheld her master then, she saw a rainbow.

Jewel opened her eyes and shook herself. Finally, the Wendy was gone. The master had been right about that, and he knew where she would go. Would he take the girl today? She clamped her lips together. Patience, Jewel.

And he was right about the boys, which ones to choose for today's adventure. As she primped her hair one last time before the mirror, she tinkled as alarmingly as possible, then zipped out of her room to work the wiles she'd recently acquired.

She buzzed over Nibs.

"What, Tink? What's the matter? I thought you were asleep."

She nodded, then traced a circle above her head.

"You had a dream? About Peter?"

"Who else?" Michael asked, looking up from the basket he was dismantling and rolling his eyes. But Jewel shook her head and dashed to Wendy's lion skin. She grasped two hairs and tugged.

"You think Wendy's in trouble?" John's eyebrows went up, then came down. "Or are you just making trouble *for* her again?"

Jewel seized Nibs by the knot of his pirate kerchief and dragged him toward the tree shaft.

"All right, all right, I'll come!"

She dropped him and selected Tootles, jabbing at him with her elbows.

"Here's your knife, Nibs. Looks like I'm coming with you. Where, Tink?"

Pausing for effect, Jewel made sure all eyes were upon her. She smoothed her skirt, then she danced a hornpipe in mid-air.

The boys stared at her, horrified, and shifted to look at one another. It was what they had suspected, and all too easy to believe. John spoke first.

"Wendy's never lied to us before."

"But she never met a pirate before, either," Nibs countered. No one had to say, *The* pirate.

"You saw how different she is today," Michael said. "She's wearing Jill's belt. Or one very like it!"

Lifting the strands of his own new belt, Curly indicated his missing weapon. "And carrying a knife."

Jewel waited, drumming her fingernails on her shoulder. It was Tootles who said it. "She's gone to parley on the *Jolly Roger!*"

Grabbing up his knife, Nibs issued his command. "You three wait here for Wendy. We'll send Tink with news. If Wendy comes back, tell her we'll——"

" . . .be careful." They said it in unison. Nibs' grin held no cheer as he followed Jewel and Tootles up the chute.

Jewel sparked them through the trees, flying fast. They swept through the thick of the wood, stomachs knotted with anticipation, Nibs and Tootles at once elated and fearful. The mere mention of the pirate ship made their blood flow faster. Of all the Lost Boys, Nibs and Tootles were the most bloodthirsty. They were the ones who craved attack on—or indeed, attack by—pirates. Nibs pulled the knot at the back of his head tighter. Tootles ran a finger down the edge of his knife.

The sound of breakers burst between the last few trees, and Jewel paused at the end of the forest. The boys righted themselves to settle, tense and erect, on the cliffs overlooking the sea. Neverbay was still out of sight, but the smell of the sea blew in, stinging their noses. The boys inhaled, scenting adventure. Jewel let them revel in the atmosphere, then prodded them to jump off the cliff. She took the lead again, hugging the rock face, anticipating the view when the cliffs would fall away and the bay would open up—There!

Neverbay looked luscious. Its sparkling waves and featherbed clouds, its circling seabirds surrounded its prize. The sails, though bound now, were long and rippling, the crow's nest hung like a jewel upon her ear. Her flag beat the breeze, the skull over crossed swords grinning welcome. Carved and decorated, her decks lay adorned with gilt, and her figurehead held out a sickle, reaching toward the waves to reap the wind.

The *Jolly Roger*, that beautiful ship, sat sweetly in the center of life, every boy's dream.

Jewel performed a somersault in the air and flew backward to see their faces. Her light flamed. Their rapt expressions confirmed it. He was right about that, too!

When Wendy opened the door of the house, her pistol sat snug at her waist, alongside the dangling bags of powder and shot. The gun was hot from its trial, and she still smelled the tang of gunpowder. Her hand spread on the pistol. She half expected the swinging door to reveal a man in black sitting at the table, stirring her tea with an iron claw. She thought nothing would surprise her, but she made a new discovery, and this one was not a gift, but a loss.

She found the teacup on the table, untouched. The sugar bowl lay broken in splinters. Sugar covered the table, rifled, pawed, its sweetest property stolen. Although she sifted it again and again with her own fingers, someone else's had unburied her treasure.

John's and Michael's baby teeth were gone.

Nibs and Tootles flew slowly toward the ship, skimming the water. The waves sent up a greeting of salty spray that they licked off their lips. As the fairy led them nearer, they saw that her hunch was correct. Wendy was aboard the *Roger*.

But there would be no need for parley. Every inch of their mother belonged exactly where she was.

She leaned off the prow, smiling woodenly at Nibs and Tootles. Her breasts were bare and her hair clung to them. Her mermaid's tail looped along the keel. Her arms were raised above her head so that her elbows framed her face. Her right hand grasped the sickle. Her left was open, beckoning to them, *Come aboard!* Her smile, so regal, kissed the wind.

Tootles couldn't resist touching her lips. Nibs fingered the sickle. Jewel sat on her nose and tweaked it. A rapping sounded above their heads. The boys flung a look at one another, then their eyes turned upward to behold the scar-covered face of Gentleman Starkey. In his fist, a ruler threatened.

"Don't let me catch you late for lessons again, mates, or you'll get ten of the best!"

He winked.

Dark Hunting

Rowan rapped his hands against his thighs, clenching his teeth as the blood flowed into his fingers. It had taken time to free himself of his bonds, but the trail was clear. Willow branches prickled his face as he followed Lightly and the Golden Boy. Two sets of feet had made their impressions. One set was firm, the size of his own, one set lighter and the size of the boy's. They led him up the creek to the apparent end of its journey, then vanished into rock. Other, older tracks, those of a beast, and much larger, hung about. Rowan's face stiffened.

Like the air here, the waters appeared to be stagnant, but Rowan discerned a hint of current where the core of Lightly's apple floated. It bobbed ever so slightly among willow blades and scum, as if something bigger than fish lurked below the surface. He watched a little longer to be sure, frowning, then turned his attention to the end of the trail. The branches drooping against the rock were crippled. He brushed them aside to reveal a wall of stone, and studied it.

The odor alone told him more was here than could be seen. It smelled dank, the stench of swamp and decay, and it oozed from an opening low in the rock. The footprints were obscured by smudges where bellies had rubbed against the earth to wriggle into the opening. The hole's upper edge was jagged. It was wide as the span of Rowan's arm, not quite as tall, and half as thick. Easy enough for a boy to enter, if he could stomach the stink.

He saw the smaller footprints leading away again toward the water, where a deeper impression showed the toes of both feet had pressed down before disappearing. The Golden Boy had flown. Inside the rock, Lightly was alone. Rowan didn't like the feel of it, the smell of it. Like an entrance to the Dark Hunting ground. Wasting no time, he dropped on his belly and slithered in to find out what he didn't already know.

In the darkness he paused, his hand reaching to feel for his tomahawk, emptily regretting its loss. He allowed his ears to explore while his eyes adjusted, hearing nothing but the water outside trickling into its groggy pool. Daylight from the hole didn't penetrate the grotto; the only source of light was a flickering within a shell. It glowed on a ledge of rock to the right, at Rowan's waist level. Next to the shell sat a wooden bowl, and a circle was painted in what appeared to be mud on the craggy wall above, with daubs of more mud at regular intervals around its inside. He counted twelve daubs, evenly spaced around the inside edge of the circle. Rowan cocked his head. He thought the image might represent a spirit, but one only vaguely familiar to him. One sacred to white men, who strove to divide the sun's day.

He could stand. The roof arched well above his head, and he stepped several paces toward the light. Now he could dimly see what was in the bowl. Teeth? Or small white beads, unevenly shaped. Perhaps they were the pearls he had heard his mother describe in her stories of pirates. Yes, it might be pirate treasure, for next to the bowl a tawny footpad lay, severed from a lion's pelt, one of its claws stuck through the hoop of a finger ring magnificent with jewels. Rowan recalled the legend; the crocodile had swallowed the Black Chief's hand, rings and all. And Rowan had seen jewelry like this only once before. On one single hand. Yesterday.

His gaze fell to the floor as he looked around for chests or bags of loot and signs of digging. There were none, but there was treasure enough for Rowan. A friend stood in the corner, and it was not a boy. Against a patch of mossy wall lay his tomahawk. Rowan smiled and snatched it up, wondering what spirit could have flown it here to him, before he himself arrived. This was no place the Black Chief was likely to visit, and the man had been on the far end of the Island last night. Who or what had carried it here?

Rowan rubbed his fingers over the familiar surface, flaking the mud away. But when he touched it, he knew in his bones the crust upon it wasn't made of earth. It was dried blood, although not human blood. Still, it made him anxious to find his friend, somewhere in the blackness. He called out, cautiously. "Lightly." The only response was the echo of his voice, trailing into the darkness.

He had seen all there was to be seen. The light of the shell burned too feebly to venture into the recesses. But Rowan was at one with life, and he sensed more than his own within this place. He turned around and followed the echo, seeking whatever waited in the farther shadows.

He shoved his feet forward one length at a time, feeling his way along the floor for Lightly. The earth was clammy underfoot, and as he stepped deeper into false night, the smell of putrefaction grew more repugnant. Rowan's lungs resisted intake of the fetid air. He covered his mouth and nose with his hand. At last his right foot met a mat; his left met flesh. Rowan knelt, set the tomahawk down, and reached out for his friend.

The mat was woven of supple strands. The flesh was cool, unmoving. It was Lightly's shoulder. Rowan's hands traveled it, searching for the right place, and he leaned down to press his ear against the frigid chest. The boy must be sleeping.

Rowan shook him. He didn't wake. He slid his hand up to Lightly's neck, to measure the pulses of the blood. Lightly wasn't sleeping. Rowan felt the cold, like the stench, creep throughout his veins, but he didn't freeze. Instead, he gathered Lightly in his arms and stood unsteadily. The weight of friendship was good, it brought warmth to Rowan's limbs. He searched the darkness for the faint sign of the entryway and headed for it.

He laid Lightly down by the hole, then lay on his own back, hooking each of his feet under Lightly's shoulders. Stretching out, he grasped the rugged wall on either side of the entrance, then he drew a breath and closed his throat, and with an effort, hauled himself head first under the rock, dragging his friend with him. Shady as it was, the light under the willows dazzled him. The boughs scraped his skin as he emerged, but he pulled with feet, then hands, until both bodies were free of the tomb in the fresher air of the swamp. Out here, Lightly's stillness made Rowan more apprehensive.

The brave bent over the boy, who he could now see was white as birch bark. Lightly's skin contrasted with the circle of mud drawn on his forehead and the dots spaced evenly around the inside of the circle. Rowan knew what he had to do. He straightened and inhaled deep breaths, sucking in what life forces existed just outside the grotto—in the air, the mud, the water, the light. Warmth returned in full, spreading rapidly, quick as lightning through the crooked pathways in his body, all the way up to tingle in his scalp.

Rowan captured the last breath, then bent over Lightly's face, his fingers prying at the boy's lips. He shoved his own mouth down over Lightly's, and exhaled.

It was said that Rowan was the Life-Giver. He hoped it was true.

Because the silence that rang in his ears was rent by the subtlest of sounds. A swish of water, and a steady beat not imagined in nature.

White man's Time.

War of Attrition

The life-breath was potent. As soon as it surged through his lungs, Lightly's eyes sprang open. He beheld Rowan's face above his, felt Rowan's fingers pressing on his jaw. The fog of confusion quickly dispersed as his ears awakened to the tick of oncoming death. Recognizing it instantly, Lightly gathered his wits. With no time to lose, he pushed Rowan aside and sat up, scrambling forward and leaping into the sky, leaving Rowan to read the imprints of his toes on the stream bank.

Fighting dizziness, Lightly swooped and hollered through the air, plunging at the crocodile with outstretched fists, then veering toward the water. The beast pursued him, snatching at his limbs. Half in the water, it stretched to snag a heel, but Lightly proved too nimble. With a clap, the jaws closed on emptiness. Its tail thrashed the pool, dredging up clods of muddy debris. Sweating with cold, the boy gulped breaths of swampy air and circled back, diverting the croc while Rowan scaled a tree to sit in patchy sunlight, taut brown skin among stiff brown blades.

Once assured of Rowan's safety, Lightly left the croc to fester. He lowered himself to a branch, and the two friends hung, panting. The color returned to their faces. And swiftly the grins spread, and then the laughter, and they were a brace of eagles who had outsmarted death. Beneath them, in its own purgatory, the crocodile snapped and snarled, moving in irregular rushes against the rhythm within, a gash on the crown of its head.

"It hasn't a hope of snaring these birds! Not until it learns to fly!"

"Your totem is surely a bird."

"That's what I was thinking yesterday." Lightly looked down again and grimaced. "Look at that ugly cut on its skull."

"The mark of my tomahawk. It was taken from me, then returned to me in the tomb. But I left it there."

Lightly felt along his belt. "I don't have my bow or knife, either."

Their eyes met. "Our old friends are gone, exchanged for new."

"It's a good trade."

"Even without weapons, we have paid each other life-service."

They heard the sibilance of the croc below, intolerant of their freedom. The young men watched its red eyes glare at them, then, grudgingly, it dragged itself through the rock into its cell. Once again, the ticking was swallowed up.

Lightly was still a bit fuzzy. "How did we get here?"

"I saw you by the small dwelling-place and tracked you to the cave."

"I was following Peter to your mountain camp and we stopped to take a look inside. I'm not sure what happened next. I got so sleepy . . . " Lightly's eyes opened wider when he became aware of his surroundings. "Look!" His recent adventure faded as his astonishment grew. "These leaves are the same as Peter wears! This must be the skeleton tree."

Rowan studied the brown and brittle leaves. "I have never seen anything like this growing before. Truly, this place is an entrance to the Dark Hunting ground." With a grim expression, he wondered, staring at Lightly but reserving comment. It was not Rowan's way to question good fortune. He reached out to Lightly's forehead and rubbed the circle of mud with his fingertips. It smeared in the sweat beaded there.

"What are you doing?"

"You are marked with mud. A symbol of Time, like the one painted above the altar in the crocodile's cavern."

Lightly felt his forehead. Their fingers joined and both boys wiped the smudge away. Lightly spied the grooves on Rowan's wrist and grasped his arm to study them. "You are also marked!"

"Tell me first of your experience."

Lightly tried to remember. "I was glad to find an excuse to visit your camp. I thought you'd be there by now. Peter and I were going to talk with the People about fighting pirates."

"I can tell you about pirates. I saw many boots yesterday."

"You were captured?"

"Soon after you flew away. The great dark man would have killed me, but the captain's claw stopped him. Now I am bound by more than rope. I owe the pirate captain a life-service."

"He could have killed Peter, too, yesterday, but he only wounded him."

"That is strange. Their hostility is a legend on this Island."

Lightly seemed to examine the skeleton leaves again, but he wasn't contemplating the strange tree. A new idea had occurred to him. Now that he was separated from Peter, he found himself thinking it through on his own. "Maybe Hook's holding back because of Wendy. He wants her to join him. He nearly took her from us yesterday."

"I have heard my mother say that change in a man may often be attributed to a woman."

Lightly smiled. "I think your mother and mine could be friends, too." Then he grew serious, thinking again. "Wendy is almost grown-up, isn't she? Peter may have to change, too, if he wants to keep her. Especially after yesterday."

"Much has happened since we parted at the camp. We will speak of it on our way up the mountain."

"I should go back to Wendy, she'll be worried if I don't come home."

"Then she need not worry. Home is where you will be." Rowan had worries of his own for his new friend. "Come." He began to descend, a few of the branches snapping under his weight.

Lightly hesitated, considering Wendy. He knew what she'd want him to do.

He didn't question it. Using make-believe one last time, he flew through the open window without looking back, and waited for Rowan by the half exposed roots of the skeleton tree.

"Show me the way!"

The Twins balanced the arrows on their fingers, then shot a few off to try them out. Their innovative bow design was working, too, launching their missiles to hurtle through the air and thunk into logs a good distance away. It would function even better when they'd attached new heads to the arrows, shaped like those they'd found at the Indian camp yesterday. The Twins had slipped one or two into their Wendy-pockets while Peter's hawk eyes weren't watching. Like conspirators, they smiled at each other.

"Wendy looked fine with her new pistol!"

"So it was her gun we heard. She's a crack shot! Right through the eye of a parrot, like Jill the pirate."

"These feathers will be dead useful on our new arrows."

"Hope she'll give us a chance at firing it."

"It'll be a while before we can cast metal for our own guns. We need more workspace than we have underground here."

"The Indians have nickel, I know. Can we trade for it, do you think? Wonder where they get it?"

"Must be a vein somewhere. We'll ask them once Peter and Slightly have established relations with them."

The two boys already had so many questions to ask the Indians once truce was declared. About the theory of papooses first. Then metals and arrowheads, lodges, canoes. They couldn't light a peace pipe fast enough.

A speck of fairy sunshine danced in the tree above them, eavesdropping. Jewel didn't linger there another second; now she was a ray of light, shooting into the forest toward the clearing, in the opposite direction from which she had dawned. Her master's business was urgent.

The Twins stored the parrot feathers in their pockets and trooped together to a log, where methodically, they dislodged their arrows. A few moments later, they sucked on their scraped knuckles and straightened, peering into the forest.

A tapping had started up in the vicinity of Wendy's house. They looked at each other. "Drums, do you think?" They listened. Soon they heard flutey music floating toward them.

"Peter's pipes!"

"Sounds as if Peter and Slightly are at the clearing, with friendly drums. They're celebrating by the house."

"They must have made peace!"

"Let's go see."

"Should we tell Wendy first?"

"She'd want us to be careful. We already know to do that."

"Right. Grab up those tools, I'll get the bows."

And so, unceremoniously, the enterprising Twins left home, without looking back.

The three boys expressed relief when Wendy dropped into the hideout, landing on all fours. Then the questions began.

"Where did you get the pistol?"

"It's a beauty! Can I see it?"

"Wendy, where were you?" John took the lead. "Did Nibs and Tootles catch up?"

Wendy answered with a distracted air, as if hardly hearing any of them. "Nibs and Tootles? No, I didn't see them." She headed straight for her workbasket and drew out a swath of fairy gauze.

Curly followed her. "They went looking for you. On the ship." The boys watched with curious eyes as she tied the material around the stock of the weapon, concealing her initials. She knew without thinking that Peter mustn't see them.

"Is that where you got that gun? And the book?"

"No." Suddenly, Wendy paid attention. Her face blanched. "No! I was at the house. You don't mean to tell me Nibs and Tootles are on the *Jolly Roger?*"

John looked down, then rallied to meet her eyes. "Tink told us you'd gone there, and they all three went to get you back."

"But why would you believe Tinker Bell? I told you not to worry!"

John became aware of his duty to his sister, and from their expressions, it was clear the two younger boys were counting on him. He planted his hands on her shoulders and looked into her face. "Wendy, we didn't know what to believe because things have changed since yesterday." With solemn resolve, he steered her to the fairy's niche and took hold of the mirror. "Look at yourself."

Wendy gave John a questioning gaze. He placed the mirror in her hand. "You're not just our Wendy any more." She lowered her eyes to the glass.

A lady reflected there. She had Indian beads in her hair, and the seam of a wound on her throat. Wendy touched her neck, awakening to the echo of a silken voice . . . *marked by her experience* . . . This lady was.

She tilted the mirror. The lady wore a fairy gown, and a knife and a pirate's pistol hung at her waist, with a newborn secret, a burning message smoldering under green gauze. Her hand moved to stroke it. The remnant of a feral old friend hugged her middle, still wild, at odds with the book reposing in its embrace.

Wendy turned the mirror back to the lady's face. The reflection of her brow creased. The most remarkable change was on her lips. The kiss no longer hid at the corner of her mouth—her fingers traced it—wanton now, it spread over her lips, making them fuller, more regal, and all the more impatient, as if her kisses husbanded abundance. . . . *having partaken . . . of both joy and pain. . .*

Wendy held the mirror, a half-smile stealing into it as she watched, when a firm hand closed over her own and angled the glass to the side. A new face smiled back at her, its voice confident and questioning.

"Do you like what you see?" His eyes looked into the mirror from under a fringe of dirty golden hair. "I do. Except for the pistol."

The Twins had followed the music to its source, flying straight to the clearing where, seeing no threat, they ran to ground and dropped their gear.

"We were right about Indian ladies, they're lovely!"

The Twins' assessment was accurate. The ladies *were* lovely, soft dresses swaying as they moved, the fringe lapping their legs. Their colored beads and the kisses that hung on their lips reminded the boys of Wendy.

"Lots more fun than nurses with prams in London!" They bounded into the air again to land in the middle of the ring of dancers, sparking their laughter. The three native women had been waiting for them, pacing in shuffling circles. One played pipes, another murmured in singsong, mimicking the brook in the wood behind the little house.

"We're the Twins. We'll help you settle into the house." They began hopping to the beat of tiny tom-toms, pounded by two tiny Indian children. The girl and boy blinked bashfully as they drummed, and the women smiled greeting to the well-mannered lads.

"Hello, Little Men!"

"Put your own things in the dwelling, as well."

"We welcome you to the ancestral home."

The Twins raised their eyebrows at one another. It was true. This house had been their mother's abode, commissioned for her by their father, built by their own hands, and their brothers'. They were at home here.

The music flowed like the stream. Two of the ladies turned their backs as they danced, so that the littlest ones, the papooses with their bobbling heads, could smile, too, at the sons of the house. The Twins' eyes lit up. They goggled, curiosity satisfied at last. "So *that's* how it works. Papooses are babies!"

The little men trusted their fingers to the fists of the babies, and were surprised by the strength in the grips. They admired the brown eyes, like their own, but were utterly captivated by the slate-gray gaze of the wee little girl with spikes of red hair.

The Twins were in their element. "We'll be needing a nursery for our new brothers and sisters, one with a nice big open window."

"And several bedrooms for our mothers. And a totem pole of our own right in the center of the clearing."

"A fire pit! Also a much stouter door, remember the croc."

"A real door with a lock and a key!"

"Where shall we build the workshop? Over there, so as not to disturb the babies?"

"Yes, and we can install a wheel in the stream for power. Oh, look! The chimney's smoking a new color."

"I like that, very welcoming."

"I'll bet it can be seen from the natives' mountain camp to Neverbay."

"Maybe farther."

"A sort of smoke signal."

"So everyone will know where the lovely ladies live."

"It's a nice, homey shade."

"Just right."

"Our favorite color."

"A lovely shade!"

They said it together. " . . .Red!"

The Twins' mother and father had brought them up well. These little men were accustomed to sharing.

"Peter!" The lady in the mirror turned to look directly at him. She replaced the mirror in the darkened niche. She had to wait for Peter to release her hand. "Michael, take Peter's things for him. Curly, here's your knife. I won't need it any more."

"Where did you get the gun, Wendy?" Peter lifted off his bow and quiver, watching her as he passed his weapons, and a knife, to Michael.

"I found it at the house. The pirates left it behind."

Peter's face dimmed. "That's where I found the Twins, just now. They wouldn't come home."

"But they were just outside! What happened?"

His voice became bitter. "They said they'd found new mothers, Wendy! I saw *them*, too. The outcasts have moved into your house. The Twins are planning to fix it up for them. When I left, the boys were digging a fire pit with papooses on their backs."

Michael's confusion wrinkled his face. "What are the outcasts?"

"They're the ones who've broken Indian law." Peter stepped next to Michael, his gaze sweeping over him. He could still look down at him. "Like what you'd be if you grew up."

The flush left Wendy's cheeks. "Are you saying the Twins are with outlaws?"

"They're not so much outlaws as just too free. They're nice enough to me when I see them. But those ladies are friendly with anyone. Including pirates."

Wendy dropped her gaze to the floor. "So the Twins have gone, too. With strangers, who seem to need them. . . . But Peter!" She ran to the tree trunk. "Where is Slightly?" She suddenly wondered; was Slightly outcast, too, for breaking the law? She bent, angling her head upward, expecting to find Slightly cramped in the chute.

"I left him."

Wendy whirled to stare, disbelieving. "You left him where? With the Indians? Are they that friendly—so soon?"

Peter shrugged and flung himself into his chair. "Slightly thought so. And I'm not worried. They agreed to discuss my idea in council. The pirates ambushed them the other night, that's why they left the river camp. We'll hear from them in a day or two." He locked his hands behind his head. "Michael, that's your knife."

Michael's mouth dropped open. "Thanks! John, Curly, look!" Rotating the knife in his fist, he admired it, then brandished it in the air. It was worn, but he didn't care.

"We'll all need to be well-armed soon. We're going to war with pirates! Tootles will get his wish for boots to polish." Peter looked around. "Where is he? I need him to sharpen my sword."

Curly shot a glance at Wendy. "I'll do it. Your knife, too, Michael." But he didn't move toward the grindstone yet.

Peter dropped his hands from behind his head and sat erect. Swiveling right and left, he inspected the hideout. "Is Tink off again? And where's Nibs?" He turned to direct a stern look at Wendy. "I told everyone to stay close to home."

"So did I. But it seems they made their own decisions."

Peter tensed, his eyes tightening. "Where are they, Wendy?"

"John,—"

"I asked *you* to tell me. Where are my boys?"

Wendy looked down and took her time, spreading her skirts to sit. She smoothed them and folded her hands in her lap. She looked Peter in the eye. And then she lied to him.

"Nibs and Tootles went out to scout. I wouldn't expect them back before dark."

Michael started to speak, but John and Curly quelled him with frowns. Michael shifted his gaze between them, then appealed to Wendy. "Will we really be fighting a war soon?"

Wendy held out her hand and as Michael took it, she petitioned Peter, her voice earnest. "There's no need for our boys to fight pirates, even now. There is another way."

Fire lit Peter's eyes. "Hook's gone too far this time. And you heard him. He said he's only begun!"

"I know he pushed you unmercifully yesterday, but he's ready for you. He knows exactly what he's doing."

Peter studied her. "You know what he's doing, too. Why is that?"

Wendy sat Michael on the floor in front of her, and her hand settled to rest on her pistol. "Remember that I made up his story in the first place. Far away in London, I dreamt him into life, and if there is some kind of connection because of that, I'll use it now to stop trouble."

Peter shook his head. "I can't share you. First thing when the boys get back, we'll form our battle plan."

Wendy's own battle plan had been forming in her mind. Her fingers lingered on the barrel of the gun. "Leave it, Peter. Everyone will be all right. I promise." Her pulse sped.

Illuminating the tree shaft, Jewel appeared. She jingled into the hideout, hovered, then flew to Peter's shoulder.

"Hey, Tink! You're awake. Seen Nibs or Tootles anywhere?"

John caught Wendy's eye and jerked his head toward Jewel. Catching his meaning, Wendy cut in before the fairy could report the two boys' whereabouts. "Shall I tell a story while we wait to hear from them?"

"Yes. Why not read one from your new book?" Peter's eyes glinted. "I think *that* was left behind by pirates, too?" He sat back, smiling in his mischievous way. "Let's hear Hook's idea of a good tale." Jewel glittered, but as always before story time, she made a dash for privacy.

Wendy's heart skipped a beat. She signaled to John and Curly to sit down. "Did you have any adventures today, Peter? I'd like to hear about yours first."

"I did. It was great fun. But it seems you've all had adventures of your own today—without me."

Jewel poked her head out of her curtain. Wendy confronted his accusing face.

"Peter."

"I knew Slightly had to go. But suddenly the Twins are gone, too." Slowly, he wagged his head. "And you won't tell me where Nibs and Tootles are."

The boys stirred uncomfortably. Wendy didn't move.

"Even you, Wendy. You're going, aren't you?"

She gazed, unswerving, into his green eyes. "Does growing up mean going?"

"You know my law."

The three boys gasped.

"I have to follow other laws. Natural laws. I can't help it, nor can the boys." She leaned toward him. "Peter. All children grow up." She thought her heart had stopped. "Except one."

"Except one. I'm all alone."

Jewel held her breath, watching as Wendy reached out her hand and laid it over the wound on Peter's arm. "Things do seem to be changing. It takes courage to face change."

His face was grim, his words forthright as ever. "I have plenty of courage. But I won't be alone. I won't let you go away."

The fairy drew her head back and squeezed the curtain.

"I'm here now," Wendy said. "Some part of me will always be here."

"I don't ever want to be without you, living alone."

Wendy drew a sharp breath as she heard another echo, words in the woods . . . *weary of living alone. . .*

Dropping her hand from Peter's arm, she sat up straight to stare into the darkness of the corner, concentrating. She focused on it until her gaze penetrated the shadows. At last, she expelled the breath. Hue by hue, the truth revealed itself, its colors blazing to life. It all fell brilliantly into place. And at the end of the spectrum she beheld them, just as he had predicted she would. They did exist. They had been there all the time.

The shades of black!

The tension in her body relaxed, and she lowered her regard to the wondering boys. She counted them. . . . Three left. And they must go soon, too. Hadn't he told her?

She turned her gaze to the tiny shrouded room. Only the glimmer behind the green curtain would remain. The envious glimmer.

"Peter." Wendy kept her eyes on the glow. "I finally understand."

It was a master plan. A so subtle plan. Why hadn't she plumbed its depths before? She had been rocking on the surface, while the current worked its purpose, pulling, pushing, fathoms below. Plunging herself into it now, she felt it moving her, swirling all around her, filling her with wonder. And yes, with admiration.

Clearly, the direction it would take next was up to her. This was no mermaid's trick. Wendy would swim right along this time, with her eyes wide open. And she gave herself permission.

She drew a long breath and released a sigh. Relieved, she slowly nodded. "Your Wendy will make everything all right." Her wanton lips smiled. A new adventure.

The niche darkened, but even that den of envy wasn't completely black.

A scarlet drop bloomed as tiny teeth bit a little pout. *Patience, Jewel.*

Revelations

W endy plunged off the cliff, laughing as the salt air whipped her hair and stung her eyes. She swung away from the cliffside until the rocky gates of the bay opened and expanded in front of her. The *Jolly Roger* was a jewel, glimmering in the dim setting of Neverbay as the sea tried to steal her away. She burned lights enough to display her shape, but unlike Wendy, all was quiet within her as she rocked there in the night.

Flying toward Hook's ship at last, Wendy approached with caution, but confident she would find no hostility there. Hook would have given orders that she be watched for and made welcome. Long Tom lay darkly at rest, the crew disposed in similar fashion below, with one exception.

Mr. Cecco was on duty that evening. The light of his lantern shone on his bracelets as he extended his arm to Wendy, assisting her to descend to the deck. His hand was dusky, warm and clinging—like his eyes. She easily returned his smile, unaware as yet of the effect her own might have on a sailor.

"Ben trovata! Bellezza." He bowed gallantly and, retaining her hand, escorted her across the deck and up the steps of the companionway. Its rail and ornaments were carved to perfection, painted in gold. She felt the grain of the planks under her bare feet, cool, and just damp enough to secure her footing on the tilting surface. Attentive to the lady, Cecco lingered outside the captain's quarters to see that her knock would be answered.

But Wendy was in no hurry to knock. She stood outside the door, trying to absorb the image of black lettering on the brass plate: *Capt. Jas. Hook.* The lantern reflected to precision within it, as if engraved there itself. Smee must polish this plaque every day. Or a cabin boy. Tootles? She blinked the thought away and glanced at Cecco. He smiled encouragement, kissed his fingertips, and backed away. She was alone at the door of decision.

Or so she believed. When she rapped, the door opened in a rush, letting out a wedge of light to dawn over her form, creating her shadow. The silhouette of what could only be Mr. Smee bent to greet her. "Good evening, Miss." Wendy stepped through the door. As it shut, the light squeezed itself back into nothing, but her shadow remained, took on the shape of a boy, and flew up and away over the water, speeding blackly toward the Island. Mr. Cecco perceived him, and now that the lovely girl was out of sight, increased his vigilance.

On the other side of the door, candlelight surrounded Wendy, and that scent of tobacco she now associated with Tinker Bell. She glanced about the cabin. Underfoot, the Oriental carpets. Dining table, harpsichord, and desk straight ahead across the aft section, and all along the stern a cushioned recess beneath the windows. The silken couch behind its curtain on the starboard side, on her left now. His four-posted bunk, sculpted and tapestried, to port. Her survey stopped there.

Further examination was unnecessary. The room was rich, glowing, inhabited by taste and luxury, just as she had furnished it faraway in that place called Long Ago. But the evidence of her pulse informed her that, like Hook himself, knowing of this room and being possessed by it were two very different experiences.

Fine as they were, the trappings dwindled in significance. Wendy was compelled to focus not on his surroundings, but on the man himself. Hook's presence commanded one's attention, she found, whether in other settings or gracing his own ship. At once his beautiful blue eyes captured hers, and everything else melted away.

No, not everything. She felt the churning start up again inside her.

He had risen to stand behind his desk as she entered, and now inclined his head to her. "Welcome aboard." He wore golden brown tonight, and a pleased expression that grew to a satisfied smile. He had, indeed, been waiting for her. She was learning about Hook, catching up.

Mr. Smee stationed himself behind her. "Will you sit, Miss?" He offered a chair before the desk, but she shook her head. She was too keyed up to sit. She suspected she had walked into another trap, but her courage found an opening through which to flow. Determined to turn the current Hook had set in motion to her favor, she wasted no time.

"Hook. You said you had accepted my terms. Are we agreed then?"

Hook was more than gracious. "If you doubt it, I will accept you again." He waved Smee away and stepped around the desk. As prepared as she thought she was for this meeting, Wendy was caught off guard; without warning Hook held out his arm and she slid within his reach. His hand stole into her hair, grasped it at the base of her skull, and pulled her toward him, persuading her to join him in another kiss, warm and wanting, but all too brief.

He released her, and as his support withdrew, she felt the shifting of the sea again.

"I am impressed." His eyes continued the embrace, then he spoke over her head, to Smee. "Walking into the lion's den, with only a pistol to protect her!" His smile returned to her. "It must be my Jill tonight." He dropped his gaze to her gun. "I see you received my letters. And tied them up with ribbon." Mocking.

No, she hadn't been ready for this at all, and it thrilled her. She mirrored his mocking tone. "I was afraid to come to you—afraid, I mean, that it might be bad manners to come to you armed."

At once Hook fell serious. He stood close to her, spreading his hand over the gun and pressing it to her side. "This is your weapon now, more powerful than your stories. Don't think of being without it again. You must use it against any who threaten you."

Looking up at him she smiled, half-way. "Even you?"

But he granted no answering smile. He raised his hook into view and caught a strand of hair on her face. He stilled, and his blue eyes bound her. "Never give up power, once you hold it." Caressing her hair with his hook, he combed it back, making music on the strands. Near to her ear, and entrancing.

Hook himself appeared fascinated, watching it, listening to it sing. He caught another curl and played again. She closed her eyes, but sought the answer. "Isn't that what you've done, giving it away to me?" The ship swayed, and Hook gripped her elbow to steady her as the anchor cables yawned.

"When you've decided who you really are, you will understand that I give nothing away." He let her go and turned abruptly, resuming his place behind the desk, standing. "Let us get to business. It is, after all, rather late in the evening for a mother to be away from her children." A touch of sarcasm.

"I've learned that they can take care of themselves. They seem to be flying from the nest."

"Like their mother before them. And what else have you learned? I'll wager your boys are wondering what is becoming of their Wendy."

She raised her chin, still meeting his gaze, but her nerves would no longer permit banter. He was right. It was best to get to the point while she could think clearly.

She said, "I've just visited the Twins where you've placed them. They're happy; they've decided to stay with the native women. I believe Slightly will wish to stay on where he is. And I'll be sending John, Michael and Curly home to London in the morning."

"And how do you propose to guide them there?"

"With the aid of your accomplice. Tinker Bell." She watched, but he gave no indication of surprise, no emotion at all. He spoke evenly.

"I see I am not to be disappointed in you."

"It suits her purpose to help me, this once."

"And you'll trust her, this sweet little impkin—with poison in her pocket?"

Wendy turned ashen and pressed her hands on the silky surface of the desk. "Poison!"

"Oh, yes. That was the first time I saved you."

"The first time?"

"When I caught up to her, she was preparing to brew you a tonic."

Wendy's face betrayed her shock. She had underestimated the

creature's determination. Foolishly. Then, remembering that her rescuer once plotted this very demise, she looked on Hook with amazement. "But you stopped her?"

"Certainly. And I must insist that from now on you be more selective in choosing your companions. As I refuse to spend all my time rescuing fair maidens, I shall, in future, require you to exercise a full measure of prudence."

Too stunned to sift his words for their full implication, Wendy scanned the desktop, searching among the brass, crystal and leather for some kind of help. "But I can't ask Peter to guide the boys home!"

"Once again, you must rely on me. Ironic. I'm the one who advises you to trust no one. But you may rest assured." He waved his hook. "I agree to grant safe passage, with the fairy. Do go on with your demands."

The floor moved with the sea. Wendy adjusted her stance and peeled her hands from the desk. With the first point agreed, she paused to discipline her emotions.

"I want you to release Nibs and Tootles. They can go to London as well, or with the Twins, or Slightly. Wherever they choose, except back to Peter."

No reaction, only one raised eyebrow.

In the face of his silence, Wendy continued. "You will soon have your way, with all of us. You've made good your threat. There will be no more boys for me to mother."

"No, no more boys, and no girl. Only men, and their women. Mothers, partners . . . and paramours."

Why couldn't she keep her balance? "Clearly, your end game has changed," she said. "You could have killed Peter, or maimed him. But what you want now is to keep me away from him."

Hook nodded slowly, assessing her. "I see you have begun to perceive the more subtle shadings."

"I see that you meant to frighten me yesterday. But I believe you do intend to end your pursuit of the blood feud, after all."

"I do intend to have my vengeance. The decision as to what form it will take rests with you."

"Then I choose mercy. I choose to leave Peter. Will that satisfy you?"

"You will find I am not easily satisfied." Hook appraised her again, hungrily, then settled his gaze on her face, approving all he had observed. "I'd not have troubled with you, however, if I didn't believe you capable."

"You are watching me betray him, just as you anticipated. You were right. It's much sweeter this way, isn't it? You needn't bother to kill me to make Peter alone."

Hook's smile was icy. He took his time, tasting the words. "My best revenge. Not only will Pan be deprived of your company, he will be completely deserted. The boys will have flown, all his family will have grown up, and one way or another, his worst enemy will hold his treasure, his Wendy. Pan will know without doubt that you, all of you, were not forced to leave him, but *wanted* to leave him . . . utterly alone." He paused, savoring it. "Exquisite torture."

Wendy stared. So that was his purpose! She had guessed its direction, but not its depth. She faltered, astonished. She hesitated. Then she had to ask. "But . . . what of Tinker Bell?"

His smile warmed by degrees. Pointedly, he reached for a crystal vial on his desk. Its contents glowed golden in his hand. He tilted his head. "You are referring, I believe, to my Jewel?"

Wendy exhaled. She stood, rocking with the sea, taking it all in. The scheme was even more ingenious than she had divined, with a neat twist of the knife. It made her lip curl. She looked at Smee, by the door. He wore a look of pride.

She turned back to Hook. He set the vial down with a deliberate chink. He waited. The ship lurched, groaning. This time, Wendy remained steady. As ever, it had only been waiting for an excuse to appear: her face relaxed, and slowly, irresistibly, her lips accepted the smile, and when it finally assumed its proper shape, it matched his own. "Exquisite."

All her boys were safe. She had been right to trust that. "Exactly how I needed you to do it. . . . You *have* been protecting me, on several levels." Her feet dragged on the rug as they drew her toward him. "You could have destroyed us all, but you chose a more civilized course."

He closed the gap between them and looked down into her eyes. "I chose the course that led most directly and most deliciously to my desires." His fingertips brushed her cheek. "I could so easily have taken a more ruthless route. That was the original plan. And I was attached to it. Passionately." His passion lingered in his look.

"What changed you?"

He took one step back, and swept a gaze from her feet to her face. "An eagle, and a mermaid."

Something, not the waves, tested her balance again. "You'll have to tell me the story . . . one night."

"I shall be charmed to tell it, but it will have to wait for morning light. Shall we consider it another article of your terms?"

"Yes, I insist." The mention of terms recalled her, however vaguely, to business. Struggling to remember the reason for this interview, she managed to think one last time of the boy. "We have only to determine Peter's fate now."

"That's done." His voice was velvet. "We have only to determine your own, Beauty."

"Yes." She was in shreds again.

"Don't forget to breathe, love." He was smiling at her, gratified. But he considered her, and his expression intensified, like that of a starving man beholding a banquet. Eagerly, he drew closer. "What is your conclusion, then? How will the storyteller give me what I want, so I can live happily ever after?"

She took his advice, breathing before she plunged. "I swear to join your crew as you requested, in whatever capacity you command. . . . Swear to me you'll free Nibs and Tootles."

"No." Geniality vanished. Hook lowered his chin, his eyes narrowing as they bored into hers. "I take no martyrs aboard the *Roger*, to suffer virtuously. No one joins my crew to be *noble*." A hint of anger.

Wendy struggled through her shock. "But what more do you ask? I'm right where you wanted me. Aren't I? Isn't everyone?"

"And are you where *you* want to be?"

"I am where I have to be! Where you demand that I be!"

"I can read your heart, remember? What I ask, what I demand, is the truth that is reflected in your eyes."

"But you—"

Swiftly, he hoisted his claw, snarling. Wendy's frightened eyes followed it, caught it flaring above her in the candlelight.

"Come to me honestly, or leave me alone!" On that hated word, he swung toward the desk and with a savage stab, splintered its top. The contents trembled; Wendy flinched, blinking.

He leaned toward her. His voice came low and forceful now, through clenched teeth. "Come to me to satisfy the pirate in *you*." He ascended to his full height, warning. "Otherwise, stay away!" He freed the hook with a violent yank, then strode to the door. Smee hastened to open it and Hook swept from the cabin, into the familiar Darkness of night. Smee followed, sending Wendy a regretful look before closing the door behind him, leaving her alone.

She stared after them, then turned to the desk, trying to see sense in the contrast between the hideous gash and the fine polished wood. Needing to understand, as if it was her own wound gouged by that stark metal claw, she lifted her hand to touch the splinters, feeling them prick her fingertips. Courage draining away, she pulled herself back, ebbing into the chair.

Hook was not going to make it easy for her. He wanted something she hadn't prepared herself to offer. He wanted her absolutely—not just a willing sacrifice to gain her own ends, but committed to his. She must become a real pirate, like Hook. Like Jill. She must never look back. It was a decision to be made for herself only, not for Nibs or Tootles, or any of the boys. Her time of protecting them was over. Whatever her choice, she would have to choose it completely, with no guarantees, and for herself alone.

But she wouldn't be alone, if she chose piracy. She would be with Hook. He would make her his woman in every sense. He had made it very clear; her own reaction to him affirmed it. They both knew. She didn't want to be alone any more than he did. And his terms were simple, he demanded only one thing. The most potent part of any creature. He had even cut it free for her so that she could give it to him. Her heart.

What options were left to her? To go home with the boys, narrowing her life, hacking at it until it fit into her parents' conventional world. To hover with Peter, yearning and afraid on the edge of completion, never knowing who would be safe. Or sail rough seas with the crew of the *Roger*, throwing care to the four winds and unfurling her own colorful barbarity—as Red-Handed Jill. She raised her pale palm and stared at it.

She wasn't fit for any of these choices. One look in the mirror this afternoon told her she could never go home. One look in Peter's eyes told her she would never be free. One look at Hook, just one more, and—

"I'm to see you off, Miss." Mr. Smee towered over her, apologetic. "The captain sends his regrets."

Seeing her sinking, he offered his hand to help her up. "Oh, and he says you're to have this back, if you're wanting it." He retreated to the table and picked up a humble object that had been sitting there all the time, overshadowed by a plush green pillow. Smee put her basket into her hands. Wendy looked down at it, her heart aching and her suspicions confirmed; knowing her weaknesses, Hook had been thorough, ensuring she would come to him. In the basket she recognized the baby teeth she had missed that morning. To each little pearl, a few grains of sugar still clung. She had forgotten to ask for them.

"Someone had a sweet tooth, eh, Miss?" Smee peered over his spectacles at her and smiled.

"Yes, Mr. Smee. Thank you. My parents will be happy to have these tomorrow."

"Begging your pardon, Miss, but you're fair breaking my heart with that long face!"

"Aye, Smee. Begging *your* pardon."

"Will it cheer you a bit, if I tell you?" He bent down to share a significant look. "The boys are both happy in their boots."

The floor finally dropped away. "You mean—all this was for nothing!"

"Oh, no, Miss. Cap'n never does something for nothing."

She dropped the basket in Neverbay as she sailed over it, bound for the hideout. Its pearls were secreted, tied in one end of the gun's sash. The basket floated for a while, then scuttled itself, like Wendy's dreams. She didn't look back to watch it. She would think of it later, derelict at the bottom of the bay, one more wreck of things that might have been.

Why was it that as she swept upward along the cliff and hung poised at the brink, she didn't feel the wind at her back, she didn't feel the moisture of the forest, or the grip of her belt or the weight of her weapon? Her only feeling was one of disappointment.

Everything she could do she had done for her family, for herself. She was no longer anchored by any obligation. But she didn't feel free, even now, for the one thing she considered, the thing she found herself wishing as she glided through the trees and the ground pulled her lower and lower, was that the captain of the *Roger* had returned to his cabin to bid her goodbye. Her single desire was to look into those beautiful eyes. One last time.

Deliverance

The shadow left the ship and the salt air behind, whipping into the wood and across the Island to a place of peace. It settled upright in the grass, silent as the breeze, reforming into solid boy. He grinned. Healing and joy lived here in the fairy garden, indiscriminating, alongside other more sinister flavors. Free to all, and all were welcome. Peter almost laughed. He drew his knife, never more happy than when hunting.

Not until it had raped the border bush, the wild holly with its soft-edged leaves, did his blade return to its sheath. The leaves looked mild, but like the fruit of the plant, they were potent. He'd gleaned enough to upset the toughest of stomachs, leaving the spills on the ground, the berries, black and deadly. No need for them yet. Let the parrots have them, they needed thinning out anyway. This time he did laugh, and the lights within the fairy ring flickered, then continued their dances, ignorant of the blade.

The boy opened his Wendy-pocket to receive the cuttings. They were sacrificed for her benefit, an offering from the garden, a much better gift than the flowers blooming, scenting and dying around him to no purpose. Flowers were fragile, but these pickings would redeem her from a beast more vile than the one he would unleash this night.

Peter pushed off and upward, his feet forcing the berries down, receiving their stain, returning them to the earth to seed it and spread their poison to a new generation. He and his shadow doubled back to haunt the banks of a chanting stream, slipping past a clearing where burned the embers of outcast fire. They ended their journey at a pool choked with willow and slime, where ghosts of breezes sighed among the branches and the lonesome skeleton tree rattled its leaves.

Pulling his knife again, he parted the boughs and sounded a low whistle. He got down on his knees, listened, and slunk into the grotto. In his pouch he carried golden dust, and deliverance for his ally, the one with fire in its eyes and a ticking god in its belly.

Peter smiled his wicked smile. The creature might never get to Paradise, but it would die trying.

Dawn awakened the mountain encampment, shrugging off a gray light that muted the colors of Rowan's blanket. His mother wasn't there to search beneath it for the twin she had foreseen for him, but even as he regretted her absence, he was satisfied with his companion's presence. His night and his tepee had not been empty. Now it was time to rise and initiate the quest.

Lightly was ready. He threw open the tepee flap. He'd outgrown the entrance to the hideout, but he had no trouble fitting through the tepee's opening. It was large enough for two men. "We will act as braves today. Our weapons are waiting to be found."

"Yes. Old friends, like new, deserve rescue from the tomb."

As they emerged into the morning, the cooking fires warmed to their work and sleepy children clung to their mothers' skirts. Old men leaned against the lodge, their blankets snagging on the logs, and peered at the sky. Young boys watched them with sharp eyes, learning. As the sun climbed, the camp took on its color, and its people their purposes, Rowan and Lightly among them. The two young men gathered necessities for their journey, rolling their packs and slinging them on their backs.

The old woman picked her way toward Rowan, her balance no longer in her feet but in her back. She hailed him and he hurried to meet her, to save her steps. Lightly followed, eager to greet again this Old One who had scrutinized him upon his arrival at the camp yesterday evening, laying her papery palm on his forehead and pronouncing him welcome.

"Rowan. The council will meet today concerning the request of the Golden Boy. He has asked us to join him in war." She leaned on her staff, and her faded eyes turned toward Lightly. "My dreams tell me not to trust him any more than the crocodile. But you are his friend. What is your opinion?"

Lightly harbored misgivings about the plan, now. He didn't want harm to befall his new people, and what Rowan could tell him of yesterday's adventure at the croc's lair made him wonder if Peter could be trusted in the world beyond his hideout. After one day as a grown-up, Lightly no longer felt sure of the notions he'd accepted as a child. "My mother counsels peace between Peter and the pirates. It is good advice."

"Rowan?"

Rowan's eyes glinted with respect for his friend, and for the Old One. "We are honored to speak to you about such matters. I agree with Lightly. I have watched the Golden Boy. He is careless at best, and one who would surely lead us into turmoil. We are safest here on the mountain until their trouble dies down."

"You are both growing into thinking men. Soon the elders will be considering your futures." She touched Rowan's arm, her hand no weightier than a feather. "And Rowan, the council will think on your mother's actions this afternoon as well. What would you tell me now?"

Rowan stood taller, straighter. "My mother can speak for herself. I would have the council invite her so that she may." It was Lightly's turn to feel respect.

The old woman smiled. "You are just like her." She shifted her gaze to Lightly. "Rowan must take care not to be outcast along with her. Taboo is not easily overcome. Not for the mother, still less for the son and the one who shares his blanket. I caution you both." She looked to each of them again. "Do not share your new affection with the world." Exhibiting neither sanction nor censure, she moved off in her uneasy gait.

"She is wise, she will bring your mother back one day, Rowan." Lightly watched him, but received no answering look. With a troubled expression, Rowan was standing on the dusty earth, staring after the woman. "Rowan?"

"You don't know the ways of my mother. I will tell you, if war erupts between the People and the pirates, she will stand in the middle, with my sister. And if *she* cannot return to live among the tribe, there is no hope for you and me to remain."

Lightly threw an arm around his companion's shoulder. "Then there must be no war. Come on. Maybe we can find her when our quest is done."

They wound their way out of the village, through the dogs and the children, and began the descent, hiking down the mountainside together, armed with fire, arrows, and determination.

Again Wendy glanced at the niche, but the fairy's dwelling remained dark. "Peter, did you send Tink on some errand?"

"No, she's just on one of her outings, you know how she is. Why do you want her?"

"I don't want to lose track of her again. She gets into such mischief when you don't control her."

He laughed. "I do control her, that's why you're still here!"

Wendy looked sideways at him. He was impossible to read, and she stopped trying. "Please go on lookout duty."

He aimed a knowing smile at her. "From what you told me, Nibs and Tootles are doing that, still! They never came home. Or have you seen them?"

Standing by the bed, John caught the tone of Peter's question, and looked up. He sent Peter a keen look. Michael and Curly formed a huddle under the covers, searching for something.

Wendy reached for the medicine bottle to water the willow chair, as she had done so many mornings. "No, I haven't seen them. Why don't you look in at the Twins' place? Maybe they have news."

"I hope they'll have a good story to tell us!" Shouts among the boys on the bed distracted him, and he swung around to demand, "What're you two up to?"

"Here it is, I found it first!" Curly held up a small white bead. "I knew I felt something under my back last night."

Michael tumbled off the bed. "Let's see the gap, John." He stood on his toes to peer as John opened his mouth and pointed. Peter strode to the boys and held out his hand for the tooth.

"That's the first baby tooth you've lost in a long time, John. . . . Right, Wendy?"

Wendy paused for breath, but didn't falter. "Yes, I suppose it is. I've lost track of Time."

Pocketing the tooth, Peter followed Wendy with his eyes as she moved to tidy the bed. He continued to watch her as he instructed her brother. "Grab your knife, John, and come with me on lookout duty."

Wendy straightened. She turned as calmly as she could manage. "I can't spare John just yet. I'm giving everyone haircuts this morning. Yours has gotten very long, shall I start with you?"

Peter returned the teasing, and his smile grew sly. "No, you don't. I think you *like* long hair now, Wendy. I'll let it go."

Her smile froze, but she really looked at him. "You're right. You look very handsome." He also looked pleased; she had said the right thing.

"Shall I stay and wait while you borrow my knife?" Drawing it from its sheath, he tempted her with the hilt.

She had to stay a step ahead of him. "No, thank you. Michael is anxious to lend me his. Will you ask the Twins if they've heard from Slightly?" This time it was Wendy who watched for a reaction. The discovery of John's last baby tooth gave her that shuddering feeling again, and she was increasingly concerned about Slightly's whereabouts. Peter must have realized his oldest boy was nearly a man. If she could just see Slightly one more time . . . She hoped, and at the same time didn't hope that the Indian messenger would arrive this morning. News of Slightly would be welcome, but talk of war would be awkward.

With a casual thrust, Peter replaced his dagger. "I already told you, you worry too much. Even with five boys flown." He sent her a quick dark look, then just as rapidly, he lit up. "Now that we have fewer boys to look after, we can go on more adventures! John can watch these two and we'll go out tonight like real mothers and fathers, the way you always wanted." Moving closer, Peter brushed her cheek with his. It was smooth, she noticed, with not a hint of a man's whiskers. He whispered in her ear. "You can wear the eagle feather in your hair."

Surprised, Wendy drew back to consider him. "That will be lovely." Maybe he was beginning to understand, a little? A little too late.

"The Fairy Glade, that's where we'll go first. And tomorrow, the waterfall!"

"Peter . . . you're right to accept that things are changing. It isn't clear yet what will happen. But we'll talk about it later. For now, let's just think about this morning." Hook would be watching, she knew it. She wouldn't cross his will, nor her own. And the endless circle of the question looped around her, and it was no longer what did she want, but what did she dare? If only—

John nudged her. Peter was standing by the entrance in his usual posture, bold and poised to fly, but staring at her with doubting eyes.

"Wendy? Where did you fly off to? I said goodbye!"

But she couldn't bring herself to say it. She smiled instead and watched him as he ducked into the tree and shot up and out of sight. He was far too clever. How much had he guessed? And what would he do when he learned the rest?

John had been bursting with curiosity, and he seized his chance. "Did you see Nibs and Tootles? I thought you might bring them home last night."

"No, but I heard news of them." Hurriedly, she turned to include Curly and Michael. "Get ready to go as soon as Tinker Bell comes back."

"Go where?"

"Home, to London."

Michael whooped in excitement. "I'd forgotten about London, it'll be a new adventure!"

"London! Today?" Curly brightened. "I've wanted to see it since Peter first hunted there!"

All expression fled from Wendy's face. "He *hunted* there?"

"Oh, yes! He boasted about finding you, and he told us all about you and your stories."

"You were right, Wendy, it has to be today." John's look was alarmed but unyielding.

His sister nodded earnestly. "It has to be today. It's not just the pirates. You're much taller than Peter now, almost as tall as Slightly, and Peter has your last tooth! I wish we had news of Slightly—but you'll be fine, I've arranged it all." She sat down and gestured the boys nearer. "John saw me leave, but everyone else was asleep when I slipped out last night. I held parley with Captain Hook, and we agreed on terms of an accord."

Curly and Michael gasped while John shook his head. "I wish you'd let me come along. Did he call you Jill again, and ask you to join him?"

"Yes. But in the end he ordered me away." Wendy's heart quickened at the memory, and warmth rose within her as she said, "But there will be no war. If we do as I promised, Captain Hook will grant us safety." Looking toward the willow throne, she lowered her voice. "Even for Peter."

"Wendy . . . you're the best mother ever!"

"Soon you'll have a new mother, Curly. My own mother." She untied the end of her sash to free the hoard of teeth, then poured them in his pocket. "These are Michael's and John's, I saved them for her. Give them to her from me. You'll have to explain because . . . I won't be coming with you."

The excited expressions vanished and Michael clutched her hand. "No, Wendy! If we have to go, so do you!"

John leaned forward, frowning. "We can't leave you here, or Nibs and Tootles, either."

"Don't worry. I've worried about everyone all along, and Peter's right. That's enough. But Nibs and Tootles must stay behind. Hook demands that they join ship's company on the *Jolly Roger*."

The three boys dropped their jaws. Michael stammered out, "Pirates—in the family?" and Curly's wide eyes filled with disbelief.

"You couldn't get Captain Hook to let them go?"

"I made my best offer, and he refused it." The pang of his rejection shot through her again, and she barely heard Curly as he persisted.

"Can't they just fly away?"

"As it turns out, they want to be pirates. But I've been thinking about Nibs and Tootles." She understood now and she faced it, the truth Hook had recognized at once. "They were brought up to piracy, weren't they? They simply decided to go on that way."

"Won't you be lonely?"

"Yes, I'm learning how Mother and Father must feel since we left home. They'll be so glad to have you back! But I've already made friends with the Twins' new mothers. Now get ready, and I'm sorry, but you can't say goodbye to Peter. He'd never let you go if he knew. He's still expecting to battle Hook."

John looked as grave as if he were already a grown man in London. "It isn't right for us to leave you."

"John." She addressed the man, and her eyes communicated a message she didn't want the younger ones to hear. "I need you to stay with Curly and Michael. Your first responsibility is to make sure the window closes. Keep it barred for a while, but only until you think the time is right."

"But what shall I tell our parents?"

"Mother and Father are grown-ups. They can handle the truth."

Michael, with plenty of time left to grow, bounced with enthusiasm. "We'll have lots of stories to tell them!"

"Yes, Michael," John said, and he turned to face his sister. "But the one they'll want to hear most is Wendy's story, about why she can't go home."

"You made me see it in the mirror." Wendy's kiss played along her smile. "The Neverland is my home."

Tipping his head, Michael peered at her. "I can see it, too. I doubt our other mother would recognize you any more."

With a wise look Curly said, "You've grown up."

"Almost. And I can't go backward. But you'll finish growing up in London. You'll be fine men, if you always remember being children . . . in this colorful place."

Curly took his mother's hand and bowed over it, and then he laughed. "We'll always remember the Wendy lady!"

John grinned, a boy again, but knowing the answer before he asked. "And *is* it a great adventure, Wendy?"

"Yes, it is! Curly, John, Michael." She gathered them up and gave each one a helping of her kiss. "Don't ever be afraid. Just follow your hearts, on whatever side of the window you choose."

The young men looked at each other in the limp green sunlight. They heard it. Lightly's voice was hushed. "It's louder than before."

"Shall we climb up the tree and watch?"

Lightly shook his head. He crept to the stream and searched it for a stone. It left a trail of damp circles from the water to the wall where, drawing aside the curtain of greenery, he pitched it into the opening. They listened, tense. The rock thumped. They heard ticking, and nothing more.

Rowan slipped his pack from his back and held the bowl of embers to the torch. "We won't know until we see." The glow leapt to the pitch and hissed into fire.

Lightly dropped his bundle, too, and gripped the torch above Rowan's fist. "I'll go first. Get your arrows ready." He bent down, thrust the torch in the entrance, and elbowed through it. Rowan slithered after, weapons in hand.

They recoiled from the stench but kept their eyes open. The tick echoed in the chamber, bald and inexorable. They bunched their bodies to spring upright, while the torchlight dimmed and flickered, gasping for air in the reek of the cavern. Lightly held it out, hardly breathing, spreading the feeble light in a half circle. Its aura revealed only two things. Neither was the monster they dreaded.

"The clock!" Lightly crouched, holding the torch above it. His voice bounced back from the walls. "It's lost the clock!"

"Now there will be no warning of its coming." Urgently, Rowan's spirit probed the darkness, but sensed no life there.

But there was magic. The flame jumped, illuminating it. "Look what else." The glitter sparked to life in the torchlight. Lightly's face lit up as well. "Fairy dust! Just what we need." He scooped it up, filtering the dirt through his fingers and hoarding the gold in his pocket. "Now you can be a bird, too!" Then his smile faded. Their eyes met. "But you're not the only one."

Rowan's face hardened. He understood. "I have an obligation to fulfill. Without question, we must move quickly now. Let us find our weapons." They surged into the dank recess where the mat lay rotting. Rowan grabbed up his tomahawk, Lightly his own bow and quiver. Pressing their hands to their mouths and noses, with no time for reverence or horror, they kicked at decaying remnants of many kinds. But they found no hint at all of the remains of a knife before the torch died, too, and became part of the refuse.

Contrary to the captain's mood, Neverbay lay becalmed. Hook felt a need to keep moving today. He ranged the deck of the *Roger,* fencing in shirtsleeves with Gentleman Starkey.

"As you see, Mr. Starkey . . . one must keep up one's skills. . . . Swordplay with boys has made you rusty." He aimed his final thrust. "It's too easy." He nailed Starkey, figuratively, to the mast, to the acclaim of the men around him. "As I know from recent experience." He yanked the rapier free, hanging it to dangle from his claw as he tidied his throat with a handkerchief. Near to hand on his belt reposed his finest pistol, one half of a perfectly matched set.

"Yes, Sir." Starkey touched a respectful hand to his forehead, then addressed his pupils. "Listen to your captain, mates! Wise words. Take my sword, Mr. Tootles. Now, Mr. Nibs, fetch Mr. Smee's needle and thread."

"Aye, aye!" With his orange kerchief bobbing, Nibs dashed down the deck. His clomping feet halted as a cry escaped the crow's nest.

"Ahoy! Two approaching, starboard, Sir! In the air!" Swiftly, all deck hands moved to defensive positions. Returning his sword to his grip, Hook raised his gaze eagerly and squinted at the sky. No . . . but not boys, either. A dark form, and a light.

"Hold fire! Let them board." He saluted the pair and the sailors backed from the rail. The rare birds flew nearer and touched down, accompanied by an unsettling cadence. The Indians' gazes darted around the prickly sea of swords, exchanging astonishment with the two youngest crewmen before settling on the captain, where he stood darkly inspecting them. He spied the tomahawk even as his head jerked up and his eyes widened. He cocked his ear to catch the abominable noise. The crew fell silent, fingering their weapons.

There was no mistaking it. The relentless beat of Time. And the source of the beat lay wrapped in a blanket in Rowan's arm. Mindful of their peril, he and Lightly jumped to the deck. Hook held his sword ready and strode across the boards to tower over them.

"You have news for me."

Rowan ventured, "News, and a messenger." He unwrapped the bundle and held out the timepiece. Hook snarled, baring his teeth.

Everything about the thing was offensive, from the overloud ticking, to the stench, to the coating of sludge obscuring the face. Hook seized the handle with his claw, ripping it from Rowan's grasp. His sword clattered on the deck and he flung the clock into the air, drawing his pistol. The crewmen covered their heads and backed away, their gazes locked on flying Time. The gun exploded, the young men cringed, hands over ears, too late. As the shot assaulted the senses and its echo repeated over the water, the clock burst into a hundred metal shards, pelting the deck and crunching under Hook's enraged boots. The messengers held their elbows over their heads and stared wildly, uncertain of their own fates. Hook rounded on Rowan.

"What do you mean by this? Where is that infernal croc?"

Rowan salvaged his composure, all eyes upon him as, shaken but unblinking, he faced the captain. "We found your clock in its lair, but the beast was gone. I repay your life-service. You are warned."

Hook studied his face suspiciously, then thrust his gaze at Lightly. "You were Wendy's boy, the first to grow up. I advise, for her sake, that you both get back to the mountain. And tell your council I am aware of the proposed pact with Pan." His earring swung as he turned to glower at Rowan. *"You* are warned."

But Lightly squared his shoulders. "There's more news, Sir. The crocodile is no longer earthbound."

Hook looked him up and down. "Well? Explain yourself!"

"We think Peter gave it the power of flight, Sir. You're not safe anywhere."

Hook froze for one moment, his knuckles whitening on the stock of his gun. Then he pivoted, shouting. "Smee!"

"Aye, Captain!" Smee shoved his way through the company toward his commander's side.

Hook's eyes burned. His every muscle seizing, he rasped at Smee through gritted teeth, "Take the girl! Now!"

Smee never stopped moving. "Aye, Sir, right away!" He sprang to his duty, signaling two mates to follow him to the dinghy where they began its launch, working together in practiced motions.

"Triple the watch! Roll out Long Tom!" His eyes were red now, aiming at the Indians. The hook raked the air at their bellies. *"And get them off my ship!"*

His men scrambled to obey as Hook whirled and shot toward his cabin, mounting the steps three at a time. Gentleman Starkey winced as the door slammed, then picked up the forgotten rapier and goggled, red-faced, after his captain, running a finger around his collar—and hoping to hell he'd given satisfaction.

Jewel chimed in impatience, but kept her promise. She arched over the treetops like a shooting star, eager to snatch these last growing boys from the Wendy. Time for them to go! Her orders were explicit: only boys. He had been in uncertain temper this morning. She wouldn't dare help the Wendy escape.

Wendy waved them off, carefully not telling them to be careful. Blinking tears away, she sent kisses flying along with them, then tossed her care for them after the kisses. She would never have to fear for Curly, Michael or John again. When the boys had sailed too far to call back, she breathed easily, until she began to consider the next move and the most cunning way to tell Pan the situation. It would have to become his own idea. . . .

She turned to slip down the tree trunk, then stopped, surprised. Her hand flew to her pistol, but her expression had no time to change and her hand no chance to draw. As the fairy's trail faded to memory, Wendy crumpled to the forest floor, dazed by a brutal blow.

She could see his shadow on the wall, twisting together with her own.

Wendy lay on the bed, her arms behind her, his arms around her. Her breath came shallowly. She felt the tickle of his beautiful hair at her cheek. She ached. His shadow was whispering in her ear, satisfied at last, his anger assuaged.

"We're alone. Alone together now. Your boys are all gone, aren't they? Nothing more to distract you." Warmly, he pressed against her back, cradling her. His scent surrounded her, like his arms. The razor-sharp blade began to toy with her hair. Her eyes rolled toward it, but she didn't dare turn her head. Nor did her shadow.

"You belong here, with me. I swear that I'll go right on protecting you."

She willed her body to lie still. Only her lips moved. "You don't have to do this. I won't fly away."

"I'll have to make sure of that."

Singing softly, the metal withdrew from her hair. She felt the bed resettle itself as he rolled off of it. He pulled her shoulder, shifting her to lie on her back, on her hands. Then he mocked her, his eyes laughing. "I spent all morning working out how to get you to take this." He held the bottle up, toasting her. "Then I remembered how much you like kisses."

The room spun around her. He took a long swig and set the bottle down. With one knee on the bed he bent over her, his lips pressed together. Resting on his elbows, he held her face between his arms. She wrenched her head to one side, grimacing, but his pursued. Her legs began to flail, and he stretched out to lean his whole weight upon her. He shoved her face upward and then his fingers forced her lips apart and his mouth pressed down hard over hers.

The fluid flowed into her and trickled warm down her face and neck, moistening the scar at her throat. She spluttered and choked, pushing it out with her tongue. He bit her tongue and lifted his face, his lips wet.

Amused, he shook his head. "You'll never grow strong like Jill Red-Hand if you don't take your medicine, my Wendy. Once more!" And she turned her face away from him, only to watch with her eyes wild as his shadow reached for the bottle and filled its mouth and then he forced himself down on her and did it all over again, imposing his will on her, and his body, and his liquid, and she swallowed and gagged, her stomach retching.

He raised himself off her then. He stood, spat the dregs from his mouth and wiped the moisture from his lips on his naked arm. "But it's only water, isn't it? Nothing to harm you, or heal you. Just make-believe."

Wendy twisted her head to the pillows to dry her face. They smelled like him. She struggled to sit up. Her head hurt. Bitterly, she swallowed again. The tone of her voice matched the taste in her mouth. "What do you think you're doing?"

He sat on the bed and leaned toward her. "The question is, what did you think *you* were doing? When you were with him last night? I can't have you flying off like that again."

"I wanted to talk to you, you wouldn't allow it. You didn't have to hit me!"

"You know I'll never hurt you again, Wendy. I'm your family. Your only family, now."

"I wasn't leaving you."

"Yes, I made sure you stayed. But it doesn't matter anymore." He stood and gestured grandly. "I have been cleaning. There's not a speck of dust left."

"Dust?"

"You won't be flying anywhere from now on." He snatched the bottle and flung it away. He was still smiling as it hit and splintered. "That was your cure." He watched the horror transforming her face. "And you should know, it isn't safe outside any longer. The croc has lost its tick, and it's smelling around for anything that stinks like a pirate. You'll have to stay in here. Even the air isn't safe for you now!"

She had to whisper it. "Peter . . . what have you done?"

"It's the magic of fairy dust, Wendy! The last of it. *You* can't fly anymore, but my ally the crocodile can! He'll hunt my enemy down and slay him for me, while I stay home and keep you safe."

The hideout slid out of focus, Wendy's ears stopped up. Her stomach contracted again and her eyes burned. But she wouldn't allow herself to collapse on the bed again; she had to stand. She tried to keep the panic out of her voice. "Then you can untie me now, untie me."

Peter pulled out his dagger and scooted toward her. She calmed her stomach, concentrating on summoning a smile. It came to her, shivering. Dizzily, she turned her back to him. He sawed at the bonds on her wrists until she reminded him, "You can't cut fairy fabric like that. You'll have to undo the knots. Hurry, it's hurting me." While he worked she caught glimpses of his pleasant face over her shoulder. Her own face felt like ice.

When the strip of gauze came free, she drew it from his fingers, hand over hand. "I'll put this where it belongs. Will you light the nightlight? It's part of the medicine ritual, you know." She draped the crumpled swath over her shoulders, catching from the corner of her eye her own shadow mimicking her motions on the wall.

Grinning, he darted to the fire. "You don't need to disguise Hook's present with that gauze any longer. The gun makes a nice trophy, doesn't it? But I'll put it away soon. Can't have you using it."

He crouched to light a twig. Looking above him, she scanned the mantel, her stomach convulsing again. Pistol and pouches, the book and the feather. But the Wendy wasn't sitting up there yet. When Peter turned again, she was tidying the bed.

He rotated once as he flew to the table, as if to flaunt the power of which he had robbed her. Disregarding the gesture, Wendy crept close to him, watching with all her old affection as he lit the shell, and pressing her fists to her belly. She made sure to stroke his fingers with her own as she took the light from his hands and settled on the bed. "Peter, sit here." She set it on the table and pulled him down next to her. "Listen." He folded his legs, ready to hear her story.

"You are clever, so clever. You were right, I do appreciate medicine." She smiled, teasing. "I'll be making you take yours, next."

He grimaced happily and wrinkled his nose. "Too bad I broke the bottle!"

She looped the swath of gauze forward and over his head, to lie at the back of his neck. She cocked her head. "I'll just have to be clever, too, and think up a way for you to take it." She drew him toward her, and his shadow complied as well. Her smile was genuine now, as she guided him down her path. "So, you see, I can't give it to you yet." Looking down, she played with the sash, crossing it in front of him. "You'll have to wait until the time is right." Her eyes were bright and her throat acid. Pulling the ends, she coaxed the cross of the sash toward his neck, laughing. "You made *me* wait, didn't you? I waited and waited for the time to be right." Her insides churned.

A foot shuffled at the top of the tree chute. Peter swung toward the sound, and Wendy sped into action. She launched her body against Peter's, shoving him back until his head hit the bed post with a crack. Yanking the sash tight, she crossed it around the back of the post and tied it off under his chin. He choked, his hands at his throat first, then grabbing at her, his fingernails scraping her arms as she snatched the dagger from his belt and lay back. She rolled off the bed, spun to the hearth and seized her gun.

She was standing, arms together, legs apart, aiming at the chute when—boots first and swords drawn—into the hideout rushed Nibs the Knife and Tom Tootles.

Wendy lowered her pistol, breathing a sigh of relief. She wore a wonderful smile.

"Thank goodness. . . . Pirates!"

And she trusted them to plunder the place while she climbed clumsily to the wood, to find relief for her stomach as well.

She hoped they would rob him of everything.

Even his shadow.

Workings of a Damaged Man

Hook prowled his cabin, his features wild, his angry tread silenced by the carpets. He'd have Starkey's back in shreds if the new sailors botched it. They'd sworn their oaths, rather sooner than most, and signed the articles, but that didn't mean those two boys wouldn't make mistakes. It was a man's job. But Pan, hiding in his pit and hoarding his plunder, prevented men from entering his front door. Hook snarled. Hindering men was the point of Pan's existence.

The sea was dead calm, waiting for Wendy. Not a hint of wind stirred his ship. The men on deck were watchful, but mum. Sunlight jabbed itself into the cabin windows, darting in watery patterns where it bounced off the sea onto the ceiling. Points of light on the desk caught his eye. Impatiently, he brushed the fairy's glitter into a mound, to be recaptured on Smee's return. Hook had spilled it trying to fly again, but didn't bother with the effort of gathering it up. He held absolute control over the creature; he could make her give him more without ever turning its power against her. In any case, the trial had been a failure. He needed *her* here, belonging to him, to make the magic work.

Under threat of the crocodile, his first instinct had been to pull the girl in, to protect her. Even as he'd shouted the order to Smee, the intensity of his own reaction had surprised him. But that boy had set a monster loose and endangered her, again. Hook could fight that beast, but she was like an innocent playing with fire, and ill prepared for its ferocity. He couldn't lose her now.

And he couldn't go after her, either. Enraged again, he swept the mound off the desk with his shirtsleeve, sending a shower of sparks flying to the floor. He stepped on them, resuming his pacing.

His eyes still burned. He'd nearly gutted those Indians where they stood. Flying effortlessly over his ship, light as the breeze, and with that reeking clock! The image they'd conjured of the crocodile, and the crash of his sword on the deck had carried him to the edge of his worst memory, sorely tempting him to breach the accord. But her boys were to remain unharmed. She didn't have to be happy in order to serve him, but Hook was adamant. He would have her no other way. She was no ordinary girl, and only taken willingly would she suit both his pleasure and his purpose.

Hook paused in his pacing to fix his focus on the sea. A gull swooped and dove, rising again with its writhing prey. He mocked himself, smirking. Only he would think of this particular class of warfare as one of his purposes, to be strategized and pursued like victory at sea, another bountiful ship to be grappled, boarded and plundered. He had applied his famous wiles to catching this prize, and relished the thrill of every skirmish. But the winnings this time were too precious to be looted and squandered. Following the custom of the legendary Captain James Hook, he sought only the richest, rarest prize. His eyes blazed with their bluest intensity now, their burning gone from them to spread throughout his body.

He had resumed his pacing without knowing it, stopping this time to observe his reflection in the glass of his bookcase, his face superimposed over the leather-bound volumes. Transparent, his image blended with the books. He might be real, or he might be a story. A twisted smile slipped over the titles. She was quite a storyteller. *The Pirate King fell in love with her, made her his Queen, took her to Paradise.* . . . Not as simple a tale as it sounded, but he had lured her to the brink of Paradise already. She had only to connect the segments and speak the tale. Darkness vanquished. The end.

But a hungry, screaming seabird recalled him to the present. His victory wasn't accomplished yet. She was out there now, at the mercy of his enemy, her enemy. He had forced her there himself, demanding nothing save the truth, teaching her another lesson. He would be glad to have done with children for good and all. As soon as she removed the final obstacle—and drew blood. Red-Hand. He grimaced, and then he laughed. He had already identified the weapon!

He heard boots on the boards, and Smee's knock.

"Come!" Hook was already there when the door opened. He didn't stop, he commandeered her along with her shocked expression and swept her in, kicking the door shut with a crack like gunfire. He felt his arms surrounding her softness, smelled the sea in her shining hair, bent to taste her lips, felt her hands pressing against his chest and her head shaking refusal and he didn't think again at all until he could finally hear her speaking to him.

"Hook . . . Hook—Captain! Don't kiss me. I believe I'm poisoned. . . ."

"Did you see his eyes? Wendy was right. They turn red!" Lightly had tangled with the pirates beside Peter before, but never witnessed the killing fury of the captain.

Rowan flew low to catch a splash of water and rinse his hot face. "I have heard of it from my mother's tales, but never believed until today. We must bring his warning to the People, before the sun sets." They veered away from the water and up the cliff.

Lightly touched down at the top and caught Rowan's ankles as he passed over, pulling him to earth, laughing as they both tumbled and rolled. Their relief at escaping the pirates lent intensity to their activity, and for a time they gave themselves up to it. Clasped in young lovers' embraces, they brought each other to the edge of the precipice, where the wind shot up and cooled their faces. Below, the sea sparkled and the spume flew high to fall back against the rocks. When Lightly sat up, he was breathless.

"Now that you can fly with me, we are truly twins of the heart, as your mother foresaw in her dream. And it won't take long to get back up the mountain. Let's stop and see my mother on the way."

Rowan picked himself up and offered Lightly an arm. "It is wonderful to be a bird!" Grabbing on with both hands, he swung around, dragging Lightly in a half circle and flinging him off the cliff.

Lightly hung on and they both plunged, feeling the wind whipping their faces and whistling in their ears, relishing the freedom of the fall until the last moment, when they threw out their arms, skimmed over the crests and arched back up to the woods.

They hoisted their packs, and Lightly led Rowan toward the hideout. "We'll fly over the trees, this time. I don't care about being seen so much as I care to watch the air."

"Yes," Rowan agreed, "We must keep our eyes sharp for both hawk and crocodile."

"Hawk? Is that what you call Peter?"

"It is the symbol we use for him in magic rites. Again, I am glad I can fly."

"I'm not afraid. He's just a boy."

They dropped down to approach the hideout on foot, looking around for its inhabitants. No sign of life was evident, and no sound of voices.

"They must be lying low because of the pirates." Lightly called down the tree chute, "Wendy?" Bending to listen, he received no response. He picked up an acorn and sent it rolling down. He didn't try to slide down himself; he knew he didn't fit anymore. "Wendy, it's me, Slightly!" He might have seen a shadow dart by the bottom of the chute, but he heard nothing. "Let's go. She's not there."

Rowan's eyes became guarded again. "Lightly. The pirates have taken her, as he commanded."

"I'm not so sure. Peter will keep her if he can." But Lightly cast a doubtful look at the secret entrance. The place was too quiet to be the home of boys.

Rowan kept silence, hoping for Lightly's sake Wendy had accepted no green apples today. "Come. We can do nothing here."

They rose up over the trees, and Lightly pointed to the red plume in the sky. "There it is again, the smoke we saw earlier. It's coming from Wendy's house."

"I know that place."

But neither of them knew it now. A parrot screeched as they slipped down into the woods. They stole to the edge of the clearing, spying.

Below the flapping of the chimney hat, the Little Men were

sweating, their shoulders broadened and their new muscles working as they hauled lumber to the house and stacked it. They squinted in the direction of the parrot, then turned to smile greeting, standing proudly by the structure that was already emerging from their labors. Two native children were climbing in and out, giggling and pretending to fly through the skeleton of a window. Their two mothers could be seen through the open door preparing food at Wendy's table, and a dark-haired baby slumbered in a basket in the shade, to the lullaby of the singing stream. Its music had changed, along with the house and its inhabitants.

The parrot floundered down to perch on one Little Man's shoulder. "Do you like our scout? We trained him to do lookout duty. Come see the place!"

Lightly walked toward them, studying the house. "We were just at the hideout but no one was there. Have you left home, too?"

The Little Men answered in turns. "No, we've *come* home. When we're done improving the place, there will be plenty of room for our whole family."

"We belong with three ladies, now! They treat us a bit differently than Wendy did, but they're very nice."

The children stopped their play to stare at the strangers, their pretend wings folded. Rowan joined the others and Lightly gestured toward him. "This is your new brother, my companion, Rowan. We live at the mountain camp, for now."

Rowan offered his arm to each of them. "I know these women. You are lucky to have found family with each other."

The women heard, and hurried from the house to greet Rowan with embraces and flashing smiles. One lady sported dimples, the other, long, dark hair. "Rowan, you are here! She is at the stream, getting water."

Rowan's gray-glass eyes gleamed. "She is here, as well?"

And then she was next to him, his sister on her back, and Lightly took her pail so she could wrap her strong, soft arms around her first son, and kiss him. But it wasn't Lily's nature to stop there; she turned and kissed Lightly, too, and the cold water sloshed over his feet. "Rowan, you have met your twin!" she said.

Lightly set the pail on the ground. "I'm called Lightly now."

His identical brothers grinned at him. "We have new names, too."

"We're called the Little Men." The parrot flapped its wings as it accepted a nut and fluttered in a rainbow to its tree.

The first two women looked at the twins sideways, flirting. "Not so little, any more!" And they laughed, shooed the children back to their game and returned to the house.

"Come, sit down." Stepping toward the fire pit in the center of the clearing, Lily beckoned the four young men to follow, and they sat on the logs arranged in a circle around it. Rowan lifted his sister from his mother's back and set her to crawl in the grass at their feet.

"She is growing!"

Lily observed her son, and his three brothers. "So are you all. Your new lives are bringing you up quickly. You are nearly ready for your rituals." Her eyes lingered on the twins, and the two young men blushed at the admiration in her regard.

Lightly leaned toward them. "Nibs and Tootles have chosen new lives, too. We saw them aboard the *Jolly Roger*. They've joined Hook's crew!"

The Little Men looked at each other with raised eyebrows. For a moment they pondered, then they turned to Lily, who spread her hands in encouragement, and they made up their minds. "We have joined the Indians . . . "

"Why shouldn't they join the pirates?"

Lily looked pleased. "Each must follow his own path to happiness. As you see, even brothers may choose different ways. Yet you remain brothers."

Rowan had been considering Lightly. "I, too, have seen us growing. As for my sister, look at her red hair! When you come back to the People, Mother, she will be a flame among burnt logs."

"She already is, Rowan. That is why we are here." She smiled, and Lightly missed Wendy again.

But Rowan's features set, and he straightened. "Mother, the council is speaking of her today, and of you."

"Let them speak. I knew the meaning of my choice."

The baby began to fret and Rowan picked her up. "Shall you come back if they invite you?"

"Not to wear ashes and raise her in shame."

Rowan bounced the little girl and she sucked on her fingers. A shadow dimmed his face as he watched her, thinking. "You have brought forth life. How does this bring shame to any of us?"

His mother chuckled and reached for the baby. "My Rowan, questioning the elders? You *are* growing!" She pulled up the waist of her dress and put the baby to her breast, but her smile quickly faded. "Those who look for shame will surely find it." The red head bobbed as the baby suckled. "Especially in those things that bring pleasure."

Rowan said hopefully, "The Old woman may yet prevail over the council. But I am glad to find you in a good place."

"We managed well enough before, but it is better now that the good captain has seen to our needs. I have no worries, except for you." Her gaze moved to study Lightly, and then she decided. "No, Rowan, I have no worries even for you any longer."

Lightly was studying Lily, too, uncertainly. "The good captain? Hook?"

"Yes, He of the Eagle's Claw. We had no true home until he directed us here, to our Little Men. Now we are all under his protection." The former Lost Boys exchanged glances, confused. Rowan read their expressions and turned to his mother.

"Like your Little Men, Lightly used to be one of the Golden Boy's pack. His mother is the woman who came to tame the wild boys. She belonged to the boy, as well. Her sons are concerned because the Black Chief has laid claim to her."

As understanding lit her face, she nodded. "Then she is a lucky woman. To have so many sons, and the attentions of such a warrior!"

"But he's a pirate!"

Lily laughed at Lightly's frown. "He is a man, and your Golden One is not. That is the real difference. But I have met Wendy. She is a treasure. I can see why the pirate hunts her."

Seeing the others' concern, Rowan said, "The Black Chief has spared my life twice. And my mother is a wisewoman. She sees no danger for Wendy."

But Lily's eyes lost their gaiety and she shook her head. "I did not say there is no danger for her. Even his own men fear him. The legends say, he lives on the edge of crossed swords."

Rowan stood. "I know there is danger to you, if the People join forces with the boy to fight the pirates over her. We carry a warning from the Black Chief. We must go now and deliver it." He bent to kiss his mother and touched his sister's cheek. "Here is treasure, also." With his hand resting on the stone of his tomahawk, he turned to the Little Men. "A warning, too, to you and your family. Do not seek the end of the stream. It is the haunt of the crocodile, and a place of death."

Lightly unfolded himself, rising to his full height to add his caution to Rowan's. "The croc no longer ticks warning. But from what we witnessed today, I think losing its clock means its time is at an end."

Rowan jumped up on the log. "Your vision came true, Mother. Watch the skies for our return!" And they both leapt into the air, to wave goodbye and laugh at her astonishment. The Little Men whooped and the parrot screamed again, and then they were gone.

Hook listened in silence to every word. He left her to Smee's ministrations then, while he saw to business, interrogating Nibs and Tom, dividing their booty and inspecting preparations for sailing. And battle. He had never doubted that battle was imminent. But which animal would attack first?

He scanned the sky and turned his steps toward his cabin, to give her an opportunity to prove her valor. Again.

Wendy reclined on the day bed, concentrating, examining the details of the world behind the curtain. They were illuminated by the sun shafts that forced their way into the cabin, the plunging light of the sunset on the sea. Wendy blinked, lying there, under the sunlight's violation.

She no longer felt the stomach ache or the sting of the scratches along her arms. Nor did she feel the freedom of her hair since it had been unbraided and the beads removed, nor the damp scrape of Mr.

Smee's sponge on her lips, nor the heavy strangeness of her body. Her observations crowded out the sense of shock, and while she observed, she felt nothing.

She tried to feel nothing when she thought of the weapon she won, at last and too late, from Pan. Smee had cleaned and polished it for her, and now it lay next to her pistol on the desk, a bright silver dagger. It meant nothing.

Pushing away the encroaching emotion, she scrutinized the couch. The long, raised side was carved in dark wood, a swan, the feathers of its wings locked forever in the glossy finish, half spread and poised for flight. But looking at it only reminded her; like this bird, Wendy was unable to fly. Nibs and Tom had supported her, just as John and Michael did, that day she should have run away with the pirates.

Too raw, she rejected the feelings. Wendy pressed her lips together, concentrating again.

The fabric of the couch was shiny, woven in patterns of medallions and laurel leaves. The pillows were of crimson silk, with golden tassels. Next to the couch, the Oriental runner swirled with exotic shapes in varied colors, fringed with wool. It was too detailed to remember perfectly, and it troubled her. If she could just fill her mind with these little things, instead of—

She began again.

The room was elegant. It was polished and padded. Its contents were so well tended that, apart from the mutilated desk top, she believed only six inches of ragged material existed in it—the edge of the curtain where the nap of the velvet was shorn away, evidence of its master's grip. That single flaw held her attention for quite a while.

She heard swift footsteps on the companionway, then voices outside the door. It opened, then closed, and the curtain was hooked at the very spot to which her gaze was attached. The velvet was gathered, and cast aside. Hook stood stone-faced, high above her. She sought out the details: blue eyes, golden earring, black hair, white shirt—

Brown bottle.

Wendy stiffened.

"I have the antidote," he said. "Will you trust me to administer it?"

"I want you to kill him."

"That was never an article of our accord. The first thing to purge must be his poison." He stepped toward her and inclined the bottle. "Open it."

Repulsed, she sat up higher on the pillows and looked at him, questioning. His aspect remained stern. She didn't want to look at the bottle, not any bottle, didn't want to touch it. But she had trusted him; she came here willingly. There was nowhere else to run. No way to fly.

Hook nodded, commanding, and she forced herself to focus on the neck of the bottle, her face creasing with revulsion. She fixed the image in her mind, then reached out, steadied it, and pulled the stopper. She held it before her eyes, driving out the sensation the sight of the bottle invoked, intent instead on memorizing the pattern of pits on the cork.

"Wendy. Drop the stopper."

Reluctantly, she released it, hearing nothing as it bounced on the runner. Hook sat down at her side and locked her gaze to his. He raised the bottle to his mouth, then tipped it up, taking a long draught. He brought it down. Still watching her, he swirled it with his tongue before swallowing.

Her heart pounded and she went cold. "No."

"It is rum. You'll not have tasted this kind of spirit before."

Sitting up further, she inched back, raising one knee to secure herself on the slippery silk. Scarcely moving, she shook her head.

"I will warm it for you." He put the bottle to his lips again, filled his mouth, then set the bottle aside. He leaned toward her, raising his hand to her cheek. With gentle force, he pushed her down upon the pillows. His hand slipped into her hair, his other arm moving beside her head so that the hook hung harmless above her. His face bent over her and his lips barely brushed her own, then pulled back.

She could smell the potency. His lips brushed hers once more, and once more, pulled back. His eyes were solemn, encouraging her to join with him. The lips touched again, more insistent, and his hair draped around their faces and fell trickling down to the scar at her throat. He pulled back.

Her own lips parted, breathed in, and he lowered his again to enter them and when the drink was warm enough, he released it to her, a gentle, fiery stream. Burning rum flowed into her mouth, overwhelming every taste that had come before. She swallowed, its flame purging her throat, the vapor cleansing her lungs. It was pure power. His tongue followed the fluid, making sure it was gone. He kissed her, and she pressed against him, burning like the drink. Lifting his face, he drew the sweetness from his lips with his tongue. He took it from her lips, too, and then he sat up and let her catch her breath, his own chest rising. His fingers followed the path of the rum, from his lips to hers, over her chin, down her throat and between her breasts, finally coming to rest just below her stomach. His hand lay on her, as fiery as the drink.

And then his hand left her and her skin was cold where it had lain.

"Once again." He reached for the bottle. His eyes intense, his breathing hissing through his teeth, he toasted her. "To your good health!" And then he did it all over again while her arms rose to welcome him and wound around his waist. And this time, she opened her lips and admitted him as he imposed his will on her, and his body, and his liquid.

She drank him in, and her hands moved upward, dragging in circles on the tautness of his back. Seeking his shoulders, she inched her hands higher, and stopped. She had found a barrier to his shoulders, a rigid line that wrapped around him, under his shirt. She traced it with her fingers across his back and around to his chest. Capturing her hand at his breast, he sat up abruptly.

"So. You have discovered the inner workings of a damaged man. Shall I leave you now? Give you time to recover?"

Wendy sat up, turning her hand to clasp it in his. She shook her head. "Time doesn't exist here."

He smiled stiffly. "How you tempt me." Satisfied for the moment, he stood to yank the ends of his shirt from his waist. He hauled it over his head, one-handed, shook his mane from his face and freed the claw from its sleeve. He bunched the shirt and sent it flapping over the wooden swan.

Wendy sucked in her breath. Beyond the thrill of his honed physique, she felt the panic rising within her. She pushed herself up off the couch to really see him, and she stared. She saw, now, how in her storytelling she had made him suffer. She hadn't imagined this. It had never occurred to her to describe it. But it was so basic to who he was, who she had made him—why hadn't she?

Because she had been a child. Believing innocence could do no harm, she had never questioned. As a result, a man stood before her, wounded, mutilated, incomplete. Here was the consequence of championing a white knight, blindly, unthinkingly faithful. Filled with dread for the next, more ghastly revelation awaiting her, Wendy braced herself. But, no longer a child, she accepted that it must come.

His hair veiled part of the harness. The leather was segmented, laced together, to allow movement. His opposite shoulder was strapped as well, but less so. Its bonds didn't hide his contours, proclaiming instead the strength beneath his trappings. He bore a tattoo there, the black flag of the Jolly Roger, rippling between and linking the mounds of his upper left arm.

The leather cup on his right shoulder was held in place by the strap she had discovered around his chest, with one clip securing the harness to his body. It connected to his wrist by means of more straps, reinforced by a cross-band near his elbow. All the pieces worked toward a single purpose—to anchor the wooden form into which was driven his wrist at one end and the disguise for the damage at the other. His infamous hook. She recalled the shock of the first time she'd seen it. She believed she knew better now, but it struck her exactly the same way, and she swayed.

Hook had been observing her. He held his arms out at his sides. "Barbarous, is it not?"

She tore her gaze from the workings of his wound and met his eyes. "I won't lie to you."

"Hardly what a girl looks to find in her first lover's arms."

"Hardly." She fought the panic down. "I expect to find much more in . . . his arms." And shutting her eyes to his hook, she moved herself into them. He closed them around her, pressing her cheek to his chest, her temple to the strap, so that she caught both the rich scent of his skin, smooth under its black fringe, and the dry smell of the leather. But only momentarily.

He held her away from him, and studied her with narrowed eyes. "What has changed since last night? I have not. I am still a pirate. My ship is still a bird of prey. Is it that you now have no where else to go? Is your new love, in truth, a port in a storm?"

The rum must be affecting her hearing. "You can't believe that of me!"

"And what can you believe of me? Anything? Everything?"

"I believe you have saved me, again."

"So you are merely grateful, repaying me for my many kindnesses."

"Kindnesses?" She recognized him again now, the ruthless sea captain of her stories. "In showing me kindness you have sacrificed little, and gained everything."

"It seems not quite everything, yet."

"But a moment ago—"

"A moment ago, last night! Questions of Time. My question remains. What has changed?"

She looked at him and lifted her shoulders. "Nothing. Except that I admit it."

His eyes became hard, like ice. "If you think to enter my game, I can change your mind, and very quickly. Shall we test your strength? Shall we see the truth, in all its glory?" Raising his hook, he regarded it, then smiled at her, coldly. "Yes, I believe it is the moment."

She backed away, her hands at her mouth. Had she been wrong, again? And when he suddenly raised his hand to her face, she flinched.

His sneer was swift. "I thought as much. No matter what I see in your eyes, you harbor doubts. As do I." He reached out again and snatched her wrist. "Put my mind at rest, girl. Show me that you really want to know me." He pulled her roughly against him, slapping her hand on the clip at his breast. "Once again I will command you. Open it."

Her hand clutched the clip, her resolve slipping away. "I will." She believed she was trying, but it shook in her fingers. The metal tongue was too stiff for her thumb to bend. Entreating, she raised her eyes to his. "Help me."

Hook looked down at her and shook his head, his silken voice reproachful. "My hand is no more. It is yours that must open the way, for both of us."

"But I don't have your strength."

His remaining hand covered hers. "You're wrong. But how can I share what you will not accept?"

"I will accept it, I do. The scars you have to show me . . . and the consequences of what I've done to you, the horror of it. I was a thoughtless child!"

"Ah! Now go on. Connect the story." Still, he pressed her hand against the leather.

She thought, and she remembered, and her eyes widened. "You said—you said you'd been after the wrong fox!"

"So I did."

"You knew even then that I wove your story."

"Tell me."

"*I* dreamt it up, *I* spoke the words—"

"Golden words!"

"And they came true!"

His grip tightened. "Just the words?"

"No . . . you. You came true, too."

"And what else is true, Storyteller? What words will you speak to me next?"

She had to say it. She had to speak the truth. "It was I, not Pan, who did this to you."

"Yes."

"And it is I you want to punish!"

"Yes, and?"

"That is the reason you ended your blood feud against him."

He turned his ear toward her, raising an eyebrow. "Against whom?"

She barely whispered. " . . .Me."

He pulled her hand from his brace and presented it to her with an exaggerated gesture. "Half right, but full marks for effort. I had other motives as well. Knowing what you now know, what next?" Casually, he waved the claw. "Pray continue your narration."

In shocked calm, she studied his eyes. "But this is the end of the story. You will kill me now, or punish me until I wish you had."

He smiled, satisfied, and caught her in his arms. "Now you are thinking like a pirate! Yes, it is the end. The Wendy will die here." She felt the tip of his hook boring into her back, just behind her heart. Gasping, she pushed herself further toward his chest, clutching at his arms. This was the moment she had dreaded, the crisis she strove to avoid since the first time she saw his ship and felt the blow of Long Tom, since she discovered with its bone-shattering blast that Hook was more than a story.

But strangely, she was not able to believe in him yet. "You're right, I believe anything and everything of you. But I can't believe you'll kill me."

"Yet that is what you would have me do to *your* enemy."

"Yes, it was my first urge, but . . . "

The hook fell away from her heart. His good hand stroked her cheek and traveled to her neck, and his thumb pushed her chin upward. "Tell me the tale. How will I satisfy my dark urgings for Wendy?"

His touch was still warm, and something in his eyes sparked her courage. She looked at him shrewdly now, thinking. "You don't really want to punish me further, or shame me." With a sharp intake of breath, she realized, "If you did, it would already be done." He inclined his head. Her face cleared. "You want me to learn."

"I have told you. Wendy will not leave this room alive." Once again his ear turned toward her, and one eyebrow rose. "*Whom* do I want to learn?"

Her mouth fell open. "Jill!" Two stories merged.

He smiled, nodding once. "Excellent! Shame cannot satisfy me, nor tutor you. Experience will do that." He gripped her arm and hooked the shoulder of her gown. Leaning toward her, he searched her eyes with a hunger in his own. "I offer you all the experiences of which you dream, what you have called your adventures. Will you grow up to be a pirate? Will you redden your hand and sail with me, Jill?"

She was relieved, alive, ready to promise anything. Here was a man, waiting to accept her, a ship waiting to sail. She cast about to find the answer, then turned her face to the hook at her shoulder. She laid her hand on its rounded edge. Touching it, her panic leapt up within her, but excitingly so. She ran her fingertips along its curve. She couldn't close her fingers over the blade of his hook, but she longed to. It had dealt death, she knew it, and she suddenly desired to possess it. It electrified her. She was learning already; she could be ruthless. "Jill killed the beast that stalked her. What must I do?"

The victory that lit his eyes only excited her further. "You are the storyteller. You decide!"

Again, she vowed, not caring whether she meant it. "I will!"

"You will follow your legend?"

"I will color my hand with our lifeblood . . . mine, and the blood of the 'beast' that stalks me!"

He slid his arm down to circle her waist. "There's my bold Jill."

She touched his arms. His leather straps were supple, soft over the firmness of his muscle. She grasped him. She raised her chin. "Last night you demanded truth, and again today. I demand nothing less from you. I was half right about your reason for ending the feud. Why else?"

His eyes softened. "Everything I disclosed to you last night was, indeed, truth." The seductive wave of his voice washed over her. "I am merciful because I desire you."

"You hated being alone—"

"Do not underestimate yourself."

"I know because I can feel it. I am more to you than just a desire."

"*Just* a desire? Desire should be pursued with all our abilities. It is the elixir that brings us life, the muse who inspires our endeavors." He pulled her closer. "Deny your desire and you end your story."

Her eyes burned bright. "I came to the Neverland following my desire. I won't deny you any more."

His grip on her waist was so tight it pained her. "You declared it when first we met. *We have found each other.*" He bent to kiss her. Her toes dug into the carpet and her hands dug into his hair as she reached up recklessly to join him. She would have him now, she had entered his game, and its risks set her blood to pounding. Just one of his kisses was worth the price she would pay. She thought of the cost, and when he let her go, she was shameless. His half-smile slipped to her lips, taunting him.

"I followed someone else, thinking he was you."

He matched her. "So now you are playing with your power. Very good! Now you are *my* mistress. What is it like, at last, to taste power?"

"Like your rum, like nothing I've ever tasted before." She was drunk with it. "Like you."

"Then drink deeply, and savor every drop."

She did, dragging him toward her, tasting the liquor again on his lips, but she couldn't get enough. Craving sensation now, her nerves all on edge, she was breathless, and demanding. "Show me how to get my fill."

"Ah, that is where *my* will comes into play. I want you never to be satisfied."

"You would have more revenge? More of your exquisite torture?"

"Exactly! And for myself as well. Sweet agony, and may it never cease."

"I *am* learning. I warn you now, you may get your wish."

"My mistress grants my wishes. An ideal type of slavery! But are you really ready to take me on? Let us test your mettle again. Since you command it, you shall have the truth. All of it." Still afflicted, she sobered as he held her at arm's length, his gaze raking her face. "I have yet another reason to show mercy." His smile could not contain his satisfaction. "My vengeance on Pan is complete. More than that, I am grateful to him! Very conveniently for me, he tempted you out of your safe little bed behind the window, and seduced you into mine."

Gazing into his triumphant eyes, she stood engulfed in fever, breathing hard, anchored in his damaged arms while the room pitched and her thoughts careened. He had hunted her, tempted her, and seduced her. And so had Pan. And, in truth, she had tempted each of them, to gain her own desires.

And she regretted none of it. It was all part of her experience. She concentrated and pushed her emotion away, and in its place sprung a new desire. In the end, her nails tearing at his chest and at the strap imprisoning him, one leg winding around his and her body clinging to him, she uttered one brutal fact. "But I didn't have the strength. I couldn't open it." Her eyes challenged him. "I'm not in your bed."

He laughed, leisurely, and the dark, sculpted posts and woven tapestries of his bunk loomed behind him. "You think not?" He closed his hand over hers, over the clip. "Yet again, vixen, you tempt me from my purpose."

She was ruthless. She sneered in his face, and hissed at him, "It is just as well, if your purpose is to murder Wendy!"

He stiffened, but she ignored the warning. Filled with a barbarism she didn't understand, she thrust again, "Will you flinch when I pursue *my* purpose? When I draw your blood to stain my hand?"

But he read her heart, again. "You're feeling it already, aren't you, Jill? It's the blood-rage. But we will kill your Wendy with kindness." He shoved her away from him, snatched her bodily into his arms, and strode across his cabin. He flung her onto his bunk.

"Now you're in my bed. Have your fill of *that*. Alone!" He turned his back as she rolled over and raised herself up to crouch catlike on her hands and hip, spitting fire.

"But I want you to—"

"Smee," he interrupted, calling coolly toward the door. Mr. Smee entered immediately.

"Aye, Sir."

"Fetch me a shirt." Hook turned to her, stone-faced once more. "The 'lady' in my bed needs to sharpen her new claws." Hook lowered his chin to stare at her, darkly. "And gather her strength."

It was not long after they left her there that the lady, her features wild, prowling the cabin on silent cat feet, noticed the bottle. It had tipped over, rolled on the runner, and spilled most of its not make-believe but very real contents onto the swirling patterns and varied colors of the exotic Orient.

She closed her eyes, tense. The design was too detailed to remember perfectly.

And she didn't care. She picked up the bottle and toasted the door, staring at it. Darkly. "To your good health!" Then she snatched her dagger from the desk and took the bottle to bed. She could use a good, strong drink while she designed the details of her first kill.

All or Nothing

Peter yanked the curtain open again. "Tink! Tink, where are you?" He knew she couldn't hear him, but it felt good to hear a voice. A good, strong one. A wonderful voice, belonging to a wonderful boy.

He had heard another voice today that he hadn't expected to hear ever again. A young man's. Slightly, returned from his final adventure. And he had called not for Peter, but for Wendy. Well, she wasn't here. Peter had pitched Slightly's acorn into the fire. Now he rubbed his sore head and stepped over the broken shards of the medicine bottle to throw himself into his chair. All alone.

Slightly lost, then found, and grown away. The Twins at the clearing. Wendy's brothers and Curly flown back through the window. He'd bring them back soon, and a dress for Wendy, one of her mother's. She'd like that. She'd say it was lovely. And he would bring back a new medicine bottle. But Nibs and Tootles . . . his green eyes smoldered. She had given his best fighters to the pirates! Probably in a silly effort to save himself in some kind of accord. And she gave herself up, too, as she promised Hook that day. Only now she couldn't fly away from Hook.

It would make her rescue more difficult; he'd have to get more dust. "Tink!" He jumped up and circled the room, then stopped by the tree trunk. Placing his hands on its bark, he slid them around the back. In the shadows behind the tree his fingers bumped along until they found the crack. His nails pried at it. With a groan, the hidden panel fell open. Peter grabbed up a candle and smiled to himself. He had something even better than fairy dust. His secret cache. His armory.

Here amid the stockpile, Peter hoarded his most prized trophy. It shone in the glare as it had shone that day in the sunlight, when it blinded the tyrant of the *Jolly Roger*, just long enough for Peter to mutilate him . . . the rapier he took from Hook along with his hand. And here were knives, many knives. All belonging to Lost Boys, truly lost now. But the two boys Wendy gave to Hook were worse than lost. Peter swore to himself that in his bold attack tomorrow he would win them back, and their loyalty too, along with their boots. He smiled. He had always promised them boots and he'd kept his word. And he had promised Wendy the *Roger*. She would own it by tomorrow!

Peter tucked the best of the knives in his belt and gripped the rapier. He would wield this one in place of the old sword plundered by Nibs and Tootles. Falling back, he swung it, making it sing in the air. His arm felt fine, the scar didn't trouble him. It was another trophy, like a tattoo! He danced with the sword, feeling its power, getting to know it. He thrust his way across the room, and then he spied the golden lion skin on the bed. "Dark and sinister man, have at thee!" And he pierced it, dragged it up on the sword and drove it into the wall. The hide hung there, the firelight casting its massive shadow over the bed. He had brought this lion down; he would bring down the lion of the sea, too! Bunching his fists, Peter punched the air. He felt his muscles swelling, pulsing with strength, and he filled his lungs and crowed. The sound of his voice crowded the underground cavern, and then it was gone. Like his boys.

There was only one way. A duel. Kill the captain, and the crew would be his to command. Tamed at last! Wendy would look at him with stars in her eyes, as she did the night he first awakened her. She would be grateful to him for ridding the boys of the pirate threat. He would rescue Wendy. He would save them all. He couldn't wait for the Indians, nor for the croc. He would challenge Hook in the morning, when the sun was blind-bright again, and the next sword he won he would cross with this one, and Wendy would see them every day over the mantel and know that Peter Pan was far more clever than any pirate king. She had asked for a weapon. He might even present the new sword to her. But not for keeps.

Peter took up a stick and poked the fire until it crackled, then he shoved the fairy gauze into the flame, to blacken. He had unknotted it from his neck, but only after Tootles held him at sword point while Nibs looted his trophies. The two of them—the traitors—had stuffed his treasures in a bag and struggled up the shaft. The mantel was nearly bare now, and his sheath was empty. Wendy had borrowed his dagger! Angrily, Peter sprang up to search the shelf again. The acorn was there. Nibs had left that, and the jar with its hawk and crocodile design. Peter grabbed the acorn, rubbed his finger along its scar, and tossed it in the fire to roast with Slightly's. He had given Wendy real kisses this morning. That was enough. He watched her green strip of gauze as it shrank back and curled, a viper in the nest.

Beside the hearth, he spied her workbasket. He opened it and scrabbled through its contents until he found it, the thimble with which she had kissed him. He slipped it on his finger, as he had watched her do countless times in the evening in front of the hearth. Settling in his chair, he stared at the fire, his eyes and his hair glowing in its light, and tapped the shiny thimble on his chin.

Thimbles and acorns. Kisses and swords. He shook his head.

Girls were so hard to understand.

She heard him calling her. It broke her heart, again. Peter needed her. He needed her now! Jewel perched, a twinkle on the dusty bark of the tree, and she covered her ears and dimmed. He had a wonderful voice, although nothing like her master's. She had followed the instructions her master's voice outlined, guiding the three boys to London and watching the window close, and on her return she was commanded to watch the hideout, yet had nothing to report except his crowing.

She would slip down in the night, when the crickets chirped above and he slept below, and she would nestle in his hair. That was allowed. But Peter mustn't see her and he mustn't feel her; she must be just another cricket. The time wasn't right. She trusted her master to tell her when. He knew best. Stretching her wings, she sighed. Until then, she would carry out her orders, hungry and hopeful.

But the Wendy was taken at last! She was a prisoner aboard the ship. It wouldn't be long now. Once the Wendy turned pirate and became his slave, too, he wouldn't need Jewel so often. But Jewel's light sharpened as a familiar pang of jealousy pierced her soul. She wished she knew. Why did her master want that Wendy? Why did Peter want her? She shook her head.

Girls were so hard to understand.

The monster dragged itself forward, strangely alone. The companion tick was absent now, and prey was easier to trap. Having gorged its purged and empty belly on waterfowl, the crocodile had turned its lumbering steps toward the forest. Victims were readily snapped up here, too, and the Island was fast becoming Paradise for this reptile that had been so long the victim of its enemy's cunning.

It had been far too dependent for its meals on the quick creature with the low whistle and the shining blade. The larger prey had not been impossible to snatch, but required much stealth. Only the unwary—the fledglings, cubs and children—had been easily snared. But the constant smile on the animal's face assumed meaning now that the tick had been exorcized. The green hide slithered along the floor of the forest, in a direct line to the last place it had scented out and confronted its favored meat. The beach on the bay. Insofar as this beast could think, its thoughts were very pleasant.

Creeping through the mottled light of the underbrush, it was invisible but for the blood-red eyes. Unblinking eyes. The squawkings of the parrots and the roarings of big game affected it not at all. More interesting to its ear were the sounds of monkeys overhead, chattering among the trees. A family jumped and quarreled above, too noisily to hear the swish of flesh on the grass. These plump primates were entirely too free, plucking at one another, frisking and irreverent, and unaware of the predator below. The leaves among the branches rustled and the limbs bounced, and not one of the family saw—nor heard—the murderous log rising.

Parallel to the forest floor, inches above it, the smiling monster looked up in silence, parted its jaws and floated higher. The monkeys raced up and down their branch, innocent of evil. They never had time to scream.

"Rowan. Lightly." The Old One beckoned from her post on a shady blanket outside the council lodge. Her granddaughter leaned down to support her as she adjusted to sit upright. The old eyes didn't miss the look the maiden aimed at the men, black-lashed and coy. The girl was learning to use her weapons. The woman gestured to the braves and they sat down cross-legged in front of her, politely ignoring the girl and waiting respectfully.

"Trouble stirs your spirit. What have you seen?"

Eagerly, Rowan answered, "We have been at the mercy of the Black Chief, and he allowed us to go in peace. He said for the woman's sake, Lightly and I must stay on our mountain."

Concern etched Lightly's face as his gaze sought the crone's. "Hook sends warning that he knows of our talks with Peter. Two of my brothers are now among his crew. They must have told him."

The Old One closed her eyes and leaned against the lodge. White wisps of hair straggled in the breeze. "So now it is brother against brother?" After a moment she opened her eyes and shook her head. "No, the council has acted wisely to deny the boy's request. You will bear the message to him in the morning."

The friends' shoulders relaxed and they sent each other relieved glances. Rowan turned to the woman to lay down the other matter that troubled his spirit. "Old One, we have seen my mother. I ask what the elders decided."

She blinked slowly. "Rowan, Lily and the others have broken with tradition. It will take time for the tribe to understand." She looked from Rowan to Lightly. "Always, there is fear of the new."

With a heart too stout for silence, Rowan frowned. "Fear of a new baby?"

Her bent posture grew rigid. "It is not like you to take advantage of my good will. But I understand that you begin to think for yourself, and that is well. No, not the baby, but the father. We have never allowed relations with the pirates, and the People distrust the unknown, the untried. But it is my hope that by her example Lily will teach us to open our minds." She reached up to her granddaughter, who slipped her hand in the wrinkled one. "And our hearts."

Rowan set his hand, strong and brown, on his partner's knee. "She has already taught me that much."

She patted his arm, her touch skimming his skin like a whisper. "You have the courage of a warrior. I need no naming ceremony to understand that. But it will take place at the next moon."

Lightly smiled at Rowan, and watched him grow taller. The girl with black lashes giggled.

The young men ignored her, politely.

When she woke, she was in his bed, on his ship, in the sea. The wind had risen and the ship rocked her like a cradle. Through the open window floated the endless hushing of the bay waters. Alone in the captain's quarters, Wendy's wild energy had been directed into a plan of action, and over time she eased into the rhythm of the waves, soothed by the long, reassuring words of the sturdy wooden beams that held his world together.

She sat up, alert to her situation. Here, in this place that knew him so intimately, the force of his presence lingered. Yet even as she had lain with his nearness, he allowed her solitude and reflection. Now the flame he had ignited was steadier, but it still burned.

Once again her flesh began to prickle with both panic and anticipation. Her heart sped. She seized the bottle and tipped it up to drain the last swallow of rum, tasting it thoroughly before releasing its fire to flow all the way down to the pit of her stomach, and lower. She couldn't stop herself from writhing in its heat, nor did she wish to, and her back arched and her legs moved instinctively, while the palms of her hands pushed at them. She was alone, waiting for the mystery, and he whom she had chosen to guide her through it.

Feeling under the pillow for the sharp metal of her dagger, she reassured herself, then rolled off the bed to stand for an uneasy moment, regaining her sea legs. The cabin was dark, with one thick candle shining in a lantern. It hung near the day bed, and her heart sank as she perceived the carving of the imprisoned swan. She remembered now; she was no longer the Wendy-bird. And soon she would no longer be Wendy. She was locked in this beautiful cage by her own desire. And his. Her lip lifted in distaste; Pan with his medicine had, ironically, sealed his Wendy's fate.

Other changes had occurred while she slept. The Oriental runner vanished and in its place were satin slippers. The couch appeared to be recovered in splendid colors. Wendy pushed herself away from the bed and stepped toward it, light-footed. There on the couch were her things, the plunder from the hideout—her pouches of powder and shot, her book, even her eagle feather.

Softening, she lifted the book, handling it as if it brimmed, like a cup full of wine. She touched it to her lips as if to sample it. And then she embraced it with all her heart as she smelled the dry scent of leather and it carried her back to the hours before, and ahead to the hours to come. She shivered, releasing a cascade of warmth to flow into her limbs. Tucking the book in her palm, she raised her green-gauze skirts in both hands and held them to her face, closing her eyes, breathing in his scent and falling in with the motion of the sea.

Wendy dropped her skirt to reach for the feather, drawing it across her cheek with bittersweet pleasure. She looked toward the bookcase waiting by the door, then paced to it and back, and back once again to stand in front of it. Lifting the glass cover, she ran her hand along the leather ridges until an opening showed her fingers where to shelve the volume. She slipped it in, her fingertips assuring it was set all the way back, intact and in line with the others, as if it had never gone adventuring. Then, betraying its secret, she laid the feather along the shelf in front of it. The glass caught the candlelight as she replaced the door, and her reflection fell across the books. Just a silhouette, a shade of a storyteller, anonymous over her tales. Quite naturally, the darkest one of all came to mind, and his counterpart. She knew the ending, now, and she looked at her black self and, once again, smiled darkly.

Now that the familiar was set aside, she turned to examine the unfamiliar. The slippers were soft and delicate. Not much use. Wendy laughed and cast them away. She'd have boots made soon, of a much tougher material—smirking, she shifted her gaze toward the doorway—the hide of an enemy.

Next she handled the hair brush, tortoise-shell. Hours ago, Mr. Smee combed her hair with his fingers, and Wendy had shied from them. Yet as the man unbraided and smoothed it, his hands proved as tender as his features were rough, and he tamed her tangles, to a degree. But she hadn't seen a brush since Long Ago, and never one as fine as this. It fit into her hand. She ran it through her hair, once, to try it, then over and over until it didn't catch any longer and her hair lay sleek and shining in the lantern light, spilling over her shoulder. Her head tilted, her eyes closed as she repeated the motions. The brush and the bo'sun reintroduced her to a ritual. She had forgotten, living with boys, the pleasure of brushing her hair.

Then the gowns. The gowns were exquisite. Simple, fine. She had only to choose a color. She found it right away and held it up, her back to the others. Its sheen invited her to touch it. She hugged it to her body, one hand on her breast, the other making free with the fabric, coarse texture under deceptive luster. Taffeta, sturdy but gleaming. She danced it to the bed, laid it out, and shed her doeskin girdle.

"An admirable choice."

Wendy whipped around, her tension rebounding at once. His hand came out of the darkness, becoming solid as he lit the candles. His robe fell open to reveal his skin, golden in the growing light, marred only by his leather strap. Hook was sitting behind his desk, one knee up, one foot resting on the edge.

She drew breath, unnerved. "I should have known you were here."

"You would have known, had I wished you to know." He lit all the candles before he spoke again. His beard, his face, were black and bright, a charcoal sketch, and his golden earring pierced the night. His mouth was grim. "You have not been completely alone, after all."

For the first time she noticed his boots standing ready by the bunk, and her pulse surged within her. Their presence reinforced the fact she had finally come to accept: Hook was real. Searching for distraction, delaying the inevitable, she allowed something else to catch her eye, on the shelf of the bed. She picked it up and approached the desk, skirting his boots. The contents of the crystal vial glowed in the candlelight, as brilliant as the leather was black.

Wendy met his stare without shame. "I stole it, but the magic didn't work."

He raised one eyebrow. "Stealing from me?" He clicked his tongue. "No honor among thieves." Then he smiled, satisfied. "So you are truly ensnared in my net. Had you wished to leave me, you would have flown." His eyes reflected the candles, watching her.

She set the crystal down with a clack and scraped it forward over the desktop, past the ugly gash. "Then you know what fairy dust can do! And you allowed it?"

He gathered his long legs and sat up. "I allow it, I insist upon it. It is the only way for you. But we are no longer talking terms of an agreement. Like the other members of my crew, you are free," his smile was sardonic, "as a bird."

"But I thought . . . I described you as the tyrant of the *Jolly Roger*."

"So I am. And like all pirate captains, the authority I wield is given me, not by law, but by my men." He stood and stepped around the desk to look down at her. "They, like you, have chosen me over other masters. And whatever power you and I hold over one another we have placed in each other's . . . hands." He reached for hers and held it fast.

Her cheeks warmed. She knew it now, just as she had known in the moments before she gave him her hidden kiss. Another waiting time was at an end. "Our time alone is done. Show me what I have placed in your hands."

Pulling her closer, he searched deep in her eyes. After solemn study, he dropped her hand and swept past her, his robe sending a draft that guttered the candle flame and rushed against her bare arms. He plucked the dress from the bed and crossed to throw it on the couch. When he had shed his robe it followed the dress, sprawling on top of it. Hook turned to her, the glorious conqueror she had made him, shining in the flaming light. "No more delays, then. Come to me."

She caught her breath. "Aye . . . Captain." And with her insides in tatters again, she moved to his side and gave herself up to his will.

"Look at me." She did. She looked to his handsome face, stern now as he shook his head. "All of me."

She obeyed him, her blood beating against her skin. But before confronting the harness, she concentrated on his tattoo, the black flag. He followed her gaze. "You know my story. Blackbeard was not eloquent, but as a young man I found his arguments persuasive."

She remembered his history. The details were becoming clearer now. "You impressed your own mark upon him before the end. But Roger was a perfect choice for you. He has been your closest friend."

Hook placed his hand on her upper arm, considering. "He will look well on you."

"Me?"

His eyes barely narrowed. "Once aboard my ship, it is all, or nothing."

"I want nothing less than all." And she touched his mark, and stroked it. Then she slid her hand to his leather strap, following it across his chest. She braced her back and fixed her grip on the clip, but he stopped her with his own.

"My hook will tear just once tonight." He slipped his arm behind her shoulders. "My fairy has taught me the charm." She looked at him, puzzled, then felt his hook dragging at the back of her dress. It sank, cleaving the uncleavable fairy gauze with only a whisper. He yanked the remnants off her shoulders and left them to shiver in shreds to the floor. Hooking her hair, he pulled it forward to lie on her breast. His lip twitched; his eyes swept over her. "Yes, you are my mermaid." And before she could feel anything, he kissed her into carelessness.

Until he recaptured her hand, and directed it to the clasp. His whiskers scraped her ear as he whispered, "Know me, now!" She gazed into his dark blue eyes and next moment found she had opened the clip. His chest swelling with a slow intake of breath, he shrugged his brace away, to drop on the floor with a sullen beat. She looked down at the hook, inert at their feet. She sensed Hook himself lost nothing by its absence, and her heart was pounding. He raised his empty wrist and caressed her shoulder. Shuddering, she felt the ship pitch, but when his arm circled round again, she lifted her eyes to behold it. He watched her face. And then he smiled.

Her face was set, but she didn't flinch. As panic coiled in the pit of her stomach, she took it all in, the rude ending of his arm, his ragged flesh, the scars tearing every direction—and his pain. She winced, and her arm jerked as her own wrist flared with flame, white hot. Searing.

Far sooner than the torture he had endured, hers was over. The tension eased, and the coil of her belly relaxed. She raised her hand. Gingerly, she placed it under his arm and forced herself to look until she ceased to feel the shock and his interrupted limb became her own. With her fingertips, she touched his scars. Tough and tender.

Her head tilted as her gaze traced its way up. There, beginning just above the cut, was another tattoo. His mermaid wrapped her tail around his arm. In her hand she held a sickle. Her tresses floated about her shoulders and clung to her breast.

"She is the mermaid of your story." The name came to her. "Your Beauty?"

"I gave you my word. You will hear the tale and know her better in morning light." His eyes were changing, subtly, to violet. "But before the light, we must pass through the Darkness. I swore I would have revenge, that I would tear the enemy who took my hand. Before I can honor my promise to you, I must honor that vow to myself."

"And I promised you. I will accept the consequences." But she was shaking.

"And then you will be released. But I also swear . . . " He held up his wrist, placed her hand on the mermaid, and covered it with his own. "She is you."

The rush of emotion overpowered her. She reached for him and took his face between her hands. "You must take her now, before—" But he shook his head, cutting her off, just as she wanted him to do, and he pressed his broken wrist upon her lips. Then he let it fall, so that he touched her only with the black velvet of his voice and the purple fire of his eyes.

"Let me bring you death, and life."

She had stopped breathing already. "I will."

And he swept her away in his mutilated embrace, and laid her down in his bed. The sea rocked them as he lay down beside her. Her legs wrapped around him and clung to him, she stroked his face, dragged her fingers through his hair. He rolled with the waves and pressed her beneath him, his damaged wrist delving under her back to raise the gift she so willingly gave to him. And when at last he took his lips from hers, his eyes burned red and his teeth were set and he unsheathed his weapon to satisfy his passion and fulfill the vow he had sworn so long ago when he hissed into the Darkness at his unseen enemy. As a pirate on his prey, with a single savage thrust that forced the breath screaming from her body, he tore her.

And then, as a man to his woman, he made love to her, passionately.

Rites and Rituals

A long way away, the river twisted behind the braves, a living shadow. Even farther away, they could see the flickering orange of light thrown upward by outcasts' fire. Seeming not so far were the silver stars, shedding their blessings on the mountain while the breeze swept over it. Rowan and Lightly had climbed to the pinnacle and sat looking down like gods on the passion below. But they were not above it.

Lightly was still adjusting. "So Nibs and Tootles are pirates! And the Twins are the Men of the clearing, arranged by Captain Hook."

"Lightly, I believe he has arranged more than we know. He discovered that you and I became friends the very day it happened."

"How do you know that?"

"He had a man watching us at the camp, the one who captured me. And although I didn't answer the captain's questions, he could read my eyes. He was very interested in the Golden Boy's companions."

"You were lucky to get out of there alive."

"I do not think it was luck. I think the captain spared my life, knowing you would one day come away with me."

"Before we knew it?"

"So it would seem."

"He knew who I was when he saw me. The first of Wendy's boys to grow up. But why would he want to find places for Peter's band? He wanted to kill us before. Wendy worked hard to keep us all safe from him."

Rowan shook his head. "The man is deep. He must have his reasons."

"You think he changed his course because of Wendy?"

"It would seem to work in his favor. He wants her."

Lightly shifted uncomfortably on the rock. "Wendy knew we were growing. She worried about us breaking Peter's law. I saw it in her face every time we lost a tooth. And look at us now, almost men! It must be because we're away from Peter, as if we're making up for lost time. I'm sure none of the brothers we saw today will fit down the hideout's chute by tomorrow." He stretched his long legs. "Wendy must miss us."

Rowan watched Lightly in the cool starlight. "When we bring the council's message to Peter tomorrow, we will know for certain if the captain's men took Wendy. We will also learn whether your remaining brothers are safe."

"If the pirates captured Wendy, Peter will be determined to battle, with only John, Michael and Curly to help him. They're no match for that crew. Knowing Peter, he'll challenge Hook to a duel, but he'll bring his boys along. You're right, they aren't safe."

"Lightly. You aren't understanding what I said."

Uneasy, Lightly tried to absorb his friend's words. Rowan's carved face was uncompromising.

Rowan said, "The captain arranged to take you and your brothers away from home. Not to harm you, but in order to save you."

"To save us?"

"After listening to my mother today, I am certain. Wanting to be sure I spoke truth, I didn't tell of my suspicions before."

Lightly shivered in the wind. "Suspicions." It wasn't a question.

"Like me, you never questioned the ways of your tribe until now."

Lightly sat still as he thought, and then he spoke slowly. "But why would Hook want to save us, and from what?" He knew the answer. He wanted to be wrong.

"Why? As he told us today, for Wendy's sake. From what?" Rowan straightened and turned away. "I do not wish to speak ill of your family."

Lightly looked over the end of the mountain, over the end of his childhood. His feet dangled in the air. "I already know. I just don't want to believe."

"No, Lightly. You want to continue to believe."

"Yes. . . . It's hard to let go." It was just as difficult to speak. "I loved Peter."

"It is disappointing. An occasion for great sorrow."

Lightly watched the wind swirling the fringe on his leggings. "Even Wendy couldn't help him. Hook saved her, too. She tried so hard to love Peter, and he almost slit her throat."

"She is also a brave."

"She believed in him and nearly died of it. Just like me. When I couldn't help growing up, he left me to the crocodile."

"I have not doubted it. You were a sacrifice to the Spirit of Time. But you had to discover it for yourself."

"I was an offering, to keep him from growing older."

"Like those little teeth in the bowl on his altar."

"Rowan, if Hook hadn't spared you, you couldn't have rescued me."

"And we repaid the life-service to him. I see now." Rowan lifted his chin. "It is not an obligation. It is an honor."

Lightly's nod was brief, as if it hurt. "Peter's boys and I lived in fear of Captain Hook our whole lives. Now he's the reason we live at all."

"The captain has granted you a future. Peter is the past."

"He is just a boy, and he always will be."

Rowan lent his strength. "But you are a man. You will endure this, and be stronger."

Lightly drew a deep breath. "Yes." They were silent. The stars blurred. Lightly ran his arm over his eyes. He gathered in his legs and set his feet squarely on the rock of the mountain. "I have lost Peter, and I will mourn him. But I mourn for more than that." He blinked before meeting Rowan's eyes again. "You asked me when we first met. Where my other brothers went—the older Lost Boys."

Rowan waited.

" . . .Now I know."

Rowan's arm firmly surrounded his companion's shoulders. "Tell me about them."

Tom Tootles and Nibs the Knife outdistanced Mr. Smee and his lantern in the dark woods, despite his longer stride. He had informed them that they acted well today and that the captain was satisfied. Now Nibs was trying to keep his mind on business. "Our training paid off. I could see Mr. Starkey was relieved."

"Good thing the captain sent us for Wendy when he did. Getting down the chute was easy, but we sure had a hard time of it getting back up." The new britches squeezed Tom tighter today than the old ones had done.

"She was happy to see us!" Nibs rubbed his hand over the prickly stubble on his chin.

Tom made an effort to follow the conversation at the same time he followed the pulsing beats of sound. "She was shaken up, though. But the captain cured her of whatever Pan did to keep her. As if she could be kept!"

"No more than we could be." Nibs tripped on a tree root and had to slow his steps. He dusted the dirt off his hands, looked up to locate the orange glow above the trees, and tightened his kerchief. "She tried to get the captain to release us, can you imagine?"

Tom smelled the smoke of the bonfire. "I can imagine her doing anything, since she trussed Pan and held us at gunpoint! She's proved her valor. I say she's a match for him, all right."

"For Pan?" Nibs scented the smoke too, and he wasn't thinking clearly at all.

"Get your head on straight! For Captain Jas. Hook, as engraved on the brass plate we polish every day." The throbbing drums reverberated within their chests. They were getting closer.

"I knew it when we saw Wendy's face on the *Roger*'s figurehead, Tom. They're mates." Something in their words made the blood hammer in their ears and their necks hot, in spite of their open collars.

The place was easy to find. They stumbled into it, halting abruptly. Several of the young braves had brought their drums and flutes and they sat in a bunch around one of the logs, pounding and piping out the rhythm of their hearts, free of restraint in this place of red smoke. The women spread the blankets within the circle, stoking more than one kind of fire there.

Mr. Smee caught up to his charges and placed a restraining hand on Nibs' shoulder. "Hold up, mates. Mr. Starkey can teach you many skills, but listen to me when it comes to the ladies. Doesn't do to look too eager." And in his hurry he pushed past Nibs and Tom, leaving them waiting on the edge of the clearing. They stood fidgeting, listening to a parrot squawk in the trees where once upon a time they had played hide-and-seek.

But the ladies wouldn't allow hiding tonight. They held out their slender brown arms. "Come, we are waiting for you!" The young men felt their feet trundling them forward.

"You can't dance in these. Set them here, with your swords."

Nibs and Tom hesitated until Mr. Smee nodded, his spectacles flashing in the firelight as he turned away. The two women eased them down. The ladies drew off the prized boots and, knowing the ways of pirates, set them at the ready.

Like the boys, the clearing was changing. The house was growing up, too, and a totem pole stood beyond the fire. It appeared to waver, springing to life in the heated air above the flames. Its wood showed only two symbols carved in it so far—at the top a lion with a fierce expression; under that a tiger bearing a subtle smile. Tom knew the work. "The Twins!"

Two heads stooped so that two sets of brown eyes could peer at them from the viney window of what used to be Wendy's house. Smiles followed. The beat of the drums was too much to resist. It was a force of nature, and they all began to move to it. The twins left the little house to the sleeping children; young men belonged outside tonight. The braves and the brothers hailed one another, while the women smiled and began to move as well, sinuously, around the fire and over the blankets.

Mr. Smee laid a hand on Lily's arm and coaxed her from the cluster of braves. "Are you free, love?" She laughed, then looking back at her admirers, she touched the nearest on the cheek with her fingertips, and as his black eyes watched regretfully, she left him.

"Smee. You are late."

"And I'd not let the boys fly ahead, I'm that stubborn!"

Lily's feet slid through the damp, cool grasses as she led him around the old house, past the stacks of lumber, and into the adjoining frame of the new. Inside, in the warm light of Smee's lantern, she bent over a basket, her hand resting on the knotted edge. Smee set down the lantern. Disregarding the basket and its sleeping infant, he tugged her arm away from it. "The captain sent you this." He slipped three golden bracelets onto her wrist.

Lily held up her arm to view them and her smile stiffened. A cooling breeze swept through the house frame, and her manner matched it. "The captain's generosity has already proven bountiful. Please tell him that my sisters and I accept these as gifts only. As for all who come to us, it is our pleasure to assist him."

Mr. Smee's eyes twinkled over his spectacles. "And this." He pulled from his pocket a cord on which dangled another shiny object. Lily studied it. Slowly, her eyes lit with comprehension, and her smile softened. Smee hung it on her finger. "He said to tell you your builders should know what to do with it."

She clasped it. "A key. For the front door when it's ready! It is a message, isn't it? He tells us that the place will be truly our own. The good captain grants us the gift of home."

"Aye, Lily. He asks nothing more of you. I'm glad to see you happy. I know how much you've wanted a real home since leaving the village."

She rested her hand on his brawny arm. "Smee, I ask no more than you can give." She looked out the door to the alluring light and listened to the drums that called her back. "And you do the same for me." After a long moment, her eyes shifted back to his admiring face.

"Aye. We're a pair." And with an effort, Smee freed up his gaze to cast a glance about the place. "That's a fine big window! Almost another door, you might say."

"Yes. Our young men tell us the window must never be closed. It is a tradition."

"You'll be wanting some curtains for it. I'll bring back some fine kind of cloth this trip, and run you up a set."

Lily smiled, but her voice was subdued. "So the time of parting is come, then? Your captain has won Wendy from the boy?"

Smee grinned. "We'll know in the morning, but I've no doubt. And then we'll be weighing anchor." He scooped her into his arms while she dropped her treasured key to the pallet on the floor. His red beard burrowed into her neck and she giggled like a girl until the baby began to mewl, pudgy elbows flailing at the air. Smee's rough smile struck his face. "Go on. I've a job to do, anyway, getting these cursed boots off."

"Will you hold your daughter again?"

"I'd rather hold you. Give her these." He unhooked his spectacles from his ears and tossed them to Lily. "I'm told children like such things."

Lily looked askance at him and set them down by the lantern. "Take your boots off, man, and hold peace about things you don't understand." She shook a mellow-gold bracelet off her wrist to dandle it over the child, who grasped it and quieted. Lily drew off her dress, swaying to the drums, and when she turned back to Smee, the blue-white drops were beading on the tips of her breasts and rolling down in lines that clung to her curving skin.

Throwing off his shirt, Smee dropped to his knees on the pallet. With his big hands on his Lily's hips, he pulled her toward him. "Aye, woman. You make good sense. This is something I understand!" Her arms cradled his red head and it bobbed as the strong, sweet man lapped up the mother's milk and suckled at her breasts, bringing her to a tender ecstasy before he tucked in to feast on the heartier fare also offered him by the generosity of his hostess.

Outside by the fire, the flutes breathed music through their shafts and the drums beat on, slowly and steadily now, stretching Time to make the night last. The flames of the beacon fire whipped in the breezes and the orange kerchief weighed anchor and went sailing, flagship of a fleet of shirts, skirts and breeches. Soft brown hands beckoned and lingered on bristled chins and smooth, muscled chests. Tougher hands responded in kind, and the dance settled onto the blankets. Kisses were learned, then given and taken freely, and brown thighs opened to receive curious caresses, and later, one by one, the knowing hands guided virgin timber into lush forests, to the happiness of all.

And on the colorful blankets in the clearing and up to the windswept pinnacle of the Indian mountain, there were no boys left to mother. Only brothers, partners, and paramours.

On the ship, in the rolling waters of the bay, the woman in the captain's bunk lured him closer with a not-so-hidden kiss. With all her heart, she gave it to him while her left hand wound his hair around her fingers, imprisoning him. Her right hand wound snakelike under her head. Between the sheet and the pillow she sought her weapon, then clutched it at the hilt. Before she could strike, his hand followed the contour of her arm. His grasp was casual as he encircled her wrist, yet it rendered her dagger impotent. Pinned beneath him, she struggled while he took his time to end the kiss, and then he raised himself up.

"I will use it first," he said.

Her breath came in ragged bursts as she gripped her knife and dragged his arm downward. She rolled with him toward the middle of the bunk, above him now, still clutching his hair. "The legend of Jill decrees what I must do. If you can't give me what I need, I'll take it!"

"The blood of the beast that stalked you?" With his hideous wrist Hook forced her chin up. "Or the one that caught you?"

"I want the one thing you can't abide. The letting of your own blood! Do I demand too much?"

His gaze was fierce, touching every curve of her face. "You have shed yours for me. I am purged of that. I flinch at nothing now." He sat up, bringing her with him. "You needn't steal from me. I will give you everything, and never miss it."

He wrapped his hand around her fist and kissed her palm, just below the handle of her dagger, then held the stump of his arm over the red-stained linen, the bloodied bedclothes where she had lain when he tore her young life away. "Mark me again!" He pointed the knife at his mangled flesh. Her legend commanded; she narrowed her eyes and bared her teeth, and together they cut a crimson line and he bled, his lips set in a twist. She went cold, her eyes burned, and she watched his dark blood mix with her own, and the cold turned to heat and pounded in her chest, firing the wound he had ripped open to bleed deep within her. She dropped the dagger, splayed her hand and set it in the pool, smearing the colors together, her eyes wide, her face rapt in magical trance. She convulsed when he touched her, gripping her wrist. He raised her hand, still spread stiffly, then he set it on the sheet, pressing it down, lifting it up, and then releasing her. He held out his open hand to her and she grasped it by the wrist and when the ritual was done a set of crimson handprints marked the white linen, left and right, male and female, commingling their blood—an emblem of their unity.

Then Hook threw his head back and laughed, long and loud, while she wrapped herself around him, her scarlet fingers scratching at his skin and the blood-rage of her legend still possessing her. The sound of his laughter went ringing below, where the crew lay on their bunks and hoisted up on their elbows to leer at one another in the lantern light. The echo of it hurled itself up the mast high over the sea and set black Roger to flapping as he grinned at his captain's triumph. And Hook flung the dagger away, wrapped his wrist and laid her down, to take her offerings again while she burned.

The night wore on, the candles flamed lower. When he was sated, Hook fell onto his back and breathed the sweet smell of the sea. Then he drew his own jeweled dagger from under his pillow. He ran the blade once through her hair and she clawed at it, lusting for it. But he raised it out of her reach, and the colors of the gems shone in the candlelight, wild and blazing, like their eyes.

"Victory is ours tonight!" He swung the dagger down at her back, tearing triumphantly at the sheet. The shriek of rending cloth made her flesh crawl; she cringed and clutched at him, in her savagery a creature of instinct, hardly human and beyond understanding now. But Hook smiled when it was free, a rectangle of stained linen, a standard of red to fly below his black banner.

Then he held her, his whiskers scraping against her ear over and over while he called her his Jill, and he stroked her and sponged the blood-rage from her heart. And together, gradually, they eased into the rhythm of the waves, soothed by the long, reassuring words of the sturdy wooden beams that held their world together. Her queen's smile came to her, and she looked to him, and to their dark and light locks twining together on their shoulders, and all the while their red blood stained her hand.

He rose up and covered her with himself, his black waves hanging over her. Silkily, they dragged down her body, moving slowly, while she laughed in pleasure. His one hand and his naked wrist slid behind her knees, his beard and his lips tickled her softest skin, kindling the sensation within her thighs, building and fueling the flame there. Her hands and heels delved into the bed as her rapture intensified, and when she could bear his torture no longer, Hook raised his face to her, lifting an eyebrow in mock surprise.

His voice was velvet. "Why, Jill. I have found another kiss."

Red-Handed Jill didn't understand him, but she believed in him. And when her Pirate King took that kiss, he took her to Paradise.

They lay in the last guttering light of the candles. Hook watched the flickers play upon her features, and then he woke her.

"Tell me the tale now. The beginning of it all."

She remembered it, like recalling a dream, and sat up to weave her arms and his story around him. Her eyes were as clear as her voice.

"Young James was born into one of the finest families in England. He was away in his last term at school when his beautiful black-haired mother was murdered. She had been vibrant, and corrupt in a very charming manner, and he had adored her.

"He had earned a reputation at school for his hot, quick temper. He wounded his fencing master at the very moment his mother was slashed and left to bleed to death on the ancestral bed in which she gave birth to him. James was not quite the last thing she thought of as her life ebbed away.

"There was another, a younger brother with a complexion of the very wrong shade to suit a dark father. James rushed from school when the authorities came calling. He burst into the mansion and surged up the stairs to the nursery, where the silly servant girl sat teary-eyed, clutching a little nightshirt. She wouldn't speak until he struck her with the back of his hand, the first time he ever loosed his temper on a woman. Looking fearfully into her young master's changing eyes, she admitted that the golden-haired boy fell from his pram in the park that very morning. Recounting his Lordship's rage against her Ladyship, the nursery maid sobbed into the nightshirt, confessing that the frightened child must have run away, when she wasn't watching.

"His passionate, arrogant father left the country with the family fortune and blood on his hands, never to be seen again. The scandal broke, and with his brother lost and his prospects ruined, James jumped a schooner and hired on, bound for exotic lands, learning to live, and live well, by his wits and his charm.

"A young man fallen from grace, he slipped into the Neverland, where lives the stuff of fantasy and of nightmare. James fit easily into both, a strong, handsome, brilliant man, cultured and callous.

"He left shame behind him on the shore the very first time his eyes beheld the sea. But he lost everyone he cared about in a single day. From that time to this, he was terribly alone."

Everything connected, as he had known it would. Hook was satisfied. He drew a deep breath. "From that time to this." They looked into each other's eyes. The last candle sputtered out, and Hook and Jill lay not alone, but together, in the receding Darkness of dawn.

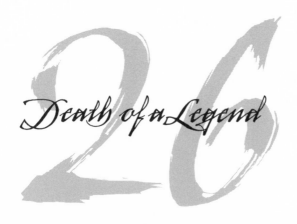

Death of a Legend

Jewel awoke to the raucous sound of chirping. But night's crickets no longer sang; now she heard the birds of dawn. Rubbing her eyes, she yawned. She smiled in contentment, lying tucked in Peter's golden strands. Thinking she heard grass rustling at the top of the shaft, she swiveled toward the entrance. Wide awake now, Jewel listened, her little ears intent. . . . Nothing. She sighed.

Then came the skittering of an acorn rolling down the chute. Jewel leapt from the tangle of Peter's hair and crouched to fade among the tree roots forming the wall. Peter awakened, jumped off the bed and caught the acorn as it tumbled across the floor. They both heard the call. Slightly's voice, fully grown.

"Peter! We've come with word from the Indian council."

Peter cocked his head toward the shaft but remained still.

"Peter?" A pause followed, then another voice murmured and mingled with the first. Peter strode soundlessly to the fire and pitched away the little brown nut. He plucked a knife from the table, sheathed it, then grabbed up a sword.

Jewel's eyes opened wide. She recognized the gleaming rapier Peter had won from Hook. She hadn't seen it in ages, she'd forgotten all about it, she hadn't warned him! But surely her master would remember that Peter had confiscated his weapon?

The voice echoed down again and Peter listened.

"The word is this, Peter. The Indians will remain on the mountain. You're all alone." A red clay object clattered down the shaft, the grasses stirred, and then there was silence. Even the birds had flown.

Peter dashed to pick up the token. It was a peace pipe, long, feathered and painted with symbols. His features clouded. A moment later, his face became a mask of determination. Exuding all the entitlement of an aristocrat, the boy rested the sword on his shoulder and paraded to the mantel. With ceremony, he positioned the pipe where his arrow used to reside. He tested the point of the rapier on his fingertip, crossed to the niche and swept the curtain open with the blade.

"Tinker Bell!"

He said it so commandingly Jewel nearly popped out of her hiding place to fly to his shoulder. Only just in time did she catch herself lighting up, and she hunkered down again, biting her lip. She had almost disobeyed her master!

She should never have stayed here! He was gracious to allow it. But he had made it clear what punishment would befall her if ever she betrayed him. Too well she remembered her frantic attempts to stay afloat in the Lagoon as her precious dust became saturated and swirled away. Compelled by her bondage, Jewel had confessed when he questioned her that, of all the elements, only water could end her powers. If enough of her grains of magic fell into the sea to lump and wash away, she really would be like some kind of cricket—with no light, no flight, and no music.

Jewel acknowledged the truth now. Her master had made her see it: the Wendy saved her at the Mermaids' Lagoon, in spite of everything. But Jewel was certain that once that girl became Jill the pirate, she would never intercede for her, especially if the master's fearsome wrath was spurred to its height, as any mistake with Peter would do. Jewel's wings began to tremble. She folded them farther out of sight, cramping herself deeper into hiding.

Peter stood as if undecided. He banged the sword on the table and glared at the chute, then paced the length of the cavern, his expression dark. He opened his pouch and upended it, shaking the contents over the tabletop. A lone tooth fell with a tiny clatter, and a few waxy leaves floated to scatter. Jewel caught the glimmer of a flake or two of her dust, but Peter shook his head.

"Not enough!" Replacing the pouch, he lifted his chin. He stood stock-still for a moment, then, as his new-idea look illuminated his face, he skipped to the shaft. Jewel blinked and Peter was gone.

Mr. Noodler saw it right away in the morning. He smiled and elbowed his fellows, pointing his backward hand. "See the new standard, mates!" It flapped in the wind under black Roger, a red and white banner printed in familiar ink. Two bloody hands, proclaiming their captain to be whole again. Noodler's gold teeth glinted. "He's finally found his right hand!"

Bill Jukes' tattoos lost their symmetry as he smirked. "Aye, and that flag will serve right well to bait his enemies, too."

"The croc'll be sure to rise to that!" Laughing aloud, Cookson pulled his knife from his belt. The pirate crew sharpened their steel and fell to their chores, making ready for some sport.

Nibs and Tom were grinning all over themselves this morning as they stowed Mr. Smee's sewing machine. "What a night! The Wendy lady was right about growing up. It's an adventure, all right."

"Aye, Tom. Remind me to thank Pan when he comes, for choosing us a wise mother." They laughed heartily together as they swaggered back to report to Mr. Starkey.

On watch in the crow's nest, Mr. Cecco bellowed down in his accent, "On deck there! Two approach starboard side, from above!" No one scrambled this time, for the crewmen already manned battle stations. Jukes and Cookson raised Long Tom's iron barrel and set its sights.

Mr. Starkey squinted at the sky. "Mr. Tootles, Mr. Nibs, stand by! These are friends of yours." He gave them the nod and the young men hailed their oldest brother and his partner from the rail. As the pair descended to the deck, the pirates made out a stripe of black paint across their faces, over each of the Indians' eyes. The braves scanned the deck. Seeing no sign of the captain or his claw, they relaxed and clasped their brothers' arms.

The smile Tom gave Lightly stretched broad like his shoulders. "I see you've got your wish. You're a brave."

Lightly returned his smile, gesturing toward the boots and swords. "You've both got your wishes, too. And look at you. You're sturdier than ever, Tootles, and Nibs is nearly as tall as me!"

With a curious stare at the Indians, Nibs studied the changes. "You're different today, too. Why the black paint?"

Lightly's voice quieted. "It's a sign of mourning. I'll explain." He addressed Gentleman Starkey respectfully. "We ask to speak with the captain. And Wendy, if she's here."

Starkey's eyes never left the Indians. "Fetch Mr. Smee, Nibs, and tell him it's the same messengers as yesterday, requesting to see the captain. And his lady."

"Aye, aye. Right away!" Nibs hustled over the deck in his new long stride and up the steps of the companionway, two at a time.

Controlling his reaction, Lightly merely tugged his vest straighter. "So Wendy's his lady, now?"

Tom Tootles' barrel chest expanded, and he smiled. "She's changed, like the rest of us, but you'll know her. She's truly Red-Handed Jill now." Rowan and Lightly followed the glance he shot to the standard waving at the top of the mast.

Rowan kept his voice low. "So the captain has won her. Now he must settle with the boy." He and Lightly exchanged looks from under their marks of mourning, but Lightly shook his head.

"No. I don't know Jill yet, but I knew Wendy. It is she who must settle with him. It seems she's finally broken his law."

"Good morning, Madam."

The woman who used to be Wendy Darling opened her eyes, and a shock surged through her. The man who was Captain Hook sat smiling smugly on the edge of the bed, dressed in dusty blue velvet. Like his rings, his hook gleamed in the morning light. He tilted his head. "I regret that I must leave you. A little matter of a battle to be won."

Jill regained her composure and strove to sit up, gripping her stomach as a pain jabbed her insides. Hook offered his arm, and when she was sitting upright, he drove off discomfort by pressing an ardent kiss upon her fingers. "Our Mr. Smee will attend you, my love."

Mr. Smee's rugged red countenance beamed upon her as he bobbed his head. "Morning, Madam."

She blinked, still trying to determine if she slept or waked. "A battle?"

"How flattering. Really, you shall cause me to blush in front of my boatswain." He turned a wry look on Smee.

"Oh, aye, Sir. One night with yourself and the lady's forgotten the lad who came before!"

Hook turned back to Jill, his smile fading, and regarded her keenly. "Yes, battle, with your former beau. He is sure to want to avenge your honor." His fingers still possessed hers.

"My honor? No. Only his own. And I *had* forgotten. But you're right, he won't let me go without a fight."

"I am yours to command, Madam. Would you have me kill him?"

"But would you want to, now that you've recalled who he is?" She darted a glance in Smee's direction.

"He is the same boy he has always been since entering the Neverland. A childish menace who would slay us both if given the opportunity. Yes."

"But you wanted to protect him, once upon a time."

"And once upon a time, I wanted to destroy you. Another ironic twist of Fate. It makes life so interesting, does it not?"

Her eyes caught the spark within his own. "Yes! Far more interesting even than a good story."

A hesitant knock interrupted. Hook glanced at Smee, who excused himself to answer it and exited.

Jill laid her hand on her lover's velvet sleeve. "But Hook, what of the fact that Pan is your brother?"

"Half brother. Even blood ties mean nothing when honored by only one party. And like my other family members, he has proven himself untrustworthy. In spite of his dubious paternity, a true son of the house."

"But if he knew——"

"If he knew, he would have more reason to resent me. I am everything he hates within himself."

"Yet he will never acknowledge it." She bowed her head. "He will never admit how similar you are."

Hook raised an eyebrow and dropped her hand. His reply was barbed. "I shall endeavor to be complimented." Another knock intervened. "You may enter, Mr. Smee!"

"Sir, Madam. Two Indians to see you, the same pair as yesterday."

Hook stiffened. "I will leave you to Mr. Smee's tender care once again."

Smee cleared his throat. "Cap'n, they've asked for both you and the lady."

"See to her. They can wait." Hook held out his hand again and she nestled hers within it. "It is your eldest son, and his . . . companion."

Her eyes lit up as she smiled. "Slightly! He *is* with the Indians, then, and he's all right."

"You may judge for yourself when you see him. When you are ready . . . " He leaned over her to brush her cheek with his lips. Deciding that wasn't enough, he kissed her fully, and then his blue eyes warmed her as he lingered over her hand, and her name. "Madam Red-Hand . . . Jill."

She had stopped breathing again. He relinquished her hand and stood, swept his hat off the desk and with a nod to Smee, strode from the room.

Jill held her hand to her cheek as she watched him go, and then she raised it and stared at it, drawing in her breath. She hadn't dreamt it after all. The inside of her right hand, from palm to fingertips, was stained a deep blood-red. She threw aside the comforter and wondered at the ravaged bedding.

Mr. Smee's kindly voice broke into her thoughts as he took her hand in his own, surveying it and the linens through his spectacles. "Begging your pardon, Ma'am, but it looks as if the battle's already been! There's naught to be done about your marking, but I've brought a basin for the rest of you. And would you be wanting a nice cup of tea?"

She grimaced with another twinge of pain in her middle as she straightened, then she half-smiled at him. "No, Mr. Smee. Better make it rum."

"A woman after my own heart!" As his hearty grip retained her hand, he brushed a stray strand of hair from her face. He squeezed her fingers and bent to look into her eyes. "If it's not being too forward—was it a rough night you had, Ma'am?"

She was mistress of her emotions now. "Oh, no. Everything went smoothly. All according to plan."

He laughed his rollicking laugh and freed her hand, turning to lay out the gown and other necessaries. "You're sounding like himself now! You've made a fine choice of the dress, it matches your eyes. And I'll get you whatever else you're needing. You've only to ask."

"The captain promised me a story this morning. But business must come first."

"If he promised, he'll be true to his word. One way or another."

"Aye, Mr. Smee, I've learned that. But you know him better than anyone."

"No, Ma'am. I know the captain's ways. It's you that knows his heart."

Jill spoke softly, more to herself than to Smee. "He's known mine all along. I just didn't believe it."

"Ah, and who's to blame you? There's no guarantees in this life. Best we join the captain on deck now and see to the Indians. And then we'll have to be ready for a fight!"

"I had hoped that last night was his happy ending."

Mr. Smee's jocularity withered with his grin. "Now, Ma'am. I'll not be betraying my captain, but I'll tell you this much, for 'tis no disloyalty." He peered over his spectacles. "Don't ever be telling him the end of the story."

"But he's a legend. It must go on forever!"

Smee smiled sideways at her. "I'd not be telling him that, either."

"Aye, Mr. Smee. I'm learning why ship's company respects you." She gazed out at the sun on the sea and her voice was firm. "So a battle is to be fought. My first. And I'm ready." She turned back to Smee, her eyes steely. "There is one thing I'll be needing, Mr. Smee, if you'd be so kind. To continue the story of Jill. I'm sure you can find it for me."

"Anything, Madam. The ship is yours."

"Aye . . . "

Mr. Smee liked the smile on Red-Handed Jill's face. So cold it warmed him.

It lay on the beach of the bay all night, cooling its blood and gloating on its surfeited stomach. The tide pulled away from the shore, leaving a saturated strip of sand and a green log to bask in the early light. And as the sun rose, the beast's faith and patience was rewarded. The fresh morning breeze came to it, the salt-scented air, carrying with it another smell. The enticing aroma, not only of flesh this time, but also of blood. Out across the water, toward the sun.

The crocodile blinked and hauled its bulk forward. The sand scraped its belly until it floated up to buoy in the bay waters. Its powerful tail shoved the water from side to side and its legs paddled. Unwittingly, the green sea concealed the monster as the beast swam silently, pleasantly, toward bliss.

Tom Tootles waved a dismissive hand. "We've all broken that law. Pan is no threat. Captain Hook sent Nibs and me to fetch her from him, but we had an easy time of it. She'd already put him in his place!"

Under the black paint, Lightly's eyes remained somber. "All the more reason for him to come after her. And another grand adventure, to win her back."

"Aye, he never learns."

Rowan agreed, "The boy holds the courage of his convictions, but little wisdom."

Nibs bounded back to the deck and joined them. "We're to wait here, Mr. Starkey."

Gentleman Starkey retrieved a handkerchief and mopped the back of his neck. "I hope for everyone's sake you two haven't brought more bad news to the captain." The Indians' eyes grew wary as they looked past Mr. Starkey. Nibs the Knife corrected his posture. Tom Tootles tucked in his shirt. Stowing his kerchief, Starkey blew a breath. "We were all much too near to death's dark door when you left us yesterday!" Then he froze.

The silken voice flowed over his shoulder. "Quite right, Mr. Starkey. But I shall be content if only one passes through that door today." Hook rolled his eyes upward to behold the new banner, and his claw blazed in the morning sun. "No. Make that two."

In Peter's cavern under the ground, Jewel clambered out of hiding and smoothed her feathers with shaking fingers. Her wings were nearly as crumpled as the day Mr. Noodler captured her in the Fairy Glade. But she had flown again that day, and she would fly today. She beat them, testing, and rose an inch or two. Edgy as a fledgling, she flitted toward the entrance, hesitating only a moment in order to peer up.

Peter was nowhere in sight. She plunged up the chute and surfaced among the trees, rising high to see which direction Peter had flown. She spotted him, as she had oftentimes, not by sight but by the waving of the telltale foliage in his wake. He was headed away from the hideout, in the opposite direction from Neverbay. Ducking down into the forest, she followed, creating in her agitation her own stirring of leaves.

Jill waited confidently, now prepared to cast off from the cabin and set sail into her new life. With a nod to Mr. Smee she indicated her readiness, but he stood gripping the door handle and didn't open it for her. Stately, she lifted her eyebrow. "Mr. Smee?"

"Will you wait, Madam? Captain's orders." He stepped away to open the wardrobe door instead. "And you'll be wanting to see yourself, I think, before you go out." The mirror hung on the inside of the door. Jill looked, and watched herself glide toward it. She gazed then with pleasure at the woman there, the woman she had wanted to be. Her dreams were still coming true. And it continued to be true of her as this new lady—she didn't need enchantment to call her smile. She herself was enchanting, and the royal smile flew irresistibly to her lips.

Although she selected her raiment for quite another reason, Mr. Smee was correct. The gown she chose last night did match her eyes, perfectly. The neck was cut square, the bodice tight; the shimmering skirt was loose enough but not too flowing to interfere with the movement her pirate life would demand. Her arms were bare, and begging for bracelets. Jill's smile deepened in anticipation.

The sash Mr. Smee had fashioned for her served her well, hugging both the polished pistol and the silver dagger to her hips. She ran her fingers over the weapons and inspected her trim reflection. She chose to remain barefoot for now, but her hair was brushed to a sheen, and as she watched, her lips parting, Mr. Smee's big hands suspended in front of her a dazzling string of jewels. He hung it round her neck, an opal and diamond necklace, not quite hiding her scar, but sparkling with all the colors of the Neverland. With her fingertips she stroked the cold, smooth opal surfaces. Her tongue touched her teeth as she beheld the gems' reflection, and aroused, her pulse beat quicker. Her first heady taste of pirate treasure. Almost imperceptibly, her lip twitched.

Smee caught the lust in her eyes, and he smiled. "A gift," he confided as he fastened it, "from the captain's own coffer, chosen himself as his lady slept."

Breathless, she slowly shook her head. "He knows my heart." Jill's eyes glittered like the diamonds, until she remembered the battle ahead. Then her eyes changed to resemble the stones in a more solid way. Her voice, as well. "Time to go, Mr. Smee. We've work to do."

Peter reached into the twisting tree to pluck two of the most succulent apples, round and green, and pocketed them in his pouch. His countenance glowed with expectation as he snatched another apple, a fat red one. He jumped down to the grass and bit into his fruit to sample its sweetness. Then he flung it to the fairy garden and bent his knees to push off and away. From the cover of surrounding trees, Jewel's troubled eyes watched the butterflies scatter from the thud of the apple, then she flitted just like them after the boy, an uncomfortable swelling doing its best to enlarge her heart.

On deck Mr. Starkey, with a sense of relief, abandoned his pupils to his captain and the visitors. The legends of the claw were as nothing to its reality, and Starkey liked to keep well away from it and its bearer, the more so as Hook appeared none too pleased to greet the Indians again. The captain's tone revealed his displeasure.

"Well gentlemen? What accident of fortune brings you back to us today?"

Diplomatically, Lightly raised his hand in Indian salutation. "Sir. We bring word from the People. Rowan and I just delivered the message from the council to Pan. He'll have to fight you on his own, without our help."

Hook scrutinized him, interpreting the mourning paint. "And? Something else, I think?"

Lightly paused, reassessing the formidable face. "A family matter. I felt that Wendy—Jill—should know what we've discovered about Peter." With curious gazes, Nibs and Tom watched their brother and their captain. Their captain tossed his head, and the feathers on his hat quivered with impatience.

"I should think she knows him rather well enough by now."

The young man stood resolute. "I believe *you* know him well enough. But she might never guess the full truth."

Hook raised an eyebrow. "I see. . . . Yes, I will allow it, as she has expressed a desire to speak to you. The lady shall join us presently."

Drawing himself up to his tallest, Lightly said, "And Sir. Something I would like to say to you." He looked into the piercing eyes of a former nightmare. "I owe my happiness to my mother. But I owe my life to you." He turned his head to include his brothers and his partner. "All of us do."

Regarding Lightly with tightening eyes, Hook dropped his voice. "Shades of black." It seemed all Pan's brood could distinguish them now. He assumed a wintry smile, tasting it again. "Sweet revenge."

The door to the captain's quarters opened and the lady pirate stepped onto the companionway. She moved discreetly, with only a whisper of skirts, but even so, an immediate hush fell and Hook swung around, his earring a golden arc. The sailors' elbows jostled their shipmates and all heads pivoted, even that of Cecco in the crow's nest, who should have kept on watch but imprudently forsook the horizon and his duty to train his spyglass on the Beauty instead.

The crew of the *Roger* had anticipated her emergence. Seeing her now, they no longer begrudged the wait. With jewels at her throat and her hair shining, her weapons at her side and a dress of royal blue, she stood on the top step, regal, one hand on the rail, and returned the stares. She knew these men.

Her sons recognized her still. They straightened, their chests swelling with pride. Lightly, Nibs and Tom adjusted to her as they had adjusted to their own grown-up selves. Rowan studied her, and identified the capable woman he first glimpsed at his people's camp. Ship's company smiled and inhaled a collective breath; this vision was a captain's share of treasure, indeed. Every man was certain of the punishment the master would exact if they acted on their thoughts. Every man was certain this lady was worth it. Then they remembered the triumphant laughter ringing out in the middle of the night, and forgetting caution, one and all turned their heads on their craning necks to witness the captain's reaction.

They almost missed it. He was in motion, his rolling gait catching up to the stairs, the plumes on his magnificent hat rippling in his haste. His eyes bore the glitter his men had witnessed time and again before boarding to plunder a rich prize of a ship. Hook's posture was supreme, his jaw jutted, and he barely smiled. He placed one foot on the stair and thrust his hand out, reaching to escort her. As she descended to the deck she smiled on him, and it was his answering smile—the one with a kiss that hung waiting—that finally gave evidence of his emotion. Clearly, he believed this woman to be his soul.

It was when she accepted his support that the inside of her right hand became visible, blood-red, stained and in contrast to her beauty, a blot, like the mark that marred the captain's own perfection. Barbaric, it appeared incongruous with her loveliness—an intriguing hint of the mysteries she cloaked.

Jill looked up at Hook. Her clear voice touched all his men, though her words embraced him alone. "Captain. Sir. I thank you for the jewels."

"You honor me, Madam, by wearing them. You honor me also by your choice of color. I thank *you*." His smile and something else matched her own. . . . "Forget-me-not blue." Their identical eyes exulted.

Her expression shifted subtly then, as she settled her red hand on her gun. "And we both carry our pistols. Two halves of a perfectly matched set."

Hook bowed. "Not unlike ourselves." He moved to turn toward the assembled sailors. But Jill was a consummate storyteller; she knew her audience. She touched his shoulder and drew him back, and he fell into her kiss. The silence broke into cheers, and only afterward did she allow him to turn his back to her to address his jocular and expectant crew. Then, in habit born of instinct, she surveyed the surroundings for signs of peril while he stepped forward.

"Ship's company! I would have you recognize yet another new shipmate. Your mistress, and my lady." His hook cut an elegant gesture in the air and his lip curled just enough. Even the new men didn't miss the velvet threat in his voice. "And she will be respected as such." He turned to present her. "Red-Handed Jill."

The men snatched off their hats to wave them, they whistled and hollered. Their captain faced them all with both dignity and elation, experiencing for the first time in his legendary career the triumph of unity aboard his ship, his own *Jolly Roger*. These were his men, and they were ready to celebrate, stamping and shouting out their glee; but in the next moment they stuttered to silence, the expressions on their faces transforming from jubilance to horror. Nibs, Tom, and Lightly lowered their jaws in disbelief. Nothing in Wendy's stories had prepared them for this. Rowan's stolid frame went rigid. Mr. Smee, watching within the doorway to the cabin, marooned his grin there and lurched forward along the companionway, gripping the rail at last to hurtle his bulk down the stairs.

All eyes had turned toward Jill again, for behind the captain's back, her face hardened to an icy satisfaction. Only her eyes flamed as she bared her teeth and yanked her pistol from her sash. Her pirate lover with his quick reflexes swiveled around and his visage transformed from victory to astonished rage as he realized that the pistol with which he had gifted this lady now hung suspended in her scarlet hand—and pointed at his head.

Louder and more ominous than the stomp of Smee's boots on the boards, the click of the hammer resounded through the waiting ship. And in the space of a heartbeat, before any man could stop her, Jill squeezed the trigger and fired. And as her captain fell away, she tossed her gun into her left hand, seized its companion from his own belt, and fired that, too.

In two blasting concussions, Red-Handed Jill had proven to the astounded company assembled there on the deck of her own fearsome pirate ship that her legend was true, as well. She was a crack shot, and she left terror in her wake.

With a vague realization that she had somehow learned to be careful, Jewel concealed herself among the root walls of the hideout. It was an unsettling feeling, matching the others she traded in her heart today.

In increasing distress, she watched Peter dig the two green apples from his pouch and position them on the table. He grasped the sword hilt, raised the blade to his face, straight up, and turned his back to the fruit, marching three paces as if preparing for a duel. Whirling back to the table, he impaled one of the apples. He grabbed it and twisted the sword, sliding the apple up and down the blade, watching as the tender insides oozed to the floor. Jewel could smell the tang of the juice. When Peter withdrew the blade, the sticky drippings ran down it, coating it with a film of fairy sleeping draught. He flicked the seeds off, laughing as they flew through the air. One hit the wall and stuck not far above the fairy. Her forehead furrowed while panic shoved every other feeling out of her heart. But she no longer feared discovery; she had taken care so he couldn't see her. Rather, a bigger struggle grew within her small space of a heart, a conflict it had no room to contain, and Jewel was in agony.

Peter had smeared the potion generously. Jewel knew that too much of this sleeping draught would make a fairy sleep forever. And she had never witnessed its effect on people. What might it do to a man? Her man!

The boy dropped the savaged apple and thrust the sword in his belt. He whipped his dagger free, plunged it in the other apple, and did the same to it. As Peter tucked the knife into its sheath, his sly smile spread across his lips and Jewel's worries compounded with his words.

"If I can't use fairy dust, I'll use fairy medicine. Oh, the cleverness of me!"

Red-Handed Jill held the pistol at arm's length. Dirty gray smoke rose from its muzzle to twist its way into nothingness. The eyes of all aboard the *Roger* followed it upward as the echo of her shots resounded in staccato over the deck and across the water, diminishing until only the snap of whipping flags could be heard. It became the whipping of a monstrous tail beating the air, and an agonized hissing ejected from an open throat.

Captain James Hook stretched out flat on the boards, rolling away from the beast. He abandoned his hat and its jaunty feathering to be crushed by the brutal weight that slammed onto the deck, at the spot he had fallen as he dodged the shots—his Jill's redeeming shots. The ship shook with the blow, the animal grunted forcefully, and Jill stumbled forward to keep her balance. Now the tail of the crocodile slammed against the gunwale. The open jaws waved, lashing out with raking teeth toward Jill and the scent of her lover. Blood streamed from the sockets of its two empty eyes.

Jill backed from the swinging snout, shoving Hook's burning pistol into her sash and drawing her dagger. It felt small in her hand, and she bent and parried, her eyes darting over the hide, searching for the strategic point to stab. But Smee finally stumbled to the bottom of the steps, and he reached out with both hands to snatch Jill off her feet, dragging her up the stairs and out of harm's way. Clutching her knife and her pistol, she stared wildly toward her captain. On reaching the top step she strained against Smee, who, sure of the captain's wishes, only gathered her more securely in his arms.

Hook sprang to his feet and he drew his sword singing from its sheath. The crocodile rose up and swung its head in his direction, smelling its irresistible prey, tempted even in its pain. It lunged at him. Hook's eyes blazed red. Fixing them on the monster, he gripped his weapon in his one good hand with its sparkling jewels. Loosing a long wordless yell, he hoisted his blade and slashed it at last across the throat of the crocodile. He allowed the force of his motion to spin him around, his coat flaring about him, and he directed the bloody point forward to plunge it with all his weight into the heart of his surging enemy.

Skewered upon the blade, the crocodile belched and lurched again. Hook's face contorted while he planted his feet wide and leaned, his hand edging close to the hideous teeth as in its lust, the croc drove the rapier deeper into its body. The animal lunged once more, then stopped. The thrashing subsided and it collapsed, its jaws snapping closed one last time, condemned to silence for all eternity.

Hook relaxed his stance and straightened, inhaled, then with a gratified smile, dragged his blade from the carcass. In savage sensuality, he lingered over it, deriving pleasure from the yielding of his enemy's flesh. When it was free, he raised his sword and looked up and down its length. Then he stared at the beast.

Mr. Smee released Jill from his hold. Hook swung around and, breathing again, raised reddened eyes to meet her earnest gaze. Slowly, their faces smoothed and their expressions cleared. Hook hung his rapier on his claw, lifted his hand, and with a graceful flourish, saluted her. And amid the uproar that erupted from the throats of their shipmates, relief sank into their perfectly matched hearts. Together, Hook and Jill had killed the beast—the beast that had stalked them.

Over the bobbing sea of congratulatory heads, they nodded to one another, once. And they read each other's thought.

One left.

Duel on Deck

Of all the emotions battling through her heart today, Jewel had only one left. The problem was she felt it for two people. And very awkwardly, she was feeling it for both of them at the same time. Her master, and her boy. She acknowledged it; she needed to love them both. But her heart hadn't burst apart yet. It was expanding. It hurt.

Peter had kicked the lion hide to the floor. Now, while Jewel spied from the cavern wall, he snatched the pelt and bundled it up. He slipped behind the tree chute and Jewel's jaw dropped in surprise as he pried the back of the hollow trunk open to reveal an unsuspected cupboard. Peter stuffed the hide into it and before shutting the door, he pulled out a knife. Watching shrewdly now, Jewel supposed this hiding place was where her master's rapier had been stowed for so long.

The boy grasped the knife in one hand and a hank of his hair in the other. He sawed at the hair, cutting until it was roughly the length he kept it before. It was untidy, but it was Peter. Straddling a pile of golden clippings and mutilated apples, he shook his head, satisfied with the feel of it. At last he was ready. Peter drew back his fist, then flung the knife. It spun through the air, striking the wall with a thump and a shower of dirt. Jewel shuddered as the knife quivered, the point inches above the opening of her niche. Peter stared at it, puffing out his chest. Setting his face in a grim smile, he swiveled and swept up the chute, a golden, green-eyed fury, the sword at his side scraping wood as he went.

Jewel flickered out of the tangled roots. With a spate of music, she shivered her shoulders, then reached out to catch the cascade of fairy dust. Trying to calm her anxious breathing, she hesitated before blowing on the powder. Within moments she controlled herself and sent the warning to her master. As she blew, her wrinkled wings illuminated, and the hedonistic heat began to pump through her veins. Her eyelids wanted to close to indulge in its rapture, but she couldn't stop to luxuriate. She had to move. But first she clapped her hands together, trapping the dust. None must be found here in Peter's lair. She blinked and forced herself into action, her aching heart fluttering as madly as her wings. Hoping Time would be with her, she launched herself toward the entrance.

She inhaled moist air from the woods, dispelling the lingering languor of her summoning, then she streaked over the trees toward Neverbay as if her own life depended on it. Maybe it did!

Once upon a time, Tinker Bell would have taken poison for Peter. Today, Jewel would take it *from* him, if she had to.

The celebration aboard the *Jolly Roger* was cut short. Hook tore at the air with his claw and his boatswain hollered, "Avast, lads! Let the captain speak!"

Jill tucked her weapons away and swept her skirts aside, making her way down to the deck to take her place at the captain's side. Still on guard for her, Smee followed at her heels. Nibs, Tom, Lightly and Rowan approached too, more cautiously, to stare down at the dreaded crocodile and look in awe upon its slayer. He presented his bloody rapier to Tom, who pulled out his oiled polishing cloth and wiped it clean.

Hook raised his head, commanding more loudly than necessary so that all hands—below and above—would hear his order. "Mr. Smee. Change the watch."

"Aye, Sir." Smee turned to Mason. "Up you go!"

Jill startled as a clang of metal hit the deck. It rolled, sending shards of glass spinning toward her feet. The spyglass.

Hook didn't blink. He'd seen it coming. He was still staring at the crow's nest.

Mr. Cecco was looking down, clutching the ratlines, the bracelets on his arms glaring in the sun. He swung out and descended, moving quickly but reluctantly. Mason passed him on the way up, shaking his head. "Bad luck, mate." By the time he set his feet on the boards, Cecco's swarthy face was sallow. His jewelry jingled as he made a sweeping bow. He dared to speak first.

"Captain, I apologize. I deeply regret my failure to watch for the crocodile. I should have given warn—"

"Mr. Smee." Hook turned his back on the sailor. "Kindly have the carcass removed."

Not one of the company could deny that Cecco was a strong man, but at the captain's words his striking features blanched. Jill's color deepened, and her face set as she addressed the captain. "Sir." She spoke through her teeth, staring at Cecco. "I want the hide."

"Very well. It shall be yours. Mr. Cecco. You may do my lady the favor of flaying this beast. She has need, I believe, of a pair of boots for her lovely feet."

Cecco's face relaxed in relief. "Aye, Sir!"

But among his crew, Hook's treacherous courtesy was legend. He smiled. "And by all means, take your time, Mr. Cecco. Because all the while you are performing this admirable service for your mistress, it is my especial wish that you should anticipate the flaying *you* will receive. At the hands of our very capable, very thorough Mr. Smee." The captain's chilly regard transferred itself to his boatswain. His jaw clenched. "The *instant* the job is finished."

Mr. Smee's nod was curt, his lips a frozen line. "Aye, Sir. It'll be done." He was just the man for the job. Cutting and stitching.

"Mr. Tootles," Hook commanded. "Fetch the cat."

It lasted only an instant, but Cecco saw it. So did Hook. Out of habit, Tom looked to his mother for sanction of the captain's command. It had become second nature for the boys to seek her approval of Pan's more dubious orders. But now Jill regarded Tom impassively, even coolly, yielding to him no indication of her opinion. In the next second, Tom checked himself and hurtled away to the armory, making up for his mistake by speed.

Bowing again, the handsome Italian seized his opportunity, applying every ounce of charm at his disposal. "My lady. *Bellezza.* As the captain says, you are my mistress. Such a fair one must have a heart to match her countenance. You will surely demonstrate your compassion, and speak for me?"

Hook's eyes narrowed. He watched Jill closely. Tom's boots pounded the deck in his haste to return, and a moment later he offered the handle of the cat-o'-nine-tails to Mr. Smee.

Jill shifted her gaze from Cecco to Tom. Slowly, she opened her crimson hand and held it out. "Mr. Tootles. Thank you." Her hand closed on the cat and she smiled on Cecco. "Mr. Cecco. Your words are beautifully chosen. And you are correct; I have every intention of acting fairly. I *will* speak for you." No one dared utterance, but the sailors rolled their eyes to observe the captain's darkening displeasure. Only Mr. Cecco's dread was allayed.

"*Grazie*, my lady."

"I speak for you when I say I feel certain you do not mean to question the captain's authority." The lady's smile turned cold.

Relief vanished from Cecco's face. He demurred, gesturing. "No . . . no, Lady. I meant only—"

"Because if I believed you did, before seeing you excused I would request that our captain allow me to administer your punishment—*myself.*" She paused for effect, then lowered the whip so the knotted ends dangled on her feet. The leather tingled on her flesh, sending a thrill surging upward. She turned pointedly to Hook. "Sir, you are most kind to promise me those boots."

A murmuring arose to die down just as quickly, and although Cecco's broad shoulders slumped, his dusky eyes followed her like all the others', and fired with admiration.

Grim but satisfied, Hook removed the cat from her hand. "Not at all. And there will be no need for you to exert yourself." He tossed it to Smee. "Our boatswain will handle it."

"Yes, I trust Mr. Smee. His loyalty is beyond reproach. I also trust that he and all my shipmates know, if they didn't before, that the thing I hold most dear is my captain's life." She sent a questioning look to

Smee, who nodded firmly.

"Aye, Madam, my apologies. Force of habit." Smee's gaze traveled purposefully among the men and he raised his voice. "We'll none of us doubt it again!"

"Nor will I, my love." Hook wound his arm around her waist and swept her toward the companionway, indicating to the four young men that they should follow. They obeyed, shaking their heads and breathing freely again as the tension aboard the *Roger* found release. Jill heard Smee bellowing as she ascended the steps.

"Back to your positions! We've yet another battle to fight!" And amid the jumble of aye-ayes and the hurrying footsteps, the odd-assorted family adjourned to the captain's quarters.

"And so I ask you again. Would you have me kill him?"

Jill sat in the captain's chair leaning her elbow on the warm, silky surface of the desk, her eyes glistening with unshed tears and her red hand on her forehead. She had remained calm throughout the telling of Lightly's tale. She listened in silence to every word, accepting her own role in its unfolding horror. But she refused shame. She garnered its lesson instead.

Hook had sent her sons away, his sober young crewmen to their duties and the Indians with their black-painted faces to their people. They had all fulfilled their obligations, and more. They were good men.

"Kill him? I will know when I see him." She slapped the desk and sat up, suddenly fierce. "I may do it myself!"

"I'll not begrudge you that pleasure. Indeed, I go so far as to recommend it."

"And you knew what he was doing?"

"I suspected he was eliminating the older boys, thinning out his own crew. It suited my needs," he gathered her up from his chair, "until I needed you."

"And then you placed us all under your protection."

He held her chin and forced it up. "And have been well rewarded for my pains."

"If I had known the truth, you wouldn't have had to fight for me."

"The fight was rewarding as well." His thumb caressed the corner of her mouth, where her kiss used to hide. "But I did warn you about him. You didn't believe in me."

"No, I was living a fairy tale. Yet I suspected a mystery. . . . Nothing close to the truth! How very near Lightly came to death."

Hook felt his eyes burn as he viewed the scar at her throat. "Every bit as close as you, my love."

"Yes. But to harm his own band of boys, the boys he named and raised." She shook her head. "Pan must surely never be allowed to grow up. He would make a vicious man."

Hook's words were steeped in irony, "He comes by it naturally, however."

"Imagine what he heard, that morning he ran away from home. What must they have said to one another?"

"My murderous father, and our cheat of a mother? Until the fatal day, they were discreet in front of the servants. But I assure you, there was nothing I didn't hear."

"He claims he went back home once, and found a baby boy in his place."

"No doubt a new family in the house. He wouldn't have known the difference."

"How very sad." But it was the thought of her own motherly affection for her boys that made her breath shudder. Her lover's arms took possession of her, and he comforted her. And she wept into his fine linen handkerchief for the poor Lost Boys. Someone had to mother them, at the last.

At length Hook lifted his cheek from her hair. "You will soon have your opportunity to change his story." With a satisfied smile, he reached for the carved crystal vial on the desk. The fairy's dust glowed brilliantly, transmuted once again to a royal peacock blue. Hook and Jill drew apart. Their eyes met, and matched its brilliance. "The fairy's warning has come. Pan approaches!"

"He thinks to tame us!"

"To slay us."

Mr. Smee had already furnished the item Jill ordered. She slid it off the desk. "Captain, I require your indulgence."

He raised an eyebrow. "What is your wish?"

"I've just one, insignificant request." She angled her head. "Promise me . . ."

"Anything, my love."

"About Pan."

Hook regarded her, questioning, then his features relaxed and he smiled. He had never admired her more than at this moment. Truly, the woman was his mistress. For with eyes half closed and a smile that could melt gold, she sidled up to him. With one finger of one red hand, she stroked his velvety shoulder, and Red-Handed Jill did what no woman, save herself, would ever do again.

She commanded him.

"Don't touch Pan, Hook. He's mine!"

Jewel had no trouble catching up to Peter. Her wings seemed to exert more force as she beat them. They were stronger! Each stroke sent her sailing farther through the air. She streamed along, lagging just enough behind so that he wouldn't notice her. He never looked back anyhow; it wasn't Peter's way.

The exquisite sword whipped through the air at his side, glinting with sunlight, the same bright sunlight that blinded Hook before, to Peter's advantage. Or disadvantage, now, Jewel thought. That battle, the one that maimed her master, still raged. Below the boy and the fairy the sea shimmered, and the pirate ship buoyed into sight. Peter grinned. Jewel's spirits sank.

The colorful clothing of pirates caught the morning light, bedecking the *Jolly Roger* with a cheerful show of force. Men lined the rail, evenly spaced and surrounding the deck, each exhibiting a blade in his hand and a smiling mouthful of teeth. Three men hunched over Long Tom, one holding a flaming torch from which an acrid smoke snaked upward. The red Irishman manned the bow, and the muscular sailor sporting jewelry and dark red stripes on his back stood stiff at his post beside him. Even the crow's nest was fortified. Two men perched there, with pistols in their belts and two daggers drawn. The sound of Mason's voice flew over the water as he pointed with his knife.

"Ahoy! It's the lad, to starboard, Cap'n!"

As he ranged lower, Peter assessed the situation. The Jolly Roger flapped in the breeze, and below it a new flag, two mismatched bloody hands. Peter smirked. That flag was vile, like Hook himself. Then his expression waxed fierce. In whose blood had Hook dipped to paint it?

He searched the deck for his Wendy and his boys. In the center of the ship played a scene that puzzled Jewel, but fortified Peter's resolve.

Not surprisingly, Hook was prepared for his coming. The captain stood before the mainmast, two hearty pirates flanking him with swords drawn as he casually chucked the point of his rapier under the lady's chin. She stood in proud resistance, her back up against the mast and her hands behind her. She wore a new dress, not green this time like Peter's eyes, but dark blue like her own. She was still armed; Peter saw her pistol, and his own dagger pricked her sash. She was even smiling at her pirate captor—she was no ordinary girl! And bloodstains smudged the deck before her. What a story she would tell the boys tonight! Smiling broadly, Peter circled the mizzenmast, crowing.

Alighting on the edge of the crow's nest, Jewel wondered how best to warn her master of the potion that coated Peter's weapons. He had ordered her to stay hidden from the boy, even aboard the ship. Mason greeted her genially, "Miss Jewel! Come to see the sport?" Emitting a nervous jingle, she hunched over the railing, her elbows up and her wings down, to watch for her opportunity. But Mason interrupted her efforts with a disturbing observation. He nudged Noodler, in his vehemence nearly dislodging the man's tri-cornered hat. "Look, mate. The fairy's grown!"

Jewel's eyes opened in shock. She rotated to gape at Noodler's bizarre hand reaching toward her. Making no move to grasp her, he merely held up his fingers to measure. "She *is* bigger! Look, Miss Jewel, an inch at least."

Jewel did look, and it was true. The thumb to which she had clung that day to recover her wings had shrunk. She flattened her hand and patted her chest. Her heart didn't pain her so badly anymore. It, too, must have grown! She loved *two* people.

And she feared for two people. The sound of Peter's crowing terrified her, as did the answering laughter that surged from Hook. He flung it up to Pan, a challenge, and then he smiled.

"Well, Pan, so you've come at last! To rescue your ladylove. You're a bit late, boy. She *is* a lady, now. A lady pirate. Do you still want her?"

Peter settled on the yardarm halfway up the mizzenmast, legs apart, folding his arms and completely at ease in the air. "You know I do!"

"Yet you claimed you'd rather see her dead than turned pirate."

"So I would! But I'll tame her."

Jill lost her smile and clenched her hands behind her back. The men arranged all round the deck stirred, murmuring disapproval.

"All by yourself, boy? Where are your new friends, the Indians? Not enough fairy dust to bring them along, too?"

Peter's comfy stance went rigid. "You forced my boys to talk, then." He unfolded his arms and balled his fists. "I saw your bloody flag. What have you done to them?"

"Why, they are right here, Pan. I haven't harmed them in any way. Don't you recognize them?" With his hook, he gestured toward the two pirates at his sides. His sword point still played at the lady's throat.

Peter squinted down at Nibs the Knife and Tom Tootles, and he laughed. "You don't fool me! They're no boys of mine. Those are your own men." A chortle arose from the pirates.

Hook smiled in satisfaction and waited for silence. "Exactly." He watched the grin slide from Peter's face. "But I'll send them up to you. With your famous charm you may win them back." He jerked his head and the two young men pushed off the deck to fly up to Peter's perch.

Peter drew his dagger as Nibs and Tom grabbed at ropes and settled on either side of him. Nibs adapted to the yards as easily as he used to light in the trees, but Tom's bulk set the rigging to swaying. Peter kept his footing with no trouble and looked up at first one, then the other. His brows drew together as recognition dawned. "I still say you're no boys of mine! You're pirates now. I won't waste my time trying to take you two back after all." He looked to the lady. "I've got better things to do."

With twice his customary respect, Nibs called, "What are your orders, Captain?" Peter opened his mouth to respond with a command, then his eyebrows rose. He saw that Nibs had swung out and was looking down at Hook.

The rigging rocked and Tom bellowed as he balanced, "Shall we chase him off, Sir, or shall we leave him to die in the croc's grotto . . . " His cold stare reproached Peter. "Like our brothers."

Peter's face grew defiant. "I told you none of my boys has ever grown up. This is why!" And he hurled himself and his dagger toward Tom. Tom expected it; he hoisted his sword in time to deflect the blade. Peter fell back in the air, then twisted to launch himself at Nibs.

"We're not children anymore, Pan." Nibs' cutlass threatened and Peter pulled up short at its tip. "We know what you've done, and we want none of your make-believe. You'll never get any of us back."

Hook's velvety voice drifted up. "You seem to be all alone, Pan. If you please, Mr. Tootles."

Tom hovered at Peter's back. "Captain Hook has fixed it so your last friend won't help you, either." Peter spun to face him, then rolled his eyes upward to see where Tom's blade pointed.

Peter dropped all expression. High in the rigging spread a new sail, swelling in the wind. A green one, stretched uncomfortably. It strained at its moorings as the breeze battered it. Only the tail swung loose, as if the beast still lived and strove to swim away the way it came, on waves of air. The wind carried a hint of the stench still. Peter knew it. What was left of it.

"The crocodile!"

And he smiled. "At least it was loyal to the death." He aimed a piercing look at Nibs, who returned it.

"If we'd stayed loyal to you, we'd be dead, too."

The boy's eyes flashed with pride. "But I gave you a glorious childhood, in Paradise!"

Tom and Nibs looked at each other, and laughed. Tom said, "You did! But now we're sorry for you, stuck there all by yourself."

Nibs had recaptured his good humor. "You'll never know how glorious growing up can be. Ask our mother, she can tell you." The crewmen slapped their thighs and guffawed.

Hook struck an elegant pose, leaning on his sword. "Excellent point, gentlemen. Take your positions. The lady in question begs to be heard."

The young sailors abandoned the yardarm and leapt to the deck to stand guard at their captain's back. Peter wrapped his legs around the mast and slid lower, seeking a better view of his Wendy, but she shook her head at him with that look that warned him to be careful. "Peter!" True to form, he ignored her caution, swooping down to land on the deck three paces from her, and from Hook. Peter shifted his dagger, gripping it in his left hand to rest his right on his sword.

"Don't worry, Wendy. I'll set you free."

"Oh, no, Peter. I'm not the least bit worried. I knew you would come." Her smile was warm and gracious. She could melt him with it. But her heart was cold. "Now I'll be able to finish your story."

"This is the part where I win the *Roger* for you, Wendy!" A lusty laugh blew among the *Roger*'s crew.

Jewel circled down from the crow's nest to flutter uncertainly behind Peter, watching her two loves. Hook frowned at her, but she remained suspended, pleading with her eyes. Her captain barely shook his head. When she persisted, he curled his lip in irritation. Hanging his sword on his hook, he reached into his inner coat pocket to draw out a vial. "Mr. Nibs. Take charge of this and stand by for further orders." He tossed it to his sailor. Jewel stiffened and covered her mouth with her hands. Disregarding her, Hook took up his rapier again. "I told you before, Pan. You may call the lady Jill Red-Hand now."

Peter's green eyes sparked as he drew his sword. "She'll always be my Wendy. I've come to get her back. Use the hook I gave you to cut her loose—now."

Jewel's heart wasn't big enough yet to admit the Wendy, under any name. Peter's determination to reclaim the girl jarred her jealous nature, but jealousy wasn't reason enough to risk her master's displeasure. Jewel was desperate to inform him of his peril. What should she do?

She must risk it. He had to know! Gathering her courage, she pressed her lips together and chimed, loudly.

Peter whirled to find his fairy. Smiling, he grabbed for her. "Tink! You're just in time!" With her new speed she dodged his hand, then floated almost near enough to touch.

Hook leveled his blue stare at Jewel, menacing. His admonition fell soft and cool, like snow. "If the fairy is wise, she will not interfere."

Jewel flitted to Peter's shoulder, her light burning to match the intensity of his face as he watched Hook and Jill. Appealing to her master, Jewel plunged her hand in her pocket, the one that once held poison. Then she pointed to Peter's blade, violently shaking her head. Hook's eyes darkened with suspicion and he studied his sword in Peter's hand.

Jill eyed the fairy while a note of doubt entered her voice. "I suggest you send her away. She may do something foolish."

Again Peter opened his mouth to answer, but Hook interjected, "Like sprinkling fairy dust on my lady! But Jill is not bound, Pan. I have already 'cut her loose,' as you so eloquently phrase it. Since she can no longer fly, she has chosen to sail—with me, not you, as her captain. I must thank you for making her escape impossible at precisely the critical moment. I do appreciate your assistance. You've been so helpful in advancing my plans all along. . . . You've been like a brother to me!"

With a quick intake of breath, Jill drew Peter's attention, and Jewel's as well. The sprite who had used to be Tinker Bell perceived that this was no longer the girl she despised. Like the fairy herself, she was mysteriously transformed by her master's influence, and for the better.

Peter gave the lady an assessing look before he grinned at her. "I see you've gotten your share of booty! A new dress, and a nice necklace. What did he make you give him for those? Another kiss?" Jill's eyes flared. Her shipmates exchanged lewd glances, but didn't dare further.

Hook clenched his teeth. "Another man would slit your throat for that, Pan. But I will tell you that a woman's regard cannot be purchased or plundered. *That* precious treasure is earned."

"And hatred is, too. I challenge you, Hook! To a duel. Winner takes all!"

Jewel jumped from Peter's shoulder to hang in the air, ringing with alarm. Hook's eyes remained on Peter. "Calm yourself, Jewel. I won't have to hurt him—badly." He smiled. "I'll leave that to the ladies." His sword hummed as it whipped up and plunged at Peter. The boy sprang backward, parrying, and leapt up high. Catcalls from the pirates showed their scorn for this tactic. Peter scowled and lowered himself. He dove at Hook, their two blades flashing in the sun just as they had done so long ago, clanging together, beating up sparks of sunshine.

Jill's face was serene; she set herself against care. Resolute, she smiled as she watched her champion, transfixed by his skill. The fingers of her left hand toyed with her glittering necklace. Once upon a time, someone told her she worried too much. She didn't worry anymore.

Nibs and Tom backed away to make room for the duelists and stood sentry on either side of Jill. Knowing Peter's tricks, they held their swords ready. The other pirates kept up their banter, urging their captain on against his longtime adversary.

Fighting with language, too, Hook taunted Peter, "I see you've brought me my rapier back. A pity you can't return my hand as well. But I'll make do. . . . Jill has given me hers." He thrust again to engage Peter's weapon, parried it, and wheeled, his silver sword belt blazing. The jewels on his fingers flashed as he stopped Peter's blade and hooked it. Then he stood firm, scratching the razor edge of his claw down its length. Peter gritted his teeth as the jolts rasped against his sword and shuddered through his arm.

Bobbing above him, Jewel shook her head in panic. Did Peter realize his enemy was scraping away the apple's nectar? The master had gleaned enough potion on his hook to close Peter's eyes. How much did Peter's blade retain? More than enough to drop a fairy. And the dagger was fully potent still. Peter wielded it in his left hand as he battled with Hook. He jabbed it at the man now, but the claw had already released him and Hook's sword pushed the boy away.

Peter couldn't find another chance to strike Hook's flesh. He couldn't reach him. He'd have to knock the sword from Hook's hand—or slice away the hand holding the sword! "I'll fetch her hand back from you, Hook!" Brimming with mischief, Peter bounded skyward. He set his feet against the mast and pushed off again, arching back to dive with all the force in his strong young body, hardened by adventure. Swinging the blinding-bright rapier in his scarred right arm, he hollered, and targeted Hook's last remaining wrist.

Jewel clapped her hands to her eyes, guarding against the glare. But she could still hear. A blade screamed as it cut the air. Her master raised his voice in a peal of rage, and metal met flesh with a horrid, dull smack. One sword clattered to the deck. The pirates exclaimed; Jill gasped.

Then something limp and heavy slapped the boards, and Jill shouted, "No! Not another one!"

Jewel dragged her hands from her face and gaped. The three figures stood on the blood-smeared deck, their breathing unsteady, their shoulders heaving. Peter posed in his bold posture in front of the master, his face twisted, but his green eyes glowing with expectation. He clenched his tainted dagger in his fist, threatening to stab through the gorgeous fabric of Hook's coat, aiming for the heart.

Hook's eyes glowed red. His claw hung poised to rip Peter's throat. Red-Handed Jill had shoved herself from the mast. In both her hands, she'd caught the captain's wrist—his left wrist. She held it upraised as if he were wounded. Jill struggled to hold him stationary while the pirates crouched to spring, cold steel raised. Then Jewel saw Hook's sword blazing above Jill, still gripped firmly in an uninjured hand.

Weak with relief, Jewel spied the second object she'd heard fall. It was not Hook's last hand after all, but the whip Jill had been hiding behind her back when she leaned against the mast. It now lay curled, potent but dormant—and beyond Jill's reach.

Jill stared at Peter, thinking fast, then she stopped struggling and looked to Hook. Her face cleared. In a guarded motion, she lowered Hook's arm, and his sword along with it. She released him. She stepped over Peter's rapier where it lay harmless on the deck, and the woman placed herself where she had stood so often in her heart: between the boy and the man.

At the mercy of their weapons.

Taming the Boy

J ill faced Peter with her back toward Hook. The weapons—dagger and claw—hung only inches from the bare skin of her neck. She seized a breath and planted her feet on the boards. Her voice rang clear, and calm as death.

"No. I've decided. No more boys will die."

"Hook will die." Peter's empty sword hand throbbed from Hook's blow as he jerked his head at her. "Move away, so I can finish him."

"No, Peter. I'm going to finish it. The story of Peter Pan, Wendy, and Captain Hook."

Hook remained wrathful, his sword at his side and his poisonous claw upheld. "You must back away from him, Jill. Do not trust him!"

"Let's hear the story," insisted Peter. "It should be good, now that you really know him!" He smirked, ready to listen, but didn't relax his stance. Jewel dangled over them, her gaze darting from hazard to hazard.

"All three of them shed blood, and the feud came to an end. Peter Pan took Captain Hook's hand, Hook slashed Peter's arm, and Wendy bled at wounds from both of them. That story is done."

"It can't be done. No one wins!"

"Everyone wins. We all go on to new adventures."

"But Hook's a pirate." Peter shrugged. "He has to be slain."

His talk didn't shock her any more. "I made up the adventures, for you, and for Hook. I'm as black and as bright as either of you." Her gaze shifted to Peter's dagger, then back to his face. "I accept the consequences." Jill stood firm. She had the audacity to smile. *"I'm* a pirate."

"I'll change that!" Knife in hand, Peter feinted toward the claw and kicked off from the deck. Hook merely snarled, holding himself in check as the boy rose backward into the air and twisted to grasp at Jewel. Quick as he was, she leapt away quicker, evading capture.

"Tink! Give Wendy some fairy dust!"

Hook had kept his word, allowing Jill to handle Peter in her own way, and Jill breathed more easily. She directed her voice upward. *"Both* Peter Pan and Captain Hook dropped the blood feud."

"I don't like your ending."

"You may not like it, Pan, but you hunted me and you chose me. I'm your storyteller. Now I have the end of *your* tale all ready to tell. Come down and hear it."

Peter shook his head, his tousled hair shining. He tucked his dagger in his belt and posed, hands on hips. "You can't make me!"

Jill's half-smile graced her lips. "All right. I'll tell you *my* story again, while I . . . wait for you." She began to pace the deck, watching him, keeping her scarlet secret in her fist. Without losing sight of the boy, Hook set his boot on the fallen rapier and shoved so that it scuttled toward Tom, who snatched it up. Allowing Jill Red-Hand room to work, the captain and his men backed away to stand sentinel at the rail. Jewel sped to the shelter of the mizzenmast yardarm and perched, alert. She attended Jill's words, wondering how that smile had come to match her master's, and hoping to discover at last why he strove to win this lady.

"You remember. The story of Red-Handed Jill. I'm known for my prowess in swordplay, and I'm a crack shot. The first time I fired my pistol I shot the eye of a parrot at fifty paces. And that's how I brought the crocodile down."

Peter glanced at her gun and his face darkened. Jewel eyed the weapon, too, and nodded to herself, remembering the parrot feathers in the Twins' hands that day. But surely the master had men enough to fight alongside him?

Jill strolled to the mast. "It's the croc's blood that stains this deck. The Pirate King and I killed that beast, the one that stalked us both.

But it's the blood of the beast that stalked *me*, mixed with my own, that stains my hand." She bent to gather up the leather coils she dropped during the duel. Drawn into the tale in spite of himself, Peter hovered, rapt. As Jill had anticipated, he was playing his part in the story.

"I cut myself a lion's tail for a belt. My shipmates tell me I'm beautiful, too." Peter beamed. Jill dropped the loops of leather to slap and snake along the boards as she shook out her lash.

Jewel studied Jill's face. The girl *had* grown up to be pretty.

"And I've taken to carrying a whip. I use it to bring down anyone who tries to tame me." She flared the whip to one side and snapped it in the air, locking Peter in her deep blue gaze as it played. Jill was pleased; supreme in his self-confidence, Peter hadn't stirred. His strength was his weakness, and she used it against him.

"And now I've gotten out to sea and joined up with pirates. Of course, as I'm a lady, I had to prove my valor first." Hook smiled complacently. The crewmen passed looks to one another, chuckling, and Jewel observed them. They seemed in accord with their master's opinion of the lady. Laughing at Jill's last words, Tom Tootles remembered the first time he'd heard this story, and he winked at Nibs with an understanding he now owned completely.

Jill's lips curved as she coiled the whip again. Still concealing her crimson stain, she slid her hand down the long leather grip. The sunlight on her necklace needled Peter's eyes. "The Pirate King doesn't even try to tame me. We're about to sail together and have lots of experiences—what you call adventures." Jill sauntered to the rail. "And the Pirate King . . . "

He surrounded her whip hand with his own. His eyes took hold of her and his silky voice completed her sentence, speaking low, to Jill, "Has fallen in love with her and made her his Queen."

Peter grimaced, but Jewel popped upright. She blinked. Now she knew! Jill had lost the train of the story for a moment, enchanted by the magic of her lover's words, but now she had recovered and stood unashamed as her fingers caressed his cheek, lingering on his beard. Jewel caught the luminance in the man's eyes. Like the full moon behind stained glass. Like her own wings! The master wanted Jill to light him up, to touch him, the way he touched Jewel! He wanted the woman for reasons very different from Peter's.

The Pirate Queen roused herself to conclude her tale. "The Pirate King has taken me to Paradise . . . " And they kissed, just like the end of all great stories. Jewel's happy sigh tinkled. Jealousy banished!

The kiss was a bit much for Peter, but Jill knew her audience and pulled away on cue. She resumed her pacing and cracked the whip again. Undaunted, Peter cocked his head. She judged the distance.

"There's only one place for a wonderful boy like you in my story now, Pan. At the happy ending," her smile enticed him just a little lower, "of my lash." She hurled it out, snared his ankle in its grasp and with a sharp tug, reeled him down to the deck. Peter flung out his arms and landed with a thud.

"The end."

Raucous laughter broke from the pirates. Shaking his foot, Peter tried to free his ankle from the coil, shouting over the sailors' hilarity. "I like the story of Wendy better!" He sat bending over his foot as he worked it loose, then scrambled to stand, ignoring the sting of the swelling welt.

"Yes!" Jill gathered her whip again while she stared at him, speaking more quickly. "The one where Wendy grows up, falls in love and sees the world, independent and free."

Peter scowled. "That was never real!"

"Not until now. But I'll finish your story first. This is how it will be—"

"I don't want to hear it. I don't like your stories today!"

"But everything is just that to you, isn't it? Only a story. And it's about you."

Peter brightened. "Then give me the whip and let's go! We can hang it over the mantel. I'll set you free from Hook, no matter what story you had to tell him. I'll let you fly again and you can be my Wendy and tell me tales about us." When the fairy jangled at him from her perch on the yardarm, he tossed his golden head. "And Tinker Bell."

"I can't live in childhood with you any longer. And I've learned I don't want to be entirely free, after all." Jill tucked the whip handle in her sash. She held her wrists out, together, her hands in fists and palms down. "But as you see, I'm not bound by ropes, as you first believed.

I am bound by affection." She turned her fists up. Then, watching his handsome face change, she opened her hands. The scarlet coloring assaulted Peter's eyes. He jerked away, flinching.

She lowered her arms. "Hook told you the truth, Pan. I have chosen to sail. I have chosen him."

Hook stepped to her side, his head at an arrogant angle. He didn't take his eyes off Peter. "Jill. Time to get under way."

"Aye, Captain."

Peter's eyes thinned to slits. His hand slipped to his dagger. Hook tensed and held his weapons ready. Peter shot him a guarded glance. "You're not thinking clearly, Wendy. Hook's done something to you. You're not yourself." Sensing danger, Jewel slid down from the mast to drift closer.

"Yes. I'm not your Wendy any more, if I ever was. I've grown up." She held up her hand, splaying her crimson fingers. "I'm Jill." Peter turned his head away.

Jewel watched her boy suspiciously and glided nearer, so close now that her light reflected in the blade at Peter's belt.

"What's wrong, Pan? You didn't want me to keep secrets from you." Jill gestured toward the top of the mast. "Even our standard proclaims it. And I have far less blood on my hands than you have on yours."

"Pirate blood. What's that matter?" The pirates grew restless, agitating their weapons with sinister jingles. Jewel stared intently at her master.

"And the blood of the boys who broke your impossible law!"

"Better to die nobly than live like a pirate, with no rules!"

Jill lifted her jaw. "I think for myself, now, to decide what is right and what's wrong. And so do our boys. We can be proud of them." She held out her hand to him. "We still have much in common. Let us part today, as friends."

"No. I'll go. When I've cut this hand, too!" Peter's knife flared from his belt to swipe at Jill's red hand. But the fairy knew Peter. She, too, had been thinking for herself, deciding what to do when he acted. Her larger wingspan aided her purpose. Beating blue feathers, Jewel shot through the air to throw her body between Jill and the blade. Her aura pulsed with her heart as she clutched the steel and clung there, causing Peter to halt in mid-swing. Jewel held fast, saving Jill for her master, saving Peter for herself.

Hook lashed out with his claw, snagging Peter's hair as the boy ducked sideways. Snatching her hand back, Jill stepped away unscathed and loosed her whip again. Peter tried to shake the fairy off the dagger. She tightened her grip; her wings drooped. Two drops of blood smeared the edge of the blade. It was Jewel whose hands were cut.

The captain strode forward, hooking Peter by the back of the belt but careful not to cut it in two. He dragged Peter toward him. Driving the point of his rapier into the deck, he set it to stand at attention, within easy reach. Then he seized the boy's hair at the base of the skull, persuading a stretch of neck to lay itself bare. Hook pulled him against his chest, and his claw circled around to threaten that tender throat. Peter Pan was now exactly where the pirate had always wanted him. With a grim smile, Hook hissed in his enemy's ear, "Lower the knife."

But Peter didn't lower it. He stared at it, his eyes filling with panic. Jewel was weakening. Her head lolled to one side, and she was slipping down the bright metal toward his fist. Jill cried out, "Jewel! She's fainting—catch her!" But Peter's left hand was trying to free his hair from Hook's grasp. Seeing Jewel's condition, Hook relented and let go. Deftly, he captured Peter's wrist instead, and twisted the boy's arm behind his back.

And then Peter did lower the knife, and his expression blackened as he looked at Jill. " 'Jewel?' " He could almost read the truth in her eyes. He threw a glance at Nibs to confirm it. A vial full of golden dust shone in the young man's hand. It was glowing like a feeble fire in the wind, flickering. Dying.

Peter clenched his teeth and his breath came in bursts. He looked down at his weapon. Jewel's light was flickering out, too. Peter snapped the dagger forward, flinging the fairy off the blade. "Traitor!"

Unconscious now, she was helpless. Jill's whip thumped on the planks as she dropped it to catch the limp little body. Peter stabbed his knife backward over his shoulder, raking the air at random, reaching for the flesh of his foe. "You've stolen her, you pirate!" he hollered. Hook snarled, yanking his own head and shoulders back.

But amid shouts from the other sailors, Nibs and Tom closed ranks. Tom grabbed Peter's wrist.

Hook's warning came sharp, "Be careful. The blade is poisoned. Remove it."

"Oh!" Jill gasped. She stared at the fairy in her hands. Tom pried the dagger from Peter's grip and flung it overboard. It revolved, flashing, and Jill sighed in relief as it disappeared over the railing, like a silver seabird diving after prey.

Peter squirmed, trying to slither out of the pirate's grasp. "What have you done to my fairy, Hook?"

"What have you done to *my* fairy, Pan? Mr. Nibs, open the vial. Quickly." Nibs drew off the stopper and looked expectantly at Hook. So did they all, and the ship's company fell silent.

"Blow on it, gently. Don't move a grain!"

Anxiously, Nibs held the rim to his lips and blew. The dust was dull now, the lower half of the bottle colored gray. A few of the particles stirred.

Hook tightened his grip on Peter. The boy struggled in his hold, shouting, "She'd be all right if she'd been loyal to me!"

Tom glared. "Like the crocodile?"

Hook ignored them. "Softly! Breathe on it!"

Concentrating, Nibs tried again, more gently. Jill covered the failing fairy with her other hand. The little limbs were growing colder. "Jewel, come back to us."

Every eye on the ship fastened on Nibs. He found it difficult to control his breathing. Jill felt the wings stiffening. Tearing her gaze from Nibs, she looked up at Hook. His face was marked with concern as he oversaw Nibs' efforts. He turned to his servant, commanding her.

"Jewel! Wake now!" At the same moment, the powder in the vial began to brighten. Jill felt the fairy wings soften. Soon they wavered between her palms.

"Stroke her wings. She must feel your touch."

Jill lifted a finger to brush the faded feathers. Little by little, they were illuminated. Working together then, joining in a sense of wonder, Jill and Nibs performed magic. Jewel's wings responded one plume at a time, assuming their former hue. Jill smiled as the fairy stirred, and Jewel smiled weakly to herself. Her wings trembled. She flexed her shoulders, sighing with a grace note. Her back arched, and she breathed deeply, luxuriating with her eyes half open. After a moment, Jewel blinked. Sitting up in Jill's red palm, she looked about her. She gazed quizzically at the lady pirate, searched for her master, then gripped Jill's thumb to stand.

Peter grinned. "Tink! You're back! Come on, I'll take you away from him."

But Jewel paid him no heed. With an air of delicacy, she clung to Jill's thumb; the tiny wounds on her hands pricked. And when she pushed off to fly, she left another dot of red on Jill's hand, and a gift.

A gift of golden dust.

Jill beheld it. She clamped her fingers together and hugged her hand to her breast. She raised her gaze to her Pirate King, and then she laughed. The heaviness slid away. She felt airy again. Light as a cloud! Hook caught her expression and inclined his head.

Jewel hovered in front of Jill and nodded to her. Spreading her wings, she rang out her joy, then flew to Nibs' shoulder. Nibs shoved the stopper in the vial and grinned at the fairy, laughing as her feathers grazed his cheek. "Welcome back, Jewel!"

"Well done. Now, Pan. What shall we do with you?" Hook's claw threatened once more, poised at Peter's throat. "A taste of your own medicine, perhaps? I have a dose right here on my hook, as it happens." The pirates chuckled but the beaten boy, although mute, persevered in his defiant scowl. The fairy maintained a haughty silence.

Jill could barely keep her feet on the deck. "Captain. Whether or not he will admit it, Pan now knows he has lost everyone. He is completely alone. Do you have everything you want, Sir, so you can live happily ever after?" She wanted to fly!

"Have you, Madam?"

The smile came, unbidden. "I believe I do!" Then Red-Handed Jill, the Pirate Queen, brought her thoughts down to earth to fix a bitter gaze on Peter. Sobering, she moved toward him with menace in her eye. Her gaze was drawn to the brilliance of Hook's sword hilt where the sun struck it, and then she turned again to Peter. Reaching out, she fanned her fingers, wrapping them around the grip of the weapon.

"I want vengeance, Pan. For your betrayal of the Lost Boys." With the strength granted by her unity with its master, Jill yanked the point from the planking. "And for betraying me." She guided the tip of the rapier to his throat and stroked it. Peter winced.

"I want you to suffer for what you nearly did to our boys." She pressed the flat of the blade under his jaw. She spat her words. "That is only one of the consequences of your actions." Pushing the steel against his chin, she lifted his head, angling her own as she studied his face—so familiar, so foreign. At last Jill raised her eyes and looked above him, to her lover.

She drew a long breath. "And of all people, it took a pirate to teach me mercy." Dropping the rapier's point to the deck, she regarded Peter once again. "I will allow you to live your story. And I will live mine. Like my pirate, you are a legend, Peter Pan. Legends rarely die . . . but they do grow." As Peter opened his mouth to object, she overrode him. "I don't want you to grow up. What I want for you is to learn. As I am doing."

Peter perked up. "Learn a new story?"

Placing both hands on the hilt of the sword, she leaned on it. "Yes. Your new story. I'll tell it differently from now on." Her deep blue skirts billowed with the sea air, swirling to caress the blade. "Listen, Peter."

Hook relaxed his grip on Peter as the boy stilled, always his habit at story time, to attend Jill's words. Jewel plunked down to sit, folding her legs on Nibs' shoulder and resting her chin on her fists. Ship's company stirred, leaning forward in expectation. They were learning to appreciate the yarns spun by Red-Handed Jill.

"As the blood feud ended, Wendy and the boys grew up and away from Peter Pan. But he went on living happily, having adventures in the Neverland. He never made peace with the pirates or the Indians, but he learned to beware of them. And from that time, any Lost Boys he found, he cared for and raised until they could no longer slide through his front door. When this happened, Peter brought them to the House in the Clearing. He himself was never allowed to enter there, but the young men were welcomed by grown-ups, and guided into their futures. And all on the Island remained forevermore under the protection of a certain sea captain and his lady, who still return from time to time to assure that all is well."

The silence that followed was filled by the yawn of the ship as she tugged at her anchors, stretching and pulling herself awake. A stiff breeze set her flags to snapping and pushed the sea sloshing against her hull. Her sails ruffled along the yardarms like tapping fingers, anxious to be unfurled and spread against the wind. The *Jolly Roger* was ripe to sail.

Jill was ready, too. "Captain, does the new story satisfy you?"

"Perfectly, my love. Your reputation is well deserved." Hook looked down on his captive, savoring victory for one long moment. Then he released his hold on his mother's son.

Peter pulled away from Hook and swiveled to study Jewel. "Tinker Bell?"

She turned up her nose. The boy strode with his accustomed confidence toward her roost on Nibs.

"You have to come back with me."

She chimed threateningly.

"That medicine wasn't meant for you, it was for Hook!"

Not deigning to drop him a note, she blazed.

"You can't be his fairy. You've always been mine."

She turned her back to him and swung her legs around to dangle off the backside of Nibs' shoulder. Her heels thumped, but she watched Peter out of the corner of her eye. Peter perceived it, and grinned.

"All right. I'm sorry."

Her head snapped back and she studied Nibs' big ear. His hair stirred in the hostile draft of her wings.

Peter spun to face Jill, questioning. "Isn't Tinker Bell going to be part of my story any more? Ever?"

"Sir? What are your orders?"

Jewel whipped around to plumb her master's expression, hope lighting her wings. But Hook's aspect was stern. He gestured to Nibs, who returned the vial to his captain's outstretched hand. "Jewel is not at liberty to join you now, Pan. You know very little about her, after all." He pocketed the vial. With sagging feathers, Jewel loosed a dispirited tone. Hook listened to it, then raised his chin and sent a message to Jill.

His thoughts were open to her, and she voiced them. "It is unlikely Pan will gain enough insight to reach accord with such a divine creature. But perhaps, in another chapter, he will be clever enough to pay attention to our Jewel and to learn about her." The divine creature lifted her wings and glowed.

Peter grinned slyly. "I *am* clever!"

With all the grace of her breed, Jewel rose to her feet, casting off to circle Peter once in a sparkling ring. She cruised up to the crow's nest, where Mr. Noodler welcomed her into his hand. He lifted her to the brim of his hat, and she consented to climb aboard to man her position there and take up watch alongside the other sailors. It was her turn for lookout duty.

Hook and Jill watched Peter goggling up at her, a surprised expression on his face. Was he learning already? Jill turned to Hook and presented the hilt of his rapier. "With my compliments." She watched as he sheathed it, then she plucked Peter's dagger from her sash. "Captain, with your permission?"

"You are the storyteller." But he moved to her side to stand guard as Jill held the handle out to Peter.

"I give you your weapon, and I give nothing away." She tucked the bright silver dagger into Peter's sword belt, next to his Wendy pocket, " 'For he was never without his knife.' "

He flashed a smile at her, and she could just see his bright green eyes, almost covered by his golden hair. Like the first time she'd ever seen him.

He laughed. "It was a good idea I had, for Wendy to borrow it when she was captured by pirates!" He secured it, then he sprang from the deck. Jill smiled, getting used to him again. He moved so swiftly through the air that one couldn't distinguish the features that had fascinated his Wendy. Soon he became a familiar blur. And so, unceremoniously, Peter Pan left for home, without looking back.

Jewel looked up from her duty to listen as he crowed. Then she settled in with her shipmates and regarded the horizon, like black Roger above.

The captain's order rang out. "Mr. Smee! Weigh anchor!"

The vigorous reply shot back from the bow. "Aye, aye, Sir! First shift, to your positions! Haul away, lads, and drop sails!" In a chorus of ayes, Hook's men surged into activity. They tucked their weapons away to man the capstans, straining to heave up the dripping anchors. Swarming up the rigging, they unlashed the blossoming canvas, relishing the rock of the *Roger* as she yielded to temptation at last and broke from the arms of the bay. Like their captain, they were men of appetite, as eager as the ship herself to sample the offerings of the open sea.

As Mason deserted the crow's nest, the whistle of a precisely aimed whiplash rose from the deck. Mr. Noodler stole a glance over the rail at the activity below, then with his backward fingers smuggled a flask from his pocket. He turned his eyes upward and cocked his head, but slowly, so as not to jar the sailor in his hat.

"Have a little nip, Miss Jewel?"

Leaning over the brim, she ascertained the direction of her master's attention; a coil of leather snaked itself about his boot, and with a sultry stare, hand over deliberate hand, Jill was reeling him in. Jewel hopped from the hat. Flitting toward the flask, she smiled conspiratorially at Mr. Noodler. From the looks of things, Time was on her side.

The captain's eyes were luminous again. With one ankle tangled in the lash, he leaned his lady against the mast. Jill's red hand had already tossed away the whip handle and was ardently engaged elsewhere.

The master wouldn't be needing his Jewel for quite a while.

Other Oceans

The Pirate Queen retained her dignity with difficulty. She fairly flew to the cabin. Her feet just grazed the boards as she ran over the deck, and engaged not at all the wooden grain of the steps. The pitch of the ship became meaningless as she transformed to a creature of air once again. As if they could fly too, the captain's boots behind her tapped the stairs lightly, and only every other one as he sprang up them to catch her. Slamming the door required only a moment, but turning the key in its lock became a labor to savor as, with deliberation, he turned to her and smiled half-way, suffering her to wait on the anticipated click of the bolt. She nearly dove for him before he ended her torment.

"Sir, you try my patience!"

"Madam. We have all the Time in the world." Leisurely, he discarded his belt and sword. He drew out a handkerchief and wiped his curving blade clean of poison. And then his hook took possession of her, plucking her from the air where she hung, her feet dangling over the carpet. His arms caged her. "A lovely bird, you are. My bird of Paradise." For once he didn't have to bend down to claim her kiss. But still he made her wait. He tilted his head and studied her face. "Open your lips, and speak to me—" But he didn't take it.

She gave it to him. Impatiently, breathlessly, like the very first kiss. And also like the first, she wanted it never to end. Hook stood with his feet apart, solidly on the floor, his own kiss delving in her lips. Weaving his fingers in her hair, he tethered her securely. He was familiar with the ways of fairies now, and surely this winged thing could not be captured except with love, and a steadfast hand.

But hurried as Jill had been to bestow that kiss, she took her time afterward in slipping her hands downward, over his velvety waistcoat and into his pocket, to mine for sparkling treasure. Hook regarded her indulgently. Searching the warm recesses of his person, her ruby fingers lingered until she found the vial and gathered it up. Her eyes shone like the crystal. Holding it out, she asked once again, "Captain, with your permission?"

But his indulgence was at an end. "No." Hook seized her wrist, and dragged her, floating, toward his bunk. A shadow fell over her face as her feet came to rest upon the floor, but Hook was adamant.

"I'll not enter so lightly into the workings of magic. Too many times it has failed me already." He directed her hand to the bed shelf where he compelled her to set the vial down. "We will perform the rite, and afterward I will allow you to fly wherever you will." She smiled solemnly then.

His eyes transfixed her as he eased her pistol from her sash and laid it aside. Gradually, he shrugged away his coat. Jill descended to the floor, gracefully, and with ceremony relieved him of his waistcoat. He lifted her skirts and ran his hand about her hips, searching for the fastenings, eventually letting fall her petticoats. She waited for them to settle, then knelt on them at his feet. Setting her hands on his thighs, one at a time, she drew her fingers down the velvet from its widest to its narrowest points. Her hands settled onto the cuffs of his boots, and she drew them off by degrees to position them precisely in their place by his bunk. He reached down to her and with deliberate consideration, raised her up again. Leaning toward her inch by inch, he cradled her face in his hand and when their lips met at last, he kissed her forever. Time meant little to her any longer. Less than nothing, to him.

The ship reached open water and, flying herself, kicked up her heels in liberty. The pirate pair listed to the bed and sank into it. One good hand unlaced her dress. One red hand loosed his breeches. Together they served each other with reverence, freeing one another of clothing. But he stayed her hand at the clasp of his harness, and the hook and its trappings remained intact over the sculpture of his chest. "My mermaid is already free." He ran his fingers over the jewels where they glinted between her tresses.

The lovers fitted their limbs together, lingeringly, as the lovesong of deepening water serenaded them and the prospect of the sea's expanse opened to their view. Hook responded to the promise of the horizon; he kissed Jill ardently, thinking of her, and of yet another love. His eyes strayed. "You must rise now, to meet my other, older mistress." He lifted her, turning her to the window and supporting her as she leaned back against his chest. Delicately, his hook parted the hair draping her eyes.

Jill clasped his wooden wrist on her shoulder and looked out, gazing in awe upon his other lady. Her changing contours were charming, and mysterious. The *Roger* sailed upon her, solitary, within a great circle of undulating current. No petticoat of cloud or vapor restricted the sun from ravishing her with its kisses. The sea accepted the light, lifting and plunging at will, according to her whim. The crest of each green wave formed a gem to adorn her, and dazzled the woman's eyes.

"It is no wonder you took to the sea. She is rich in every way."

"And makes us even richer. You shall see."

"I little thought I'd ever leave the Neverland."

"But you aren't leaving it. You have seen a single port. Once you have awakened here, the only way to forsake it is to abandon your desire."

"But to leave the island of my dreams . . . "

Hook's eyes drank in the prospect of the sea, then he looked down and filled his soul with the sight of Jill. "There are other islands, my love. I will show you them all." He turned her in his arms and drew the curtain of her hair aside to kiss her throat. "Follow me."

Arching her neck, she received his caresses, so very contented. But the vial glittered with temptations. Her eyes wandered to it and soon she caught it up. Then the golden rain showered their bower, east, west, north and south; the air wavered with it. Bearing a scent of morning gardens, it settled like dew on their mouths, and tasted like roses. It spangled the man's hair and emblazoned the woman's jewels. Hook and his Jill fell together and rolled in the residue, their bodies glistening in the sunlight. Their eyes were struck, bedazzled with the brilliance of each other yet refused to close against the magic, and shimmering, their bodies joined together as they kissed with golden lips. Even the strappings of his brace became encrusted with gilt, like the bridle of some winged horse. Locked, glimmering, in the freedom of each other's embraces, the two ascended effortlessly, floating on shining currents of air. In their exalted bed, mounting to heights of scintillating sensation, they fused into one another, and as unmeasured moments passed, their passion exploded into stars. By the time they bumped against the beams, their breathing surging through their mouths, the feathery air on which they reclined seemed the most natural couch in the world for lovers to share.

Hook drew his lips from hers and even his laugh was gilded. "I used to envy the birds. Even they cannot match us now!" Trapped in the grain of the beams overhead shone more little stars, scraped from his glowing shoulders and twinkling down on their magic circle. The lovers reclined together, suspended, their hearts soaring, their eyes still blinded to everything else.

But the sea was calling. At length Hook's ears attended it, and Jill, though not yet understanding the liquid language, was drawn, as ever, to the open window. She pulled him with her and flung the casement to its widest extent. "Come, Hook! Fly with the birds. Fly with me!" Her radiant arms stretched longingly, one toward him, one over the sill.

But he stabbed his hook in a beam of the ceiling and anchored himself. Reaching down, he seized her round the waist. "Hold, my love. I see now how very easy it was to entice you away from home." He gathered her into his arm. "You feel the power of flight and you forget your position. But I have made you a queen over men this time. You will find them easier to govern than boys." His eyes appreciated her splendor. "And easier to tempt."

Jill looked at her lover in surprise, then laughed at her state of undress. "Forgive me! I'd no thought of anyone but you."

"A fault for which I shall never upbraid you. Fetch your gown, before I forget myself. I've an obligation to discharge. We've yet to complete the terms of our accord."

"You were generous. You granted all I asked and more—except for Nibs and Tom."

"You demanded their freedom."

"Which you refused."

"It didn't occur to you then that they desired to join me."

"Even though I meant to join you, too."

"And I had already granted their freedom. I couldn't give to you what belonged to them."

"Nor could I give you what belonged to others. You worked ruthlessly to free my heart so that I was at liberty to grant it."

"The only thing in the world for which I lacked. Except for the tale, the accord is sealed."

"The story of your Beauty. Yes! I hold you to our agreement."

Reluctant to descend, they settled on the floor to leave footprints in the fairy dust as they waited upon each other, donning only essentials. Once Jill had coaxed his claw through its lacy cuff, Hook led her to the couch and took her into his arms. The flightless swan supported their backs, catching a little glitter of its own. Their eyes, blue as sapphires, met and held. Hook noticed that her eyelashes still sparkled with magic. He began.

"You told me the story of James, the young man who entered into the Neverland to mold his destiny. Here he found everything he desired. Skill, experience, wealth, women, respect . . . power. He didn't court companionship, for ignorant of its charms, he had never sought it. By day he lived his fantasies, and by night he gathered strength. In the form of Beauty.

"She came to him in his dreams and whispered to him shyly, like a maiden, through the veil of sleep. Growing ever bolder, still she declined to join him—yet she taunted him with his incompletion. He reached for her but she tormented him, hiding within his soul behind a curtain of Darkness, torn just enough for the light of her smile to enter. As he dreamed, he could see her smile, a ray of loveliness, but intangible, unkissable. He could hear her voice; she spoke to him in golden words, but when she told his tale, she dictated that he should suffer loss and pain and interrupted passions. But also, ultimately, love.

"Over time, her features became refined, her voice clearer. She swam like a mermaid in and out of his sleep until one morning he netted his desire, fixing her image in his waking mind. He caused her likeness to be set in his skin. He commissioned her face to be carved in wood. Having gained this power over her, he ordered that she should bear his weakness and turn it into strength. And he hung her, his sweet tormentor, at the fore of his ship—the prow of his life. Now her hook plucks the waves, her hand summons the unattainable. Like the interrupted man, she seeks to grasp what she cannot hold.

"The Beauty has sailed with me forever. And the day I watched her forsake the water to follow an eagle and catch the sky, the moment I stood in Darkness beholding her face in sunshine, I knew that she is you, and you are me."

Jill's tear collected gold-dust granules as it cleared its path down her cheek. "She is your storyteller." She took his face in her hands and looked into her own eyes. "She dreamed her life into you, all her desires. But she had to grow up before we could become one." And, inspired and inspiring, she kissed him.

He pressed her hand to his cheek. "A story and the truth. A perfectly matched set." Hook abandoned the couch and plucked her from it, drawing her toward the door, but in front of the bookcase, she paused. In the full light of day, their reflections bounced back rich in color. The books behind the glass were real, clothed in leather, and the letters clearly legible. Neither the books nor the lovers took precedence; the images did not supercede, but enhanced one another. Opening every door of every shelf, Jill uncaged the contents, sending sunbeams flying. She snatched up her feather and twined it into the Pirate King's hair, alongside his earring. "Our stories have woven together, and it is I who have come alive, here in the Neverland."

"My dream, alive."

The lock slipped easily now, and the door opened to favor their escape. A trail of magical sand marked their progress, ending where their feet kicked the deck of the companionway out from under them. Unnoticed except by a similar light twinkling in the crow's nest, Hook and Jill flew, hand in hand, into the blue sea sky, up, and over the starboard rail. Hook flew as if he had always held the power, not a skill to be relearned, but a memory awakened. They dove down, rolling once, and flew ahead, past the forward anchor still coated in the moss of Neverbay and dripping with moisture. Here Hook pulled himself upright. Drifting alongside the ship, the pair kept pace with her, and their feet were dewy with the spray she tossed as she harvested the waves. Hook shook the blacker waves from his face. The feather flapped in the air.

"Follow me."

Jill followed, flinging herself along with him to face the dipping bow, with the wind leaping into their arms and filling the sails all above them. And then she saw the sickle, reaching for the sea. She saw the open hand. She grasped it, letting the wind flutter her against the hull as she stared at the figurehead. The captain linked his own hook with the wooden one and braced a foot against the ship where it glistened with damp. His white shirt billowed like the sails as he watched her face.

"My Beauty, carved from my visions."

It was like looking up into a beloved old mirror, brown and aged, but still reflecting truth. The Beauty leaned eternally, yearning for the edge of the horizon, her eyes clear and seeking the adventure that waited there, longing, perhaps, to tell its story. Her hair swam in the air, and at the end of a lovely looping pathway, her tail trailed in the sea. Her smile, Jill's own regal smile, bade the sea to claim its kiss. Everything about her was tempting, was true.

Jill looked closer, and her lips opened in surprise. Her hand rushed to her throat. There, on the Beauty, every bit as dark and weathered as the carving of the face, was her scar. Jill reached out to feel it, a gash smoothed by the trickster, Time.

"Has it always been there?"

Hook inclined his head. "Like my hook. A mark, blending with your beauty to form your soul."

She remembered. "The end of my story, as I wish it. As you told it."

"No, only the beginning. You are a work of art that lives on forever."

Her eyes beheld the mermaid again, and she held her head erect. "Am I really so beautiful?"

Hook smiled wryly. "Yes. We are." He bent his knees and shoved off from the hull, and like the perfect pirate she had made him, he stole the woman away. He took her soaring then, cleaving the air with his hook and spiraling high into the shoreless ocean of the sky, where even the white wings of his ship could never venture. He looked down where it skimmed below, spreading its feathers of spray, a water bird promising flights to spirit Hook and his Jill onward to other oceans, other islands.

Hook had won the few things he held dear. Now he secured them in his heart like the treasure in his coffer. The legendary captain of the *Roger* locked his Beauty in his arms while she leaned back and spread her golden wings, and they danced as one in the wild music of the heavens, and would not be captured by the wind, or Time, or blind monsters, or even little boys who just want to have fun.

The Seas of London

The London moon rode high and bright on the waves of the sky, crisply casting the boy's shadow. Legs wide, hands on hips, the familiar image pressed against the curtains. Closed curtains.

The shadow cocked its head, listening. A stutter of hooves on cobblestone bounced up from the street. Like the moon, the midnight clock floated in the heavens, ticking inaudibly, and having struck the hour, its gonging dissolved in a sea of stars. No further stories could be heard.

Black arms reached out and felt at the sash, secured a grip and pulled to lift the window. The arms were strong, but the casement declined to yield. The fingers flew to the latch and worked at it, rattling. Immediately, a dog barked within the recesses of the nursery. A glow leapt up and shone through the fabric of the drapes, as if it had been waiting for Peter. Approaching slowly, it refined itself. Its gleam burned through the insubstantial belly of Peter's shadow. He grinned, expectant. The candle's light glided up to the curtain, and there it stayed, a constant little fire unruffled by any errant breeze from any open window.

Peter waited. He peered at the light. It abided. Peter rattled again. The dog barked; the dog hushed. The mischievous boy pounded the glass with the flat of his hand, but to no avail. Like the flame, the parent holding it remained resolute, unwavering.

Peter's face tensed and he sprang back from the window. He hovered. Not a breath stirred the candle's light. He shook his head, then he stilled and hung there. All alone.

The sky shimmered around him. Something wet rolled down his cheek, something he'd felt before. He dashed it away. Then he felt something he'd never felt before. It lifted the golden hairs off his forehead and rustled through his leaves. It whistled a little as it touched his ears. It was cool, even refreshing. He couldn't help but feel it, and it stirred him somehow, like Tinker Bell's wings. Like Wendy's words. It dried his tears.

The wind.

Peter lifted his arms to welcome it, to let it in, to inhale it deep in his lungs. He sensed that this was his only opportunity; it would never catch him again. And when the wind released him, he turned away, arms still upraised, falling back into the ocean of the London sky. He didn't look back, but he determined to return. He'd remember. He would always remember.

Behind the curtain, Mr. and Mrs. Darling would remember, too. The unflagging flame sustained them. They had traveled through darkness to understanding. They were grown-ups, and they had to accept the truth, however disappointing. They now harbored no hope of retrieving their Wendy. Except in memory, except in myth, she was lost to them.

They told her story, over and over again. In their fondness for the girl they embellished the tale, they made up legends about her. But the family knew: these new stories weren't real. Not without the magic of the Wendy.

For she was no ordinary girl. From the time the fairies spied the open nursery window and returned her to Number 14, the Darlings had known she was only on loan. It was just a question of Time. As the first little girl ever to venture from her pram in the park, Wendy had nonplussed the winged creatures of air. The fairies hadn't known what to do with her. They had brought her home.

The Darlings had opened their hearts to her, however briefly, and Time had not been on their side. While she lingered, dreaming dreams and weaving stories, Wendy kept strict track of Time, gazing over the sunken city at the clock tower and listening for its chiming; rocking her baby brothers to the rhythm of the pendulum on the mantel; counting the minutes to grown-up, and never knowing why. Some thing, maybe some one, called to her, demanding her presence elsewhere. Whatever it was had hooked Wendy's heart and pulled with a powerful grip. Fearing she would fly too soon, the Darlings never reminded her of her first adventure in the park. Now it was too late. Time had run out.

Their own spinnings were only stories, phantoms, like the Darlings themselves must seem to a bunch of boys who lived in the Neverland. Only the Wendy's words were golden, infused with arcane powers, like grains of enchanted dust. Wendy had been touched by the fairies. Some of their magic rubbed off on her, and all unknowing she had spun dreams into reality, truth from tales. Her fantasy had come alive, in the Neverland. Now its waiting time was over, and she had answered its call. And wherever she was now, her parents still believed in her.

But Mr. and Mrs. Darling had learned. They were taking no chances on losing the three colorful youths she'd sent to them not in her stead, but with her love. From now on these boys would fight pirates in the park, they would bubble and bob about mermaids in London's lagoons. They were whole and happy. They were home.

Peter Pan and his shadow could come and go. He could rattle like the skeleton tree at the door of Dark Hunting, he could pound until the ill-omened leaves dropped from his clothing to litter the doorstep. The nightlight would burn, steadfast. But until young men chose to fling it open, the nursery window would remain closed.

Peter had to go hunting again. He needed weapons. Michael had flown home with the dagger that had been Slightly's. The hidden cache hoarded plenty of knives, but Peter prided himself on keeping an even score, one for every Lost Boy. And another dagger and two swords were missing in the recent engagements with pirates. One plundered, two confiscated. They had to be replaced.

Peter knew where to harvest them. A visit to the wharves under cover of night, and he had plucked a brace of knives. A speedy foray across town to the palace guardroom, and Peter gleaned two sturdy swords. He tucked them all in his belt, a steely bouquet he might once have presented to his Wendy—he smiled shyly—his ladylove. The wind had told him what she was to him, and it was safe to admit it now . . . she was gone. He remembered that she'd thought weapons were romantic, she'd once requested one in exchange for a kiss. But he hadn't given it to her, and now she was gone. Peter's smile waxed grim. There was plenty of steel aboard the *Roger*.

And two new men. Hook played a dirty trick on him, stealing his boys. A worse trick, unforgivable, to steal his fairy! Peter would never make peace with him. Nor with the Indians. They'd taken his boys and left him all alone to fight their enemies. As well as things worked out, it could have been better if he'd had braves behind him.

Being alone was no fun. He missed Wendy, he missed his band of boys. Peter had already visited the House in the Clearing. He'd gone there to get the Twins back, but he hadn't found them. Pungent ashes smoldered in the fire pit and footprints danced around it, small, medium and large. Wendy's little place still stood and the chimney poured out its smoke. Red, now. Peter could see it wherever he flew on the Island. When he landed in the clearing, he'd heard a parrot squawking in the trees, and over the lusty laughing of the stream rose a sound of children's voices. But he didn't seek out the muddy stream bed. After the wind departed to leave him alone, he had known. He wouldn't be following that path again.

Peter had paced all around the big new house the Twins had built and seen no one. The nursery window was open and draped with an Indian blanket woven in vivid colors. Peter had listened outside in case one of the native women was telling a story, but he'd heard nothing.

Yet the boy had been determined to find the Twins. He'd stalked back over dry sprinklings of sawdust to the face of the house and confronted the door. It was a handsome one mimicking those in

London, made of oak, and warm in the sunshine. The door boasted a shiny brass plate with a knob and a keyhole. Peter peeked through the keyhole and all he saw was the stub of the key. Someone had to be at home, but when he knocked on the door there was no response. He tried the knob and it was smooth and solid in his hand, but although it turned easily, the key had done its work. The Twins' door was bolted.

Peter had stepped back from the doorstep to the long grass of the Neverland that tickled his ankles. He looked to the second-story window. It was open and a lazy green curtain waved at him, but no one else. Above it, the red smoke steamed its way over the clearing and swirled above the trees. In its own kind of cursive it spelled out its message: many would be welcomed here, but except in story, not the wonderful boy. Peter Pan must never enter here.

So Peter missed his boys, all lost again. And right now he missed Tinker Bell as he made a quick round of the park. Tink and Peter used to visit her cousins here, collecting the boys they'd found. Now it was after hours and the gates were closed. The park was lit by fanciful moving lights—fairies, stringing ribbons along the pathways to mark passage to their ball. They fluttered their bright little wings, like matches struck and flaring. One of those matches was a bit brighter, bluer, a bit broader than the others. It flamed in a secret spot surrounded by greenery and shed its rays on the withered remnants of little discarded sweaters. Lost sweaters.

Peter blinked. He slowed his flight and descended to the dewy grass, then jumped in the air to perform a back flip. "Tinker Bell!" She'd come back to him! She must be glad to be back, her aura shone more intensely than ever before. Even her wings appeared fuller somehow. "Tink!"

She jingled when she saw Peter. She zoomed up to meet him, and the two swirls of gold circled and chased, speeding over the treetops. They skirted the boundaries of the park, rattling the cage of its fencing, and as they rushed over old haunts, their draft stirred feathers on the nesting birds in the trees of the island. The pair of pixies dove and coasted, and they grinned at their reflection in the pond as it broke into silver pieces under the plinking of the fountain. Peter crowed, and Jewel laughed her shiny-bell laugh.

His voice was bold. "I'm glad you're back, Tink!"

But at his words she slowed to a halt, becoming strict with him. In musical terms she let him know who she was, and who he was. She was Jewel, and he was her boy.

Peter scoffed. "Tink, you don't mean it."

She leveled a stare at him.

"Why didn't you come with me? Why did you sail away?"

With her chin in the air, her language resonated. Jewel had responsibilities. She had people who relied on her. She might be called away; she might perform important duties elsewhere from time to t—

"You just had an adventure. I'll keep you with me from now on."

Jewel narrowed her eyes and rang out as plain as speech. *Watch yourself.*

When Peter's laughter subsided, he struck a pose in the air, grinning. "Make me!"

And she did, easily. She flew away from him.

"Wait! . . . Tink . . . Jewel?"

The fairy stilled.

"Jewel."

She straightened.

". . .*Jewel!*"

Jewel smiled. She turned around.

"Does Hook still think you're his fairy?"

Her light pulsed and the smile curved her lips. Then she grew cool. She drifted toward her boy, eyebrows raised, trailing a frosty vapor of snow stars. Icily, she folded her little arms and intoned the lesson. *Some things a girl keeps secret.*

Peter laughed. "Let's see what we can find in the garden!" He turned tail to race her back. With her new wingspan, she eclipsed him.

Jewel's light led the way through the shrubbery. It was a hidden circle, the secret garden where the park fairies tended Lost Boys. There were plenty of decomposing sweaters and a blanket or two, which the birds mined for nesting material. Once arrived at the heart of the ring, Jewel's radiance illuminated something Peter hadn't noticed before. A compact face. The face of a new one, a smallish one, with restless feet and the air of a miniature knight errant bound upon a quest. Jewel hailed him with music, and the new one put out a fist. Peter touched down and cocked his head, regarding the fist and its owner for a moment. Then he shook it, saying, "Hello, green eyes!"

The little boy, too, cocked his head, and looked sideways at Peter. "I been waiting. That pretty fairy told me you'd come for me." He grinned. He had a bold little voice. "She can cuss like a sailor!"

Jewel piped up as if to prove it.

Peter's voice held a touch of pride. "I named her Jewel."

The child tossed the hair out of his eyes. "Where are the adventures?"

As he grinned back, Peter's eyes flashed under his own hair. "You're in one now!"

The boy almost crowed in his excitement. "Then I'll be needing one of those weapons!"

"We'd better get on home, now, Chip." Peter hunched down. "Hop on. I'm your father."

Chip scrambled onto Peter's back. Before he got a grip for traveling, he raised himself up and pecked Peter on the cheek. "That's a kiss for you." Then he hung on tightly, ready to go.

But Peter stood with a ghost of a smile on his face, unable to move for a moment. Like an arrow, Chip's kiss darted straight through his heart. Peter's weak spot, since Wendy went away.

Chip urged him with a leading question. "Are we going to the Neverland, Father?"

Peter's smile came fully alive. "There isn't anywhere else! Hold on."

Jewel whirled around Peter's head as he hiked Chip higher onto his back, and she blew a handful of golden sparks over the little boy. Having thought it through, she was sure her master would allow it; all Lost Boys should be able to fly. And her fairy dust matched the child's hair perfectly. Jewel wasn't surprised Peter took a shine to this new one. Chip was a tiny piece of Peter. . . . Almost as if he'd been made to order, by some clever storyteller.

Peter took a running leap and called over his shoulder, "Your knife is sharp, Chip, be careful with it."

Jewel halted in mid-air, and her grin fell away. Eyes wide, she chimed in alarm, *Careful?* She shook herself and beat her wings to catch up to Peter, contemplating an idea identical to his own at that very moment.

Maybe, they each thought as they skimmed over the islands of London and dipped in and out of cloud currents with their hearts swelling. *Maybe the Wendy isn't so very gone, after all!*

Chip shouted into the wind. It ransacked his golden hair, but left Peter's untouched. "Will you tell me a story, Father?"

"If you promise to call me Peter, and take your medicine."

"I will!"

"Which one do you want to hear, Chip? I know them all!"

Chip had his answer ready. "A pirate story!"

Peter's green eyes ignited. "I'll tell you all about my favorite pirate. On some adventure in the Neverland, you may even catch a glimpse of her . . . The Pirate Queen, Red-Handed Jill!

"Be brave, my hearty, for you never know when you'll meet her. You must be prepared, if anything can prepare you for that kind of shock . . . "

Never, Again

In the bed on the ship in the sea in the night, the never-ending lovers are entwined, swaying together, and the rhythm of their intricate dancing slows. Ebbing and flowing, the sea's own time takes them over again. They fall back to lie at rest, Hook and Jill, while the moonlight swirls in wavering pools on the ceiling. Their earrings gleam, their eyes are lustrous, like the dusting of stars shining overhead in secret recesses of wooden beams. The ship purls as she flies through the darkness, her hungry wings swelling with every breeze she seizes.

Rent apart and recreated, Red-Handed Jill seizes her breath, too, and whispers silently, like the sea.

"I know what you're thinking."

Complete, replete, he waits.

"You're thinking about Time."

Hook smiles, all the way this time. "I am thinking about Forever." He gathers his treasure in his one-handed grip. "And I am not alone."

They roll together again, on the ship in the night, sailing past the ever-after end of once-upon-a-time, loving and living with all the passion only pirates can know.

Acknowledgements

With an ocean of gratitude, I salute ship's company . . .

Jolene Barjasteh, Stacy De Coster, Victoria Everitt, Linda Ford,
Greg Gressle, John de Guzman, Erik Hollander, Maureen Holtz,
Barbara Kaufmann, Kim, Mary Lawrence, Christopher Mabrey,
Sarah Meehan, Krista Menzel, David Mertz,
Deena Sherman, Ginny Thompson,

and my first officer, Scott Jones.

My highest compliment to the genius who engenders genius...

Sir James Barrie

About The Author

Combining a career in media with her literary and dramatic grounding, Andrea Jones reaps the result in writing.

As a producer-director, writer, and manager in television, she has worked for CBS, PBS and corporate studios. She also performed as on-camera and voice-over talent.

She holds a B.A. from the University of Illinois in Oral Interpretation of Literature, with a minor in Literature. A continual student of the arts, history and humanity, Jones finds her work informed by such sages as Carl Jung, Robert Graves, P.G. Wodehouse, and, of course, Sir James Barrie.

Jones is an enthusiastic patron of her public library. She dedicated several years to promoting a non-profit children's organization, and is active on stage in local theatre. Having outgrown the "hideout under the ground," she lives near Chicago.

Hook & Jill is her first published work, and the first in a series of "grown-up" Neverland novels. Book Two is *Other Oceans*.